MICHELLE GRIEP

A
HEART
DECEIVED

A NOVEL

David C Cook®
transforming lives together

A HEART DECEIVED
Published by David C Cook
4050 Lee Vance View
Colorado Springs, CO 80918 U.S.A.

David C Cook Distribution Canada
55 Woodslee Avenue, Paris, Ontario, Canada N3L 3E5

David C Cook U.K., Kingsway Communications
Eastbourne, East Sussex BN23 6NT, England

The graphic circle C logo is a registered trademark of David C Cook.

This story is a work of fiction. All characters and events are the product of the author's
imagination. Any resemblance to any person, living or dead, is coincidental.

ISBN 978-0-7814-1101-1
eISBN 978-1-4347-0726-0

The author is represented by and this book is published in association with the
literary agency of Word Serve Literary Group, Ltd., www.wordserveliterary.com

The Team: John Blase, Caitlyn Carlson, Renada Arens, Karen Athen
Cover Design: Nick Lee
Cover Photo: Shutterstock

Printed in the United States of America
First Edition 2013

1 2 3 4 5 6 7 8 9 10

052013

For Aaron, my encouragement;
For Sal Pal, who knows my voice;
And as always,
For God, my redeemer from deception.

1

Deverell Downs
Bedfordshire, England, 1795

Sunlight slanted a direct route from heaven through the sanctuary windows. Were the dust motes riding that beam sturdy enough to carry her weight, Miri Brayden would mount up and fly out of there in a heartbeat.

In the pulpit, her brother droned on—and on. And on. Probably something about brimstone or eternal wrath. Who knew? Her mind floated from speck to speck as she zigzagged her eyes up to the glass panes. Beyond, a few small clouds roamed free. What would it feel like to drift away on one of those? A lot softer than the wicked pew that numbed her backside, to be sure.

Half a rebellious smile twitched her lips, then disappeared. If God singled her out for her lack of attentiveness and incinerated her on the spot, she shouldn't be a bit surprised. Not that she didn't deserve it.

But that would be too easy an out.

She forced her gaze back to Roland, who aimed his finger like a weapon of God, firing musket balls of scripture into the congregation. Stifling a yawn, she blew out a long breath instead. Several other sighs chorused around her. From behind, a suspicious snort-snort might have been a snore, but she resisted the urge to turn and confirm it. If Roland didn't end Sunday morning prayers soon, the whole of Deverell Downs Church would meet with a fireball of judgment for dozing off.

Or maybe Roland *was* their judgment.

For the third time in the past eternity, she tilted her chin sideways and stole a glance two aisles over at Mr. Mystery, as she'd dubbed him. The man sat alone, in the seat usually inhabited by Mr. and Mrs. Harper. He was likely tall, for his broad shoulders and head cleared the top of the box pew. His hair was the color of winter wheat, pulled back and fastened in a queue. Straight nose, neither too long nor too short, a clean-shaven face with a square jaw … she might just change his name to Mr. Handsome instead.

"All rise."

Roland's voice caught her in the act, and her face burned all the more when the mystery man stood and turned his head, meeting her gaze straight on. The deep blue of his eyes asked questions she wasn't sure she could answer.

Then he cocked his head and winked.

Miri snapped her attention to her feet as she rose, stomach twisting. Had Roland noticed the exchange from his high perch? Daring a peek, she moved her lips along with the final hymn, though no sound came out. Her brother lifted his face to the ceiling, arms poised for benediction. Miri's muscles loosened, all the way down to her clenched toes. God had been gracious indeed.

At the final amen, pew doors flew open, and bodies rushed into the aisles. Shouldn't people be running to God instead of away from Him? Miri bit back a smirk. It wasn't God they ran from, but rather her brother. She'd run too, if he weren't currently her sole means of support.

Though Roland would label her as brazen, she draped her pelisse over her arm and shouldered into the press. The thought of the outdoors was far too tempting to take the time to don and button the cloak. Merely thinking of trading the stuffy sanctuary air for the brisk spring breeze hastened her steps.

Nearing the vestibule, however, she stopped. Those behind her flowed past like water around a streambed rock. Ahead, standing on tiptoe, Clive Witherskim looked over the shoulders of taller men, no doubt hoping to spy her. Fresh air lost all appeal at the thought of sharing it with him.

She spun and bumped flat against the squire, Mr. Gullaby.

"Oh! Forgive me." Stepping aside, she backed against a pew, allowing plenty of room for the squat man to pass.

Instead, he tugged on a long gold chain, swagged from a vest pocket inside his waistcoat, and retrieved a filigree watch. Flipping it open, he made an exaggerated point of studying the thing, then lifted his dark little eyes. "It is commendable that during your brother's retirement he has graciously chosen to fill the pulpit for Mr. Eldon. However, I am wondering, Miss Brayden, if perhaps you know when the vicar will return?"

Miri angled her face, keeping track of Witherskim with one eye. "I am sorry, sir. I have no idea when Mr. Eldon will return, though I will pass along your commendations to my brother."

"Humph. Then you can pass this along as well." He held up the watch and snapped the lid shut inches from her nose, making her flinch. "Mr. Eldon always kept Sunday morning prayers to fifty-five minutes. Fifty-five, Miss Brayden, not two hours. Your brother would do well to remember that if he ever serves again."

She nodded, for her own aching backside could not argue with the man. "Of course."

"Good day, then … what's left of it." The squire dismissed her with a flick of his wrist and disappeared into the crowd of remaining parish members flocking around the entryway. Witherskim no longer stood amongst them. Had he finally tired of the waiting game?

Pausing, she tucked a stray curl behind her ear. If she took her time, Witherskim might give up and leave the grounds altogether. The afternoon could yet be salvaged with a few of the cook's biscuits and a hot cup of chamomile.

"For God's sake, Miriall, why are you still here? You dawdle as a common slackard. Come along." From behind, fingers bit into the fleshy part of her upper arm, heeling her into step with her brother's long stride.

She opened her mouth to protest, but Roland cast her a dark look, a clear warning that he'd brook no quarrel. Upsetting him in public, especially in full view of Miss Prinn and Mrs. Tattler, who stood gaping from the doorway, would be madness—exactly what she'd been trying to avoid the past month. Pressing her lips tight, Miri swallowed her dissent and quickened her pace.

"Ladies, excuse us." Roland nodded at the women as he swept Miri beyond the sanctuary's threshold and into the bright spring morning. Ahead, on the road leading to town, the flanks of a black mare disappeared around a bend.

Roland pulled her up short. "You see what your dallying has done? Master Witherskim has ridden off already. You missed a prime opportunity, Miriall."

"Thank God," she said, then wished she could pull back the words and cram them deep into her reticule, so fierce was Roland's scowl. "What I mean to say is, thank God that I have you to look out for my welfare, brother."

"Yes, you should. Daily." He rubbed the back of his neck with one hand, then slowly lowered his arm to his side. "I suppose I shall have to step up my intervention. Master Witherskim is your best, and I daresay only, prospect."

"But Roland, if we could simply find Will. Maybe he would—"

"Enough!"

From the corner of her eye, Miri caught a flash of a grey shawl and dotted yellow skirt edging closer. If Miss Prinn and Mrs. Tattler soaked up any of this conversation, they'd wring out every drop and wash the entire town from one end to the other. Miri lifted her lips into her brightest smile and raised her face to Roland's. "As you wish."

"All right, then." He tugged on his shirt cuffs, straightening his sleeves, and eyed the remaining congregation. Most had fled, but a few grouped in conversation next to the greystone walls of the church. None paid him any mind, probably fearing he'd let loose another sermon.

"See to it that you are not late for luncheon." He turned and crunched down the gravel pathway toward the rectory.

Tattler and Prinn immediately swooped in, the scent of lemon verbena and ripening curiosities filling the vacuum left by Roland's departure. "Oh, Miss Brayden! Such a lovely day, is it not?"

Miri curtsied to the ladies, then hurried after her brother, calling over her shoulder, "My apologies, ladies. I am needed at the rectory."

Better to have lunch with a madman than suffer dissection by the town gossips.

❧⁂❧

London, England

Ethan Goodwin leaned against the stone blocks of St. Mary Woolnoth Church, tired of debt and thievery. Weary of breathing, actually. The feeling had been with him for some time now, like a tooth gone bad—one that needed pulling. Life just didn't glitter anymore. He blew out a snort. As if it ever had.

Carriages rolled by. Horses and wagons and people darted one way and another down the London street. Near the corner, a young miss, with a pert little nose and hair all in ringlets, clutched a book in one hand. A stringed pouch dangled from the other. Easy pickings—but much too dangerous. A red-coated dragoon stepped beside the girl, tucking her hand into the crook of his arm.

The last of the great tower bells rang, pulling Ethan's gaze to the opening church doors. Parishioners poured out like spilled holy water. His eyes moved from one prospect to another, but something was wrong. Very wrong. No thrill raced through his veins with the coming conquest. His heart didn't even accelerate. A sooty feeling, black and heavy, tamped out any embers of anticipation.

Even so, he glanced from a fat madam to her fatter reticule. Sequined. Satin. And no doubt lined with silver coins. Humming an old bawdy song, a favorite of his friend Will's, he clasped his hands behind his back, then stepped into the departing congregants. Raising his face to the sky, he studied what might have been blue beyond the smoky haze, and bumped square into the woman's shoulder.

She gasped. "Good heavens!"

"Watch your step, man!" The fellow next to her lifted a single glass lens to his eye. If murder were possible by the sharpness of a squint, Ethan's lifeblood would be pooling in the gutter.

"Dreadfully sorry." Ethan shrugged, holding out both hands. "Afraid my mind was occupied, which is more than shameful, being that I've upset you both. Please forgive me."

The woman sniffed.

The man curled his lip. "Shove off."

"Again, my apologies." Ethan bowed, touching his fingertips to his forehead in a salute.

Then snatched her bag as they hurried past him.

Judging by the weight of the spangled pouch, the thing held a ransom's worth of coin. Practicality shouted at him to pocket the booty and run, fast and far.

So why did the world blur to a stop?

His feet froze. The sound of his own breathing echoed in his head. He gaped at the treasure nestled in his hands, and the longer he stared, the stronger a foreign urge welled. Burning. Incessant. Slightly nauseating and—

Overwhelmingly compelling.

"Excuse me!" He broke into a dead run. "Madam!"

He didn't stop until he tapped her on the shoulder.

"Didn't I tell you to shove off?" The fellow turned, puffing out his chest. "I've a mind to call a constable—"

Ethan held out the reticule. "I believe this belongs to the lady."

The woman's eyes widened, her lips forming a large O. She seized the pouch and clutched it to her chest. "Oh my! I didn't realize I'd dropped my bag. Thank you, sir. Thank you so very ..."

Her voice faded into the street clamor as Ethan wheeled about and stalked off, angry at her gratitude. Angry at himself. That sweet bit of fortune would've paid off his debts. What was he thinking?

As he stormed by the church, an old gentleman, thin as the cane he white-knuckled, descended the final step. From the tip of his silk cravat tucked into a sateen-breasted waistcoat, down to his glossy leather shoes, the man smelled of money.

Ethan slowed his steps. Could he pull off the act without another appearance from his long-lost conscience? Did he even want to? He flexed his fingers, trying hard to conjure up some kind of zest for the task, and … nothing. Not one thing in him longed for the rush of a fruitful theft.

"You there!" A bulwark of a man, draped in a black cassock, stood at the church's threshold, pointing a finger at him.

Ethan lifted one brow while slipping a glance to the left and right.

"Aye, I said you. Come here."

Frowning, Ethan hesitated. Oh, it would make a right fine tale to laugh about with Will should he answer the reverend's call, but he'd learned long ago that churches and jails were best avoided. He opened his mouth to cut the fellow off, then pressed his lips shut. Slowly, almost imperceptibly, the reverend's finger had nudged upward, aiming just beyond Ethan's shoulder.

Glancing backward, Ethan followed the trajectory with his eyes. Seven—maybe eight—paces away, a constable folded his arms and widened his stance, gaze fixed on Ethan.

Bypassing the old fellow with the cane, Ethan took the stairs two at a time. "Ahh, yes, Reverend. So glad you asked me here today." He embraced the man, clapping him on the back. That ought to give the constable something to think about.

"In truth, lad, I think you have God to thank for this appointment." The reverend whopped him hard between the shoulder blades in return.

Coughing, Ethan didn't protest as the man led him inside. He couldn't. He could barely breathe. He followed the clergyman to the back pew, where the fellow stopped and held out his arm.

Ethan sank onto the oak, falling into memories he hadn't known still existed. The smell of beeswax votives and linseed-oiled woodwork jarred loose fragments of verses and a lifetime of sermons.

"Scoot over, lad." The reverend's voice boomed, expanding to the farthest corners of the high ceiling.

Ethan nodded toward the closed front doors. "I appreciate what you did out there. But honestly, there's no need to waste your breath on the likes of me. I'll just sit here awhile and then be gone. Don't worry. I won't pilfer your candlesticks on my way out."

A slow smile spread across the man's face, tightening his weathered skin. He shook his head, grey hair shorn like an over-mown pasture. "I don't care about lost candlesticks, lad. I care about lost souls. Now … move over."

Blowing out a long breath, Ethan slid aside. The constable would have been better company than a clergyman. He gritted his teeth and waited, hoping the reverend's lecture would be mercifully short.

The wood groaned as the fellow lowered himself next to Ethan. "The name's Newton, lad. John Newton. And you are?"

"Ethan Goodwin," he ground out.

"That vein in the side of your neck is going to pop if you don't relax, lad." Newton's voice had a smile in it.

"Look, Reverend, allow me to be plain." Ethan angled to face the man. Better to get this over with in a direct manner than beat around the burning bush. "I don't believe in God. Not anymore."

Newton laughed. Outright. Large and toothy and genuinely delighted. His shoulders shook, and he ended up wiping moisture from the corners of his eyes.

Ethan's jaw dropped. He'd seen a lot of queer sights on the London streets, but never a clergyman laughing as lustily as a sailor.

"Hah! None of that matters, lad. God believes in you. Your belief or lack of it doesn't change His existence."

Ethan scrubbed his face with both hands. Maybe he was beyond tired. Surely this conversation was a dream. Where was the reverend's condemnation? His holier-than-thou judgment? "Look, Reverend, you saw what I was about to do out there. What I am." He lifted his chin and locked gazes with the man. "I, sir, am a thief. I won't pretend otherwise."

The reverend didn't flinch. "I'm not asking you to."

A smile twitched Ethan's lips. "Oh, I see. Of course. You ask nothing of me. Very clever. It's what the Lord asks, eh, Reverend?"

"The Lord?" Newton's brows rose like a swell in the sea. "What does the Lord require of you? Is it to make your own peace? He would as soon require you to make a new heaven and a new earth. Is it to keep your own soul? No more than He requires you to keep the sun in its course. His own arm has wrought salvation, lad, and He will secure it. None but this does He require … to do justly, to love mercy, and to walk humbly. The methods of His grace will enable you to do so, not anything I have to say."

Stunned, Ethan sank back, grateful the pew upheld him. Slowly, he shook his head. "You would not say such things if you knew fully the wretch that sits here before you, sir."

"Nor would you remain in the same room with a sinner such as I." Newton reached out his hand, placing a calloused palm on Ethan's leg. "Which is neither here nor there, for God knows."

God knows?

Ethan's mouth dried, teeth tasting like bones. Sudden clarity struck him a powerful kidney punch, and he slipped forward, knees grinding onto the floor. He clutched the pew in front of him, holding tight to keep the world from tilting.

The awful truth of the man's words was cold and unyielding, relentless as the stone floor and as hard. He grasped tighter, digging into the wood as it splintered into the virgin flesh between nail and finger. No hellfire, not one word of gnashing teeth or eternal pain cut into his soul as brutally as those two little words.

God.

Knows.

His blood rushed. Hairs prickled. Just like he'd felt earlier, something was not right.

Or maybe it was. Maybe this was what rightness felt like. For the first time in his life, *he knew.* Ethan Goodwin knew. Truly.

God help him.

"Take all the time you need, lad." The reverend gripped his shoulder, then stood. "All the time you need."

Ethan squeezed his eyes shut. Newton was right. He did have God to thank for this appointment.

2

If men's heads were roses, she'd lop them all off. Gripping the shears in a stranglehold, Miri squeezed them until her arms shook. Clip. For Roland's sharp words. Snip. His obsessive control. Slice. If only she could as easily be rid of the problems her brother was causing, but things had only worsened now that he'd imbibed a heady drink of power from the pulpit two days ago. Do this. Don't do that. Chop. Chop. Chop! She'd like nothing better than to nick off Roland's tongue.

One by one, dead branches collected in a thorny heap at her feet—spiked and tangled as her thoughts. Obviously working in the rectory's garden would not be a diversion. Not this evening.

Spent, she sank to the ground and laid the shears in her lap. If she couldn't keep herself composed, how would she ever succeed in keeping Roland calm? She breathed in deeply, savoring the early evening smell of dirt and worms and possibility. Like the possibility of running away to live with Will. Forget about Roland. Leave the bones of her past here in the rectory garden to bleach in the sun.

She exhaled, long and low, until nothing was left. Maybe she was the one slipping into insanity, for it was crazy to think she could find Will and more than madness to think he'd take responsibility for her. Responsibility wasn't exactly a prodigal's hallmark.

"Miss?"

Miri startled at the cook's voice, shoving anger and hurt down into a dark cellar in her heart. No doubt they'd keep. Glancing over her shoulder, she forced a pleasant tone. "Yes?"

Mrs. Makin's raisin eyes were set deep into her face. Mobcap askew, she looked like a shortbread taken too soon from the oven. "Beggin' yer pardon, miss. I hate to be interruptin' ye, but Master Brayden, why he's a mite ... well, if you don't mind me sayin', I'd as soon ask you about the meals for the rest of the week rather than him. Master Brayden is ..."

"Cantankerous?" Miri smiled. "Or surly?"

"Oh, miss!" The cook's brows rose. "I never said—"

"Of course not. I did." Brushing aside a stray curl with the back of her hand, Miri cocked her head. "Though I vow I won't own up to it. Now then, what was it you wanted to ask?"

Mrs. Makin clucked her tongue, a censure belied by the sparkle in her eye. "I'm wantin' to know if the vicar will be back soon. For all his skin and bones, Mr. Eldon is a hearty eater. I've been wastin' a fair amount of time and food, cooking and serving as though he might come to table." The cook took a step closer and lowered her voice. "But it's been four days now, miss. You know I tend to my own affairs and all, but I was wondering if you knew ... what I mean to say is ... that were some scuffle I heard the other morn."

Miri's smile faded. So it hadn't been a nightmare, not if Mrs. Makin had heard the same ungodly sounds in the predawn gloom last week. Angry voices, hushed and low. Crashing furniture. A cry. Then silence, smothering and weighty.

Her own careful search of the rectory had yielded nothing amiss, except for her own shredded nerves—which Mrs. Makin now deftly minced yet more.

The cook glanced over her shoulder, then, with another guarded step, drew nearer. She bent, her words clearly meant only for Miri. "I've been meaning to ask if mayhap you knew something about the vicar's disappearance."

Hah. As if Mr. Eldon, her brother, or any man for that matter, would confide in her. Men hoarded their secrets like casks of wealth. Miri shook her head. "Sorry. I know as much about Mr. Eldon's situation as you."

"Well then, I suppose there's naught to be done about it." Mrs. Makin straightened and patted the flour-coated apron stretched across her wide midsection. "My girlish figure has suffered enough. If it's all the same to you, I shall stop cooking as if the vicar were here. Leastwise till he returns, eh?"

"By all means, Mrs. Makin. Do as you see fit."

"Thank you kindly, miss." The cook tucked her chin and turned, her skirt billowing up dust swirls on the walkway.

Miri watched her go. Just past Mrs. Makin's shoulder, a dark cloud hung low on the horizon. Frogs ribbited, their sound bass and throaty, swelling with the coming night and promising a rainstorm. But peeking over the edge of the thunderhead, the last of the sun's rays reached out. Miri pushed off her bonnet and lifted her face. Orange light soaked into her skin, dappling a spotted pattern on her closed lids. The evening breeze, while damp, hinted that summer was not far away. If God could change the seasons, why not her life?

Please, Lord, would You?

Working out a kink in her neck from her strained position, she opened her eyes and caught sight of a thick sucker near the base of the shrub rose. She lifted the shears, tilting them first one way, then another. Such an angle would make this difficult. Must even her chosen pastime present nothing but trouble?

The stray curl fell forward again, and she blew it back. Gearing up for a quick, powerful slash, she leaned forward, spread the wooden handles wide, then slammed them together.

"Miriall!"

The blades slipped, gouging into the branch's flesh. A jagged gash cut deep enough to wound but not to sever, opening the door to disease. Miri stared at it, sickened for a moment, then shot to her feet. The shears clattered onto the gravel. She tugged on her bonnet, brushed bits of soil from her dress, then inched both hands behind her back, hiding the dirt beneath her nails. "Yes?"

The spasm in her brother's clean-shaven jaw did not bode well. His grimace deepened while his gaze swept her from head to toe. "Return to the house."

"I shall, shortly."

"Now." He turned, the tails of his greatcoat flapping.

Miri glanced at the barren rose bush. There would be few blooms if she did not finish pruning before buds appeared, especially since she'd butchered the poor thing. "Pray, give me leave to—"

"No." He neither looked back nor paused in his trek toward the rectory.

"But ..."

He stopped and pivoted. The waning daylight threw sharp shadows across his face, and she flinched at his resemblance to their father.

He stared her down. "There is naught more to say, child. You will cease squandering your time on this garden of vanity."

Child? Of all the arrogance. At nine and twenty, he was only five years her senior. Miri lifted her chin and flashed a prim smile.

"I fail to understand how caring for the Creator's handiwork can be construed as vanity."

"Consider whom you address. I do not recall your face among the dons beneath me at Pembroke."

A vein protruded on his temple. For one wicked moment, she entertained the crass thought of it bursting.

Remorse forced her to break the deadlock of stares, and she studied the crushed leaves at her feet. "Forgive me. I did not think."

"One of your many shortcomings. No wonder Father never found you a husband." He exhaled his disgust, the chirrups of roosting martins the only sound bold enough to reply. "I shall, however, overlook this incident."

Miri dared look up. Was he truly extending her grace?

"Henceforth you will take better care in minding your tongue and your time. This parcel of weed and sticks is incapable of producing anything of use." The frown on his lips softened, though it never quite became a smile. "I expect more from you than tending to that which is beyond salvation. Am I quite understood?"

Clamping her lips together, Miri nodded. She understood.

But she could not agree.

⌒☙◯❧⌒

Drizzle and darkness. Fog and murk. Miserable companions, comforting as death. If the grim reaper did chance to appear, Ethan would embrace the wraith with open arms. But not even that specter would brave the Old Nichol slum on a night such as this. Dank air settled into his lungs, and a tremor wracked through him. He tugged the threadbare fabric of his coat tighter and pressed on despite his wavering determination.

"What's it been now … two days? Three? You suffer in vain, my friend."

Above the clamor of London's sleepless streets, the words carried on Will's gin-soaked breath. The odor added yet one more offensive layer to the stench wafting from the open gutters, triggering Ethan's nausea. Ethan doubled over and emptied the contents of his gut, adding to the waste. Even after the half-digested remains of the small bread crust hit the muddied lane, he remained bent, dry heaves clenching his belly.

"You don't have to go through this. You know I've the cure for your ills."

Straightening on shaky legs, Ethan nodded, then wished he hadn't. Dizziness nailed him, and he grabbed Will's sleeve. "The cure is—"

"Let me guess … God." Will shrugged him off, though a smile deepened the dimple in his chin. "Believe me, in the past few days I've heard enough from you about God this and God that. Where is your God now that you shake and heave and hurt? If this is your idea of a better life, then I'll have none of it."

Pain hammered in Ethan's temples, and he closed his eyes against it. Mayhap his friend was right; his life certainly wasn't any better—physically, at any rate. The price of abstinence exacted a cost higher than he'd bargained for. Abandoning his wicked lifestyle had sounded like a good idea while sitting on that church pew, but now—he clamped his lips, forcing back the relentless sickness.

"Your newfound piety will be the death of you. Here."

Ethan opened his eyes to his friend's outstretched palm. The lump resting there looked like tar and smelled of poppy seed, settling his stomach at once. Desire shook through him, harder than the chills that had rattled his bones for the better part of the evening.

Perhaps he had been rash in his decision. Even a tot was weaned gradually from his mother's milk. He ran his tongue over cracked lips, pulse racing. He could start a new life—a good life—tomorrow.

"Well?"

No mortal could bear such temptation—especially not a man like himself. Newton would understand, wouldn't he? Would God?

Will shoved the piece closer. Relief, escape, euphoria—all within grasp, inches from his fingertips.

Ethan snatched the opium and clutched it to his chest, trembling.

"Good man." Will clapped him on the back and set off with his long-legged gait, calling over his shoulder, "Come along, then."

Ethan hesitated. The longer he stood, the more the fog condensed, beading along strands of his unkempt hair, dripping into his eyes and clouding his vision. An utterly foreign feeling of abhorrence at what he was about to do began deep in his chest and spread outward. This was wrong. He knew it.

But it would be the *last* time.

He swiped moisture and guilt from his brow with the back of his hand, then strode to catch up with Will.

His friend veered off the lane, disappearing into an alley that led to the door of their flat. Hardly bigger than a wardrobe, the lean-to housed all sorts of vermin, both human and rodent. Ethan rubbed his thumb against the silky lump in his hand. Soon it wouldn't matter where he laid his head.

Increasing his pace, he cut the corner too sharply. A coughing fit raged through him, and he stumbled over a hump of rags.

"Ye scarpin' prigger! Watch yer step." The rags shifted, then stilled.

Ethan bent, hacking until he caught his breath. "Sorry, Jack."

He should have known that the crossing sweep would be balled up about now, but his thinking had turned to wet wool—thick and heavy. Once again he brushed the hair from his eyes and wavered on unsteady feet. The rolling clouds of mist thinned in the narrow passage, and though darkness yet reigned, he could see much better.

"Well, well, just the lackey I been waitin' on nigh the better part of the eve." A deep voice, raspy as kicked gravel, met Ethan's ear an instant before a figure emerged from the side of the building. "Right fine of you to show up, Ethan boy. Not mannerly to keep a business partner waitin'."

Ignoring him, Ethan sidestepped the man. Fingers bit into his shoulder and yanked him backward, causing his treasure to fly from his grip. Anger filled the hollow in his gut. "Knicker off, Thorne."

"Surly pup!" Thorne grunted. "Pay up, and I'll be on me way."

"No, I'll be on mine." Ethan jerked free. He never should have come back. Not tonight … not ever.

Thorne spun him around. A knife blade flashed in his hand. "I said, pay up."

Ethan's heart beat erratically. Why was breathing such a chore? Mind racing, he scanned the dark alley for a bottle, a stick, a broken bit of brick. Anything. He'd lost his jackknife, his dagger, his boot blade. Everything … except his soul.

"Caught you with your britches down, did I?" A smile split Thorne's face. "Yer such a wastrel. Can't even defend yerself. Ethan Goodwin … ha! Oughtta be Ethan Good-fer-nothin'. You'll either die at the gallows or of the pox."

"I suppose that depends upon whether I embrace your principles or your women, doesn't it, Thorne?" Ethan widened his stance, prepared for anything once that insult hit home.

Thorne's smile vanished. He advanced a step, glowering. "Then it'll be a direct route to Newgate for you."

Newgate? *God, no. Anything but that. Please.*

Sweat dampened Ethan's shirt until it stuck to his back like a second skin. He'd watch his blood spill in this alley before he'd rot in a jail cell. Bare hands would have to do. He lunged for the knife.

Thorne sprang forward, slashing.

The blow knocked Ethan to his knees. A new kind of wet, warm and sticky, soaked into the front of his shirt—from the inside out. Pressing his palm against his ribs, he gasped. Drips trickled down his side as he pushed up to his feet. "You cur! You miserable little—"

Will shot past him, a dagger of his own clenched tight and aimed at Thorne's heart.

Thorne snorted, then feinted into a crouch. At the last second, he twisted. Will's blade swung wild, throwing him off kilter.

Just the opening Thorne needed. He thrust upward, a blur to Ethan's eyes. The close alley walls muffled Will's cry as he lurched backward.

Time stopped. The awful thud of Will's head smacking the ground sounded overloud in Ethan's ears. His friend—his only friend—gasped for breath like a fish on sand, an alarming amount of blood pooling on his chest.

"No!" Ethan grabbed Will's knife, rage narrowing his focus to one potent thought.

Kill Thorne.

He stabbed. Blade met bone.

Thorne's eyes widened. His jaw dropped, followed by his body. Two twitches later, Nigel Thorne lay still as a corpse.

Ethan cast the dagger aside, then turned and knelt next to his friend. With the last of his strength, he shifted Will's head to his own lap that his friend might breathe easier. But gurgles accompanied each of Will's labored breaths.

"Hold on, Will." He rocked him as a babe in arms. Will's friendship had ever been closer than a brother's. Much closer—and well did he know it. "Hold on."

"Did you ... did you kill him?" Blood snaked past Will's lips and oozed down his chin.

"Hold on!" Ethan swallowed back fear, and his throat tightened. God ... what had he done? This was all his fault, and for what? A meal's worth of pocket change? He tugged at his collar with a free hand, unable to breathe. How had everything gone so wrong when only days ago all had been made right?

"You cannot ..." Will struggled, wide-eyed. "Do not stay here. Go ... west end. Find my sister. I know she'll—" Will gasped. "She'll help you."

Beneath Ethan's grip, his friend grew limp. It wasn't fair. None of this was fair. "No!"

Ethan jerked his face to the sky. Blackness stared back, nothing more. "God! This isn't how it's supposed to be. Not for Will. Not like this. Take me, not him!"

"... not worth it ..."

Ethan bent, angling his head to catch his friend's words.

"... she will ... help." Will sucked in a shuddering gulp of air and breathed out his last words. "Seek Miri."

3

Nigel Thorne stiffened his arms and legs, playing the part of a dead sewer rat left to bloat in the alley. Ethan Goodwin's heavy breathing had long since fled into the night, but Nigel lay there just the same. No sense taking chances. He'd already wagered and lost enough blood for one evening. If not for the bag of quids tucked beneath his waistcoat, Goodwin's blade would no doubt have ended him.

He opened one eyelid to the thinnest of cracks. Complete blackness stretched into an endless void. He widened the slit. Impossible. Even with the heavy fog, he ought to at least see a lighter shade of grey.

Both his eyes flew open. The longer he stared, the harder he tried to distinguish some kind—any kind—of variation in the darkness, yet the darkness deepened more. Black crawled in and made a home behind his eyeballs. Gads! Maybe he really was dead.

He jerked up his head. His hat rolled off to the side, and, without the thick felt inches from his face, everything sharpened into focus. Ash heaps. Horse droppings. A pile of rags. And a corpse—one for which he'd rather not take the blame.

Pressing the heel of his hand against the gash near his ribs, Nigel sucked in a breath and staggered to his feet. The alley closed in on him, and he waited for the spinning brick walls to slow into straight lines. He took one step, then spewed out curses. Holy hobnails, but that hurt!

With each step thereafter, he used up every profanity he owned, then borrowed a few he'd heard down at the wharves. Slowly, leaning against shops and posts and sometimes a random drunkard, he worked his way to Shoreditch and finally climbed the stairs to Mistress Pegg's Bawdy House.

Woozy from pain and panting, he shoved open the door and stumbled into the entryway. A thick waft of perfume mixed with sweat and the soured stench of too much gin stole the rest of his breath. He banged his hip against a small table at the bottom of the stairs, toppling an oil lamp. Grunting, he hung the rest of his body against the stair rail.

"Lovey?" he hollered up the flight of steps.

Giggles from behind closed doors and a few suggestive euphemisms came from above, but no Pegg.

He tried again. "Lovey! It's me, your Nigel."

Hinges creaked, followed by floorboards flexing. Pegg appeared at the top of the stairs. Her frilly robe gaped open, revealing a long string of pearls wrapped twice 'round her neck and dangling low onto a half-laced corset. A stocking encased one plump leg. The other wore a lone garter. Nigel licked his lips. Too bad he'd wasted the evening's tussle with Goodwin instead of Pegg.

"You shoulda came earlier, luv. I'm already occupied—oh!" She narrowed her gaze on the upper half of his chest, where blood darkened the fabric. Her bare feet flew down the stairs. "What happened? Oh, lovey. Here. Let ol' Pegg help you."

She wrapped her arm around his shoulders, and he leaned into her, inhaling her trademark jasmine scent and catching a chaser of some other fellow's shaving tonic. He'd be jealous—if he didn't know he alone held her heart.

"Come along, dearie. Your Pegg will fix you up, she will."

They shuffled into the sitting room, where she lowered him onto the settee. Nigel sank against the flat cushions, grateful to land. "I knew ye'd do me right, lovey. You always do."

Finally at rest, he closed his eyes and listened to Pegg bustle about. Fatigue had nearly claimed him when searing pain cut across his torso.

"Ow! Sweet nocky, that hurts!" He scowled at Pegg, who had tugged off his waistcoat, the fabric meshed with dried and fresh blood.

"Man up now, lovey." Pegg met his gaze. "Yer shirt is next. Ready?"

At his nod, she yanked. Burning white torture cut into him, ripping, stabbing, nauseating. He grit his teeth so hard, his jaw crackled in his ears. By the time she tucked in the edge of the fabric band, he was one big throb of agony. The bandage held tight around his torso, but it still felt as if his guts could spill out at any moment.

He eased back, wincing. "If I didn't know better, I'd say ye're trying to kill me, woman."

"Dead ye'd be without my help, ye blighter." Pegg crossed her arms, and her bosom jiggled—a welcome distraction from the pain. "Don't you go forgettin' it was ol' Pegg's kind hands what set you to rights."

"No, wench." He sighed. "I'll not be forgettin'. I pays me debts, and I make sure others do the same, startin' with good ol' Ethan boy."

Chin to chest, Nigel watched red spread outward onto the binding on his chest. Ethan Goodwin would pay his debts, all right—and more. When the balance came due for the murder of Will Brayden, one well-placed accusation would transfer that debt away from himself—and instead credit it to Ethan.

Yessiree, he'd unleash Constable Duffy on the morrow to sniff out Goodwin, but for now … he nuzzled into the soft place between Pegg's neck and shoulder and slept like a babe.

∽◦⊙◦∽

Miri lay wide-eyed, staring at the bed hangings she should draw shut but never did. Same for the draperies. Closing them would remove the chill but would also seal her in like a corpse in a crypt. She'd rather shiver. Tucked beneath the heavy coverlet, her toes curled inside her woolen stockings for warmth. Perhaps a mug of hot tea would be a better companion on this sleepless night.

She scooted from the bed and donned a pair of fleece-lined slippers and a long-sleeved robe, then froze. Cocking her head, she listened until her ears hurt. She could've sworn she'd heard something. A creak, perhaps, or maybe a moan. She held her breath, stilling the sound of her own breathing.

Nothing but silence reigned now.

She exhaled and pushed aside the curls falling forward on her face. Soft light shone through each windowpane, resting in elongated rectangles on the woven rug. Following a beam to the glass, she looked over the front drive. A three-quarter moon illuminated the sky. Several clouds roamed free, competing to block its brightness. Tree limbs swayed, bending so far as to scrape the window.

She smiled to herself. Of course. The wind. She turned and lit a candle, cupping the small flame while she crossed the room. Yes, a hot drink would be just the thing on a night such as this.

Fingertips inches from the doorknob, she stopped. A slow creak leached through the wood. If a branch whapped against the window, what would explain the noise outside her door?

Moments stretched, cold and uncomfortable, silent save for the frenzied beat of her heart. Had she imagined it, then?

Leaning closer, she rested her cheek against the oak panel. A floorboard groaned beneath the hallway runner just outside her door.

"Who's there?" Her voice assaulted the night air.

No answer. No creaking. No sound—until fingernails scratched on the wood.

Miri jerked. Fear collected at the back of her throat, choking out a scream.

"Miriall." The low whisper of her brother's voice shot a rush of relief through her. Goodness. What a skittish ninny she'd become. She pulled open the door.

Then gasped.

Roland stood clad in his nightshirt, his face pale. His usual well-groomed hair spiked on end, as if he'd grabbed handfuls and pulled. Hard. Wide and wild, his dark eyes darted like a bird with no safe place to land, then at last focused on her. "Did you hear that?"

Miri's mouth dried. "What?"

He snatched the candle from her grasp and ground out the little flame with his thumb.

"Roland!"

"You can hear better when you don't see. Come." He clutched her hand and tugged her down the corridor to the stairway.

Miri followed, two steps to his one, debating the wisdom of having opened her door in the first place. From now on, she'd take care to keep it locked.

As they climbed the steps to the next level, her lungs started burning, and she panted. "Roland, please, what did you hear?"

"Shhh." His sharp exhale left no room for argument, nor did his pace.

The hem of her wrap caught beneath her toe, and she stumbled. Roland's grip righted her before she tumbled headlong.

By the time the stairs opened onto the third floor, her vision had acclimated to the dark. For one dreadful moment, she held her breath as they neared the attic door. After the death of her mother, she'd learned that cellars and garrets stored anger and punishment.

She tensed, but her brother strode on.

Two doors down, they passed the open entrance to the vicar's chamber. Though it was no doubt immoral to do so, she glanced inside. The bed was empty, the drapes drawn back. Surely, given his duty, Mr. Eldon should not leave them alone at the rectory for days on end like this, especially in light of Roland's illness and retirement.

Cold air curled around her feet and crept up her ankles. At the end of the corridor, her brother stopped. An eight-paned window punctuated the wall above a console table. He looked out at the same moon she'd admired minutes before. The dim glow lit a halo around his head, and she shuddered. He was a darker angel than anyone could possibly imagine.

He released her and raised his arm, pointing one finger toward the adjacent room. His chamber. The hallowed chamber that he allowed no one to attend.

Miri swallowed. "You want me to go in there?"

He didn't move.

What if such an event had played out between her brother and Mr. Eldon the night before the vicar disappeared? Had Roland somehow been the cause of the man's departure? Rejecting such a heinous thought, she sucked in a breath for courage and peered into the chamber. No silvery light shone from uncovered windowpanes in that oppressive blackness.

She glanced back. "I cannot see. You know I don't do well in the dark."

"For God's sake, Miriall, be quiet!"

His voice reverberated in her chest. Hot tears welled in her eyes. More than anything, she hated that even after all these years he could affect her so.

Roland shook his head, and his brows knit into a dark line. "Now you won't hear them. You won't … hear them." His tone progressively lowered until he whispered. "I wanted you to hear them this time."

He covered his face with both hands, shoulders shaking as if he sobbed, but no sound came out.

All fear melted at the sight of her brother's dignity seeping away by increments. Returning to his side, she laid her palm on his sleeve. "I shall listen. I'll try, I vow I'll try."

He recoiled from her touch, or maybe her words, and bolted into his chamber.

Miri trailed after him, arms stretched before her lest she crash into furniture or God knew what else. She crept until her fingers met brocade edged with braiding. Grasping the curtain, she wrenched it aside. First one window, then the next. The pale moonlight cast away any remaining terrors of the night—except for one.

Atop strewn bedcovers, Roland lay curled into a fetal position, whimpering.

Miri took care not to jar the mattress overmuch as she sat next to him. Times like this kept her anger in check. Stroking her brother's hair, she hummed a tune from a lifetime ago, when family meant safety and haven.

> *Hush now, my weary, my traveler, my own.*
> *Rest, peace, and slumber are yours to be known.*
> *You are my precious, my dearest, my best.*
> *You are worth more than the stars.*

One by one his taut muscles yielded, and his breathing evened. She lightened her touch until her hand no longer felt his hair, then rose, fighting her own sobs that begged release. The past several months she'd won many a battle against the madness threatening her brother, but she was losing the war—and with it, her only chance for a decent life here at the rectory. She'd be homeless.

But not hopeless. Lifting her face to the ceiling, she mouthed a desperate prayer. No doubt God could act on her behalf. The hard part would be waiting for that intervention to come.

And in the meantime, she ought to find herself a means of support independent of Roland.

4

Ethan stumbled along, now and again shoring himself up against a brownstone to catch his breath. Alternating between shivers and sweats, he forced each step. The further he advanced from the Old Nichol slum, the better chance he had of saving his life.

But was it worth it?

It should be him lying rigid and cold in an alley, not Will. Will Brayden was the only friend he'd ever had, and now he was gone. Forever. Worse, it was all his fault. Swiping a rough sleeve across his runny nose, he shoved down the pain and pressed on.

His muscles sagged. His bones ached. The task of searching the entire west end of London to find Will's sister seemed as impossible as her willingness to help a rogue like himself. Why should she? Though Will had often sung Miri's praises, Ethan doubted she'd deign so much as to speak with him. He smelled of the gutters and looked no better than a stiff dragged from the Thames. She'd be a fool to take him in. No one would help a wretch like—

A wretch? Of course. What a half wit! He scrubbed his face with one hand. St. Mary Woolnoth's would be a far easier quest than traipsing circles throughout the west end. Reverend Newton should have been his first thought—but thinking had a way of increasing the pounding in his head. Surely the reverend would take him in until he could think straight.

He picked up his pace, only to be halted again and again by cramps or coughs or chills. Morning had arrived in earnest by the time he reached the shadow of St. Mary's steeple.

Pausing before the double towers, he squinted. The stairs moved. How could that be? He rubbed his eyes with his fists, then slowly refocused. Sure enough, the steps rose and fell like an ocean tide. Slowly, he lifted one foot and planted it on the smooth masonry. Expecting the stone to ripple and roll, he braced himself for the movement. It held solid, but he did not. Flailing his arms didn't help, either. The world spun faster, until at last his backside smacked against cold stone.

A belly laugh rang out, rumbling and familiar. Not daring to stand, Ethan looked over his shoulder.

At the top landing, framed within an open door, Newton made merry at his expense. Ethan would laugh, too, if his head didn't hurt so much. He settled for a smile. His chapped lips tore, and he licked away salty blood.

"You look worse than the last time I laid eyes on you, lad. Is this the Lord's handiwork or your own?" The clergyman's voice boomed like a ship's captain, likely a habit hard to break. Despite a crooked back from his many years, Reverend Newton descended the stairs and offered a hand.

"My own, I suppose." Ethan accepted the man's grasp, disappointed that his light-headedness did not go away even with the assistance. "I've taken a fall from grace in more ways than one, I'm afraid."

"Well, well … you've come to the right place, then." Newton's hand squeezed, then loosened.

But Ethan dared not let go. Darkness edged in. Inky spots collected into blots, spreading into a blinding stain. A series of shakes rattled through him, driving him to his knees, and still he clutched the old man's hand.

If he let go, he'd be lost.

∾

Miri paused at the dining room's entry. Morning clouds hung low outside the windowpanes, grey and sullen as her brother's gaze. The vicar's usual merry greeting was still absent. His chair at the end of the table remained unoccupied—again.

Well, if providing the cheer fell on her shoulders, then she ought to be about it. She raised her chin and smiled as she crossed to the sideboard. "Good day, brother."

Roland merely kept his attention to the open book beside his plate. Thankfully he refrained from mentioning their nighttime escapade.

She turned her back to him and transferred a thick slice of brown bread to her plate, then spied a dish of fresh marmalade. Bless Mrs. Makin's soul. How the woman managed to capture sunshine in a bowl was a wonder. Miri slathered a dollop on her bread, her mouth watering, and the knife slipped from her hand. Silver clattered against porcelain, cutting the silence in the room. Eyes bore into her back, and she bit her lip.

Outside, a low roll of thunder reprimanded her.

Roland said nothing.

She let out her breath as she replaced the spreading knife. Good. Maybe he was not in as foul a mood as she credited him. Resuming a pleasant expression, she took her seat at the table.

Truly grateful for the marmalade, she offered a sincere prayer of thanks but kept her head bowed afterward. No sense risking a reproof so soon after the sideboard blunder.

"I trust you slept well." Roland's voice rumbled, ominous as the approaching storm.

She looked up, surprised to see his book closed. Was he purposely leading her to comment on his strange behavior last night? No, she would not fall prey to such a trick. If he wanted it voiced, let him speak of it.

"Yes, of course. Thank you for asking."

"I merely note that you bowed your head an inordinate amount of time."

"Ah, well …" She cleared her throat, stalling. No excuse came to mind, leastwise nothing that would meet his approval. La, as if that ever happened.

As she glanced away, her gaze landed on Eldon's empty spot—a practical weapon with which to parry. She turned back to Roland. "I see Mr. Eldon has not yet returned. Is he off on a parish call? Seems a rather lengthy absence."

"The vicar is not my charge." Roland folded his napkin, creasing each fold several times over. Once finished, he skewered her with a piercing look. "It is taxing enough keeping account of your whereabouts."

Then don't. Miri bit a mouthful of bread to prevent the words from escaping. The sweet marmalade reminded her to be thankful even for a jailer such as her brother. Indeed, though he was harsh and strict, at least she had food aplenty and a pleasant roof to shelter beneath. The church had been generous—but for how much longer?

She swallowed the question, preferring the topic of the vicar. "Should we not be concerned? It is unlike Mr. Eldon to leave no word, and it's been nearly a week."

"You place an excessive amount of interest in the man." Roland stood and pushed in his chair, resting his fingertips atop the mahogany back. "Why?"

"I merely—"

"All strumpets will have their place in the lake of fire."

Heat blazed from her neck to her cheeks. His low opinion, while not surprising or unfamiliar, still smarted. She set down her bread, no longer hungry.

One of Roland's fingers thumped against the chair, an annoying offbeat cadence. "We will speak no more of Mr. Eldon."

Fine. In fact if her brother said they'd speak no more of anything, she'd be content.

She picked up her tea.

His tapping continued. "Master Witherskim asked after you yesterday when I was in town."

Nausea filled the hollow her appetite left, and she replaced her cup without a sip. She'd done her best to ignore the man, hoping he would go away. Forever. "Roland, really, I would prefer to eke out a living on my own. I hope you told him—"

"I told him you would be happy to receive him should he see fit to call."

Happy? Just thinking of entertaining that pinch-faced lecher made her want to heave. She shoved away her plate, the marmalade's fruity smell gagging her. "I would rather not."

"Miriall!" Roland's tapping stopped, and his knuckles whitened.

A rage was there, just beneath his skin, pulsing. If she pushed him any further, it just might bleed out.

"Very well." She sighed.

"Good. It is settled, then."

A rare half smile softened her brother's face, making him look years younger. Almost like Will. The perpetual ache in her heart stabbed sharper, reminding her of how much she missed her other sibling. A lifetime ago, Will's smiles had been her refuge. No one cheered her now, least of all Witherskim and especially not Roland.

"Beggin' yer pardons, if you please, sir, miss." Nodding to each of them, Mrs. Makin stood wringing her hands in the doorway. "Old Joe is askin' for ye, Master Brayden, down at the stable. Seems the vicar's horse has returned."

Roland's smile vanished. "What concern is that of mine?"

"There's blood, sir." The cook ceased her wringing and grabbed handfuls of her apron instead. "Blood on the horse."

"Then have him bind the creature's wound. I know naught of animal husbandry."

"It's not the horse what's bleedin', sir." Mrs. Makin released her right hand and crossed herself.

Unease twisted Miri's stomach as Roland shoved past the cook and disappeared from the dining room.

Mrs. Makin whirled to leave, but Miri halted her with a question. "Is Joe all right?"

Pausing, the woman looked over her shoulder and sniffed. "I'm of a mind that Ol' Joe is the rightest of us all. You mark my words, strange happenings are afoot. Take a care, miss. Take a care."

5

Miri let the admonition follow Mrs. Makin down the corridor as the woman retreated to the kitchen. Take a care. Really. As if she didn't have bigger problems.

Still, it wouldn't hurt to question Roland about the vicar's horse when he returned. A simple explanation from him would put all their minds at rest. Leaving the dining room, Miri headed toward the study. The room's bay window gave a direct view of the stables. She'd be the first to see when her brother returned.

She inhaled as she crossed the threshold. Leather, beeswax, old books … ahh. A simple pleasure, truly. One that she savored. Outside, the clouds had finally released fat raindrops, pelting the glass in a soothing rhythm. She yawned, her whole body feeling the pull of an overstuffed chair opposite the desk. The grey morning, combined with her sleepless night, would make for a grand nap. Tempting, indeed, but utterly out of the question. If Roland caught her asleep in his sanctuary—

Better not to think it.

When another yawn stretched her jaw, she turned her back to the chair and stationed herself near the window to watch for Roland … until her head started to bob. Maybe a little movement would help.

She walked the perimeter of the room, pausing at the farthest wall to scan the bookshelves. Surely her brother would not object if she glanced at a volume from the collection, but would anything be interesting enough to keep her awake? Theology, doctrine, liturgies. Naught on the top shelf.

Running her finger along the spines of the second shelf revealed nothing appealing, either. She bent and perused the third. Dry, dull titles, one after another. Was this entire day to be ill fated? Bending farther, she looked to the bottom, her last hope.

At the very end, one book stuck out beyond the rest. Must be good to be kept at such easy availability. She retrieved it and squinted at the small print on the cover. *Praesulibus Angliae Commentarius.* No doubt a breathtaking read for a student of Latin. She barely grasped the finer points of French.

Sighing, she shoved it back, but the troublesome volume would not be pushed in all the way. Hmm. Either her strength waned from such a bent position, or something blocked the silly thing from resting flush with the other titles.

She pulled the commentary out once more, then fished her finger around the depths of the dark space. At last she finagled out a worn copy that had been hidden behind, nearly cracking her fingernail in the process. Giving in to the complaint of her lower back muscles, she stood to examine the book.

A Bible. Not surprising, really. But why had it been jammed into such an irretrievable cranny? Opening the cover, she smoothed the thin paper on the inscription page to better read the faded ink.

Grant that you will be as diligent in the scriptures
As God is in the lives of the sheep you will shepherd.

May all the blessings of heaven pour out upon you,
Bartholomew James Eldon,
With this holy Word of God entrusted to your care and keeping.
Servo Deus non vir.

> ~ *Bishop Randall Dewhurst*

This was Mr. Eldon's Bible. But why would—

"What are you doing here?" Roland's voice boomed behind her, and she dropped the book.

✧

Ethan slugged back half a mug of watered stout, trying to drive away a metallic taste that would not be shaken and satisfy the thirst haunting him. No good. He could down a keg and still feel no better. Setting the empty cup on the stone floor, he leaned forward in his chair. Even this close to the hearth, shivers ran through him. Traitorous body.

Newton's rhythmic scraping of blade on wood stopped, his whittling knife paused in midair. "How you holding up, lad?"

"I could use a healing touch right about now." He edged nearer to the fire. "Would that God might move a little faster."

Newton's blade resumed its motion. Small curls added to those already littering the floor, increasing the scent of pine. "God works powerfully, lad, but for the most part gradually and gently."

"Gradual?" Ethan grunted. "Seems to me God's work in Will Brayden was too gradual." Turning from the hearth, Ethan pinned the reverend with a searching gaze. "And where is Will now? Is he in heaven or—"

He pressed his lips tight. If he so much as finished that thought, it would be like damning Will himself.

"Who can say? Only God knows." Newton's voice, loud under the best of conditions, bounced from one wall to the other in the small room.

Ethan blew out a long, ragged breath. "It should have been me."

Newton chuckled. "You know, whenever I reach heaven, I expect to find three wonders. First, to meet some I had not thought to see there. Second, to miss some I had expected to see there. And third, the greatest wonder of all, to find myself there."

Newton's crazy declaration went down the wrong way, and Ethan choked. "But … but you're a saint!"

One of the reverend's shaggy eyebrows rose. "Who can say, lad? Only God—"

The sitting room door swung open, and Charlie, the churchwarden's son, peeked in. "Reverend?"

"Aye?" Again Newton's knife suspended its shaving.

"There's a constable at the front door a-wantin' to see you." After a few blinks, the boy vanished like a mouse through a hole.

Ethan shot to his feet, his chair crashing backward. How had they known where to find him?

"Ack, ye're skittish as a landlubber at sea." Newton rose, setting his carving aside. He righted the chair and shoved it toward Ethan. "Sit yourself down."

At a time like this? He snorted as he scanned the few bits of furniture in the room. None were big enough to hide behind. "You don't understand."

"Then enlighten me."

Ethan grimaced. How could he speak of his own hand in murdering Thorne when he didn't want to remember it himself? Worse, by seeking refuge here, he'd dragged a man of God into the scandal. Raking a hand through his hair, he settled on vagueness as the safest route. "You know I come from Old Nichol. Need I say more?"

Newton folded his arms, studying him like an obscure scripture. "What of your resolve to start a new life?"

An ember popped from the hearth, and Ethan jumped, the gunlike snap as jarring as Newton's question. "I must leave."

Drawing near, the old man rested a hand on Ethan's shoulder. "I suspect you'll do what you must, but know this … you are welcome to stay, constable or not."

The reverend's light touch ill-compared to the weight of his own conscience. Opium eater. Philanderer. Liar, cheater, drunkard. And now murderer as well. He pulled away, as surely as God must be pulling from him. It was error indeed to ever think he could lead a respectable life. He shot the reverend a heavy-lidded glance. "You would not say so if you knew the mistakes I've made."

Newton threw back his head and laughed, the irony of his humor startling. Most clerics would have seized the chance to point a finger. Not this one—which was why Ethan had listened to the old man in the first place.

"Ahh, hah …" Wheezing, the reverend paused to catch his breath. "I believe we've been over this before. We serve a gracious Master, lad, who I daresay knows how to overrule our mistakes, to His glory and our advantage."

"I don't have time for accolades!" Ethan winced at his harshness. Had that really come from his own mouth? The reverend didn't deserve to bear the brunt of his anger. "Forgive me, sir. I owe you my thanks, and I owe God—"

"No, no lad. Whatever debt you think you owe God has already been paid. I forgive you as freely as our gracious Lord has, for did He not readily give up His life for the likes of us both?"

Thick emotion clogged Ethan's throat, and he closed his eyes. The image of Will taking the knife meant for him lent all the more reality to Newton's words. He nodded, then met the gaze of acceptance Newton offered. "Thank you."

The reverend scratched the stubble on his head. "Not me, lad. Thank God."

A smile tugged his lips, a marvel truly, for how could he feel a thrill of joy with a constable outside? A wonder indeed—nay, a miracle. He glanced upward. "Yes indeed, thank You, God."

A stream of peace washed over him, seeping into the jagged places deep inside, until fear dammed it up. Urgency to leave this place pulsed stronger with each heartbeat. "Now truly, I must go."

"Where?" The reverend scanned his face as though looking for the hint of a storm cloud on the horizon. "Surely not back to Old Nichol, though I just might sail over there myself. There's a whole sea of drowning souls in that neighborhood."

Ethan blew out a long breath. Where could he go? In a different world, he might have gone home, but returning there now would be an uncharted, impossible journey. He shook his head. "I am not sure, though I have been told someone on the city's west end might help me, Will's sister. Miri Brayden."

"Brayden. Brayden." The reverend tapped a finger on his temple. "Seems to me I've heard that name before, spoken by those more learned than me. Hmm. Ask the rector at St. Giles.

He ought to know who resides in his own parish, if he's worth his salt."

"Reverend!" Charlie ran into the room, nearly crashing into Newton save for the old man's hand that halted him at arm's length. "The constable, sir, he won't be put off much longer. He says—"

"Tell him I'll be there shortly." Newton patted the boy on the head.

Ethan's pulse hammered out of control.

Charlie frowned. "But—"

"Go." The pat turned into a swat. Newton watched the boy exit, then turned to Ethan. "And God go with you, lad. You'll be in my prayers."

Good. He'd take all the prayers he could get. Penniless and on the run, he'd need them.

6

Nigel Thorne rolled over on the thin mattress, blanket tangling in a lump beneath him. Slowly, he opened his eyes, and the pounding in his head increased. No wonder that gin had been so cheap. Skunk of a barkeep. A thin shaft of sunlight breached the hole in the curtain and glinted off the broken bottle lying on the floor. He tried to focus on the resulting prism splotching a dab of color on the wall opposite him, but no good. Fuzzy vision. Fuzzier tongue. He licked his lips and swallowed.

Rap, rap, rap. Pressing the heel of his hand to his forehead, Nigel applied firm and steady pressure. Who knew? Maybe it would counteract the throbbing and even it out to a dull ache. He scrunched his eyes shut, willing it so.

Rap, rap, rap. The noise continued ever louder. Not even a beastly head-banger could sound that sharp.

Rising too fast, he winced from the pain stabbing the length of his wound. First his head, now his body. A baneful start to the day.

Rap, rap, rap.

"Hold on." Good advice. Nigel steadied himself against a littered table. When the room stopped spinning, he reached for a rumpled pair of breeches hanging half off the back of a chair. Aiming his foot for the leg hole, he caught his toe on the trousers' crotch and teetered off balance. He flailed his arms and caught himself, then shoved his foot through one leg after the other. But something sure did not feel right. Were these his pants?

Rap, rap-rap-rap-rap.

"Coming!" Oh, sweet peacock. He'd put the pants on backward. Tussling with the fabric one more time, he swapped them proper and crossed the room.

He opened the door to a hedgehog. Leastwise that's the image he got whenever he faced Constable Duffy. The man's bristly hair, peppered with white, spiked straight on end like so many quills. Loose skin jiggled when he spoke, and it took all Nigel's self-restraint to keep from poking the man just to see if he'd roll up into a ball.

"Mr. Duffy." Nigel greeted him but did not step aside.

"Mr. Thorne." Duffy snuffled as if that might clear his nasally voice. "I did what you said."

Nigel looked past the man to an empty corridor. "So where is he?"

"No one's seen him." Duffy's nose twitched, and he leaned closer. "If you ask me, sir, Ethan Goodwin's on the run, that's what. Skipped town. Wouldn't you, if you had murder a-hanging over yer head?"

Smiling at the man's naïveté, Nigel rubbed his hands together. "Good work, Duffy. Next time our boy Ethan surfaces in London, we'll clap him in irons and pack him off to Newgate. Put the case on close for now, eh?"

"Right, sir." Duffy nodded. As he retreated down the hall to the flat's single stairwell, Nigel half expected to see a stubby tail on his backside. But hedgehog or not, at least the man knew how to carry out orders, and confidentially at that.

Nigel shut the door, relieved there'd be no more active snooping into the Will Brayden killing. Perhaps this day would not be so bad after all. A drink or two to celebrate, why … he felt so light in the heels he might just pay a visit to good ol' Pegg.

Rap, rap, rap.

Now what? Surely the constable didn't expect his palm greased further. Still, it wouldn't hurt to pay for additional silence on the matter. Sidestepping glass shards, Nigel rummaged through the assorted geegaws and doodads littering the table, finally uncovering a tattered money purse. No coins jingled as he lifted it.

Loosening the drawstring, he tipped it upside down, then shook it for good measure. Nothing.

Rap, rap, rap.

"Look, Duffy …" As he opened the door, the words died on his lips—and not from a fuzzy tongue. A freak of nature filled the space. Goliath incarnate.

"Nigel Thorne?" The giant's voice rumbled louder than a lion's growl. Why did big always mean bass?

Despite wanting to appear courageous, Nigel retreated a step. "You've found his home, all right, but uh …" He glanced over his shoulder at his bed, his table, his chair, collecting just the right amount of confidence to sound believable, then turned back. "As you can see, he's not here, mate."

The mammoth grunted. "The name's Buck." Reaching out with surprising speed, he gripped Nigel by the throat and lifted him. "Not *mate.*"

Nigel's feet dangled. He clawed at the man's arm, panic increasing along with his heart rate.

The man's voice was even louder at eye level. "Seeing as Thorne isn't about, perhaps you can relay a little message for me."

Squirming, Nigel tried to pry the man's fingers from his neck.

Hah. He might as easily bed the queen herself. Any more of this and his head would pop.

"Tell Thorne I stopped by to collect a debt owed to Mr. Havisway."

Nigel's lungs started to burn.

"And that Mr. Havisway don't take kindly to late payments. Understand?"

He'd nod if he could. Blackness closed in, Buck's face becoming one enormous nose.

"I'll be back in a day or two." Buck squeezed tighter. "Mr. Thorne."

He tossed Nigel backward one-handed. When he landed, pieces of glass ground into his palms.

So this would be a bad day.

Very bad.

Sucking in air, he worked his way to the chair and pulled himself up. He sat a good long time. Coughing. Hacking. Thinking.

Where in the world would he get the guineas to pay off a gambling spree gone awry?

⌘

Miri whirled, and her skirt poufed out, covering the vicar's Bible. Pressing a hand to her chest, she tried to keep her heart inside her frame and slow her erratic breathing. "Goodness, Roland, you startled me." Truly, his catching her by surprise was turning into a disturbing trend.

"Sinners conceal their works, alarmed only when found out." Though standing in the doorway, well beyond arm's reach, he held her in place with a fixated stare. "I repeat, what are you doing here?"

Unable to contain her irritation, Miri sighed. "I was watching for your return, that's all. The study window affords the best view."

"Yet you do not stand at the window."

"Not anymore."

Her brother's jaw clenched. She would gain no information if she drove him into a foul humor.

Smiling, she patted her hair, hopefully drawing his attention upward while her toe worked to shove the vicar's Bible into the shadows at the bookcase's side. Why she felt the need to hide the thing, she wasn't certain, but it was a driving desire nonetheless. "You tarried so long, weariness gained the better of me. I paced the room and thought perhaps to borrow a book, and so you find me. What did you discover at the stables?"

"As the cook said, Eldon's horse." He crossed to the cherrywood desk, diverting his interest to a stack of scattered documents.

Just the break she needed. Her foot pushed until the vicar's Bible nestled against the wall. Still observable, but not obvious. She joined Roland opposite the desk. "And?"

"And what?" He shuffled the papers together.

"What about the blood on the horse?"

"I saw none." He shuffled faster.

"But Old Joe said—"

"Old Joe?" Roland set down the papers and planted his palms on the desk. "Whom do you choose to believe, Miriall?"

Miri gnawed her lower lip. Some choice. An elderly jack-of-all-trades or an academic bully. "Of course I do not doubt you, Roland. I simply fail to understand why—"

"Failure to understand is a deficiency in all women. It is natural, and I expect no less from you. Now if you please, I have tithes to account for." He scooped up the pile of documents he'd straightened, then sank into the chair, leather crinkling beneath his weight.

His eyes scanned back and forth as he skimmed the page. It was Mr. Eldon's role to keep the books. Why would her brother not wait until his return?

Unless he knew the vicar would not be returning at all.

Strange happenings are afoot. Mrs. Makin had never spoken a truer word.

Miri mimicked her brother's earlier stance, placing her palms on the desk. "Pray let me help you. Many a time I helped Father with his books before, well, you know ..."

"No."

"Truly, Roland, I am good with numbers." She leaned forward until the edge of the desk pressed against her hips. "Allow me to assist you. I have little else to do. Perhaps this could be the trade I might develop, something with which to support myself. Mrs. Tattler might even take me on over at the—"

"Your service is neither needed nor wanted." His eyes remained fastened on the ledger, but each of his words bored into her. "This is exactly why it would be beneficial for you to shower your attentions on Master Witherskim. I daresay he's your best chance for support. Be done with this silly notion of independence, once and for all. Now, you are dismissed."

She straightened as if slapped. Callous man! Making her hands into fists, she squeezed until her nails bit her palms. Silly notion, indeed. She'd show him. She'd polish up her bookkeeping skills in secret and instead be done with both Roland and Witherskim. Inhaling deeply, she released her tension as she exhaled, then retreated in silence.

But her stomach was not as quiet. As she padded down the stairs, a grumble creaked louder than the worn tread. She pressed a hand to her tummy, and a louder gurgle rumbled beneath her fingers. Apparently one bite of brown bread and marmalade did not a meal make. Veering right, she headed toward the kitchen.

Voices carried louder the closer she drew—one gruff with age, the other twittering.

"He can right well say as he pleases, but that was blood, I tell ye, woman. Dried blood. I'd wager it to be the vicar's, and what's more …"

Miri paused at the doorway, making sure that the tip of her skirt did not so much as sway into Mrs. Makin's or Old Joe's line of vision.

"… I seen Master Brayden's knuckles the day after the vicar went missin'. I know a-swellin' set o' joints caused by a good row. If you ask me, ol' Master Brayden had himself a knock down right afore Mr. Eldon disappeared."

The cook's voice lowered, and Miri leaned closer. "You don't think?"

"Aye, I do think, Mrs. Makin. That I do."

7

Could lungs catch on fire, sear through bone and flesh, and explode out one's chest like a flaming comet? Sure felt like it. With each labored breath Ethan drew, the burning beneath his ribs intensified, as did his exhaustion and hunger. He should have stayed in London. The hangman's noose would be a kindness compared to this torment. What he wouldn't give for a piece of opium right about now, and none of that would be found in a Bedfordshire wood. He glanced heavenward. "The reverend said You have a plan for me. Is this it?"

Skirting the village of Deverell Downs had kept him out of sight but well within range of home fires. Pots of stew, roasted chickens, fresh loaves of bread … just thinking of the aromas rained saliva into a pool at the back of his mouth. How many days had it been since he'd eaten? His stomach cramped, and he turned aside to spit. Too many. Probably four, maybe five. Seemed like forever ago that he'd met with the reverend at St. Giles. At least the man had heard of Miri Brayden, thank God.

Yes, thanks indeed. God had brought him thus far, but unless he found something to eat, he'd not go much farther.

He lowered his gaze and leaned against the rough bark of an ash tree, crossing his arms to ward off the chill of approaching eve. Deep down a cough began, and he bent, hacking until shaky and short of breath. As much as he'd like to sink into the ferns at his feet, if he didn't keep moving, he'd die here.

He willed each step thereafter. Determination was all he owned, and a pitiful amount at that. Soon, an old farmhouse with shuttered windows came into view, smoke curling from its chimney like a sailor puffing a pipe. He brushed off his waistcoat, ripped in elbow and collar and long since barren of buttons. A pitchfork would pierce his backside before he'd have a chance to beg a crust or a crumb.

Beyond the house sat an outbuilding. Small, though perhaps large enough for livestock. Worth a try. By now, pig slop would be a delicacy. He couldn't stop the smile that curved his mouth. If only his father and brother could see him now—a prodigal in the flesh.

His grin faded as he swung around to the back of the byre and entered the shadows. What a hovel. One wall leaned in at such an angle that it forced him to walk crooked, and the roof swagged so low, he needed to duck. Either the farmer was extremely short or worked with a perpetually bent back.

A single cow lowed as he batted aside a cobweb, the silk of it wrapping around his fingers. He wiped it against his breeches while heading straight for the trough, gut clenching in anticipation. His feet hadn't moved this fast in days.

Reaching the manger, he stopped and stared, pushing down an insane urge to laugh. Even the Prodigal had pods or husks or whatever in the world pigs ate. Apparently this cow had already dined and in high style. Not a grain remained.

He was left with nothing. As usual. How come running from the past never seemed to change the present?

The whiny cry of a kitten sounded near his feet. Glancing down at a patch-haired fur ball, Ethan snorted. "You look as bad as me, little scrapper." The tiny cat rubbed against his ankles, mewing all the louder.

"Would that I could help you, Scrappy." With a last glimpse at the licked-clean trough, Ethan stomped outside. "But I cannot even help myself."

Great. Not only had he sunk to speaking to animals, now he was talking to himself.

The early evening air, while fresher than the stuffy byre, set off another coughing spell. Bracing both hands on his thighs, he rode out the attack. Long after it abated, he remained doubled over, exhaustion gaining the upper hand.

"You there! Off with ye!"

Straightening, Ethan faced the owner of the ramshackle barn, hardly twenty paces from him. Short as expected, the man stood much stockier and more muscular than Ethan could have guessed possible, and he did not wield the proverbial pitchfork.

He held a scythe. The blade gleamed, honed to a fine and dangerous edge, catching the last glint of the setting sun. So that's why the farmer didn't have time to fix his byre—too busy sharpening tools into weapons.

Ethan backed up, palms raised high. "As you wish."

The farmer's scowl deepened, his wiry grey brows melding into one. "And don't ye come back."

As if he'd want to. Ethan lowered his hands and walked away, feeling the man's eyes follow him until he gained the road—if it could be called such. The thoroughfare was merely two ruts with grass worn low in between. Hah, some country gent he would make. All the years spent in London had clearly erased his rural roots.

At any rate, villagers surely would not travel so far on this rugged road each Sabbath. Making an about-face, he retraced his steps toward the Downs. Perhaps he'd missed the turn-off he should have taken.

Rounding a sharp bend in the road, he spotted another traveler en route from the small town, a musket shot's distance ahead. The man rode a black horse, and judging from the size, it was likely a mare. Mayhap he'd know the rectory's location. Was it worth the risk to ask for directions?

Horse and rider veered right, disappearing from Ethan's line of vision. Disappointment rumbled in his belly. So much for the directions opportunity—

But where the rider turned, a cloven oak stood, marking a worn trail that forked off the main road. Why had he not seen it when he'd passed by earlier? A pox on those coughing attacks!

He entered an archway of trees, following the lane until it opened onto a field. A wider path led to a grey stone church planted atop a knoll. The other wound to the right, leading to a brick-faced building, three stories high. In front, the black mare stamped as her rider secured the reins to a post. Even from this distance, Ethan could see the fancy cut of the man's coat and high-brimmed hat would allow him entrance to the rectory before his own shabby self.

Until now, he'd never given a thought to how he would approach Will's sister. He could not simply waltz up to the front door and expect admission while looking like a ragamuffin. He'd be relegated to the back door, if that.

So … why not start there?

Miri paused atop the stairs at the sound of men's voices. Surely it could not be the squire again. He'd called that morning with the magistrate, Mr. Buckle, in tow, inquiring where the vicar had been the last two Sundays. Neither Miri nor Mrs. Makin could tell him, and Roland had been out.

Cocking her head, she strained to listen. One voice sounded deep and commanding, almost dictatorial. Roland. The other was over-sweet with manipulative undertones. Witherskim. If she had taken milk with her tea, it would have curdled in her stomach.

What a dreadful close to a tiring day. With the prospect of filling her vacant time, Miri had encouraged Mrs. Makin to visit her ailing sister for a day or two. The cook had been reluctant to agree, especially with Old Joe taken abed by the rheum. After much coaxing and placating, Mrs. Makin agreed. Miri had prepared and served a cold dinner and cleaned up afterward. She'd not minded the work, but she could have done without Roland's perpetual cataloging of her shortfalls.

And now this. She pinched the bridge of her nose, hopeful of warding off the headache that was sure to come.

Laughter rang out as the front door closed, echoing up the staircase from the foyer. Miri ground her teeth at the prospect of spending the entire evening listening to Witherskim's cackles. A foxhound baying at its quarry was more pleasant to the ear. Retreating to her room was out of the question. Roland would hunt her down and likely thrill at the chase. No, hiding would not work.

She must disappear.

The voices grew muffled as the men moved into the sitting room. Now or never, then. Miri padded softly down the stairs. With one hand, she gathered the extra fabric of her skirt lest the muslin swish overloud. If Roland reappeared at this point, he'd pin her like a beetle to a display board—with Witherskim a willing observer.

She held her breath as she left the last step and prepared to pass by the open study door. If they'd keep talking, she just might make it.

Roland's voice rumbled from within. "Of course Miriall will be delighted to receive you."

Her jaw clenched. She'd sooner welcome death.

"Naturally." Witherskim's trademark snicker followed. "I would expect the same from any of the fairer sex in Deverell Downs."

Oh vomit.

"I assure you, Miriall comes from fine stock."

Fine and mad, more like it.

"Excellent. Witherskim lineage is also impeccable, a name harvested from generations of good breeding. It's a duty to my forefathers that I should plant seed in only the finest of soils."

Enough!

She dashed down the corridor, fighting the urge to rip her ears from her head. Slipping through the kitchen door, she slowed. Shadows, birthed by the approaching evening, would make navigating this maze a challenge. Good thing Mrs. Makin wasn't here to witness her flight.

"Miriall?" Roland's voice, while demanding, at least sounded far away. If he checked her chamber first, then mayhap the study, she'd have plenty of time to rush out and escape to the church. She'd take a dark, creepy sanctuary any day over spending an evening with Witherskim. And if she was found out, how could her brother fault her for spending time with the Lord in prayer?

For oh, yes, she would pray—for Witherskim to go away, for her brother's senses to be restored. Pray that, for once, life would take on some portion of normalcy, that she might live out her days in peace at the rectory.

Ouch! Her hip cracked against the table's corner, stopping her short. That would be a lovely shade of purple on the morrow. She rubbed the bone with one hand, then scooted ahead.

"Miriall." This time her brother's voice came from the direction of the study.

Hurry. *Hurry.* She yanked open the back door.

Dark eyes blinked back at her, cavernous with pain or perhaps from starvation. The man standing before her was a suit of skin hung on bones. She'd seen fatter orphans in London's alleys.

"Please, Miss—"

"Miriall!"

Footsteps from the corridor drew closer. As much as she'd like to help the scarecrow in front of her, she did not have time for a beggar. "Come back tomorrow."

"Please—" The word rattled from deep in the man's chest, unleashing a fit of coughing.

Great. Which was better company—a groping princox or a vagabond with consumption? She pushed the door nearly shut, only inches remaining to seal it. Perhaps if he thought she'd close him out, he'd leave. And quick.

But his boot filled the gap.

Frowning, she flung the door back open. "Go away!"

Startled, the man straightened, placing one hand against the doorjamb for support. "Please, Miri."

A jolt shot through her.

Only her younger brother ever called her that.

8

Miri stood tiptoe, looking past the beggar's shoulder, desperate for a glimpse of Will. Twilight painted the yard with a monotone brush, making it hard to see much past the woodpile. She squinted, yet clearly no one else accompanied the beggar. Ignoring the unwashed odor of the man, she leaned closer, giving him no chance to misunderstand her words. "Where is Will?"

He averted his gaze. "I—"

"Miriall!"

Roland's footsteps entered the kitchen, slapping the flagstone floor with determination. The last time he'd caught her helping a vagrant, she'd suffered a lecture on how poverty was a judgment of God, not something to be interfered with. Her knees yet recalled those enforced hours of repentance.

Stepping back, she pelted the beggar with directions. "Go to the church. The key is atop a grey stone set out farther than the rest." Hopefully he heard that last bit over the sound of her slamming the door.

"What are you doing?" Though the words were innocently phrased, Roland's tone bludgeoned.

She turned and flattened her back against the oak. Evening shadows twisted her brother's features into a severity that made her glad for the support. Though her mouth dried, she forced lightness to her words. "I heard you at the front door, which reminded me that with Mrs. Makin gone for the night, I'd promised to lock up the back." For an added touch, she smiled.

He frowned and folded his arms, not buying the explanation she sold.

Bolstering her resolve for the horrid words she'd say next, she lifted her chin. "I am free of duty now and for the rest of the evening."

Free? Hardly. Not if Roland and Witherskim had their way. She bit the inside of her cheek lest the thought fly out her mouth.

Roland stepped closer and grabbed hold of her upper arm, yanking her from the door and out of the kitchen. "Good. Master Witherskim is waiting."

Before she could catch her breath, Roland pulled her down the corridor and into the sitting room, where Clive Witherskim advanced.

"Good evening, Miss Brayden." He reached for her hand and planted his lips atop her fingers.

Her stomach lurched. Everything about the man made her ill, from the tip of his outmoded wig to the gartered socks covering his legs. The stench of horehound and onions hung about him, cloying as rotted fruit. His breath, hot and moist, condensed on her skin.

She jerked away, clasping both hands behind her. His eyes widened, and she realized too late that her reaction offered him a more prominent view of her bosom.

Miri scooted across the room, garnering one of the two single chairs opposite the settee, and folded her arms. From the doorway, Roland glowered at her unladylike position. Let him. Even warriors went to battle with a shield.

Witherskim proceeded to the settee and perched on its edge. If he didn't take care, he'd tumble face forward on the rug. A genuine smile lifted her lips at the thought.

And Witherskim pounced on her indiscretion. "Your brother has granted me courtship rights, Miss Brayden. I see this is acceptable to you."

Her smile vanished, and she rose. "Apparently there has been some miscommunication."

Roland flew to her side, a flush spreading upward from his neck. He pushed her shoulder so hard, she'd have a purple mark in the morn to match the one on her hip. She had no choice but to sink into the chair as he shoved her down.

With his free hand, Roland flourished a nonchalant wave. "Pray forgive my sister's insensibility. I fear she is fatigued. Naturally your attentions are acceptable, sir, and completely desirable. Do I not speak truth, Miriall?"

Roland's fingers dug deeper.

Wincing, Miri remained silent. Witherskim ran his tongue around his overly red lips. Gad … did he paint them, or were they chapped? As much as she wanted to avoid upsetting her brother, she could not agree.

"We are waiting, Miriall."

The clock above the mantle ticked. A breeze rattled the window. Witherskim's knit stockings swooshed as he crossed one leg over the other. No, she would not give in to this pressure.

Almost imperceptibly at first, Roland's hand on her shoulder started shaking. "I said here we tree flee wait for your answer, Miriall."

Miri squinted up at her brother. What had he said?

Even Witherskim cocked his head. "I beg your pardon?"

"No, I beg sweg yours." Roland removed his hand and clasped it in the other. His chest expanded and deflated several times as he gazed at the door. "I fear my sister and I are both fatigued beyond measure. Good wood hoodnight to you, sir."

Alarm screamed in Miri's mind, louder than her brother's nonsensical words. He stood straight-backed, jaw relaxed, with no corded muscles, no angry bloom. To all the world, he looked as sane and in command as when he had ruled at Pembroke.

But something was terribly wrong.

Witherskim leaned forward, a slow smile creeping over his face. A shrewd trader in the commodity of gossip, he surely must be pocketing this gem.

Miri felt faint. There was no help for it. She shot to her feet and crossed to Witherskim, offering her hand before she could recant her action. "My brother speaks truth, sir. With our cook absent and hired man indisposed by a bout of the rheumatism, we are both weary. Perhaps you should call at a different time." She placed her hand over his, looking at him through her lashes. "May I see you to the door?"

Standing, he tucked her hand into the crook of his arm and swept her from the room to the solitude of the foyer. As he reached for his cocked hat hanging on a peg, she took the opportunity to pull away.

Surprising how swift and strong the man could be. His woolen waistcoat chafed her forearms as he drew her into an embrace.

"I hope you don't think me too forward, my dear. But I feel this is acceptable if we are to be wed."

Feeling did not appear to be his problem. He felt way too much as his fingers inched down her spine. She planted her hands on his chest and pushed. "Sir, you forget yourself."

Once free, she stood tall, facing him eye to eye. "You take entirely too much liberty."

He smiled, each tooth as flat as a goat's. "Ahh, yes, your brother warned me of your coquettish ways. Never fear, dearest. I shall not hold your coyness against you, but do hope to surmount it someday … and you."

She bit her tongue, silently counting to ten. Lud! What a deviant. Swallowing the acrid taste his words produced, she reached for the door. "Good night, Master Witherskim."

He wilted into a sloppy bow. "Adieu, Miss Brayden."

His eyeballs were the last to leave, and she felt the effect of his perusal long after she shut and locked the entry. Still, ridding herself of the twisted little man brought a certain sense of accomplishment—short-lived, however.

Roland crossed the threshold of the sitting room and entered the hall, mumbling gibberish rhymes.

⌒⌒⌒

Nigel rested against the wrought-iron fence surrounding Shoreditch Church, the metal cold even through his coat. Were they locking God up or keeping people out? A bar poked into his spine, and he shifted, trying to settle between two bars instead of leaning on only one. Oh blighter! Now both his shoulder blades took the nip.

Ignoring the discomfort, he emptied the contents of a small pouch into his palm. Two, maybe three shillings at most. Pish! All that effort to extort money from Flem had not been worth it … unless Flem had been holding out on him. Nigel scrubbed his chin, itchy from two days' worth of stubble. Perhaps he ought to revisit the ol' pike.

He pocketed the coins and threw the bag to the ground, then shoved off into the foot traffic of Hackney Road. If he couldn't find Flem, then he'd collar someone else.

Scuffing along at a good clip, he took care to sidestep pools of God-knew-what and other piles of nastiness. Twilight wove a fine mesh of darkness with the sooty air. All the better. Cutpurses and dodgers would soon be bringing their prizes home to Old Nichol, anxious for the chance to guzzle some rotgut. A slow smile stretched his mouth at the irony of pickpocketing the pickpockets. But would he gain enough? His smile fled. He'd have to, or there'd be more than hell to pay.

There'd be Buck.

Reaching Brick Lane, he swung around the corner and slammed into a pile of rags.

"Dash it!" The rags jostled about as knobby legs and arms emerged, pushing up a young boy.

"Ye little squeaker." Nigel cuffed the bold lad on the head, almost tumbling him onto his backside once more. "Get on home to yer mother, if you 'ave one, that is."

The lad glared at him, spewing curses that turned Nigel's jaded ears red.

What a cur. Though truly he ought not be surprised at a slummer with spirit. If they didn't learn at a young age, they'd ne'er survive.

Midvulgarity, the boy clamped shut his mouth. His eyes went wide, and beneath the grime, his face paled as if he looked upon Satan himself.

What the devil? Nigel glanced over his shoulder, just in case a horned demon loomed out of the darkness behind him.

In that instant, the boy darted sideways and tore down the street, weaving like a barmy titmouse. Nigel glanced up at the night sky. No full moon. Hmm. Well ... not that he hadn't seen crazier things.

And likely would again before this evening was through. Old Nichol was not to be traversed by the weak of heart.

9

Sitting cock-eyed on her brother's bed, Miri shifted, loosening the knot in her lower back. The cushion behind her slipped to the floor, and Roland's head jostled on her lap. If she wakened him now, all the long night would be for naught, and she'd have to start over. He didn't stir, though dawn's grey illumination grew brighter with each passing minute. His eyes remained shut, his breathing even, his muscles relaxed. Thank God. Sleep erased the frown lines and crow's feet from his features, his boyish qualities reminding her how handsome he was without anger—or madness.

Yawning, Miri eased him off her lap and settled him onto a pillow. She snugged the covers up to his neck, then tiptoed from the room. Oh, that he might sleep through the day and know peace.

For perhaps then she would as well. *Please, God, allow just one day as none other. I am so tired.*

She passed Mr. Eldon's room, door open, bed still unwrinkled. Quiet as a vault. With Roland's recent decline, mayhap the vicar's absence was a blessing in disguise.

Descending the stairs, she paused at the landing of her chamber's corridor. The desire to wrap herself in her counterpane and recline overwhelmed her for a few seconds. If she stretched out onto her own bedding for only a moment … ahhh. But no. The moment would turn into hours. She'd miss the opportunity to feed the beggar as she'd promised, and Lord knew how much longer he could survive without eating.

A fair amount of curiosity drove her as well. How did he know Will's pet name for her? Could he tell her where Will was now?

She forced her cramped toes, still caged in yesterday's shoes, to the next step, then the next. The speedier she finished this duty, the sooner she'd sink into a soft mattress.

Filling a tankard with cider and grabbing the leftover loaf from dinner, she juggled the meal in one arm and unlatched the back door. Cool morning air blasted a fine spray of mist over her, and she shivered. Drat. She should have grabbed her shawl.

Wet grass soaked through her thin kidskin shoes, the chill working its way up past ankle and calf. If it was going to rain, why didn't the sky simply burst and get it over with—and drown her in the process?

Blowing a stray curl off her face, she trudged toward the church's stone walls, stalwart and choked with ivy, a contradiction of sanctuary and judgment. Stopping at the threshold, she shifted the tankard and bread into one hand, grasped the iron door handle with the other, then shoved open the heavy slab.

Gloom and silence greeted her. If she left the door open, drizzle would darken a puddle on the floor. So be it. The measure of light it added removed some of the shadows.

"Good day?" Her voice echoed. "Sir?"

Silence.

No head popped up from the rows of box pews, so she headed toward the screened section of the chancel and peeked over the railing. "Sir?"

Again no answer. The man had probably left, tired of waiting for a meal that had not come. She'd check the vestry on the way out, but it would be surprising indeed if he'd curled up in that small cubicle.

Passing the raised pulpit, she hesitated, tempted to stand behind it. A wicked thought, to be sure. She bit her lip before stretching her neck to view the rectory through the window. Well, why not? What with her brother asleep and the vicar absent, no one would know.

She set down the mug and bread, then climbed the steps and entered the carved-oak platform. What a position. Exalted over the nave and closer to God, one could feel powerful beyond bounds. An alluring feeling—and very, very dangerous, especially if lorded over the people. Did Roland look out, consumed with the supremacy of such an apex, and feel holier than everyone?

She shifted her gaze to the box she usually sat in, second row, and—

Her mouth dropped. No wonder the beggar hadn't answered. He was as still as the stone floor where he lay.

Dead.

Maybe he was. At any rate, this must be what it felt like to die—trapped in a black world of hot pain, more suffocating than that stint in Barbados. If his chest tightened one notch more, Ethan would cease breathing.

So be it. Truly … anything but this torture.

From somewhere far away, a hint of relief beckoned. Cool. Gentle. Caressing his fevered brow, wiping away the heat, the grime.

Sweet Jesus—could be. He forced open his eyes and met the amber gaze of a friend.

So then, he was dead.

"Will?" Ethan's ragged voice grated on his ears as he shifted to take in the high cheekbones and sculpted nose on a sprite of a woman—definitely not Will, but oh so much like him. He opened his mouth to speak more, but only a groan emerged, which elicited a sharp gasp from the angel that held him. His friend had often spoken endearments of his sister, but never once had he told of her ethereal beauty.

Miri's fine brows drew together on skin as pristine as a white rose petal. Would it feel as soft? Her lips, full though pulled into a line, were set in a face framed by ringlets of hair banded with copper strands, mostly caught up but a few loose and sweeping. She smelled sweet, the fragrance of violets fresh from a rain. Life began to seep into him, especially when he realized the cushion cradling his head was her lap.

"What did you say?" Miri's voice, while resonant and pleasing, carried an odd mixture of expectation and despair. She frowned, a thumbnail curve highlighting her chin.

The same indentation Will sported whenever he'd been agitated.

Grief welled anew, punching Ethan in the gut. How he missed his friend's banter, the camaraderie … he swallowed, trying to work up some moisture in his dry mouth. He'd have to tell her. "Will …"

Miri's muscles tensed, her forearm rigid as she ceased mopping his brow. Her eyes shimmered, large and luminous. How big the tears would be, how deep the hurt would cut.

No, he could not do this. Not yet, anyway. "Will … you help me?"

Her shoulders sank, and the grim line of her mouth softened. "I believe that I am, sir." She set down the rag she'd used to mop his brow and reached for a tankard on the pew behind her. "Can you sit?"

He must look as bad as he felt for her to ask such a question. In truth, though, could he? Forcing first one arm, then the other, he pushed himself up and propped his back against the pew edge. The effort stole his breath and began a wave of coughing.

"Here." She cupped the back of his head and held the mug to his mouth. "Drink."

Indeed, she was an angel. Cool liquid passed over his cracked lips, some leaking down his beard, but most soothing his throat and filling his empty belly. He did not stop until he drained the tankard. When she pulled away, he swiped his face with his sleeve. "Thank you."

She smiled, the light of which satisfied more than the drink. "It is a trifle."

Once again she twisted around, resettling the mug and retrieving a cloth-bound bundle. She unwrapped a half loaf of bread, releasing a yeasty, almost nutty aroma. "Are you hungry?"

His stomach constricted, and it took all his restraint to reach for the bread without shaking. He intended to savor each bite, but after the first, he lost all reserve. Within moments, nothing but crumbs remained in his hands, and he licked those off as well.

Shame set in, a slow burn beginning in the gut he'd filled like an animal. And he could smell no better. What a beast this woman must think him. His chin sank to his chest. He should leave now and never come—

Her soft laugh breached his wall of humiliation.

"I guess you were."

He shot her a sideways glance. "What?"

"I guess you were hungry." She stood, brushing wrinkles and a few of his crumbs from her dress, then collected the mug along with the cloth. Her smile faded. "But I am afraid you must leave now."

Oh no, not this soon, not when she stood there looking so appealing. "Miri, I—"

"Why do you call me that?" She stepped nearer, the fabric of her skirt brushing against his shoulder. Her head cocked like a robin about to devour a worm. "How do you know my name?"

His chest deflated. He was a worm. It was his fault her brother lay in a pauper's grave and another man lay dead. He opened his mouth to tell her. *Lord, give me strength.* Ha. If only he had a sixpence for each time he'd prayed those words the past fortnight. "I … uh …"

"Well?" The woman shared Will's tenacity.

"I …" He felt low enough without her towering over him. Gritting his teeth, he rose to his feet. What a mistake. The room spun, sweat rained from every pore, and his stomach lurched.

"You what?" she asked.

"I am going to be sick." The words barely made it out before the bread and cider. He crashed to his knees, hating his feeble body, abhorring what he was in front of her, and helpless to do anything about it—or the next bout of sickness rising from his belly. He doubled over.

"Oh, dear." The mug cracked to the floor, and Miri's arms wrapped around him from behind, supportive, strong.

Spent, he leaned against her and soaked in her strength. How long they stayed that way, he could not guess, his awareness fading in and out.

"You cannot stay here, but I fear you cannot leave, either." Her voice sounded far away. What was she talking about?

"Please. You must try to walk. Stand and put your arm about my shoulders."

He'd crush her, or at the very least sully her. He shook his head.

"Come now. You can do this." She tugged upward. "Please try."

His legs wobbled, and his head still swirled, but at least his stomach had stopped cramping. Would that he had met this woman under different circumstances.

Miri ducked beneath his arm and pushed up, bearing a good portion of his weight. "Excellent." Her word of encouragement came out strained. Though he hadn't eaten in over a week, he still outweighed her by at least five stone.

"Where are we going?" he asked.

"You'll see"—she grunted—"when we get there."

With considerable exertion, they gained the open church door, and she stopped. Her eyes darted from the rectory to one outbuilding and onto the next.

He slanted his head toward her. "You don't know where to go, do you?"

"No, sir." She gazed out at the dreary mist dampening the whole countryside. "I do not."

10

Miri hurried along the main road through Deverell Downs, her calves burning from the pace. Passing by Woods, Proprietor et al, she caught a glimpse of herself in the window. What a fright. Hair she'd hurriedly pinned up before leaving the rectory now breached her bonnet in several places. At least the pelisse she'd donned covered most of her wrinkled dress, for she'd not taken the time to change. Though Roland had remained sleeping while she'd settled the beggar into the potting shed and cleaned the mess in the sanctuary, he surely would not slumber all day. And if he woke to find her missing, she'd have to piece together quite an explanation.

She quickened her steps.

Two doors past the public house, she entered Harper's Apothecary and Tobacco. Mr. Harper's name was an apt one, for he ever loved to address a subject until the listeners would as soon stop up their ears.

A silver bell tinkled overhead, and Miri inhaled the earthy scent of clipped herbs and cherry tobacco—so much sweeter than what she'd been smelling this morn. Lamplight warded off the gloom outside and reflected from countless glass jars and bottles, some clear, others blue or green. With crowded shelves and no space to spare, the shop was as welcoming and cozy as a grandmother's hug.

"Good day." The voice from the other side of the counter did not belong to Mr. Harper. Neither did the stunning sapphire eyes of the man seated on Mr. Harper's stool. "At last we meet."

Miri blinked, unable to form a coherent greeting. How familiar was the sandy hair pulled into a queue, the noble tilt of the man's head, for she'd studied it often enough on Sunday mornings. Heat rose up her neck as she remembered his wink.

"May I help you?" he asked.

She tucked a spiral of hair behind her ear, praying she'd gotten all the dirt off her face. The man's smile captivated. A few crinkles offset his eyes, a testimony to a lifetime of winks and grins. How would it feel to live with someone like that instead of a half-crazed bully who—

"Madam?"

She bit her lower lip. Lack of sleep and a morning of foul nurse-maid duty had surely taken a serious toll on her wits. "Is Mr. Harper available?"

"I am afraid he is on extended leave, entrusting me with his business in his stead." He stood and bowed from the waist. "Jonathan Knight, at your service. And you are?"

"Miss Brayden." She wet her dry lips. "Miss Miriall Brayden."

His smile broadened. "Well then, Miss Brayden, how may I assist you"—he looked past her shoulder out the bay window—"on this fine and dreary day?"

Pleasing to the eye and charming to the ears. She swallowed back a smile despite herself. Witherskim could take a few lessons. Her good mood vanished, and she shuddered. Why think of him now?

"You are chilled, I think, miss. A bit pale as well." He moved halfway down the counter and removed the lid from an amber jar. "I believe I have just the thing for you."

La, she must look worse than frightful. Tucking up her hair, she straightened her bonnet. "I am sorry to give you the wrong impression, Mr. Knight. I have not come for myself."

He glanced up. "Oh?"

"Yes, I …" If only she could pull off her gloves and fan the heat from her face. She could not think when so fagged by the long morning—or with such an endless blue gaze holding hers. "Well, you see …"

His tone lowered as he tilted his head. "Yes?"

"It's just that …" That what? How to tell this upstanding gentleman that she wished to treat a vagabond on death's threshold?

"Our hired man has taken with the rheum." The words came out in a rush. Glancing heavenward, she shouldn't be a bit surprised if a lightning bolt flattened her here and now, though it wasn't exactly a lie. Old Joe was abed and in sore condition.

Mr. Knight returned the contents he'd taken from the jar. "Has willow bark been tried?"

"In truth, I do not know." Excellent. Now she looked foolish as well as dreadful. She wrapped tighter her pelisse, covering the gap where her creased skirt peeked out in front. How she longed to disappear—and the feeling irked her. Why care what this man thought? Or any man, for that matter? No one would have her once her brother's madness was discovered—a boon in Witherskim's case, but a death knell to any other marriage hopes.

As if thoughts of Witherskim parading through her mind weren't bad enough, from the corner of her eye, she snagged a glimpse of the silly man outside the window. Directly across the road from the apothecary's, Clive Witherskim huddled in conversation with the squire.

Miri whirled about so fast, she wobbled. Hopefully he hadn't seen her.

But Mr. Knight did. "Miss! Are you faint?" He pulled a stool around the counter and took firm hold of her upper arm, directing her to sit.

"I am—"

"Yes, you are quite pale." The back of his hand pressed against her forehead. "No fever, though."

"Really, Mr. Knight!" She pulled from his touch. "I am a bit fatigued, that is all."

He withdrew his hand but hesitated at her side, peering at her closely. "Clearly, you have overdone."

"Honestly, sir. I am fine." She took care, however, to remain with her face diverted from the window.

"Well … as you say." He resumed his station behind the counter and collected a few items, but his gaze did not leave her. "Is there no one else to see to your hired man? Perhaps I should call on him."

She shot to her feet. "No!" The thought of his discovering Roland or the beggar pushed the word out of her mouth with force.

His eyes widened. "I assure you, I am fully competent in my profession."

"I do not question your abilities, Mr. Knight. I should be happy to have you call except for …" Her mind raced to find an excuse, an exhausting maneuver having clocked only two hours of sleep.

"Except for?"

Think. Think! "You're … er … too busy." Victory! That could work. "Yes, what with Mr. Harper being gone, I would not think to impose upon you. Old Joe's not really that bad off."

"Truth be told, it's been a little slow around here. It would be no trouble on my part to see after your man. But if you think that not prudent—"

"I do not, sir. Your time would be better served here in the shop, I am sure." She held her breath, waiting, hoping to see the effect of her words. Had she soothed the savage pride beast within him?

A half smile lit his face. "Very well, you should know best."

Relief rushed through her, and she exhaled.

He ground a pestle into a mortar, filling the shop with an oddly soothing gritty sound, then formed the concoction into pills. Inspecting each one, he collected them into a small envelope and held it out to her. "Give your man two of these every four hours. That will be one shilling, miss."

As she took the packet, her fingertips brushed his—steady and strong, so unlike the beggar's hand she'd held this morn.

The beggar. Her stomach sank. She tucked the packet into her coin purse but did not remove any money. "I have one more request, Mr. Knight. What can be done for a severe cough, fever, and nausea?"

A queer look rippled across his face—one she'd many times directed at Roland.

"I thought you said your man was not that bad off."

If she said he was, Knight would make a visit. If not, then she looked like a liar. She tapped a finger to her lips, as if that might charm the right words to the surface. "Well, you see … I mean … I think …"

Mr. Knight cocked his head, studying her. "You seem a bit confused, Miss Brayden."

Not at all—she knew exactly how foolish she appeared. She straightened her back, seeking what little confidence might be found in good posture. "I do not speak of our hired man. This would be for someone else. Someone new to the parish. That's it! Yes, this fellow is rather bad off, I'm afraid."

Pursing his lips, Mr. Knight obviously tried to decide if he should purchase her poorly wrapped parcel of an explanation. "In pain?"

"Quite."

"Very well." This time his work involved no collecting or grinding or packing. He simply reached beneath the counter and pulled out a small bottle filled with liquid and sealed with a cork. "Twenty drops, Miss Brayden, no more, no less. Mix well into a half-pint of drink. Take a care in your measurements, though. Laudanum is not without adverse effects if used improperly. Administer every four to six hours, as needed. One shilling, four pence."

She pulled out the correct amount and grabbed the bottle. "Thank you, Mr. Knight. You have been very helpful."

"My pleasure, Miss Brayden. I shall hope to hear of your patients' progress. And might I recommend for yourself a bit of chamomile tea? It calms like none other. I think you could do with a bit of that."

He smiled—a knowing smile. The kind that harbored secret suspicions—one she'd seen on the vicar's face before he'd disappeared.

"Thank you." She nodded, then rushed to the door. The little bell tinkled, though not by her hand on the latch.

"Good day, Miss Brayden." Mr. Gullaby entered, standing a head shorter than she, especially when he removed his hat.

"Squire." She stepped aside to let him pass.

He did not. Instead, he eyed the bottle in her hand and lifted a single bushy brow. "I hope all is a'right at the rectory."

Miri tucked the bottle into the folds of her pelisse. If the squire learned of the beggar, he'd no doubt race to the magistrate and they'd run the poor man off before his health returned. "Simply another bout of the rheum for Old Joe, is all."

"Ahh, yes. I had a chat with your Joe a few days back. He mentioned he could feel something coming on, among other things." The squire's brow lowered, but still he did not move. "And how is Master Brayden?"

A flush of warmth flowed through Miri's body—and not pleasant warmth, at that. "He is fine, sir." True enough, at least while he slept. But why the inquiry? She narrowed her eyes and studied the man. "Why do you ask?"

"Oh, nothing." He finally pushed past her. "At any rate, likely hearsay and nonsense. Good day, miss."

Glancing both ways to make sure Witherskim no longer remained about, Miri stepped into the chill spring day, allowing the door to close behind her. Too bad it did not shut out her thoughts.

Had Witherskim gossiped about Roland's gibberish?

⌒◎⌒

Nigel's eyes stung, either from lack of sleep or the acrid Dockland stench. Probably both, though it was surprising how last summer's fire yet defiled the air with its burnt stink. Black-blistered warehouse skeletons and useless piles of rubble now made up a good half of the Wapping District. Passing the charred but still-standing Ramsgate Pub, he slowed his step. He'd give his left crown jewel to go in and chug back a few pints instead of facing Buck tonight.

Laughter and banter carried out the open door, but he flipped up his collar and pressed on. He turned into a cobbled alleyway and followed it to the top of the Old Stairs. An unusually clear night with a waning moon lent enough light to view Execution Dock. The low tide swallowed the feet of the condemned men swinging from the gibbets. Good thing he could only see their silhouettes. A shiver ran through him. Hopefully his body wouldn't soon be sharing the water with them.

But it just might.

Taking care to avoid the washed-up sewage left over from high tide, he descended the stairs, staying close to the algae-covered wall. The other side of the stairway hung open, with a drop far enough to break a man's neck.

On the bottom landing, a dark shape moved out from the shadows. Big. Obscenely big. A brief surge of fear caused Nigel's step to falter. His foot shot out, and his bum smacked onto the silt-coated steps. He slid down the rest, landing on spongy ground.

"Nice o' you to drop by, Thorne." Buck yanked him up by the collar.

Nigel teetered, shoving down his rising panic. "I told you I'd be here, din't I?" He brushed himself off, taking longer than necessary.

"Let's have it, then." Buck held out his palm.

If ever he needed his blessed mother's gift of gab, now was the time. "First off, mate, I have a bit of a proposition you might be interested in."

Buck merely shoved his hand closer.

Sucking in a breath of courage, he met Buck's gaze straight on. "Ye see, ain't no reason a shrewd businessman like yerself shouldn't profit from this little transaction as well as Mr. Havisway. He need never—"

His head hit the wall, face mashing against the rocks. Before he could right himself, both of his arms were wrenched behind his back, fettered by Buck's grip. He gasped at the searing pain in his right shoulder. Dash it! If Buck had knocked that joint out of place, why he'd ... Actually, there wasn't a whole lot he could do.

And the truth of it made him whimper.

"Shut up, ye tittering weanling. Just hand over the money, and I'll be on me way." Buck's voice rasped into his ear.

Nigel grunted. "Lemmego."

"What?"

Spitting out the blood from his cut lip, he chopped his words apart. "Let. Me. Go."

Buck's grip loosened. Nigel spun, tempted to pull the knife from his waistband, then sighed, giving up the ghost of that thought. Buck held a towering advantage. Nothing to be done for it, then. He retrieved a wad of bills. "Here, but it's short twenty pounds."

The money was out of his hand before the last of his words passed his lips. As Buck thumbed through the stack, Nigel's heart beat overloud, pounding in his ears. He resolved himself to a permanent swim in the Thames, though he was already wet from the sweat slicking his flesh. Life had sure dealt him some rotten hands. What a horrid way to—

"I said, what's yer proposition, Thorne?"

Nigel waggled a finger in his ear. Sweet nimbycock! Had he heard a'right? Perhaps there really was a God. "It's ... uh ..." His voice cracked like a downy-chinned lad. "It's like this ... I'll bring you Havisway's twenty pounds and an extra twenty for yer trouble. Plus, I'll set you up right nice at Mistress Pegg's Bawdy House. And a fine time ye'll have every night till I've paid you off."

Buck's face was granite. Not a twitch. Not an inkling to give away his thoughts.

Nigel loosened his collar, hoping these weren't his last breaths. Surely he could come up with something more. "And I'll ... why, I'll even throw in a tumble with ol' Pegg herself. Ye've not had a woman if ye've not had Pegg." How he'd get Pegg to agree to this was a mystery, but worth it if it worked.

"Triple it."

He definitely had not heard right this time. Cleaning out his other ear, he cocked his head. "Sorry?"

"I said triple it. Twenty pounds for Havisway, forty for me."

"Tr ... tr ..." Triple it? Nigel's tongue stuck to the roof of his mouth.

"Ye got seven days, Thorne. Not a day more." Buck shoved past him and took the stairs two at a time, slippery silt and all.

Nigel leaned against the wall, as high-strung as when he'd come. True enough, he'd not be drinking the river water this night.

No. He'd simply put it off a week.

11

Ethan dangled his legs over the edge of the potting shed's narrow table. Though Miri had provided him with a pillow and blanket, his body ached from a night spent on the unforgiving wooden planks. He rolled one shoulder, then the next, working out the knots in his muscles.

Light filtered through chinks in the lath. Daylight. How many hours had he slept? His chest still burned, and breathing was a chore … but the nausea and dizziness had disappeared. Actually, he felt pretty good, minus the guilt of murder and grief of losing a friend. Blowing out a long breath, he leaned against the wall and closed his eyes. How easily this brooding would vanish with one plug of opium. He licked his lips, the bittersweet aftertaste so real that he swallowed.

Sighing, he pushed off the table. Better not to dwell upon it.

On his right, shovels, a dung fork, and several grubbing hoes stood like soldiers against the wall. Cobweb chandeliers hung from the ceiling, and when he inhaled, his nose tickled deep inside. The whole place smelled like mushrooms. Atop a wooden crate sat a jug, a basin, and a tankard covered with a cloth. Not your standard garden shed fare. When had that arrived?

So … he'd not only slept—apparently he'd slept like the dead.

He reached for the jug and emptied it into the basin. The cold water bit his hands, stinging his skin as he splashed it onto his cheeks. He scrubbed his face and neck, dampening his collar. How far removed he felt from his youth, when heated water was served him from a silver pitcher. He shook aside the image. Truly there was not much he missed about his former life—except for a warm bath. Ironic that the lifestyle he'd chosen since provided neither baths nor warmth.

The door scraped open, and he looked up from his washing. Miri entered, her curves silhouetted against the outside sun—tiny waist, broad hips. What a shape. He could consume her with one embrace.

A backdrop of sunlight haloed her head. Spirals of hair glinted into a blend of tawny copper, framing her face. How might it look if he loosened those hairpins, release those curls to fall from shoulder to waist, and—

Enough. He flicked the remaining water from his fingers and wiped his hands on his pants, hoping his smile did not reveal his thoughts.

"Good morn." She crossed to his makeshift bed and set down a tray, then undraped some clothing she had slung over her arm. "I see you are feeling better."

"I am." He rested his back against the shed's wall, willing the rickety wood to hold him. "This is a curious infirmary you have brought me to, Miss Brayden, though I am grateful for your care."

She whirled, bracing herself against the table. If she were a bird, she'd have taken flight. "Who are you? How do you know my name?"

Shame raced through him. Not only had he frightened her, but the answer to either question might earn his banishment. Yet he owed her the truth. Working his jaw, he prayed that words would magically flow. "My name is Ethan Goodwin. I am ... was ... a friend of your brother's."

She frowned. "Roland hasn't any—"

"Will's friend."

The change in her expression was momentous, like a woman seeking news of her condemned husband. She stepped forward, wringing her hands. "Please, where is he?"

A lump the size of Westminster lodged in his throat. He'd give anything to erase the anguish in her eyes, especially since he was the cause. "I am sorry to say that Will is no longer ... I mean, he ..." He blew out a ragged breath and swiped his face. "Will is deceased."

"No!" All color drained from her cheeks. "Not ... not Will."

She swayed, reaching one hand back toward the bench.

Without thinking, Ethan closed the distance between them and scooped her into his arms, lest a swoon overtake her. As suspected, his embrace did consume her, so well did she fit against him. Under different circumstances, he would never let go.

As it was, she struggled, and he loosened his grip.

Her hands flew to her face, but she did not wail as he expected. Just a few, quiet, deep moans—as from one who knew well how to wield sorrow.

The lump in his throat turned to dust. "I am sorry, truly."

She swiped her eyes with her sleeve. "As am I, Mr. Goodwin."

"Call me Ethan." The request came out before he could stop it. Ridiculous timing on his part and a complete breach of etiquette, but still ... the rising desire to know her friendship would not be forced down. She must think him mad.

Perhaps he was.

Beneath a pool of tears, eyes the color of autumn oak leaves searched his. "It is not seemly, Mr.—"

"Ethan." He softened his tone. "Please, I am certain Will would have had it no other way."

At the mention of her brother's name, her lower lip quivered. The dam broke, her cheeks flooded with silent weeping. "Was he … did he … suffer much?"

Her grief hit him as a physical blow, wrenching his heart. He never should have come here. She would have been spared the pain that now etched her brow—pain birthed by him. Avoiding details that would only burden her further, he said simply, "It was a speedy end."

"Oh." Her word was a whisper.

"Miri … I …" Sweet heavens. What to say? He drew in a breath as shaky as hers. "I am sorry. Truly. Your brother … he meant a lot to me, more than—"

"Please." She turned from him and gripped the table, her body rigid as the spades against the wall. The fabric of her dress rippled as if she clenched each muscle into oblivion. "Say no more. Not … yet. Not now. Mayhap another time."

Helpless, he wove his fingers together and squeezed. So many emotions at once. Too many. One little chunk of opium would quell these volatile feelings. He licked his lips with a craving so strong he could taste it.

After an awkward silence, her shoulders rising and falling with each of her breaths, at last she spoke—and the emptiness in her voice almost killed him.

"I have brought you a few things." She pulled away the cloth that covered the tray of food, but his eyes fixed on a bottle next to the plate.

Laudanum.

Ethan blinked. Had his very hunger conjured the opium tincture? Impossible, and yet ... there it was. Close enough to reach out and grab.

His hands shook as temptation to shove Miri aside and devour the drug rattled through him. Such an act, of course, would be unforgivable, especially for a gentleman's son. He loosened his hands and planted his feet, restraining the beast within.

"Fresh clothing." She indicated the pile of fabric lying on the table. "I doubt they will fit, but it will do until I can launder yours. And here is some food, though I don't suppose you'll be needing this now." She removed the amber bottle.

His heart stopped. "No!"

Angling her head, she faced him. "What?"

The drug's bitter tang already rained in his mouth. He ran both hands through his hair. He should let her take it. Dispose of it far, far away. That's what Newton would advise, but Newton wasn't here. *God, help me.*

"Are you all right?" Miri's hand rested on his arm.

He jerked from his trance. When had she drawn so close?

"You are trembling." Concern clouded her gaze. "Perhaps you ought to sit."

He gritted his teeth. He'd already looked the fool too many times in front of her. "I'll be fine once I eat, I am sure."

She chewed on her lower lip, obviously considering his words. "Very well. Eat and rest. But if you feel the need ..." She retraced her route to the table and set down the bottle. "Use this. Twenty drops, mixed well into your drink. The apothecary was quite clear with those directions. I shall return later to collect your soiled clothing."

He stood immobile for long after she left, his eyes fixed upon the temptation. The woman had no idea what an enticement she presented—on more levels than one.

◈

The gravel crunching beneath Miri's feet grated on her raw emotions. She stopped, and the sound stopped, but the grief raging inside her roared out of control. Would it ever fade? So still did she stand, an orange-tipped butterfly flitted past her at arm's length. How dare the world continue on undaunted? She lifted her face to the sun, but even that brought no joy. Joy? Hah. The concept was as rancid as a piece of rotted meat.

Hugging herself, she closed her eyes, spring's warmth failing to reach her soul. The beggar—Ethan—could be a liar, she supposed. Maybe Will wasn't truly dead. But why speak such a morbid tale if it weren't true?

Her younger brother, her dearest, her best … gone. And she'd not been there to ease the pain or fear of passing from known to unknown. But what cut the most was that she'd never had a chance to say goodbye, not on the day he'd left home or the day he'd left the earth.

And worse, where was he now?

An eerie sensation shivered through her. Something more than grief. A fine bead of perspiration broke out on her forehead as the hairs on her arms raised.

Fear.

She whirled, facing the rectory, her skirts swishing with the movement. Other fabric moved as well—a curtain swinging back into place. Third floor, farthest window on the right.

Roland's chamber.

How long had he watched her? Had he seen her anguish? Had he seen her bringing the tray to Mr. Goodwin?

Clamping her mind against further questions, she hastened her steps to the back door. Mayhap Roland had merely been enjoying the view, though not likely. Or he could have been pondering over some obscure passage of scripture as he stared outside. More believable. Besides which, in her grief she'd stood still for so long, he might not have noticed her. It wasn't out of the realm of possibility.

Nevertheless, it would not hurt to remain in the kitchen and begin preparing another cold meal for lunch. Out of Roland's sight would hopefully mean out of Roland's mind. Besides which, busywork would put off thinking about Will ... what had happened to him. What kind of man he'd become. How he'd been killed. Had he called out her name at the very end?

As she unwrapped the last of the bread, unbidden tears watered her eyes. So much for busywork. Sniffling, she calculated that between her, Roland, Old Joe, and Ethan, the remaining crust would do for the rest of the day's meals. Thin slices, though. She grabbed a knife and sawed back and forth, trying to ignore the hole in her heart and fear in her soul.

"Miriall!"

She jerked. The knife slipped. A line of red on her finger swelled into a big droplet. Pain followed, as did a stream of blood. Just as well, for now her tears would not be questioned.

Snatching the bread cloth, she pressed it against the wound, then frowned up into Roland's face where he stood in the doorway. "Must you startle me so?"

"I would have a word with you. In the study." He disappeared before she could accept or deny the request.

With a final sniffle, she wrapped the cloth tight around the gash, leaving the bread uncovered. She scooted out of the kitchen, and with each step, her stomach twisted tighter. How to tell Roland about Will? How to explain Ethan? She crossed the study's threshold but remained close to the door. No sense venturing too deep into a lion's den.

Roland turned from the window, hands clasped behind his back. He was clad in his usual somber black, and his stance appeared more threatening than usual. "There is a rebellious streak in you."

Rebellious? She'd followed him as fast as humanly possible. Her jaw dropped, but it took a while before anything came out. "I ... I do not understand."

He stepped closer, crossing his arms on his chest. A sneer lifted one side of his mouth. "Rebellion is as the sin of witchcraft."

She clenched the rag wound about her injured hand, willing the increased pain to draw her mind from his horrid accusation.

Roland's nostrils flared as he considered her. "What have you to say, woman?"

How could she speak? It took all her will to simply breathe.

"What did I see, Miriall?"

Before she could answer, he was upon her. He grabbed her face with both hands, pulling her into the room, forcing her to look upward. "What did I see when I glanced out my window?"

Her heart sank.

"Answer me!" His hands squeezed her cheeks like a melon. One sharp twist, and he'd break her neck.

Oh, Lord. Is that what had happened to the vicar?

A burst of panic made her sweaty and clammy at the same time. Still, she refused to reveal anything about Ethan or what she'd learned about Will, lest Roland slip over the edge of sanity.

Like a rearing stallion, Roland's breaths huffed. His eyes were wide and dilated, his skin pulled taut as he glowered. For one sickening instant, her father's face superimposed over her brother's, and a black memory surfaced. This was exactly how her father had looked seconds before apoplexy felled him—the night he'd tried to coerce her into becoming Lord Shelton's mistress. It was her refusal to comply that had vexed him into paralysis. She lowered her eyes.

"You!" Roland's voice slapped her.

She winced.

"You …" He let go, and she steeled herself for a tangible blow.

Her muscles ached from the tension as she waited. At the very least, she should have already met with a cuff to the side of her head.

But no strike came. Even so, she would not engage in eye contact and stared instead at the rug.

"Your silence exposes your guilt." Roland began circling her, his polished shoes coming into view with each rotation. "As does my witness. I saw you, Miriall, coming from the potting shed. I will not have it. I will not brook your disobedience. You will give me your word that this … this … gardening is at an end."

He planted his boots in front of her. "Now!"

She jumped, more from relief than anything. Her erratic heart rate slowed, as did her shallow breaths. Dear Lord, all this talk of rebellion and witchcraft, and all because of gardening? Glancing up, she blinked. "Of course. No more gardening."

"I should hope not. You've given your word." He lifted his chin and stared down his nose. "And all liars shall have their place in the lake of fire, you know."

She nodded. Did he not threaten her with that daily? "I understand."

"Do you? I wonder. You worthless bit of baggage. There is not another in all of God's creation as useless and—"

A loud knock on the front door carried from the foyer, and Roland brushed past her. She stumbled to the overstuffed chair and sank into it to recover. La, as if that were a possibility.

"Master Brayden? Master Roland Brayden?" The words carried through the study door. Miri cocked her head at the unfamiliar voice and strained to listen.

"Yes?" Roland answered.

"I am Bishop Fothergill, come to make inquiry about the vicar, Mr. Eldon."

"He is not here," Roland said.

"Exactly. That is the matter I wish to discuss."

12

Miri's cheeks scorched as she leaned over the kettle one more time to see if the water yet boiled. No bubbles. She straightened before her eyebrows ignited. Serving tea was her best option to manage joining Roland in the sitting room, where even now he and the bishop discussed Mr. Eldon. Ooh, if this silly formality caused her to miss important information ... well, hang the proper temperature! She grabbed a cloth and removed the kettle from the fire, then poured tepid water into a teapot. No doubt Roland would later harangue her lacking hostess skills. So be it.

She scurried down the corridor, porcelain rattling. Just before she reached the sitting room door, she slowed and entered at a funeral march. Setting the tray on the sideboard rather than the tea table at center, she kept a certain distance to conceal her breathlessness.

Roland sat with his legs stretched before him, peering out the window. "Yes, I have been delayed there as well. Wallingford ought to do something about that bridge. One can hope it will be fixed when you return home ... how long did you say you were staying again?"

Miri's shoulders loosened. Apparently she'd missed nothing more than the boring details of a long journey.

From the corner of the room, the bishop signaled for a cup of tea. Interesting that he'd chosen the spindly Chippendale to sit on instead of the more stalwart settee. A man of his size ought to be more concerned. He was all belly, with legs and arms sticking out at regular intervals, topped off with a balding head. Indeed, he was so round that the bottom four buttons of his vest could not be fastened, and the rest might pop at any moment, putting someone's eye out. "My visit is indeterminate. I suppose it shall depend upon what I uncover."

Miri averted her gaze to the tea tray, hopefully hiding her dismay. With the bishop's indefinite visit, it would be doubly hard to keep Ethan's presence and Roland's behaviors a secret. She snatched up the teapot, and the lid jiggled as she poured, clattering at just the wrong time.

"Is there a problem, Miriall?"

Other than his madness, Will's death, and the vagabond hidden in the garden shed, she didn't have a care in the world. She pressed her lips tight and set down the traitorous pot, then collected the cup and saucer. Ignoring his question, she turned and served Bishop Fothergill.

Roland stood, glowering. He stalked to the mantle, watching all the while as she returned to fill a cup for him.

"I believe I asked you a question." His voice scolded harsher than a fishwife's.

She took care not to stumble on the rug lest she spill and add to her growing list of iniquities. Padding toward him, she offered his tea. "I fear I am not as proficient as Mrs. Makin. Were she here—"

"Take responsibility for your own inadequacies, numerous as they may be."

Lowering her gaze, she could not stop the burning that rose to her cheeks. She should be used to reprimands in front of company, yet her body never failed to react. "I am sorry, brother."

Behind her, the bishop's chair creaked. "May I understand this to be your sister, Master Brayden?"

Roland glared his warning for her to behave before looking past her. "Yes. This is Miriall. The church has been overly gracious in allowing my sister to reside at the rectory with me. I hope to remedy that situation soon enough."

"Oh?" The bishop gave her a kindly smile. "How so?"

Miri fixed a stare on her brother's face. Her life could very well depend on his answer, and for that she might almost hate him.

Roland refused to make eye contact. "I believe Master Witherskim, administrator of Bedfordshire School for Boys, is soon to make an offer. It is a suitable match."

Suitable! Her hands clenched. She'd sooner mate with the wretched beggar out in the potting shed. She whirled and resumed her station near the sideboard, hardly able to hear over the angry thrumming in her ears.

"I see." The bishop eyed her from head to toe, creating an awkward lull in the conversation. When Fothergill finally realized Roland's glower now belonged to him instead of her, he stifled a cough. "Well, then, on to the business at hand, shall we? It has been brought to the diocese's attention that Mr. Eldon is inexplicably absent from his post. Have you any information on his whereabouts?"

Roland took an inordinate amount of time setting his cup on the mantle. At length, he clasped his hands behind him and returned his attention to Fothergill. "I am not aware it is my duty to account for the vicar."

The bishop cocked his head. "Neither is it your duty to fill the pulpit, sir, which I understand is exactly what you have been about. Do you deny this?"

Roland pressed his mouth into a thin line.

Miri tensed, foreboding stealing the breath from her. If Roland's hold on sanity unleashed at this moment, they'd both be out on the streets.

"Perhaps you did not hear me." The bishop leaned forward. "I asked if you deny filling the pulpit."

Roland froze, a roe before a hunter. He stared at the oak molding on the far wall, the muscles of his jaw working as he must be grinding his teeth. How close was he to snapping?

Fothergill narrowed his eyes and studied him. "You seem agitated, Master Brayden."

Outside, a gust of wind rattled the windowpanes, the only noise brave enough to breach the silence.

At last Roland opened his mouth. "May I ask, Bishop, how you were apprised of the situation?"

"Not that it signifies, but Squire Gullaby sent word. He finds it rather interesting, as do I"—Fothergill lifted his chin—"that the vicar suddenly went missing not long after your arrival."

Her brother's hands emerged from behind his back, curled into fists. He skewered Fothergill with a piercing stare. "What are you insinuating? My history within the church is impeccable."

Miri let out a breath. An angry Roland was a predictable Roland.

"I insinuate nothing, Master Brayden. I state facts." As the bishop shifted his weight, the back chair legs creaked a complaint. "Your service as headmaster of Pembroke is without blemish and cannot be argued. I daresay your bout with brain fever was as much a blow to the institution as to yourself. But it is also a fact that you were sent here to recuperate, not to fill a pulpit. Do I make myself clear?"

Roland's fists loosened into splayed fingers. "Quite."

"Good." The bishop sniffed. "Until the vicar is found, I will see to this parish. Know that I plan to delve further into Eldon's absence, and I will brook no opposition on the matter."

Miri hugged herself. She did not need this inscrutable fat saint nosing about.

"Well, then, I shall attend your horse. Miri!"—Roland nodded at her—"shall see you to a chamber. No doubt you should like to refresh."

"What? Am I to learn the groom and housekeeper are missing too?" The bishop pushed up to stand, and the front chair legs harmonized with the back in relief.

"We are a bit short staffed at the moment." Roland strode from the room, dismissing the bishop with a wave, either not expecting or requiring a reply.

"No vicar, no staff." Fothergill crossed to where Miri stood near the door, the smell of talc overwhelming. "Curious indeed. I imagine my visit to Deverell Downs will prove remarkable in more ways than one, eh miss?" He elbowed her as he passed by.

Miri pinched the bridge of her nose, warding off a sneeze. The bishop had no idea what sort of prophecy he'd just spoken.

❦

Two steps from the bedroom door, Nigel ducked. Whooshing air lifted the hair by his ear as a shoe sailed past him and nailed the wall, leaving an ugly black mark. Not that he hadn't expected some resistance to his offering of Pegg's services to Buck, but this? Saucy woman. If only he could redirect that passion. Turning to face her, he softened his tone. "Listen, lovey—"

The other shoe hit him square in the eye.

"Ow!" Pressing fingertips against the sting, he growled. "Wut you wanna go and do that for? Ain't Nigel ere been your sweeting? Why, I oughtta—"

"Get out!" She reached for an overlarge crystal oil lamp.

Nigel flew out the door to the sound of exploding shards of glass. Saucy indeed.

"And don't you come back, ye hear?"

Gads! The whole neighborhood could hear. He took the stairs two at a time, rebounding between wall and railing in his haste, and did not pause to close the door behind him as he fled onto Stocking Lane. His eye smarted, and his cheek nipped where she'd slapped him. Just to be on the safe side, he kept a vigil of glances over his shoulder should she follow. He winced at the thought of the reception Buck would obtain when he went to claim his promised spoils.

Nigel blew out a big breath. When would his luck ever change?

He left Old Nichol behind and traipsed toward home. One full day, and all he'd mucked up was a measly five pounds. Five pounds! A far cry from the sixty required.

Tugging at his collar for air, he ran circles in his mind trying to come up with a new source of money. By the time he neared his flat, defeat engulfed him.

Until a sharp jab poked him in the back, pulling him from despair. He spun, fists raised.

Constable Duffy snuffled at him. "In a scrappin' mood, eh? Looks like you're already nursin' a right fine shiner."

Nigel lowered his hands. "What ye sneakin' up on me like that for?"

"Not sneakin'. Been waitin' for ye." Duffy paused to scratch a patch of greyish-brown hair behind his ear, one side of his mouth curling with pleasure. Maybe the man had fleas.

"And?" Nigel asked.

The scratching slowed until finally Duffy quit. "I happened to swing by the Chancery today, and imagine whose name I hear bandied about."

Nigel folded his arms. His thin repertoire of virtue did not include patience, especially today. "Out with it!"

"Ethan Goodwin, that's who. Seems there's a ..." Duffy rubbed his palm up and down his pant leg, watching the action with an exaggerated stare.

"Fine, fine." Nigel sighed and rummaged in his waistcoat, retrieving a shilling.

Yellowed teeth shone through Duffy's prickly beard as he pocketed the garnish. "Seems there's a genuine gent a-lookin' for him, same as you. Some kind of solicitor from up Yorkshire way, goes by the name o' Spittle, or Swindle, er ... no, it was Spindle. I'm sure of it."

"I don't give a flappety niglet about the man's name. Why, Duffy? Why would a solicitor be lookin' for Goodwin?"

"Well, that I'm not so sure of. He shut himself up with a barrister, closin' the door afore I could hear the rest, and that's the truth of it. One thing I do know, though, is that before the door shut tight"—Duffy leaned closer and lowered his voice—"I heard the word *entail*. Though mightta been impale, or exhale ..." Duffy's face scrunched, and he tapped his chin as he thought out loud. "Maybe even inhale, though 'tis doubtful, that. Most big entailments run through the Chancery, and if Goodwin's the man they're lookin' for ..."

Nigel patted the tender skin around his eye, pondering Duffy's tidbits. Hmm. If Ethan had an inheritance coming to him, perhaps his luck was about to change after all.

13

An entire day, a never-ending night, and now finally dawn's grey light slanted through the potting shed's gapped walls. Ethan lay on the makeshift bed, eyes burning as he mindlessly watched dust motes floating in midair. His right hand was numb, frozen into a claw from clutching his bottle of life for so long. Life? Huh. More like torment. Ever since Miri had brought the laudanum to him yesterday, a battle had raged within. He should drink it and be damned, but conviction weighted him as much as lack of sleep—and he was tired of both.

He pushed off the table and flung the bottle against the far wall. Glass shards exploded. Liquid splattered. A bold move, to be sure, and hopefully not a mistake.

"What are you doing?"

Startled, he wheeled about. Miri stood just inside the doorway, eyes wide.

"I …" Blinking, he tried to select one of the countless excuses parading through his mind. But as she stood there, the picture of innocence in her white day dress, he knew that each fabrication would be a further stain upon his character. He'd ruined one too many relationships by building on a foundation of lies—not this time. Not with her.

He lifted his chin. "I broke the bottle of laudanum."

His blinking was contagious.

"I see. Well … not really, but …" Her skirts swished as she took hasty steps to the table and set down a small covered dish. "My apologies. It is a meager breakfast I bring."

He scrubbed his hand across his jaw. Amazing. She'd not asked a string of endless questions—not even one. What kind of woman was this Miri Brayden? He closed the gap between them, standing near enough to inhale her freshly scrubbed scent. "Are you not going to demand an explanation?"

She remained silent for so long, he began to think she would not answer.

At last she faced him. "Look, Mr.—"

"Ethan."

She frowned. "You owe me no explanation. What you choose to do or not is entirely your own concern."

A rogue urge struck him to reach out and trace the dimple in her chin, the sweeping curve of her cheek. Instead, he clenched his hands so tight, his knuckles ached. "You are more than accommodating, for I feel I owe you my very life."

The blush of a June rose highlighted her cheeks, and she averted her gaze. "Do not even think it. I did no more than—"

"You did more than many others. Please." He laid a hand on her forearm. Beneath the fabric of her sleeve, an interesting mix of frailty and strength met his touch. "Accept my gratitude. Without you, I would have perished."

The enormity of his own words hit him hard. He owed the Brayden family his life twice over now. Without forethought, he ran his thumb back and forth along her arm.

She did not pull away. Neither did she look up. She merely stared at his hand. "I hope to return your clothing by the end of the day. I am sure you would like to be on your way."

Leave—now that he'd discovered her? "No!"

She snapped her gaze to his, fear and curiosity competing in her eyes. As much as he desired to calm her, his hand would not be stopped. He reached up and touched a wispy lock of her hair.

Miri jerked free and scurried to the door.

A pox on his street-harsh ways! He stepped toward her, then stopped. Chasing her would serve only to frighten her further. He held up his hands, palms out. "Forgive me. I fear my manners are lacking."

She paused at the threshold, rubbing the place on her forearm where he'd touched her, then slowly turned. A phantom of a smile softened her face. "Oft am I reminded of my own lack. Seems you and I have a thing or two in common, Mr.—"

"Ethan."

"If nothing else, sir, you are consistent. Good day …" Her smile grew. "… Ethan." Closing the door behind her, she left as silently as she'd come.

And it took everything within him not to follow. He sagged against the table and ran his hand through his hair. Why had no one claimed this remarkable woman as a wife?

He took up the bowl of porridge and shoveled a spoonful into his mouth. As he ate, he dug deep into his memory for fragments of conversation about her with Will. Nothing had been said of suitors or betrothals. More often, Will had fretted about her safety, such as it might have been with their father—an overbearing man who'd driven Will to the streets in the first place.

Bowl emptied, he set it down and slanted a glance toward the broken laudanum bottle. Was she really any safer with him? A long, slow sigh escaped him. Once she learned of his past, of his part in Will's death, she likely would not think so.

∽◦⊙◦∽

In the middle of scrubbing the final dinner dish, Miri paused. She'd been caught up in roaming the land of sweet memories from forever ago. Life had been a laughable journey for Will, and most often he'd taken her along for the ride. A tongue lashing from Father? Naught but a hilarious anecdote in Will's retelling. The day she'd burnt her hand on a coal grate? Will's sock-puppet show had erased that pain. When Roland had left for seminary and she'd cried because part of her left with him, Will had filled the void with a sack of candy and a reenactment of how he'd stolen sweetmeats from a fat baker who'd been far too sweaty to catch him.

A dull thudding pulled her back to the present, but the noise was certainly not from her pot hitting the side of the washtub. She tucked a spring of hair behind her ear and listened more intently. The banging traveled all the way from the front door. Someone was ambitious with their knocking this evening. Why could not Roland or the bishop see to it?

She wiped her hands on her apron, an oversized relic belonging to Mrs. Makin, then untied the strings and heaped it atop a counter. Capturing loose hair strands, she left the kitchen and sped along the corridor. Each time she tucked up one curl, two more sprang loose.

A twinge settled in her belly when she remembered Ethan fingering her stray wisps earlier that day, leaving her rather unsettled.

He was a bold man, to be sure. Bold as Witherskim, yet not nearly as offensive. There was an incongruous air about Ethan Goodwin. Something at odds. His appearance, his attire, were that of a gypsy, but looking past the outside, a gentleman resided within.

As she neared the study, an odd sound came from behind the closed door. Bass. Monotone. Foreign yet … She paused. Familiar.

She leaned closer. Inside, Roland droned on and on, quite passionate about something. His words were not in English, but neither were they gibberish.

And then he stopped. Suddenly. Did he sense her presence?

The hairs on her arms prickled. In the silence, she debated making a run for it. He'd hear the floorboards, though. She'd be a fox in a snare, her brother the trapper.

Laughter assaulted the evening air a second before the banging on the front door renewed. Perspiration dotted Miri's forehead.

What to do? Pretend no one was home? Drat. That would never work. She should not have lit that lantern in the sitting room before remembering to wash the dishes.

Speeding away from the study, she compiled a mental list of reasons why no visitors could be admitted. Plague? The pox? A nasty sniffly nose? She sighed. Much too overblown. A simple headache would have to suffice.

The front door rattled in its frame by the time she reached for the knob.

"Good evening, Miss Brayden." The apothecary, Jonathan Knight, flashed a smile bright enough to shame the sun.

But not bright enough to banish the Roland-shaped shadow looming from behind her. Her stomach sank. This could not end well.

Mr. Knight looked past her to her brother. "Good evening, Mr.—"

"What the devil is this about?" Roland's voice boomed.

Miri cringed in reflex. Yet perhaps if she might muster enough courage to divide, she would conquer. She turned to Roland. "Don't trouble yourself, Roland. I will see to Mr. Knight. I am sure—"

"And I am sure, Miriall, that I should like to know what the man has to say at such an hour." Roland angled his head. "In the sitting room, if you please."

He spun and stalked away.

Miri snuck a glance at the apothecary. Mouth agape, he apparently was speechless.

She jumped at the opening. "My brother's ways are sometimes a bit, er, harsh, Mr. Knight. You may leave now, and I will make apologies for you."

"On the contrary, Miss Brayden." He doffed his hat and fingered the brim. A peculiar twinkle lit his blue eyes. "I shall be happy to oblige your brother."

She forced a smile. The man had no idea what an opportunity he'd turned down. "Very well. This way."

She led him into the sitting room, where Roland took up his usual lord-of-the-manor-pose against the mantle. He eyed them as they entered, remaining silent.

"Have a seat, Mr. Knight." Miri nodded, indicating a chair. She sat in another, then looked to Roland. The sooner this interview was ended, the better for all of them.

As the apothecary crossed the room, the scent of tobacco and mint traveled in his wake. A pleasant smell, one that she savored, for it would likely be the only agreeable part of the evening.

Roland lifted a hand and studied his nails. He flicked his thumbnail over the others one by one, making annoying clicks. Had he already forgotten that this interview was the result of his insistence?

Miri opened her mouth to move things along—

And that's when Roland finally decided to speak. "I believe I asked what this is about, Mr. Knight."

The apothecary stiffened. If he was this put off by Roland's abruptness, how would he react if her brother totally lost control?

"Roland, perhaps we ought to first offer refreshment. Mr. Knight is a guest, after all." Miri turned to the apothecary, placating him with a smile. "Would you like—"

"Enough, Miriall. Let the man speak."

Toying with his hat brim, Mr. Knight faced her brother. "I simply came to call upon—"

"My sister is not to be called upon." Roland lowered his hands and set his jaw into a grim line.

Heat traveled up Miri's neck, settling in her cheeks, especially as Mr. Knight shot her a curious glance.

"Not that I hold any objections to calling upon your sister, sir, but that is not the intent of my visit. I came to check on your hired man, whom I understand is currently down with the rheum."

Roland stalked forward, halting inches in front of the man. "And how might you know that?"

The apothecary rose, a challenging tilt to his chin. Dread inched along Miri's spine.

"Your sister came into town yesterday and was good enough to collect some medicine for him."

"Really." Roland didn't so much as deign to look at her. Nonetheless, she felt the intensity of his anger burn through her from head to toe.

"Tell me, was she alone, Mr. Knight?" His question flew like a cannonball.

"Yes. Is there a problem, Master Brayden?"

"Problem?" Roland's chest heaved. "Quite."

He wheeled about and crossed to her, lifting her by the upper arms. "Did I not tell you to stop acting the part of a strumpet? Honestly, Miriall. A betrothed woman ought not prance about unattended as a common prostitute."

"I fear you overreact, Master Brayden. Her behavior was … agitated, not wanton." Mr. Knight's voice echoed in the sudden awkward silence.

Unshed tears burned her eyes, and she blinked. If she closed her lids, would the awful scene disappear? "Roland, you know as well as I that I am not betrothed. I merely—"

"You are. An offer was made. I accepted on your behalf. Now apologize for your behavior to Mr. Knight." He dug his fingers into her arms, emphasizing his words.

"An offer?" Goose pricks dotted her flesh, running down her arms and each leg. Though she suspected the answer, surely it could not be true. "By whom?"

Roland eyed her as if she were a babbling idiot. "Master Witherskim, of course."

"No!" Somewhere deep, sobs rose, humiliating yet unstoppable.

"Miss Brayden?"

Mr. Knight's question sounded far away. Everything sounded far away, except for the ragged noise of her labored breathing and the horrid way Roland's words played over and over in her mind. *I accepted on your behalf. I accepted on your—*

She wrenched from his grasp and tore from the room. As she raced up the stairs, she tripped, stinging her hand when it slapped against the floorboards. It did not stop her, though. Nothing would.

Once she reached her chamber, she slammed the door. A childish reaction, churlish as well—yet she took great satisfaction with the crashing noise that reached to the rafters.

She threw herself atop the covers, seeking the comfort of her bed. Just this once she'd give in to a raging good cry, then retrieve her carpetbag from beneath the bed skirts. She would leave. Tonight. Leave and never come back. Roland could rot for all she cared, and Ethan would have to fend for himself.

Poverty and death were better choices than Witherskim.

14

Ethan paced five steps to the shed wall, then five back to the other. He hesitated at the door, longing to pull it open and stroll free in the dawning light. Under Miri's care his strength increased—as did his guilt. He should tell her the full truth of his part in Will's murder, that another man lay dead because of him. She should know what kind of monster she harbored. He owed her that. He owed Will that.

Running one hand through his hair, he made up his mind. First chance he got, he'd tell her and be done with it.

But when the door creaked open and she stood framed in the blush of sunrise, the intention tucked tail and ran away.

Something was wrong.

Errant curls drooped to her shoulders, as if she'd been distracted in the process of pinning them up. Shadows darkened half circles beneath her eyes, and her lids were puffy. He'd wager ten pounds she'd not slept at all last night.

"Good day." Her voice was hardly a mumble.

"Is it?" He moved aside, allowing her to pass. "And how do you fare this morning?"

"Fine." She set down the tray, then faced him, her skin a shade paler than he remembered. "And you?"

A skilled swordsman couldn't have parried better. He shook his head. "That is no answer. Would you care to try again?"

Her nose crinkled, and she angled her chin. "I said I was fine. Did you not hear?"

He pushed shut the door, then leaned against it and folded his arms. Her words were a lid rattling atop some kind of simmering pot, one he intended to uncover.

"What are you doing?" she asked.

"Waiting."

She cocked her head farther. "For what?"

"To hear how you fare."

Her eyes widened. "You're serious."

"Sometimes, but generally it doesn't last too long."

Sunlight radiated stripes through the cracks in the wall. Several converged, casting a halo atop her head. Miri the angel—a more fitting name he couldn't imagine.

She smoothed her hands on her apron, then clasped them together. "I am not sure what to say."

"Has no one ever asked you how you are?"

"Of course, but a simple 'fine' from me is all they really want to hear." She lowered her eyes and her voice. "Do you not notice that people are generally too busy speaking of themselves to care about others?"

Shoving off from the door, Ethan closed the distance between them. He pushed aside the tray on the bench, hopped up, and patted the empty space beside him. "Tell me."

Her cheeks reddened. "Are my burdens that obvious?"

"Only to one who's looking."

The red turned to flame, and she looked away.

Ethan laughed. It was entirely too easy to make her blush, but he enjoyed the game just the same. "Come on. I'll not bite you."

She glanced at the door while nibbling her lip.

Did he honestly make her that nervous? "Miri, we've breached propriety time and again. No need to give decorum any thought. You should know by now that you're safe with me."

What ran through her mind as she stood there, statuesque and so beautiful it pained him, he could only guess. An eternity later, she turned and hoisted herself up on the bench. "All right. A few moments won't hurt, I suppose."

He waited for her to speak further, but only the outside calls of whippoorwills and chickadees spoke their concerns. Apparently it was up to him to begin. "God knows I'm the least of men to counsel you, but I've a willing ear. What troubles you?"

"Much." Her chest rose and fell with a great sigh. "Family matters, mostly. Roland and …"

Her chin sank, and she stared into her lap, silent. She toyed with the long tie of her apron, winding it around one finger, then unwrapping it again.

Ethan longed to turn her face toward his, to read what emotions sparked in her amber eyes. Surely it would be a deep, deep well. He knew better than anyone how family matters could cut into the underbelly of a soul, leaving behind a long, slow bleed. "You have not told your brother about Will, then?"

"No." The quiver in her voice hinted at much. "I want to, but … I'm not sure how."

"How about the truth?" Ethan flinched. Immediately he pressed his lips into a tight line. He was a fine one to speak of truth when he kept his own secrets so cleverly hidden.

She shook her head and pushed from the bench to stand. "Would that it were so easy. There are many things I should like to say to my brother, but he's quite … If only I could …"

Whirling about, she paced, following the same route he'd worn in the dirt. She hugged herself, tight, and slowly rubbed her arms. Either she took a chill or—

Sudden understanding washed over him. "You fear him. Why?"

She stopped and slowly pivoted, her gaze completely earnest. "Have you any idea what it is like to be at the mercy of one who sees you only as an impediment? A pawn to be discarded as early in the game as possible, giving no concern whatsoever to your own wants or desires?"

Ethan's heart raced. She could have no idea how intimately he knew that feeling. As second son, he was rarely noticed in the shadow of his older brother. Truth be told, the family butler had paid him more concern than his own father had.

"As a matter of fact"—he lowered his feet to the floor and blocked her path—"I know exactly how you feel."

"Really?" She lifted her face and studied his. "Sometimes I wonder … are you for real, Mr. Goodwin?"

Their eyes met and held, forming a bond that robbed him of breath. He took a step toward her, then planted his feet. Any closer would be a mistake he'd regret for a long time—a lifetime, no doubt. "How real do you wish me to be?"

❦

Ethan's husky tone did strange things to her. Or maybe it was the simple fact that he'd cared enough to listen. Truly listen. A tremble ran through her, though neither chill nor draft could be blamed—especially not when she felt so warm. How could she even answer him when her tongue stuck in her mouth?

She spun back to the table, confused. She must be overwrought. That was it. Disgust over the sham of a betrothal to Witherskim. Insufficient sleep. Self-loathing for her lack of courage to run away in the night as she'd intended. The gnawing sorrow over Will. All these things, when added together, made for frivolous imaginings. Ethan Goodwin could be no more interested in her than she should be in him.

That settled, she pulled off the covering cloth from a bowl of porridge and folded it beside the tray. "Here is your breakfast, along with some soap. I thought maybe you—"

"Are you saying I need to bathe, Miss Brayden?"

She bit her lip, horrified that she'd implied such. "I did not mean—"

"Because I couldn't agree with you more. I can hardly stand the smell of me."

Was he mocking her? She whirled—and his warm smile completely disarmed her. What a strange fellow. "You are very forthright, sir."

"Blunt, more like it. Forthright sounds a little too holy for me."

His humility, genuine and unstilted, surprised her. "Most men would prefer to be thought of as such, particularly by a woman."

His grin deepened. "I am a far cry from 'most' men."

"That you are, sir." The rogue tilt of his jaw and gleam in his eye—so much like her younger brother—filled part of the emptiness inside her. She couldn't help but return a smile of her own. "And I suspect that is exactly why Will took to you."

A brief yet very real wave of pain washed over his face before he answered. "I shall take that as a compliment, Miss Brayden. Now, allow me to return the favor."

He stepped toward her and didn't stop until he stood a breath away. "You are unlike any woman I've ever met. Generous, compassionate … beautiful."

Heat blazed across her cheeks, and she bowed her head. Those words, wrapped in such an intimate tone, could not possibly be for her. Such a package of endearments surely belonged to another woman, never for—

A crooked finger beneath her chin drew her face back to his. He stared at her with such intensity, she swallowed.

Then broke free and ran to the door.

"Miri, wait."

A tremor ran through her at the sound of his voice, and she paused, hand on door. "I …"

She what? What was happening to her? She couldn't put two thoughts together if it were royally decreed. She pushed open the worn bit of boards and called over her shoulder. "I must leave. I have a pressing engagement. Good day."

Before he could object, she burst outside, pressing her palms to her cheeks. Hard to tell which made her face burn more—her outright lie or the strange feelings Ethan stirred.

Four paces from the shed, she froze. Her stomach twisted, and all heat fled as she lowered her hands.

"Tell me, Miss Brayden …" Bishop Fothergill flicked his hand toward the shed. "Are you often given to bidding such fond farewells to garden tools?"

"Blazing bandycock!" Nigel's curses multiplied like maggots on a dead alley cat. Pain burned a trail from his toe up his shin. He hopped about on one foot, babying the ingrown nail that he'd angered against the table leg. Stumbling backward, he sank onto his mattress and rubbed his foot.

After a long swig from a bottle next to his bed, the throbbing eased to a bearable drumbeat.

"Slow down, Thorne," he whispered to himself as he stood. "Yer luck's about to change."

Just to make sure, he hobbled over to a chipped ceramic elephant and patted it three times. He'd won it years ago—that and a wad of bills—off a drunken sailor. He liked to think it a lucky charm, though it'd done the sailor no good.

He tugged at his frockcoat, straightening away the wrinkles. As soon as he released the fabric, the creases returned. A bit shabby for Chancery. Still, he owned nothing finer, even to be buried in.

He locked the door behind him and descended the first set of stairs. At the second, he leaned heavy to the right, brushing up against the wall. The risers didn't creak nearly so loud on this side, a stealthy path he'd learned to take when wanting to avoid old Mrs. Spankum. The landlady was a shark, and no doubt circling the waters for his overdue rent.

For good measure, he held his breath. Squalling babies behind Fanny Bridges's door masked any further noise from his footsteps. At the last set, he blew out a big sigh and trotted down the rest. Good thing he'd patted the elephant's—

"Stop right there, Mr. Thorne." Mrs. Spankum's voice was as pleasant as a hack-noted harpsichord.

Nigel gritted his teeth. The old girl blocked the door. There'd be no escaping.

"Good afternoon, Mrs. Spankum," he said. "My, you look so lovely today."

She frowned, and her chin protruded. White whiskers stood out in defiance. Nigel almost flipped her one of the few coins in his pocket to either find a good barber or buy her own straightedge.

"It'll be good when you pay up, Thorne." She held out a hand gnarled by years of work. "Where's last month's rent?"

"I—"

"And don't make up another sob story."

"Well, I—"

Her fingers closed into a fist. "You're a leech, Mr. Thorne. A free-loader. A no-good bedbug that sucks the lifeblood from big-hearted people like me. Furthermore—"

Thorne leaned against the wall and waited. Once her insults began, nothing more could be done. The smartest move when caught in a cloudburst was to hunker down and ride out the storm.

She advanced, fist raised. This was new. Did she seriously think he'd let her pop him a good one? "Now, now, Mrs. Spankum, you can't—"

"Oh, yes, I can, Thorne." She veered left and pounded on a door. "Sonny!"

Behind it, monster footsteps vibrated the floorboards, way out into the hallway.

The door swung open, the resulting whoosh of air so severe it nearly sucked him in. Buck was a flea in comparison to the horker who filled the doorframe.

"Mr. Thorne, meet my son. He's come home to help his old mum, ain't ye, Sonny?"

Sonny's thick lips smiled at his mother, then flattened at him.

Nigel loosened his collar and slunk for the safety of Mrs. Spankum's side. He patted her wiry grey hair—what was left of it, anyway. Three pats.

"Dear Mrs. Spankum," he said. "Happy to meet your, uh … little boy. I shall have that rent to you in no time at all. No time, whatsoever, as a matter of fact."

"See that you do, Mr. Thorne, or Sonny here"—she reared back and hitched her thumb toward the man—"will help you move out."

Her gesture opened up just enough space for him to scoot out the front door. Once outside, he drew in a gulp of fresh air and released a shudder. He'd been right about his luck changing.

But not about the direction.

15

Ethan paused just past the break where rectory grounds ambled into scrub brush. He lifted one hand and shielded his eyes, gauging the time. This morning, when he'd crawled out of the stream from his bath, the sun lay low on the opposite horizon. Now it hung well past its zenith. Had he really slept that long?

A leftover yawn stretched his jaw before he tousled his hair, shaking out the remaining bits of leaves he'd lain on. His stomach grumbled, and though he'd likely missed a visit from Miri, perhaps she'd left a plate of food.

But with the thunder of approaching hoofbeats, his hunger pangs faded. He looked up in time to see a black mane and tail streaming as a monstrous bay barreled around the corner of the sanctuary, straight at him.

He jumped aside moments before the riderless horse raced past. Clods of earth flew in the animal's wake, one nicking him in the shin. At such an insane pace, the beast would run himself to death. A shame, for the raw power in his muscular hindquarters and his leggy gait smacked of thoroughbred ancestry.

Ethan broke into a run and trailed him. If he could keep the horse within sight, mayhap the animal would eventually tire, and he could snag a rein.

Right before forest swallowed field, the horse slowed enough to circle back and swing 'round again. After a few revolutions, the beast stopped. The animal looked to be sixteen or so hands tall and quite fearsome with his nostrils flaring. After a final snort, he dipped his long neck to nip at a patch of newborn shoots.

"Hey now. Easy fella." Ethan held out his hands as he approached. The horse jerked up his head, twitching his ears but not flattening them. Mayhap this wasn't such a wild monster after all.

Keeping his movements fluid, Ethan edged closer. He reached to stroke the animal's neck, hot and slick from the jaunt. "There, now. You're a fine beauty."

The horse shied away, and Ethan continued his calm murmurings until he could grab the dangling rein. "Let's find your master then, eh?"

He grasped the cheek piece of the headstall and led him off. The horse danced and snorted, dampening his shirt with a fine spray. Once past the church, Ethan tugged a little harder and increased his pace.

On the road, not far ahead, a man-sized lump lay like an overturned beetle. Ethan frowned. It would be folly indeed to turn his back on this horse. But neither could he ignore the fellow lying in the dirt. What to do?

He closed the distance and ended up trading headstall for rein in one hand, then extended the other, bracing himself to bear the man up. "You all right?"

After an excessive amount of grunting and gasping, the man stood, gripping Ethan's arm until his own legs held him. "Many ... many thanks ... good ... man."

It was a wonder he spoke at all with such wheezing breaths. Ethan retreated to the animal's side and patted the beast's neck, allowing the fellow to regain his dignity and his hat. The horse leaned into him, zealous as a woman driven by passion, and he smirked at the sudden affection. "It's a fine mount, you are."

"Well …" It was more of a wheeze than a word. The man paused to catch his breath. "I see you've a grand touch with horseflesh."

"Treat them all like ladies, and you'll ne'er go wrong." He flashed the man a smile.

"Hah! Truth indeed." The man brushed dust and dirt from his breeches, then offered his hand. "Thank you for your assistance."

Ethan complied, surprised at the softness of the fellow's grip. No wonder he'd lost his mount. "Think naught of it."

"No, no, I should have been in a sorry mess had you not come along. I am Bishop Fothergill, and you are?"

"Ethan Good—" Should he take the chance of giving his full name?

"Happy to meet you, Mr. Good. You live hereabouts?"

Name dilemma solved, this new question would require a careful answer. He glanced across the field to the shed and back. "I am staying in the area."

"Oh? A traveler of sorts, then, eh? Lucky for you, your accent speaks well enough of your breeding, though your taste in clothing is …" The bishop stroked his chin, leastwise the fleshy bit that might have been a chin. His eyes skimmed from Ethan's too-short sleeves to equally shortened breeches. "Unconventional."

Ethan shrugged as he glanced at his attire. Though ill-fitting, the fabric was in better condition than his own set of clothes. "These are not my garments."

"Yes, I can see that." Pausing, the bishop cocked his head. "You offer no explanation?"

"No. None." Ethan stared him down, a trait he'd perfected as a youth when confronted by his father.

The bishop coughed as if candor was a hair ball to be expelled. "My word, Mr. Good, you are a singular fellow."

Ethan laughed. "I suppose I've been called worse."

The bishop scratched his shorn head before finally reapplying his hat. "Might I ask if you have a permanent situation? Any commitments?"

Ethan shot him a wary glance. The man asked entirely too many questions. "Not currently." He handed off the leather rein, deflecting the bishop with a question of his own. "Think you can manage?"

"Actually ... no. This rectory is in sore need of management, and so ..." Fothergill eyed him. "I have a proposition for you, Mr. Good. If you are as useful with your hands as you are with Champion here—"

The horse whickered at the mention of his name, and Fothergill mimicked the way Ethan had patted him. "I would that you consider filling in for the rectory's hired man, who is down with the rheum. I shall see to your room and board plus a stipend. What say you?"

Ethan's eyebrows shot up before he could stop them. Exchange the garden shed for living beneath the same roof as Miri? He glanced at the cloudless sky and gave silent thanks for such an unexpected boon. God was more gracious than he deserved.

"I say yes."

⌒☜◯☞⌒

Miri awoke with a start, remnants of a horrible dream suffocating her. Witherskim. Wedding night. Pale flesh with blue veins. Skinny and cold and touching her in places that ought not be touched—at least by him. A shudder shook her. Breathing heavily, she focused on the pillowcase, which was wrinkled from thrashing about. She must have dozed off a good while ago, judging from the shadows that darkened her chamber. Rubbing her eyes, she calmed her breathing.

But the gasping sound did not stop.

She bolted upright.

Roland stood at the end of her bed, panting. No waistcoat. Shirt ripped. A dark stain spreading from the center of his chest. He held out his hands, fingers glistening in the dusky light—

Blood.

Miri recoiled. Fear, the locked-in-a-dirt-cellar kind, closed in on her, and she sucked in a breath. She reached behind her, feeling for the candlestick on the bedstand, and wrapped her fingers around the cold pewter. Who knew what madness whispered in her brother's ear?

He sank, and even with the cushioning of a rug, his knees cracked hard against the floor. "Miri."

Her grip loosened, undone by the use of her pet name. She'd not heard that tone since before the dark days. "Roland?"

He looked at her like a wounded animal. "Help … me."

All sense of danger fled as her heart broke for the boy-man in front of her. She rushed to him, a flicker of hope gaining intensity that perhaps for once her prayers had been answered. "What happened?"

He opened his mouth, cavernous as if a scream from the pit of hell might emerge, but no sound surfaced.

Grasping his arm, she urged him up. Thankfully he submitted, though his stiff movement suggested rote compliance. She led him to the vanity and poured fresh water from a pitcher into the basin, then thrust in a cloth and wrung it out.

When she spread apart what was left of his shirt, her jaw dropped. Long scratches crisscrossed, layer upon layer, converging in the middle where not much flesh remained—only blood and muscle, raggedy, pooling, like a carcass picked apart by ravens.

Dizzying horror, unlike any she'd experienced, mixed with pity. Despite herself, she felt tears forming in her eyes. "Oh, Roland," she whispered. "What have you done?"

He whimpered when she set the cloth to his skin, and she recanted of ever wishing him harm. The lump in her throat choked out the comforting trifles she wanted to speak. It was impossible to reconcile the pitiful man in front of her with the phantom recollections that yet haunted her memory. Was this the same man who'd shown off his vestures with such pride to their mother? Or, as a young boy, sat up late with their grandfather, passionately discussing verses?

She rinsed the cloth again and again, each dip further darkening the water. She needed a fresh basin, but dare she leave him? Setting down the cloth, she stepped away. "Sit and wait for me here. I—"

"No!" Roland grabbed her shoulders, forcing her face to him. His whole countenance sagged. "Do not leave, Miri. Please, never leave me. Promise."

For the smallest of moments, he looked out through clear eyes, a gaze not hardened by the church or trapped behind a veil of insanity. This was the big brother she remembered—the one she and Will sought in the dead of the worst thunderstorms.

The one she'd once loved best.

And as quickly and surely as Will had slipped from her life, the look was gone. Roland released her and stepped back, the sheen of madness covering his features as a death shroud. "I cannot find it. I cannot. I look and look and ..." His words faded to mumbling as he shook his head.

Miri covered her mouth, fighting back the tears aroused by that one fleeting glimpse of her brother. Somewhere deep inside he knew, he must know, what was happening to him. So vividly reminded of the brother she'd lost, she rested her hand on his arm and squeezed. "Roland?"

His strength snapped her hold, and he crushed her to him in an embrace. "Shh. Shh." He stroked the back of her head, his heart beating erratic in his chest.

Fear barreled back, like a seven-fold spirit returning to a swept clean house. Roland could wring the life from her, and who would know? "Let me go."

"We are powerless against this, Miriall." His voice rumbled. "Powerless."

She tried to push away, but his arms tightened.

And for once, she was tempted to agree with him.

16

Nigel positioned himself outside the hanaper's office at the west end of the Chancery, strategically standing next to the clerk's tall desk. Like curing a ripe bit of Stilton, a desirable outcome would be all in the timing. As the last of eight bells chimed from the clock on the wall, Nigel began unwrapping the package he held.

The clerk, Willy, wore his clothes like a peg on the wall. Painfully thin, the lean edge about him hurt to lay eyes upon. Nigel smiled. Oh, this would work out well, it would.

Willy slammed shut his ledger so forcefully, the desk wobbled, and his quill fell out of the inkwell. "Books are closed. Make yer way out."

Groans and murmurs issued from the long line of people yet waiting to address the man, but they were fools. Let them shuffle off only to return the next day … and the next. Justice lumbered slow as a lame ox here in the court of Chancery, but Nigel knew how to feed the beast—or at least Willy. He pulled off the last of the wrapper on a steaming meat pasty, then fanned the scent of buttery crust and beef with a wave of his hand.

Willy snapped his head aside, devouring the pie with his eyes.

Nigel smiled. Just as he'd predicted. "A long day, this one, eh, Wills? Quite ran away from me, I don't mind sayin'. No time for me to eat this now, I suppose."

Willy nodded while wiping a drip of moisture from the corner of his mouth. "Aye, long indeed, Thorne."

"Hate to see this pie go to waste, but if I don't get off to old Pegg's soon, there'll be more than the piper to pay, if you know what I mean." He inched the pie closer to the clerk, who ran his tongue along his lower lip. The poor fellow probably didn't even hear him. "I wonder if you might—"

Before Nigel could finish, Willy snaked out his hand then sunk his teeth into the crust. His eyes closed, and his eyebrows lifted clear into his receding hairline. A mangy cur wouldn't have been happier with a good scratch behind the ear. "Mmm."

Hook set, Nigel started reeling. He leaned closer so Willy wouldn't miss a word over his smacking lips. "There's a certain patent I seem to have misplaced, Wills. Has to do with the Goodwin entailment. Ethan Goodwin, that is. You wouldn't happen to still have that close at hand, would you?"

Willy shoved the last bite of pie into his mouth. "Whyn't you shee da keeper o da rollsh?" Bits of pastry flew out his lips.

"I did see the keeper of the rolls, mate, but seems that particular writ ain't made it that far yet." Brushing off the crumbs that had landed on his shoulders, he stepped around Willy, then peered into the tall wicker basket on the clerk's other side. "Must still be in there, eh?"

Willy dragged his sleeve across his mouth, leaving behind a greasy smear to compliment the many ink stains. "Can't say." He grabbed a coiled lid from the drawer beneath his desk and slapped it atop the basket, all without climbing down from his stool. "Come back tomorrow."

Nigel narrowed his eyes. Greedy little hobgoblin. He reached inside his waistcoat and pulled out a gold piece, one he'd shined just in case. "Tomorrow I might not have any coins left. Why, I might just lose it all tonight a-gamin'."

The money disappeared faster than the pie, finding a new home inside the clerk's pocket. At last Willy stood and offered the empty stool. "Well then … s'pose I should take a little leg stretcher afore I pack up. You won't mind watchin' the station for me, will ye, Thorne?"

"No, no, not a bit. Happy to help."

As soon as Willy turned his back, Nigel dove into the basket. If the writ had been deposited yesterday, the little bugger would be at the bottom. Casting aside scrolls that could make or break the lives of myriad nameless faces, he searched for the document sealed with Barrister Wolmington's crest.

Spools of paper collected at his feet, none with a fancy *W* impressed into red wax. Perspiration beaded his forehead by the time he got down to the last few, all just beyond his fingertips. No wonder the hanaper's office always seemed to employ lanky-limbed clerks.

Lifting the basket, Nigel dumped it over and shook until the last scroll bounced out. The flash of a red seal lured him to follow the runaway document as it rolled past the desk. He bent like a washerwoman, scurrying after the blasted thing. The scarlet *W* taunted him with each revolution.

Finally, it rolled to a stop—at the toes of a pair of glossy black shoes with paste buckles reflecting the glow from the wall sconces. Willy couldn't afford a fine pair of stampers like those, but who else would be in this part of the Chancery at such an hour?

As he slowly unfolded, Nigel's eyes traveled upward. Attached to those shoes were legs in white silk stockings, topped by black velvet breeches edged in silver embroidery. Above that, a matching dress coat adorned with a lacy cravat at the neck—all belonging to a pinch-faced man regarding him as one might observe a cadaver.

"What goes on here?" The man's tone crackled with authority.

Mouth suddenly dry, Nigel wetted his lips. He shuffled through a deck of mental images of Chancery officials but came up short. He'd never seen this swell before. "I ... uh ... why I'm helping out ol' Willy is all. Bit of a tipover ... the basket, I mean."

The man tapped his index finger atop the carved handle of his walking stick, the lines in his face squinching tighter.

Nigel puffed out his chest, unwilling to let some tart-faced dandyprat bully him around. "Why are ye hereabouts when it's after eight bells?"

Squatting to retrieve Nigel's coveted scroll, the man then straightened. He turned the document over, examining it. "I came for this."

"No!" Nigel made a swipe for the paper. "Ye cannot take official papers like that."

The man held the scroll aloft with one hand and lifted his cane with the other, then drove the point against Nigel's chest. "I may if the document originated with me."

Nigel stepped back but refused to retreat, anger burning in his gut. "Who the nocky do you think you are, then?"

The man's lips pursed tighter than a fat madame's corset. After studying Nigel for a moment, he lowered his cane. "Spindle is the name. Mr. Spindle, solicitor and esquire, not that it signifies. And you are?"

A slow smile tugged Nigel's mouth. If he played this hand just right, he could win—more than what he owed Buck. He thrust out his hand. "Pleased to meet ye, I am. Very pleased, sir. I had no idea. Thorne's me name, Nigel Thorne, bailiff and ..."

He pumped Spindle's hand longer than necessary while scrambling for some kind of distinguishing hallmark. Whyn't his father—dirty scoundrel—have left him a fancier title? "I'm the best catch-pole and shoulder-clapper around. If there's ever a man what you need to ferret out, I'm the one to find 'im for ye. None better in all of England."

One of Spindle's brows rose. "You don't say."

"I do, indeed, sir. Nary a man escapes good ol' Nigel Thorne." He hooked his thumbs inside his lapels and struck a pose so stately, he shouldn't be surprised a bit if the man took him on as a partner for life.

Spindle snorted.

Then turned and walked off.

Nigel blew out a tirade of whispered obscenities. He'd spent two full crowns on that meat pasty and for what? To fatten up Willy while his own purse shriveled, that's what. He narrowed his eyes and swung around to grab up the scattered documents and slam them into the basket, each successive scroll an ugly reminder of how he'd wasted his time and money.

Behind him, footsteps grew louder. If Willy had the nerve to scold him for this mess, he'd turn around and pop him a good cross hook. He might anyway just to lighten his foul mood. "Keep your gob shut. I don't want to hear it."

"Very well."

Nigel straightened and slowly turned.

There stood Spindle, leaning with a two-handed grip on his walking stick, the scroll peeking out of an oversized braided pocket at his side. "But it will be most inconvenient for me, sir, to offer a proposition with my *gob* in a closed position."

⏤⏦⏤

Satisfied with Roland's even breathing, Miri turned from his bed to cross the chamber. The dark of night had long ago devoured dusk's shadows, and she shivered from the increasing chill. Dressing Roland's wound and settling him into a nightshirt had proven harder than she'd anticipated.

Exhaustion burned her eyes, and she craved the sanctuary of her own quilts. Sorting through this day's drama would require clear thinking, and that required a solid eight hours of slumber. Her shoulders loosened just thinking of warm blankets and mind-numbing sleep. She reached for the door and pulled.

To her astonishment, Bishop Fothergill stood poised to knock. "Oh! Miss Brayden." His fist lowered to his heaving chest, which he thumped several times. "You startled me."

Shadows flickered grotesque deformities upon his face. Candle glow highlighted the underside of his cheeks and jowls, freakish as a lightning-lit gargoyle. Clearly it was she who had the right to be startled.

Fothergill craned his neck to look over her shoulder. "Has your brother taken ill?"

Miri frowned. The bishop had chosen the wrong occupation, for he'd make a fine interrogator for the Spaniards. She stepped into the corridor, pulling shut the door behind her. "My brother is not quite himself this evening."

"It was the church's sincerest hope that retirement in the country would aid your brother's health, not deteriorate it." Fothergill sighed so lustily, his candle's flame sputtered. "And I had hoped to speak a few words with him. Ah well, naught to be done for that now, eh?"

"Perhaps on the morrow." She stepped past him, hoping to escape further questions. "Good night, sir."

Beneath the carpet runner, floorboards creaked as Fothergill gained her side. "Might I have a few words with you, then?"

She did not slow her pace. "Me?"

"Yes." He huffed. "If you don't mind."

"Why should I?" She shot him a sideways glance, trying to determine whether his request stemmed from civility or suspicion.

A trickle of sweat trailed the side of his face. The more he exerted, the stronger the scent of garlic. Heavy breaths punctuated his words. "Earlier this eve ... I met with ... the squire, Mr. Gullaby."

Miri stopped.

But so much weight did not easily come to a halt, and the bishop shot past her.

She waited for him to notice and return, then waited some more as he caught his breath, all the while remembering the allusion to rumors that Gullaby had mentioned at the apothecary's shop. If Fothergill's ears had been filled, she would know with what kind of manure.

The bishop produced a handkerchief and swiped his brow. "It seems the squire witnessed a squabble between your brother and Mr. Eldon ... the day before Eldon went missing."

"And?"

He shook out his cloth with a snap, then repocketed it before answering. "I was wondering if you knew anything about a quarrel."

Miri hesitated. The memory of the angry voices she'd heard the morn of the vicar's disappearance surfaced as a worm from the dirt. She promptly pecked it to death. "I know nothing."

The bishop thrust out his lower lip, clearly agitated. "You lived beneath the same roof as both these men. Did you notice frequent conflict between them? Hear any harsh words spoken by either party?"

She bit her tongue, mind whirring until she could answer in truth. She'd listened that morning with sleep-drugged hearing, sluggish of consciousness, removed by corridors and stairs and doors. The tones had been harsh, but the voices indistinguishable, and who knew what words were spoken?

"No," she said at last.

"Were threats made or implied?"

"None of which I am aware."

Like a fish out of water, Fothergill puckered his lips several times. "Well, are you aware, Miss Brayden, that Mr. Gullaby saw your brother raise a riding whip against Eldon? No strike was made, I'll admit, but what would give him cause to behave with such violent intent?"

She stifled a smirk. Knowing Roland, it could have been as small an offense as an improperly tied cravat. "I am sure I do not know."

The bishop narrowed his eyes, and she got the distinct impression that had he been behind a pulpit, he'd have called fire and brimstone upon her head.

"Have you no suppositions whatsoever, woman?"

She lifted her chin. "None, sir."

He shook his head, and flaps of skin jiggled. "You are as singular as Mr. Good."

Looking past him to the stairway, she hoped he'd take the hint. She didn't give a fig for whoever Mr. Good might be. "If that is all, Bishop, I should like to retire."

He stepped aside, allowing her to pass. "Oh ... one more thing. I expect a replacement for your hired man to arrive tomorrow. As I was not able to wrap up my business in town this eve, I shall leave promptly at cock's crow. Set up Mr. Good in some vacant quarters, would you?"

Nodding assent, she escaped down the stairs, frustration building with each step. Just what she needed. Yet another person to keep ignorant of Roland's illness and Ethan's presence.

17

Sitting in awkward silence broken only by the occasional scrape of a knife upon toast or clink of a spoon to eggshell, Miri eyed Roland over the rim of her teacup. No hint of his childlike behavior remained from last night. He sat aloof, speaking nary a word about it—or anything else, for that matter. Thus far, a simple nod when she arrived at breakfast had been the extent of his communication.

She narrowed her eyes, trying hard to see the boy behind the man. The creases at his mouth and brow blurred, lending a younger appearance. If she angled her head and squinted a bit more, his frown didn't seem nearly as austere. And if she imagined a smile, an outright grin, Will came back to life in his features.

"Are you ill?"

She jerked into perfect posture, saddened that his question broke the spell. "I am a little fatigued. And you?"

"Fine." The shadows beneath his eyes belied that statement.

His cravat rode higher on his neck than usual, and a large flourish of fabric hung lower than normal. Though he'd obviously taken pains to hide it, Miri knew what lay beneath his shirt. "Are you feeling—"

"Did I not say I am fine?"

His harsh reply threw cold water on the warmer feelings he'd stirred last evening. She set down her cup and picked up her spoon.

Taking a bite of soft-boiled egg, she closed her eyes and savored it. Gratitude that Mrs. Makin had resumed her place behind the stove filled her as tangibly as the mouthful.

"You eat as a condemned woman. Mind your manners."

Her breakfast turned to paste. She opened her eyes. "I am merely thankful for Mrs. Makin's talents."

"That is no excuse to behave as a common harpy sitting down to a plate of mutton." He dabbed the side of his mouth with a napkin, his sour countenance leaving her in doubt whether he'd ever enjoyed a morsel of food in his life. "However, I will admit I am thankful as well. Her culinary skills far outweigh yours."

Miri frowned and set her spoon next to the eggcup, resentment eating her appetite. The past three days she'd taken on the whole of the rectory's chores, for both the housekeeper and Old Joe. This was her reward? She plucked the napkin from her lap so forcefully, the butter knife rattled.

Roland cast her a dark look. "Sulking does not become you, Miriall. Please refrain from it in my presence."

She pushed back her chair, considering that as an invitation to leave his company.

"Beggin' yer pardons." The scent of cinnamon heralded Mrs. Makin's entrance into the dining room. She dipped first to Roland, then to Miri. "There's a Mr. Good a-callin'. I've seen him to the sitting room. Says the bishop bid him come, though why, I can't imagine. Rather a roguish lookin' fellow, if I say so myself, and furthermore, you wouldn't believe what he's wear—"

"Your opinion is not required." Roland slapped his napkin on the table, leveling a sharp gaze at the cook. "Do you see the bishop in attendance here?"

She lowered her eyes. "No, sir."

"Then why the devil disturb us? Of all the half-witted requests." Roland's face flushed, matching the hue of the humiliated cook's. "Tell the man—"

"Do not trouble yourself, Mrs. Makin." Miri's stomach twisted in empathy. She stood, hoping to divert further ranting against the cook. "I shall see to Mr. Good. The bishop informed me of his impending arrival."

"Did he, now?" Roland narrowed his eyes at Miri. "When?"

Mrs. Makin gave a curt bob, then dashed out, making the most of the pause in the conversation.

Longing to follow, Miri backed toward the door as Roland stood and approached, forcing a calmness to her voice that she didn't feel. "I spoke with the bishop last night."

"Intriguing." He bullied her against the doorjamb, his muggy breath hitting her forehead. "Am I to understand that you are the bishop's intimate confidant?"

Miri gasped. Of all the insidious accusations. "Of course not." She twisted aside, but there was little space to escape.

"You are not dismissed. I am not finished." He pressed closer, giving her no room. "How is it you are aware of a new staff member that I know nothing about?"

She looked up—what a mistake. With eyes wide and nostrils flared, he would disturb a king's man with his unyielding gaze. How tired she was of fear. "I fail to see why this upsets you."

"Because you do not outrank me! Your station here is barely above that of the kitchen help. In truth, the staff is more useful than you."

His words rang in her ears, and she abhorred their accuracy. "Then surely you do not object to hiring a new man."

"Object?" He smiled with all the mirth of a dog baring its teeth. "No. My objection is that you scheme behind my back with the bishop, usurping my position."

"Do not even think it—"

"What else have you been up to, Miriall?" His fists shook at his sides. "What else!"

Miri flinched. She'd read of lions, the threat in their roar from sheer volume alone, sometimes causing their prey to die from fright— and she knew exactly how that would feel. "Please, calm down."

"Calm down!" His tone bordered on demonic. "Who are you to tell me to calm down? You, who drove Father to apoplexy with your slatternly, pitiful ways?"

She lowered her head. If she could crawl beneath the rug, she would—anything to hide from Roland and the past. But she could hardly see the carpet through a veneer of tears. "You cannot blame me for Father's temper. Nor his death."

"I can, and I do."

She sucked in a shaky breath. Had she not condemned herself time and again for the very same crime?

"Because of you, Father spent the last years of his life a paralytic. You pushed him beyond his limits! You send me beyond mine. I daresay it was even you who drove Will from the house."

"Stop! Just … stop." Teardrops slid down her cheeks, darkening the fabric of her dress where they fell.

"Save your weeping, woman. It holds no effect on me. Rather you should plead for your soul before God." At last he stepped away, allowing free passage out the door if she wished.

But she stood, immobilized by the truth, sniffling and wiping tears that refused to stop.

He strode past her as if she held all the significance of a meal-worm. "Go to your chamber. I shall tend to Mr. Good myself."

"Very well." She whispered the words, catching the irony—for things were far from well.

Finally gaining some semblance of composure, she lowered her hands. Her half-eaten egg and cold toast remained on the table, the scraps a guilty reminder that she'd not yet brought Ethan any food. Temptation urged her to dash upstairs and escape to her chamber, yet compassion called for her to attend the beggar first.

Dabbing her eyes with her apron, she headed for the door. The confrontation, while ugly, didn't rankle her nearly as much as the fact that it had been set off by nothing.

Ahead of her in the corridor, Roland disappeared into the sitting room. A second later, his shout carried from the chamber. "What the devil are you doing in the vicar's clothing?"

⁓∙⊙⊙∙⁓

Nigel tugged the hem of his vest, then smoothed his lapels, straightening any major wrinkles. He'd employed much care in dressing this morn, and it would not do now to enter Barrister Wolmington's chamber look-ing the part of a rumpled lamplighter. His life—or death—might hinge on this meeting with Spindle and Wolmington, and by God he'd not let something as simple as a stained sleeve skew the results.

"You may enter, Mr. Thorne."

The clerk's words ended his primping. Nigel sidestepped the man on his way into the barrister's office.

The room smelled old. Old and tired. Years and years of docu-ments and arguments and decisions. Decades of sweaty, tearful, anguishing court cases passing in and out the same door he'd just walked through.

Or the odd smell could be from the ancient man sitting behind the desk, adjacent to where Spindle stood. Endless stacks of paper, strewn like so many legal bones spread across a desert, almost hid the tiny man. Though Nigel had never met the barrister, he'd heard stories of the giant lawyer who brandished English law as powerfully as a knight with a lance. Such a reminder was hard to reconcile with the shriveled little shell eyeing him. He didn't speak a word.

But Spindle did. "Have a seat, Mr. Thorne." Spindle stepped from his place by the only window gracing the chamber, and with a nod of his head, indicated a leather wingback across from the desk.

Spindle waited until Nigel sat before taking up residence on the other side of the desk, his height adding emphasis to Wolmington's small stature. "I have requested this meeting with you and the barrister, as you both may help me succeed in my quest."

Nigel shot a glance at Wolmington, searching for a sign of censure. His paper-thin cheeks didn't so much as twitch. If Wolmington was nothing more than a pawn in the game that Spindle played, then how powerful was Spindle? Nigel pursed his lips. It probably didn't matter, as long as Spindle counted Nigel among the players.

"Happy to help, I am, but … uh …" Nigel leaned forward. "What exactly am I helping with?"

"Recognize this crest?" Spindle advanced, holding out his hand.

Nigel squinted. The man wore an enormous gold ring on his forefinger. A rampant lion sat in the middle of a shield with some fancy squiggles decorating the top and bottom. The whole pattern was engraved, used for marking wax seals, and from the handcrafted looks of it, mighty important seals at that, for three rubies encrusted the middle. He shook his head. "No, sir, can't say that I do."

Spindle resumed his post beside the desk. "Then allow me to educate you." He lifted a brow, measuring Nigel with a critical look before continuing. "Understand, however, that what is spoken within these walls stays within these walls. Is that completely clear?"

Bobbing his head, Nigel sat back. The seasoned upholstery molded against his body, a cozy niche for what would no doubt be an interesting tale.

"The coat of arms I've just shown you belongs to the Earl of Trenton, one of the wealthiest families in all of England."

"Pardon my askin', but"—Nigel cocked his head—"if that little bauble belongs to the earl, what you got it on yer finger for?"

Spindle's lips flattened. Not a frown, really, more like the way Nigel himself might dismiss one of Duffy's comments. Hmm. Why would Spindle look at him like that?

"I am the estate's solicitor, Mr. Thorne."

"Oh, right." Nigel paused for good measure. "Righty-oh."

After exchanging an unreadable look with the barrister, Spindle continued. "Recently, the earl and his son met with a tragedy—one I would prefer not to expand upon. It is enough to say they are deceased."

Nigel nodded. Apparently he'd be hunting a killer, then. No worry. He'd track a hotheaded Frenchy clear over to the Indies as long as Spindle awarded him a fat sum. Anything to pay off Buck. But how did Ethan Goodwin fit in? He was street scum. Low life. Capable of nothing but thievery or ... murder? Of course. Nigel lifted his chin. "So the gents met with foul play then, eh?"

"Yes, but that is hardly the point." Spindle waved a hand in the air as if the question were a fly to be swatted. "As solicitor of the

Trenton family assets, and more importantly the accompanying title, it falls within my duty to find the heir of the estate. No one can inherit without me first making every effort to find this man. If he is not located, the title will go dormant. All lands and wealth will be absorbed by the crown, disrupting the lives of many a tenant. The very commerce of countless villages on Trenton land will suffer from the time-consuming length of the exchange. This is no small thing of which I speak."

Huh. Nigel tapped his finger on the chair's arm. So, as Duffy had told him earlier, this was an entailment case, but Duffy better clean out his ears. The stupid bloke had said this involved Ethan, which apparently it did not. Still, even if this mess didn't entangle Goodwin, he might yet win a full purse by finding some other nimbycock inheritor. Nigel straightened his collar then looked at Spindle. "I take it you want me to find yer lost little rich man for ye. Alrighty then. I'm game, mate. Who is it I'm looking for?"

Spindle looked down his long nose and clipped his words. "The man I seek is named Ethan Goodwin."

18

Ethan stood, drawn to his feet by a sudden sense of self-protection. Outside the sun shone, but the sitting room dimmed considerably as a dark shape filled the entryway. A man of Will's height stood in the threshold, glowering. His hair was severely pulled back and fastened at the nape, setting off high cheekbones and a defined nose—definitely a Brayden family feature. But as the man curled his fists and looked about the chamber, Ethan detected none of Will's merriment or Miri's compassion. Rather, the wildness in the fellow's eye and tilt of his head was unsettling, not unlike a frenzied stallion he'd once seen put down. Will had never looked that crazed, even after a good bit of carousing.

The broad-chested man folded his arms, barely disguising the wince that crossed his face. His waistcoat was fastened up tight as if secrets were buttoned inside.

"Well, man …" His tone might impale a victim by volume alone. "Are those the vicar's clothes, or are they not?"

"They are … uh …" Ethan glanced down. There was no denying the way his legs escaped much too early from the breeches or rationalizing why the shirtsleeves ended at his forearms.

"Please," a soft voice said from the door. "I can explain."

As one, Ethan and the man turned.

155

Pale-faced and puffy-eyed, Miri looked as if she'd not slept since the last time Ethan had seen her. What had happened to draw her so?

"Is there no end to your defiance?" The man strode toward her, a predator on the prowl. "You were told to go to your chamber."

Miri tipped up her chin, a brave gesture belied by the slight tremble rippling the hem of her skirt. "Roland, I—"

So this was the infamous elder brother, more daunting in real life than Will's descriptions credited him—and Will had been none too generous.

"You what?" Roland ground his teeth, advancing further. Were she not standing with her back to the doorframe, no doubt he would have circled her.

Ethan crossed the room, drawing close enough to intervene should the need arise.

Roland raised his hand in warning. Behind him, Miri peered over her brother's shoulder, pleading with her eyes for Ethan to retreat.

"Am I now to learn that you've conspired with Mr. Good as well?" Roland glanced back at him, the threat in his eyes razor sharp.

Ethan lifted his hands to show he was harmless, yet the stance would serve him well should this meeting come to fists. Why would any man hazard this amount of aggression toward a slip of a woman—his own sister, at that—and toward an unarmed, invited caller? He frowned. Something was not right.

Miri lowered her head.

Her movement attracted Roland's attention, and he turned back to her. "Look at me!" He pinched her chin and forcibly lifted her head.

Civility be hanged.

"Sir!" Ethan grabbed Roland's shoulder, fingers itching to spin the bully around and feel the satisfying smash of his fist against the man's nose. The brigand deserved a comeuppance, but with fear shining in Miri's eyes, now was not the time. He settled for squeezing instead, digging in his fingers.

Roland wheeled about, shrugging off the hold. His chest expanded, and he cocked his head, a calculated attempt at intimidation.

Ethan might almost smile if not for the seriousness of the situation. Coercion was a familiar friend—a commodity he could trade with the best of men … or worst, as the case may be.

He retreated a step and allowed half a smile—the comfortable mask of appeasement he'd mastered long ago. "The woman is faultless. I freely admit these garments are not my own, but I swear I had no idea they belonged to a vicar."

Roland narrowed his eyes. "Then where did you get them?"

After the harsh conduct he'd already witnessed, to admit that Miri supplied him the clothing would likely not bode well for her. He lifted a brow, praying that Roland would be calmed with the offered bait—himself. "I do not answer to you."

Roland stiffened.

Ethan continued. "Furthermore, the bishop did not stress a particular mode of dress, therefore your input is not necessary."

A deep shade of red crept up the man's neck.

"And unless these are your garments, it is hardly your concern." Ethan folded his arms. "Now then, be a good man and summon Bishop Fothergill for me, would you?"

Veins bulged at Roland's temples. His breaths came hard and fast. "You … will not … address me so vulgarly."

Ethan smiled. "I believe I just have, sir."

Miri gasped. Roland jerked as if slapped.

"Your days here," Roland managed through clenched teeth, "are numbered, Mr. Good."

"That remains to be seen." Ethan kept a pleasant tenor to his voice. "I suggest you take it up with Bishop Fothergill, for I have nothing more to say to you on the matter."

"Do not think that I am so easily dismissed. You should choose your enemies more wisely in the future. This is not finished." Roland stalked from the room.

Ethan blew out a breath. Gaining the man's dark side might prove a problem in the future, but for now, the wide-eyed beauty staring at him overshadowed any possible consequences. Hopefully this was the first of many victories in gaining Miri's trust.

And love.

⁗⊙⊙⊙⁘

Miri couldn't breathe.

In seconds, Ethan Goodwin had undone her efforts at calming Roland, and she wanted to scream with the stress of it. What kind of harm might her brother inflict upon himself this time? She dare not pursue him, lest she upset him further, but what to do? At wit's end, she hastened across the room and didn't stop until she reached the floor-length window. She pressed her burning brow against the cool glass and allowed her shoulders to sag.

Ethan's footsteps followed behind, drawing closer than she would have liked. "Miri?"

She hugged herself, refusing to look at the man. Outside, tree branches waved with the breeze. Knobby buds lost their husks and littered the ground, as scattered and disordered as her emotions.

"Are you all right?"

No matter how hard she tried to ignore him, a part of her warmed to the note of concern in his voice. Still, even if it might have been for her protection, he never should have roused her brother. She shook her head. "Why did you provoke him so? You had no right."

"You can't seriously be defending the man. I mean no disrespect to you, Miri, but your brother is quarrelsome and overbearing. He was looking for a fight. I merely accommodated."

Unable to argue against that, she unfolded her arms and smoothed her skirts. The truth of his words released some of the rising irritation she felt toward him—but not all. Obliging Roland's confrontational bent would only speed him to the asylum.

She clenched her hands, balling up her skirt fabric, then turned. "Please, do not incite him further. If for no other reason, refrain for the sake of your past friendship with Will."

A rogue flash of teeth highlighted his dark beard. "Ah, but my actions were for your sake alone."

She swallowed, nearly choking on this blunt statement. He was as forward as Witherskim.

So why didn't she feel as reviled?

He took a step nearer, bringing with him the scent of outdoors and freshly washed skin. Apparently he'd made use of the soap she'd left on his tray. His hair gleamed a brighter shade of mahogany as it rested against his collar, and his face no longer bore the pallor of sickness. Truth be told, with the layers of grime removed, Ethan Goodwin was quite dashing.

His lips parted as if he might speak, but no words came out. That she'd noticed his lips in the first place heated her cheeks, and she averted her gaze. No good could come from admiring men.

Ethan drew back. "Forgive me. I have made you uncomfortable."

She snapped her eyes back to his—then startled. He stared, unguarded, unabashed, and completely sincere. Gooseflesh rose on her arms. No wonder Will had made this man his friend. Suddenly she felt foolish and shy, repentant of the way she'd taken leave of him and for raising her voice. "No, it's not you. It's just that ..." She glanced at the door, still open from when Roland stormed out. "Roland, such as he is, is all the family I have left."

Hearing her pitiful state from her own mouth was cruel to her ear and abrasive to her heart. The pain of missing Will heightened, cresting with the knowledge that she'd never see him again. She swallowed, paving the way for words she wasn't sure she wanted to speak. "Tell me, for I think I am ready to hear it ..."

Was she? Her nails bit into her palms. "How did Will die?"

A shadow crossed Ethan's face, and Miri held her breath.

"Will was ..." His jaw worked as he looked past her, beyond the spring horizon outside, focusing on what? Some undefined point in time?

She folded her hands in front of her rather than worry the fabric of her skirt any further. That it took so long for him to reply could not be a good omen.

"He was murdered." Ethan's voice lessened to little more than a whisper. "Stabbed."

The stays of her bodice pinched without mercy—or perhaps the pain came from the breaking of her heart afresh. She should have been there! Surely she could have prevented such a violent end, somehow. "But ... why? Why would someone want to murder Will?"

He grimaced. "Reasons better left unsaid, leastwise in the presence of a lady. Would to God that you never know the ways of life on the streets."

She sucked in a breath, for that was exactly the fate she fought to avoid.

Sorrow added years to Ethan's face. Was he here in the sitting room with her, or back on the streets he warned against?

At last he shook his head and returned her gaze. The hard lines at the edges of his eyes softened as he studied her. "Will was the finest friend I've ever known. You're a lot like him, you know."

"It is kind of you to say so. Will was my friend too, years ago. I miss him … keenly." Her voice broke, along with a renewed wrenching of her heart. After a shaky breath, she continued, "All there is for me now is Roland."

"Do not fret about your brother. He will recover."

"No, he will not." She bit her lower lip, but too late to withdraw her words.

"Why would you say such a thing?"

His question hung like a snare. Though it would be freedom to share her load of worry about Roland, she knew too little about Ethan Goodwin to trust him with such a confidence.

She sighed, taking the route of vagueness. "My brother is not the man he appears to be."

"Neither am I." He spoke so low, she might have missed that statement if her senses had not been so intensely on edge.

"Who are you then, really?" She paused, cocking her head. "And what are you doing here? Why are you suddenly Mr. Good, the hired help?"

One brow rose, meeting the swath of dark hair sweeping across his forehead—roguish and unspeakably handsome.

He shrugged. "The bishop is rather persuasive."

A small smile twitched the corners of her mouth. "He does have a way of dominating a conversation toward his own desires."

Ethan laughed outright, filling the sitting room with a lightness she'd not felt since her arrival at the rectory—not for years, for that matter. She closed her eyes, relishing the sound.

"It is good to hear you laugh." The reckless thought escaped her lips before she realized she'd spoken aloud. Wide-eyed, she clamped her mouth shut.

Ethan's laughter faded, replaced with a curious tilt of his chin. "I am happy you approve."

"I meant laughter in general, of course." The excuse sounded hollow in her own ears.

"I see." But his knowing nod contradicted his assurance.

The ensuing silence stretched, long and thin. She ought to say something, or maybe do something, but for the life of her she couldn't think of what. Was she losing her mind as well?

At last a deep rumble in Ethan's belly broke into the quiet. A sheepish grin flashed across his face. "Sorry."

"Oh, dear!" Miri pressed a hand against her own stomach as it sank. She hadn't brought him a meal since yesterday, she'd been so caught up with her own life's drama. "You've had nothing to eat, and it's all my fault. Please accept my apology."

His smile deepened. "It's not like I haven't missed a meal before."

As if invoked by the mere mention of food, Mrs. Makin crossed the sitting room's threshold. "Miss?"

"Perfect timing, Mrs. Makin. Mr. Good here is in need of a plate of ..." But the sight of the cook twisting a dish towel in her hands overrode the grumbling of Ethan's belly. Fear for Roland crept a chill down Miri's back. "What is wrong?"

19

As the color drained from Miri's face, Ethan stepped to her side. Clearly the cook's words had upset Miri in a way he was hard pressed to understand. What trifling kitchen incident could possibly evoke such apparent distress—burned biscuits? Soured milk?

"Speak, Mrs. Makin." The rise and fall of Miri's chest increased. "What has happened?"

Though he already stood closer to Miri than modesty allowed, he inched nearer still. Her voice contained a curious tension, like a child, knowing punishment is required and compelled to ask what manner it might take, yet fearing to hear the answer.

The cook fiddled all the more with her dishcloth. "It's Old Joe, miss. He's taken a turn for the worse. A terrible cough rattles him so that he can hardly breathe. I hate to be askin', but what with my visit to my sister and all, I'm behind enough as is. Could you go to the village this morn and drop by Mr. Harper's?"

Miri exhaled visibly. "Of course. I shall go straightaway."

"Thank you, miss. You're a gem, you are." But the woman did not leave. She stood there, wringing the towel. If it were a chicken, it would have been long dead. "There is one other thing ..." Her dark little eyes slid his way.

"You may speak freely, Mrs. Makin," Miri said. "The bishop has hired Mr. Good here to fill in for Old Joe."

Mrs. Makin nodded but did not pull her gaze from him. He'd seen that look before—the slight curl of the upper lip and lifting of the chin translated into suspicion based upon his appearance. It used to give him a perverse thrill, knowing he could cause such a reaction. Now, his belly tightened with shame.

"Well"—he broke the awkward moment—"I'll go acquaint myself with the grounds. There's likely much to be done."

"Aye, that there is." The cook finally let her hands fall to her sides, the towel misshapen beyond recognition.

"Excuse me, then." He dipped his head before he exited. His departure greased the cook's tongue, for it slipped loose before he'd gone five paces beyond the door.

"Humph, have you ever seen the like of that? Charming as a gent …"

Behind him, the woman's voice lowered. Ethan paused.

" … somethin' ain't right, I tell ye. I know what I see, and what I see on that fellow is the vicar's clothing. What do you make of that, miss? What have you to say about what manner of man he might be?"

Ethan cocked his head, straining to catch Miri's soft tones. The hounds of hell wouldn't keep him from hearing how she'd answer.

"A pearl is rarely admired without first having been polished, Mrs. Makin. Perhaps we ought to give the man a chance."

A grin tugged his mouth upward. What a rare woman. He smiled all the way to the front door and would have worn the grin out into the yard, except for a strange chanting that pulled Miri's sweetness from his mind.

He backtracked a few steps and stopped in front of a door near the foot of the stairs. It was ajar, as if once having been slammed had bounced open a bit from the shock. Inside, a man's voice droned. Low. Monotonous. Foreign—not the accent, just the words. He leaned his ear closer.

Auribus tenere lupum ... Auribus tenere lupum ... Auribus tenere—

Ethan raked a hand through his hair. Tutored by some of the finest masters England had to offer, he identified the language as Latin, but the meaning? Drat his clouded thinking. Either he was going crazy, or the man inside the room mumbled something about wolves.

Curiosity edged him near enough to peer through the crack in the doorway. A black blur paced at the far end of the room, facing away from him. Roland. His singsong rhythm increased with each pass, faster and faster. With no forewarning whatsoever, he jolted to a halt, then slowly turned. Roland's wide, dark eyes burned into his own.

Ethan jerked away and hastened toward the front door. It opened before he reached the knob.

"Ah, Mr. Good. How fortuitous! I've had a dreadful time, dreadful." Brushing past him, Bishop Fothergill plunked down upon the entry bench. The seat groaned at impact. Hatless, wigless, breathless, the bishop fanned himself while muttering, "Trying, very trying."

Ethan glanced back at the study door, heart rate ratcheting.

It was shut. Completely.

His breathing slowed, and he turned to Fothergill. "Sorry to hear of your ill fortune, sir."

"Ill fortune, indeed. Well said, man, well said." The bishop brushed bits of soil from his breeches before continuing. "Partway to town, Champion threw a shoe, or rather lost one, in the muddiest of all ruts possible. Why, I had no choice but to forfeit my business and return here."

Ethan retreated a step as dust clouded from the bishop's clothing. No wonder the fat little man looked such a wreck. "I shall tend to your mount at once."

Fothergill rubbed his hand over his stubbly head and looked up with a half smile. "I knew you were just the man for the job. Yes, yes, do see to Champion, though with the wind knocked from my sails, I doubt I'll return to town today. Champ and I will make a fresh start of it on the morrow."

His gaze traveled over Ethan from head to toe and back again, smile fading. "I had hoped you'd give up your penchant for eccentric dress."

"Actually, sir ... you see ... I—"

"Here." Fothergill withdrew a leather pouch from inside his waistcoat and tossed it over. "After Champion's cared for, hie yourself into town and see that you find something more ... well ... fitting, I suppose."

The small bag weighted Ethan's hand, and his thoughts took a direction of their own. That many coins could buy a substantial amount of opium. He scrubbed his face with his free hand before pocketing the money. Amazing how quickly clouded thinking could turn wicked with no effort whatsoever.

Behind him, an almost imperceptible creak of a floorboard sounded from the direction of the study. Ethan shot a glance over his shoulder, but the room remained sealed.

"Is there a problem, Mr. Good?"

He turned back to Fothergill and gave a slight bow. "No, sir. I shall venture to town directly once I've finished with your horse."

Stepping closer, he lowered his voice. "I wonder, though, if first you wouldn't mind deciphering a bit of a puzzling phrase?"

Soft folds of skin jiggled as the man bobbed his head. "What is it?"

"*Auribus …*" Ethan closed his eyes, reliving the moment, then blinked them open. "*Auribus tenere lupum.*"

The bishop pushed out his lower lip. "What on earth would make you say something like that, Mr. Good?"

"Just something I overheard and was curious, is all."

Fothergill rubbed a thumb along his chin as he repeated the words. "*Auribus tenere lupum*—I hold a wolf by the ears—means 'I am in a dangerous situation and dare not let go.' There is not a more hopeless state in which to live. I suggest you beg God's mercy for the poor soul who uttered such."

Ethan nodded. Foreboding filled the hollow in his gut.

Like a smack of lips, the sound of an opening door came from behind, and Ethan spun. Through the smallest of cracks, one dark eye locked gazes with him.

⋘☙⋙

Miri snugged her pelisse tighter at the neck, wishing she'd thought to grab a muffler. Though some warmth remained from the sun's debut, the fickle spring air was decidedly more chilly than when she'd first set out from the rectory. Pewter clouds masked the sky, and countless village chimneys added to the general greyness hovering atop Deverell Downs. The closer she drew to Harper's Apothecary and Tobacco, the more her own spirit mimicked the thick and sullen heavens. Not that she minded running an errand for Mrs. Makin, nor gave a second thought to acquiring the medicine Old Joe needed.

Her steps slowed from the notion of facing Mr. Knight after their last embarrassing encounter.

She stopped to admire Mrs. Chapman's new baby. Then she waited for Mr. Foster to finish sweeping in front of the cobbler's when she could have gone around. And she really needn't have traded so much news with Miss Prinn.

Passing by the millinery, she paused, wondering if she dare dally longer to scoot in and investigate the opportunity for employment. She peered through the glass, hoping to catch a glimpse of Mrs. Tattler in the front room. Behind the window, hats of all sorts stared back at her, an emerald bonnet with a puffed crown at center. Lacy gold ruffles peeked from beneath the brim, quite the beauty.

Smoothing the frayed satin ribbon on her own bonnet, she sighed. In a life far removed, she'd kept up with London's fashions—her mother made sure she did. Clinging to Mama's hand as a little girl, visiting shop after shop, she'd never wanted for the latest pretty trifles. Miri closed her eyes, hoping to catch the magic memory. If she sniffed, she might just smell her mother's sweet verbena scent.

Instead, her nose wrinkled from a sudden waft of horehound and onion.

"Oh, that I were the bonnet you so admire," a low voice whispered into her ear. "To sit upon your head and nestle against your silken tresses."

Sickened, Miri turned and opened her eyes. She was trapped between the shop and Clive Witherskim.

"Good day to you, Miss Soon-to-be-Madam Witherskim." His cheeks, nipped by the cold, reddened in splotches.

A shiver ran the length of her. The thought of becoming his wife frosted her more thoroughly than the weather. "Good day, sir."

"Sir? No, no, my pet, that will not do. You may call me Clive, or sweetling, or your own little puddin' pot, hmm?" His lips parted into a smile crowded with too many teeth.

Miri swallowed. She'd lose her morning eggs all over his ridiculous shoes if he kept at it. "Excuse me." She darted around him.

He caught up and snaked his arm through hers. "No need to be timid with me, dearest."

"I am not your dearest." She shot forward.

He lagged, his grasp slipping off, but after a few tippity-tapping footsteps and several huffs and puffs, once again he caught up to her. "Sorry … what … was that?"

"I am on an errand, Mr. Witherskim. I have no time to dillydally with you now." Or ever, more like it. She grimaced. Why could the man not see or hear her constant rebuffs?

This time when he linked arms with her, he yanked her close. She staggered sideways, and he snatched the advantage, encircling her waist and snuggling her against his side. His breath collected on her neck like so many blisters as he leaned in. "Dillydallying is not what I have in mind."

That he had a mind was debatable. She wrenched from his grasp. "Do not take liberties, Mr. Witherskim."

He wobbled to the point that she thought a slight touch to his shoulder might tip him and he'd splat onto the mud-slogged rut in the road. As tempting as it was, Miri whirled and hurried to Harper's front door. Smoothing things over with Mr. Knight didn't seem nearly as distasteful as before. It was a lifeline.

"Wait!"

From the corner of her eye, she caught Miss Prinn gaping at the drama. Miri's cheeks heated. Fabulous. This would be gossiped about all over the Downs. She shoved open Harper's door and dashed in. The overhead bell bounced to the floor, its jingle degrading into a rattle.

Three sets of eyes skewered her—Mr. Knight, Mrs. Tattler, and the magistrate, Mr. Buckle. Miri's heart sank. Mrs. Tattler was the proficient gossipmonger Miss Prinn could only aspire to be. No wonder she'd not seen her in her shop.

The door scarcely closed before it swung open again, cracking the wall. Bottles teetered on shelves like chattering teeth as Witherskim barreled into the shop. He scooted to Miri's side, wheezing, tiny droplets flying from his mouth every time he exhaled.

Hemmed in such close quarters with Witherskim plastered to her arm, she felt all the coziness of Harper's store vanish. She was caught more thoroughly than a marmot in a snare—and felt just as desperate. She'd chew her own leg off if it would help.

She twisted violently, and they both stumbled. Mr. Buckle stepped forward to catch her arm, but there was no salvation for Witherskim. He bumped sideways into the L-shaped counter. A great, glass carboy lurched to the edge, then fell. The container shattered to bits, releasing an ever-widening pool of buckthorn syrup. Its aromatic scent immediately filled the shop.

"Oh my!" Mrs. Tattler's voice was as pleasant as the breaking glass.

Mr. Knight stepped from behind the counter, first eyeing the mess on the floor, then Witherskim, and finally landing on her. "What goes on here?"

Witherskim straightened his waistcoat and lifted his chin. "I should like to know that very thing." He stepped toward Miri, his thick-heeled shoes tracking the orange syrup across the wooden planks. "Your manner has been most displeasing, dearest."

Once again, all eyes focused on her. A sudden glimmer of understanding lit Mr. Knight's blue gaze as he put two and two together. She could see he remembered Roland's words and deduced that this man was her betrothed. Fighting a rising tide of nausea, she ground her teeth.

"Mr. Witherskim, I am not now, nor ever have been, your *dearest*." She spit out the word like a pit from an olive. "Nor do I have any intention of becoming so in the future!"

A beet would have to blush to match the shade of Witherskim's face. She should probably be ashamed to have caused him such public humiliation.

But she wasn't.

Mr. Buckle's eyebrows competed with Mrs. Tattler's to see whose could raise the highest. Mr. Knight merely cocked his head. "Is Master Witherskim not your betrothed?"

Ignoring the opening of the front door—for let the whole of Deverell Downs hear her final word on the matter—she squared her shoulders and looked down her nose at Witherskim. "No. He is naught but a foolish schemer."

"You presume to call me a fool?" Witherskim grew at least two inches, either inflated by rage or standing on tiptoe to best her height. Likely both.

"It is no presupposition, sir. It is God's truth."

"My offer is rescinded." His volume increased with each word. "I would not marry you if you were the last woman in the whole of Bedfordshire … or the whole of England, for that matter. You, Miss Brayden, are the worst sort of disgraceful tease. Furthermore," he shouted, rearing back and enunciating clearly enough to be heard in York. "A pox on you and your mad brother as well!"

Miri gasped.

He'd said it. Aloud. Her worst nightmare dragged into the light of day—before the magistrate's and Mrs. Tattler's wide eyes ... and even bigger mouths.

Everyone was speechless, except for a deadly calm voice that said from behind her, "You dare raise your voice to a lady, sir?"

20

Ethan stood at the threshold of the apothecary shop, studying the scene. All heads turned toward him. He'd been pleasantly surprised to find Miri still at Harper's. Evidently, however, the small assembly was even more astonished at his entrance.

But something other than surprise crossed the face of the primp-dressed man next to Miri. The curl of his lip and squint of his eye read wounded pride and … murder? Ethan snorted. Why would the little toady yell at Miri and then face him with unbridled rage? Amusing, in a twisted fashion.

"This is no lady I address." The man's tone was pinched, like a toddler who had been told no for the first time. He cast a dark glance at Miri. "She is a trifling strumpet of the worst kind."

Ethan's amusement vanished. His pulse quickened, and he stepped forward, straining to keep his words even and calm. "You may apologize *now*."

"Bah! Who do you think you are?" The skinny man looked him up and down. "You're no better than she, you raggedy blackguard."

Tension hung heavy, thick and sticky as the mess on the floor. Ethan cut a glance to the other men nearby. One gent was handsome in a dandy sort of way. His well-groomed hair was brushed back and fastened above a tailored white shirt collar that peeked from a black apron. This must be the apothecary. Why did he not take charge of the events unfolding in his own shop?

The other man seemed equally impotent. With arms folded over a round belly, he watched the scene with as much interest as the pop-eyed woman beside him.

And in the midst, Miri stood pale-faced and silent.

What kind of place was this Deverell Downs?

He closed the distance between himself and the fellow at Miri's side. Glass crunched beneath his boots, making him wonder what had gone on before he'd arrived. Positioning himself between Miri and her detractor, he cut off the little man from any chance of eye contact with the others. Then he bent, speaking so only the man would hear. "Either you apologize to the lady, or I shall make you into one."

The man shrank. This time when he assessed Ethan, his eyes narrowed. Despite years of debauched living, Ethan stood taller and stronger than this pompous monkey. And he'd long ago mastered the art of bluffing with deadly intensity. As if reaching for a knife, he lowered his hand.

"I beg her pardon." The words barely made it past the little man's lips before he fled out the door, mucked-up shoes making his exit a spectacle as orange syrup nearly pulled them from his feet.

Ethan couldn't help but smile. That had been surprisingly easy. He'd met street waifs with more courage than that nimbycock.

As he turned to Miri, however, his smile faded. She looked ready to faint, and the others remained speechless. Silence teetered on the edge of a cliff.

Then plunged to its death.

"Well! I never …" The other woman began fanning herself as she sagged against the counter.

"Of course you never." The man next to her patted her on the arm while slanting his eyes at Miri.

"Miss Brayden, are you all right? You look a bit, well … near hysterics, if I may be so bold." The apothecary stepped toward her.

Fine time to ask now. Ethan bit back the words with a fake cough into his hand.

"I … oh …" She glanced at the floor, the broken glass and spilled syrup, then shook her head. "I am very sorry, Mr. Knight."

"Don't fret. Think nothing of it."

But Miri could not have seen the slight grimace the man gave as he reached behind the counter for a rag and a broom. Clearly Mr. Knight thought more of it than he admitted aloud.

The other man approached Ethan, offering his hand. "I don't believe we've met."

Ethan could tell a lot by a man's grip, and this fellow's loose-fingered grasp, followed by a squeeze, screamed incompetent yet dangerous—a treacherous combination. "Ethan Goodw—"

Miri's sharp intake stopped him, bless her soul.

The man lifted his chin. "I am Mr. Buckle, the magistrate in these parts." He rolled back his shoulders, a vain attempt to appear more official. "You defend a lady's honor, Mr. Good, like a gentleman, yet your clothing suggests—"

"Yes, rather unconventional, I admit." Ethan masked a scowl, impatient with yet another comment on his attire. Thankfully, a stop at the tailor would yield a fitting set of garments within days. "Soon to be remedied, however, though likely not grand enough to match your obvious fashion sense." He gave a small bow.

"Yes, well …" The magistrate's chest swelled a full two inches. "Are you intending a long stay in Deverell Downs?"

"You maintain a very fair village, and I am fortunate enough to have taken a position at the rectory. Speaking of which …" Tired of playing the flattery game, he addressed Miri instead. "Mrs. Makin would like to add a physic to your order, Miss Brayden."

"Oh." She looked to the magistrate and the hawk-eyed woman. "Do you mind?"

"Actually"—the woman sniffed as if she smelled something rotten—"I was about to leave when you came in, though it's rather fortuitous that I did not."

A flush pinked Miri's cheeks while a wrinkle frustrated her brow. She turned from the woman and tipped her head toward Mr. Knight, who knelt as he finished the cleanup from the spill. "I came for Old Joe. He's acquired a severe cough. Do you have—"

"Of course, Miss Brayden." Mr. Knight stood and made short work of dispensing with the dustpan and soiled rags.

Ethan noted the smile the fellow directed at her didn't quite reach his eyes. He appeared the chivalrous gent, yet why hadn't Mr. Knight stepped to Miri's aid when she'd obviously needed help? Ethan almost respected the annoying little fop more than this man. The runt had been a brute, but at least he'd been real. In Ethan's experience, good looks were often a casing for decayed character.

He ran a hand through his loose hair, clearing the strange turn of thought, and waited while Miri collected and paid for her items. Opening the door for her, he allowed her to pass, noting that the three others watched her departure with narrowed eyes and pursed lips. A look all too familiar when directed at him, but this time it was not he they focused upon.

Why would Miri attract such guarded disdain?

⟡

Nigel leaned back, his head cradled between the two perpendicular walls in the corner—best spot in the whole alehouse. It made him invisible, for who paid mind to one more drunk afloat in a sea of guzzlers? He closed his eyes halfway but didn't miss a thing.

Two tables from his, a raucous bunch of coal heavers reveled, identifiable by the black powder worn into every crease of clothing and skin. With biceps thick as the ceiling beams, their muscles flexed and bulged in turn as each man took his try at arm wrestling someone called Pugs.

Opposite them sat a portly man in a patch-haired fur coat, deep in conversation with his tankard. The last of the occupants in the smoke-filled room was a street vendor whose juggling skills entertained a rosy-cheeked serving wench.

Into this mix, Duffy trotted through the door. Nigel leaned forward, willing Duffy's beady eyes to silently pick him out from the others.

"Eh, Thorne! There you are, then." Duffy's booming voice stopped the wrestling and confused the juggler's hands, sending five leather balls rolling onto the floor in different directions.

Stupid oaf! Nigel clenched his jaw. If he let one word loose, there'd be no stopping the curses that would follow.

In all his hedgehog glory, Duffy ambled across the room. Ten pairs of eyeballs followed his tottering stride, all the way to where he perched on a chair opposite Nigel.

So much for invisibility. Nigel's teeth might crack if he clenched his jaw any tighter.

Well, as long as the entire world is focused on our table ... Nigel hailed the serving girl and ordered a pint for the oblivious constable.

Duffy flashed a smile. "What's the occasion?"

Nigel slugged back the rest of his ale, taking his time to wipe the foam from his upper lip. By then, the wench resumed her giggling over the juggler, and the coal slingers once more raised their voices in wagers. The round man had not resumed his tankard talk, but instead planted his head face down on the table, passed out.

Keeping his voice low, Nigel finally spoke. "I need you back on the trail of Ethan Goodwin."

"Huh?" Duffy's yellow teeth peeked out from a peppery-bristled beard. "I told you, he left London."

"That you did, but I need to know where he went." He fished around in his waistcoat pocket and produced a small drawstring bag. Taking care to jingle the contents as he set it on the table, he met Duffy's gaze. "I'd bet my grandmother's buntlings that if you poke around Old Nichol, you'll find some bit of information that will be worth your while—and mine."

"Not that I mind—" Duffy followed the path of the purse back into Nigel's jacket. "But whyn't you go yourself and save the coins for yer own pocket?"

Nigel picked at his teeth with his thumbnail. Appearing too anxious might tip off even nimwitted ol' Duffy. Withdrawing his thumb, he studied it for a moment, then said, "Don't have the time, mate. You and me, we gotta divide and conquer, so to speak. You scour the slum, I'll scrub the docks. We'll meet up tomorrow."

Duffy nodded before draining the rest of his drink. After a belch and a scratch, he stood. "Best be on me way, then."

Nigel allowed for a discreet amount of time following Duffy's departure before he rose. He skirted the room, avoiding eye contact, though it seemed that once the hedgehog had left the premises, no one noticed him anyway.

Outside, a blast of cold night air slapped him in the face, and he turned up his collar. Closer to the wharf, the breeze took on teeth, biting his nose and cheeks. The affront to his ears was no less substantial. Masts creaked, flags snapped, catcalls and whoops of sailors too long a'sea lifted in song and revelry.

Huddled around a brazier next to a brown-brick depot, a group of dockhands swapped stories. Nigel passed them without a second glance. Much too trim and tidy to know the likes of Ethan Goodwin.

Farther down, dark figures squatted near a stack of crates. The guarded timbre of their voices suggested skullduggery of some sort, as did the strong smell of rum. Nigel slowed but did not stop.

His footsteps echoed as the walkway between warehouse and waterway narrowed. Not many inhabited this part of the docks, for clearly the merrymaking was at the other end—depending, of course, upon one's definition of merry.

From a shadowed niche, flanked by a heap of cargo nets on one side and a pyramid of barrels on the other, whispered words carried out, blending with the breeze. Nigel sniffed. A peppery scent tinged with … yes … poppy seed.

Victory.

He leaned against the barrels and folded his arms, careful to avert his head—not that he could see into the cursed blackness anyway. Still, whoever was within would surely detect the lack of threat in his stance.

Speaking just loud enough to be heard, he said, "I'm a-lookin for one of yer own. Goes by the name of Ethan. Pals around with a fella called Will. Where is he?"

A fat grey rat waddled out from a crevice behind the nets, close enough that Nigel could hear its claws scratching the wooden planks. Other than that, the usual wharf sounds filled the night.

Nigel turned and spoke directly into the black hole. "He stands to make a fortune, mates, and we all know where he'll spend it."

"Ain't seen him. But you let him know there's a right fine shipment a-comin' on the next East Indiaman ..."

The words faded as Nigel retraced his path and headed home. Defeat made him tired, and having to rely on Duffy to gather information wearied him further. Even so, sleep would not come easy this night, nor the next two, as his deadline to repay Buck loomed.

The worn stairway leading to his third-floor room lodged creaking complaints with each step. One day, mayhap, he'd woo Lady Luck and leave behind this clap-shack for finer accommodations.

Old Mrs. Spankum must have been cooking fish again, for the stench lingered in the stairwell's close air. He lightened his steps. Hopefully with a full belly she'd—he smiled at the snore ripping through her door. No worries about rent haggling tonight.

He patted his waistcoat pocket for his key, climbing the last bit of stairs. As he neared his own door, he slowed.

Something didn't feel right—and with his many years of man hunting, he'd learned to trust that queer bubbling in his gut.

Senses heightened, he jiggled his key in the lock. No click, yet the disturbance opened it an inch. A frown twisted his mouth. Someone had been here—

Or still was.

He planted his foot on the door, and it crashed open. Sconce light from the hallway illuminated a shadowy scene.

Socks draped over the chair back just as he'd left them. The table at the center was piled high with papers and dishes and a leftover crust of bread. His bed was in one corner, a chamber pot in the other. Nothing out of place. The familiarity of it all grazed his trusted intuition.

Had he simply forgotten to fasten the bolt? Maybe ... but he lit a small oil lamp and kept it burning even after he climbed beneath his covers. He was becoming as skittish as Duffy, and the thought irked him.

Lying down, he settled against the lumpy mattress, glad to be off his feet. It'd been a long day and—

His eyes popped open, intuition vindicated. A warning written in black char was etched onto the ceiling.

Two days.

21

Miri's head bobbed, and she jerked awake. It took her a moment to reorient herself to the sparse surroundings of Old Joe's chamber. Next to his bedside, a small flame sputtered like a disapproving tongue. She stood and arched her back before adjusting the wick, then bent over the old man. The tang of camphor and vinegar rose from the poultice bound to his chest, and her nose wrinkled. She held her breath. Thankfully, he did not. It appeared he rested peacefully— A peace she'd give anything to own.

She stepped away with a sigh and sank onto the chair beside the nightstand. She could not remember what parting words she'd given Ethan earlier that morning as she'd fled the scene at the apothecary's shop but recalled everything about Witherskim's horrid revelation. The timbre of his voice. The curl of his lips and fine spray that flew from them.

"A pox on you and your mad brother as well!"

Her deepest fear had come to pass, and instead of facing it, she'd run. Run straight home and hidden in Old Joe's room, expecting any minute to hear the magistrate arrive and haul Roland away. But the rest of the day passed without a whisper of threat. Serenity blanketed the rectory, albeit a delicate and brittle kind. Deep within, she knew that the tiniest tremor could splinter it to shards. She yawned and reached to massage the tight muscles at the nape of her neck. Too much thinking was the first ingredient in the recipe for melancholy.

"It's late, miss. I'll take a watch."

Mrs. Makin's voice sent a charge through Miri, chasing off her fatigue to a far, shadowy corner. No doubt it would creep out and reclaim her once she stretched upon her bed and relaxed.

She stood and faced the cook. "Thank you."

Mrs. Makin's lower lip folded into a frown as she eyed the undisturbed biscuits and teapot on the stand. "You've not eaten a thing, except for those few mouse bites at breakfast. If you don't mind me a-sayin', you look a bit peaked. I've left you a tray of food and some ginger tea in the kitchen."

Pressing a hand to her stomach, Miri was tempted to refuse, but perhaps the woman was right. She should probably eat. Who knew what the morrow might bring. This could be her last meal beneath the rectory's roof.

The cook leaned closer and lowered her voice. "Ginger tea with a bit o' yarrow is just the thing for what ails a woman." She winked in a knowing fashion, then handed off her candle lantern and shooed Miri out of the room.

If only her problems were as simple as that.

At the end of the corridor, she paused near the kitchen door, trying to conjure up some kind of appetite. Her stomach clenched, but not from hunger. What would become of her once Roland was taken away? Worse ... what would become of him?

She stormed down the corridor, her candle flickering with the swift movement. Drat that Witherskim! A disgusted sigh emptied her lungs of air, and she inhaled, then paused. Sniffing, she detected the distinct scent of elderberries. What in the world? She turned the corner—

And her jaw dropped, as her lantern nearly did. Were she four years old, she'd close her eyes and make the macabre image go away. Instead, she mustered courage and forced her arm to rise, exposing more light onto the stairway.

Roland sat several steps up, leaning back on his elbows. His long legs splayed from beneath him. Shimmering with a strange radiance, his eyes locked onto hers. He opened his mouth, but no words came. Only his tongue as he licked his lips. In a rather grotesque version of a tot playing dress-up, he wore her white cotton nightdress—and nothing else. He lurched forward, ripping the fabric, and grabbed a bottle at his side. Tipping it up, he knocked back a swig. Much of it dribbled out the sides of his mouth and down his chin. The accompanying burp tore the silence.

Miri's hand flew to her chest. Her brother, the pious master of Pembroke, doctor of divinity, was completely and totally foxed. Truly, she ought not laugh.

So she coughed instead. "Uh … Roland?"

A smile lifted one side of his mouth, a freakish blend of guilt and defiance. As far as she knew, he'd never before tippled. Why now?

Why not?

"They tol' me … they tol' me … did you hear 'em?" His words slurred, barely audible, and his head lolled side to side, as if he couldn't decide what he wanted to look at. Finally he stopped and peered at her.

What went on behind those eyes? Did he have some sense he was losing control, or had it all been stolen from him at once, like a thief dumping a jewelry chest into a sack? He blinked, pupils wide and deeply black, and then his eyes disappeared. Rolled up fast as the snapping of a shade. He collapsed backward, his skull thudding against the stair.

Too stunned to move, Miri stood rooted, unable to comprehend the bizarre scene, or what to do about it—her thoughts every bit as ransacked as her brother's. She matched her breathing to the mantle clock ticking away in the sitting room. A mindless activity, but soothing, giving her time to think.

One thick snore ripped from Roland, sawing through the quiet. She should probably get him up to his chamber before someone else discovered him. But how?

Biting her lower lip, she considered the possibilities. She was no match for such dead weight, not even with Mrs. Makin's help. Bishop Fothergill? He'd cast them out before the magistrate got the chance. And Old Joe lay abed. That left …

Ethan.

◦◦◦

Ethan sat up, groggy. The bed frame creaked, and the Book of Common Prayer he'd borrowed slid from his chest and landed on the floor. Shadows wavered against the wall of his small room, jerking one way and then another from the guttering candle flame. He ran a hand through his loose hair and yawned. Half awake and half dressed, he must have dozed off while reading.

A light rapping at his door added to the rattling of the windowpanes from a stiff breeze. Ethan grimaced. Hadn't Fothergill run him ragged enough for one day? When he'd returned from the village, he'd fully intended to find Miri and speak with her. An urgent need to tell her the truth nagged him—of his part in Will's death and Thorne's murder. If she were to shun him because of it, better now than after the rising regard he held for her could not be let go of.

Already it might be too late. But the bishop had assigned him one task after another until nightfall. By then, it was beyond seemly to approach her.

Rap. Rap.

Sitting motionless, he didn't so much as twitch. Maybe if he feigned sleep, the fellow would go away.

Rap. Rap. Rap.

"Mr. Goodwin … Ethan?"

Miri's voice, albeit soft and low, jolted through his body. He bolted up, shoved his legs into trousers, then yanked open the door. "What's wrong?"

"I wonder if … I mean to say …" She closed her eyes as if relieved to find him there, then suddenly pinned her gaze on his. In the depths of those amber pools, hope surfaced.

He sucked in a breath, resisting the strong urge to glance over his shoulder and make sure it was he—he alone—that she sought.

Candlelight added an ethereal glow to her fair skin, making a stark contrast to the shadow that crossed her face. "Would you help me?"

Help her? He'd go to hell and back for her. All she had to do was ask. He shifted his weight, pushing words past the emotion she stirred. "Of course."

"Oh, thank you!" She turned, probably expecting him to follow.

"Hold on. I've not got my boots—"

"No need," she called over her shoulder, hastening down the passageway. "In fact it's better if you don't. It will be quieter that way."

He trailed her silhouette down the corridor. Mystery hung on the night air, perfumed by her violet scent. His bare feet soaked in the chill of the floorboards as he caught up to her. "What exactly am I helping you with?"

Instead of answering, she pressed a finger to her lips, then sped down the corridor, turned at the next, and finally stopped near the front door. Nodding her head toward the stairway, she whispered, "This."

Ethan looked where she indicated, then snorted. "Well, well …"

He passed by Miri and ascended the first two stairs. Not that he hadn't seen more peculiar sights in his time, but here? In hallowed walls? He was hard pressed to reconcile the drunken man in the torn nightdress with the arrogant image of Roland when sober. Suddenly the angry outbursts and quirky behavior all made sense. Roland was a drunkard. A sanctimonious, highly educated tosspot.

"We should get him to his chamber before …" Miri's words trailed off, but she needn't finish. If Fothergill found Roland sauced on the stairway, he'd throw him out.

"You hold the light. I'll heave him up." He climbed several more stairs, positioned himself to grasp Roland beneath the armpits, then lifted. Gads! The man weighed at least fifteen, maybe sixteen stone. Putting all his strength into the effort, he strained upward, one stair at a time.

When they made the first landing, Ethan's shirt clung damp and cold against the middle of his back, and he paused to catch his breath. Little snores escaped Roland on his inhales. The man was as content as a babe in arms.

"Is there not more I can do to help?" Miri's voice was surprisingly calm. Now that he thought about it, her whole manner was calm, as if finding her brother wearing her nightclothes were a common occurrence. Apparently the man's drinking problem was nothing new.

"On the contrary"—he flashed her a smile—"this could not be done without your guiding light. Carry on."

The next flight of stairs challenged in new ways. His thighs burned, and sweat trickled down his temples as he lugged Roland ever upward. The man really ought to swear off biscuits at teatime. Breathing hard, he halted at the top of the third floor. An unspoken agreement passed between him and Miri, for the bishop's chamber was on this level. Her eyes looked from his, to the candle, then back again, and he nodded. With one small puff, darkness covered them.

Miri's rustling skirt and Roland's occasional snorts were the extent of their noisemaking. Thank God she'd warned him not to put on his boots. As they passed Fothergill's door, they held their breaths. Her brother did not.

At that precise moment, Roland sucked in a snore that tore a jagged hole through the silence.

They froze. Ethan allowed only his eyeballs to move.

But the bishop did not burst out of his chamber, nor did candlelight show from the gap between his door and the threshold.

His heart slowly restarted. So did Miri's swishing skirt. They moved on to Roland's chamber as a large, incongruous animal— Miri the head, him the guts, and Roland the tail.

Hefting the man onto his bed took some effort, but they managed to get him atop the mattress with a few grunts. Ethan turned to leave. Roland was sour enough to stomach when sober. If he happened to wake now, who knew what kind of ugly drunk he'd make.

But the slight press of Miri's hand on his arm forestalled him. "We should get him into suitable bedclothes," she whispered.

He nodded, trying to ignore the thick tension settling over him as Miri gathered Roland's nightshirt. They stood on each side of her brother. Miri propped, and he tugged. As the gown cleared Roland's calves and then his knees, Ethan stopped. For all he knew, the man could be as naked as Adam beneath that dressing gown.

Trying not to make eye contact with Miri, he said, "Leave the room. I can manage."

"You cannot do this alone. His arms are like dead eels." Though she whispered, her determination came through clearly enough.

"Wait by the door. If I get in a bind—"

"Don't be silly. I can help."

She simply didn't get it, which both pleased and irritated. Searching through a mental arsenal, he realized that bluntness was the kindest weapon he could find. "Miri"—he kept his voice low and waited for her to look into his eyes—"if you stay, you may see more of your brother than you wish to."

Deep color rose from her neck, and her throat convulsed as she swallowed. "Oh."

He waited until she posted herself at the opposite end of the chamber, her back toward him, before he started yanking and pulling solo. She was right. Roland's arms were dead eels. Eventually, he stripped off the ruined nightdress and almost hugged the drunkard for having the sense to keep his britches on—until something worse snagged his attention.

"What in the …" He leaned closer to Roland's chest. Dark scabs crisscrossed into a pulpy wound. Only once before had he ever seen anything like it, and the reminder made his blood run cold. Either Roland had tangled with a bear, or this man of the cloth fought some very real demons from within. Likely the latter. And if so, how long before his violent tendencies turned outward?

Ethan quickly redressed him, then, with a nod, guided Miri into the hallway. They retreated on silent feet, padding the length of the corridor. This time when they passed Fothergill's room, a yellow strip shone from beneath the door. Ethan pressed his hand against the small of Miri's back, urging her to hurry. It would do neither of them good to be accused of a tryst.

Either she sensed the same danger or his touch startled her, for she shot ahead and did not stop until they reached the landing on the floor of her chamber.

When she turned, her vulnerability struck a raw nerve in him, so potent he nearly flinched. "I want you to lock your door this night. Every night. Your brother"—he paused and ran a hand through his loose hair. How to say this?—"suffice it to say that I will rest easier if you do as I ask."

Darkness made it impossible to read her expression, yet the quiver in her voice could not be hidden. "You ... you won't tell anyone about this, will you?"

He curled his hands into fists at his sides, hating the fear that thickened her voice. Men he could fight against, and gladly for her, but how to slay this dragon? If it would do any good, he'd wrap his arms about her and never let go, yet at this point, that might frighten her further. So he simply said, "Your secrets are safe with me."

"It is not my secrets I worry about," she whispered. "Good night."

She whirled, leaving behind a faint violet scent, and he remained in the shadows until he heard the click of a bolt in the grate at her door. As he retraced the path to his room, he couldn't help but wonder to whose secrets she referred.

And how would she feel about his?

22

"Watch it! Ye brainless, namby-pated …" Nigel shook his fist in the air as mud splattered him where he stood. The half-witted driver careening in front of him obviously couldn't hear him above the clankity-clatter of the dray's iron wheels. A blind-eyed washerwoman could have driven those horses around the mud-holes blighting the street better than that crack-head. Irritated, Nigel scrubbed the sludge from his face harder than he should have, then winced.

"'Ere you go, mate."

Duffy's voice boomed in his ear. He'd be lucky to make it to past noontide without going deaf around here. Turning, he recoiled from a yellowed handkerchief waving in his face.

"Gimme that!" He grabbed the cloth from Duffy's hand. "You're late."

As Duffy recounted one useless detail after another, Nigel took the time to wipe his face properly, adding in a swipe to his neck and ears for good measure. He handed it back, more black now than yellowed. When Duffy pocketed the cloth, a flashy bit of lace floated to the ground.

"What's this?" He smacked Duffy's hand out of the way and held it up.

"That's mine!" Red spread up Duffy's neck and colored his whole face as he snatched it back. "Like I was sayin', me own puddin' pie come home last night. Ain't seen the ol' girl in o'er a fortnight. That last row we had was—"

"I don't give a flyin' fig about your *puddin' pie*. Get on to what I paid you for, man."

Duffy's eyes glazed for a moment, and his tongue worked his lips. Good. Thinking position. The old hedgehog's wheels were finally turning. At last, he spoke. "Right. Well, I scoured the Old Nichol, just like you said. Didn't turn up much about Goodwin, I'm afraid."

A string of curses unraveled out Nigel's mouth. "Gimme back my money, Duffy!"

"Hold on, hold on." Duffy's teeth did the working this time. "Now then, like I said, nothing new on ol' Ethan boy, but I did find out his friend Will has a sister."

"What the flippity-flap do I care about some wench—"

"A sister that lives up Bedfordshire way." Duffy leaned closer, the smell of sausage and headcheese rank on his breath. "In the country, that is. Just the place to hide out, I'm thinkin'." He waggled his hedgehog eyebrows.

"Well, well." Nigel chewed on that tasty nugget of information. Maybe, just maybe, fate's perpetual frown was turning into a smile.

He nodded. "Good job, Duff. You can go on back home to yer puddin' pie then, eh?"

Duffy grinned, his cheeks bunching so that it squinted his eyes nearly shut. "Righty-oh."

"Think I'll be takin' me a little trip north o' London." Nigel scratched his chin. Yes siree, just the time to leave behind the blasted city, especially since Buck would come a'callin' on the morrow.

⌒⌒⌒

Miri lifted her face to the warm breeze and breathed deeply, the smell of moist earth and worms a leftover reminder of an earlier rain shower. She'd have to scrub the bottom of her skirt after this walk about the grounds, but the added chore would be worth the moment spent soaking in the morning's rays. Though hiding out in Joe's room had provided much time to think, it was beginning to stifle.

It was apparent she would not be able to hide Roland's madness much longer. Witherskim had voiced it, and now Ethan had witnessed it firsthand. She must make plans. But with no money or employment—she couldn't seriously expect Mrs. Tattler to take on a madman's sister—what was there to plan?

Chinnup, chinnup, chinnup, a throaty sparrow admonished her as it sailed overhead, sounding for all the world as if it scolded her to face her situation with a good heart. The bird sailed across the garden and flew to a ball of twigs and fluff tucked beneath the rectory's eaves. Sheltered from elements and enemies alike, the little bird likely didn't give a care for its survival.

Miri frowned at the sky. "Where is my safe nesting place, God?"

No answer. Not that she expected one ... or did she? "Chin up, indeed." She sighed and cast her attention back to the path.

Nearing the cluster of rose bushes, she stopped. Some shrubs sent out reddish-brown shoots from their branches, others dark green, but the one she hadn't finished pruning showed no growth whatsoever. She crouched for a better look. Not a nub of promise dotted its branches. At least she wasn't the only one God was ignoring, then. The thought did not bring comfort.

"You look as if the weight of the world is on your shoulders."

Ethan's deep voice cut into her ponderings as he squatted next to her. "Though I don't suppose you got much sleep last night."

True, fatigue did cloud her concentration, but how had she missed hearing his approach? If she didn't pull herself together soon, she might easily be rooming with Roland at the asylum. Turning her head, she offered Ethan a wry smile. "Not the weight of the entire world, just this one rose bush. I'm afraid you ought not keep company with me. I'm a murderer."

His eyes widened an instant before he leaned forward to focus on the shrub. No further words passed between them, yet she got the distinct impression that she'd somehow indicted him.

He loosened the dirt at the shrub's base and poked around with one finger. After a "humph," his prodding moved upward. Taking care of the thorns, he felt here and there until finally he snapped off the tip of one of the longest branches.

"My mother kept flowers." He examined the broken edge, turning it over in his hand. Bringing it to eye level, he squinted, then tossed it aside and faced her. "Give it time. Rose bushes are hardier than you might think. With much patience and God's care, this one could bloom again."

Miri bit her lip, affected by his words more than she'd care to admit. His message brought good tidings for the shrub, but dare she hope it might signify future changes for her barren life as well? Not likely. She stood and smoothed her skirt.

"You scowl as well as your brother. This ought to lighten your mood, though." Stepping close—near enough that her breath hitched—he reached out. With the lightest of touches, his palm brushed against the wisps of perpetually loose hair that refused to be captured in her chignon.

She froze, wondering what he intended.

"Look." He drew back his hand and held it up for her to see. A small stone, round and speckled, sat like a jewel in his palm. "Lighter already."

She stared, as mesmerized by the deed as by the man.

He reached again, and she fought to keep from leaning in to his touch—the same rebellious urge that had gripped her last night on the stairway. How could she be so drawn to a man she knew so little about?

Retrieving another stone from behind her other ear, he said, "Surely you must be feeling lighter by the moment."

She swallowed. Oh, she felt all right, but not lighter. More like dizzy. "How did you do that?"

He cocked his head, half a rogue smile softening his face. She'd not noticed before that he'd trimmed his beard and tamed his unruly hair into a queue at the back. Cleaned up properly, his boyish good looks put Mr. Knight's to shame. But as he reached again, the muscles rippling beneath his shirt reminded her that this was no boy.

He produced an additional rock and tossed them all into the air.

"Why—" Her astonishment turned into a smile as he snatched each one before they hit the dirt and juggled them. When he spun in a circle without losing any, she laughed.

"Now"—he pocketed the stones with a grin of his own—"that's better."

"And if that would not have made me laugh?"

"Well, then." He stepped closer and lowered his voice. "I should have tried all the harder."

Perhaps his wink meant nothing. Nevertheless, a shiver tingled through her.

"Are … uh …" She scrambled for words as elusive as a handful of scattered marbles. "Are there no ends to your talents?"

A smirk lifted one side of his mouth. "I've been called many things in my day, but never talented."

"Oh, but you are. You shod the bishop's horse, fixed the pantry's stuck door, stopped the wind from whistling through that crack in the sanctuary's window, and I don't even know what else. And besides the countless times you've made me smile, you stood up to Witherskim for me and helped me get Roland to his chamber last night. Then …" She stopped, hating the way she blabbered like a moonstruck schoolgirl. Not that she was, but it sure must sound as such.

He must have thought so as well, for his grin reached clear to his eyes. "I was not aware you were keeping tally."

His husky undertone stole what little coherency she had left. "I wasn't … or rather … I am not …"

All her words, all her thoughts, stalled beneath his gaze—one so intense her heartbeat faltered, then galloped out of control.

This was ridiculous. Of course she felt attracted to him. He'd been Will's friend. Ethan was her last tangible connection to a brother she'd loved very much. The times she'd shared with this man felt as comforting and connected as if she'd been with Will himself. There was no pretension in their relationship, no awkwardness. Just heartfelt companionship. She smiled, relieved to finally categorize the odd feelings he created. "I am happy you are here. At the rectory, I mean, not necessarily standing in the garden with me, though I really don't mind, and …"

One of his brows rose as her babbling slowed to a stop. The sparkle in his eyes cut through her own rationalizations, creating more than a brotherly feeling skittering along each nerve. She swallowed at the sudden realization.

Chinnup. Chinnup. Chinnup.

Stupid bird. She wanted nothing more than to hide her burning face from Ethan's consuming gaze.

"There is no other place I would rather be"—his smile faded, and a serious flash ignited in the depths of his brown eyes—"than here at your side." Slowly, his hand rose, the back of his knuckles barely a murmur sweeping across her cheek.

Propriety be hanged. She leaned into his touch. The warmth of his skin suggested virility, and the roughness, strength. This was the kind of hand that could protect.

Or entice.

At her movement, his lips parted, and he sucked in a breath. That she'd even noticed his mouth shamed her. But that didn't stop her from wondering how it might feel to have those lips meet her own. A queer twinge jerked in her stomach—no … lower, and her face burned all the hotter.

His fingers—why had she thought them rough?—brushed along the length of her neck, from just behind her ear to where flesh met collar. Closing her eyes, she memorized their trail.

"Miri." His voice caressed deeper than his touch.

When his breath mingled with hers, warm and heady, her eyes flew open. The passion she read on his face aroused in her a powerful desire—

One that instantly sobered her. She retreated a step, guilt washing over her as thoroughly as a basin of icy water. What possessed her? "Forgive me. I should not have—"

He shook his head. "It's I who should be begging your forgiveness. Will spoke truth when he said you are a saint." His smile returned. He pulled back his hand and motioned toward hers. "May I?"

Afraid of his touch, and equally terrified of what her own response might be, there was no good reason to comply. So why did she?

"Turn your hand over and open your palm."

She shook her head. "No, really, I can't juggle."

"Open it."

His hand was hardly an inch from her own. Still she wavered. "But—"

"Do I frighten you?"

The catch in his voice suggested that her answer held great power. Was he seeking her trust?

Should she give it?

"No, you do not," she whispered. "Sometimes I get scared, but not with you. Never with you."

His eyes widened at her admission. Surely he must think her a terrible strumpet.

But the genuine smile lighting his face said otherwise. "This is just a gift, Miri, nothing more, and a poor offering at that."

Uncurling her fingers, she held her breath. She ought not trust this man, especially as his hand opened onto hers, hot and trembling … or was it her own that trembled? Her heart beat harder.

Perhaps she ought not trust herself.

He drew back, taking all his warmth and strength with him, until she realized something yet rested in her palm.

Lifting her hand, she looked closer. A rock—in the perfect shape of a heart. She shot her gaze to his. Everything such a gift implied shone in his eyes, naked and unashamed. Had any man ever truly looked at her so?

He turned and walked back toward the stables, whistling.

Chinnup. Chinnup. Chinnup.

"Yes, chin up!" She twirled around, again and again, giddy for reasons she'd later ponder. "Chin up, chin up, chin up!"

"Good heavens, Miss Brayden! Such a display."

She stopped, suddenly queasy. Clenching her fingers tight around the heart stone for courage, she faced Bishop Fothergill.

He wasn't smiling.

23

Miri eased shut the sanctuary door, pressing her back against the cool oak until her eyes adjusted to the indoor light. *Thank You, Lord, for greased hinges and heads still bowed in prayer.* She scooted down the aisle, aware that a few eyelids cracked open to see who dared enter so late. Surely peeking was as sinful as tardiness. The thought was salve to her bruised conscience. Besides, it wasn't as if she'd missed the service entirely—as she had breakfast. Spending hours well into the evening at Joe's bedside had finally taken a toll. La, who was she fooling? She wouldn't have slept anyway for clutching the heart stone Ethan had given her yesterday.

Entering the box pew, she stood next to Roland's rigid body and bowed her head. Slowly her heart rate leveled as Bishop Fothergill droned on. And on. Did God enjoy hearing the man's voice as much as the bishop enjoyed using it? She clenched her hands together—tight enough to cramp—a nominal penance for such an evil notion. Why did it never fail that her most wicked thoughts crept out in the holiest of places?

At last an "aaahhh-mehnn" rolled off the bishop's tongue, and before they sat, she sneaked a sideways glance at Roland. Between her vigil in Joe's room and the irregular hours Roland had been keeping, she'd not seen him in several days—not since his drinking spree. His dark hair was slicked back above a white collar, the scent of pomade and shaving tonic strong and peppery. When he met her gaze, his eyes looked clear, and the frown he gave her implied his usual condemnation. He appeared normal, though it felt odd to think of her brother as that.

Tension drained from her shoulders, and she sank onto the pew.

"Oh!" Pricks of pain dotted her backside, and she shot up, catching herself before regaining a complete stand. She pressed her lips tight to keep from drawing more attention than she'd already gained. Eyes burned into her back and her sides, and several heads turned from the pews in front. From his advantage in the lectern, the bishop glared down at her as if she'd recited the Lord's Prayer backward.

Reaching behind, she cleared the bench, shoving aside sharp bits of metal, then sat as far as possible on the pew's edge. As Fothergill resumed the Sunday reading, she palmed one of the objects, then opened her hand in her lap.

Beveled shaft, square head, sharp point … a horseshoe nail. Her brow crumpled in confusion. Why would there be a handful of those on her seat?

Roland leaned close to her, his breath hot in her ear.

"For want of a nail, the shoe was lost. For want of a shoe, the horse was lost. For want of a horse, the battle was lost." His foot tapped in rhythm with the singsong verse. "We've lost, we've lost, we've lost."

Miri stiffened and pulled away, all too aware that Roland's antics had been noticed this time. Whispers passed around the sanctuary like an unholy wind. For the first time ever, she wished the bishop would drone a little louder.

Perched like a stone about to tumble off a cliff, she teetered in the thin place between the temptation to run out like a madwoman or wait to see what else her brother might do. The bench's edge cut into her bottom without mercy. Next to her, Roland's fingers tapped out a crazed rhythm on his knee. Minutes passed, or maybe hours, though it felt like days. This had to be the longest sermon she'd ever suffered through.

When summoned to stand for the benediction, she wavered on her feet. Thousands of needles prickled from her thighs down, sharper than the horseshoe nails. She wiggled one foot, then the other, trying to wake the sleeping flesh without losing balance—or looking as if she danced a jig.

The bishop had hardly finished voicing his "bless yous" and "keep yous" before Roland scooped up a stack of books at his side. He nudged her. "Go."

She started to collect the nails, but he pressed into her.

"Go now, woman."

Standing, she opened her mouth to argue but quickly shut her lips. The vacant stare that met hers shouted that Roland had already left. For once, she agreed wholeheartedly with him. The sooner he exited the sanctuary, the better.

She stepped aside, allowing him to pass, then regretted it as he crashed into Squire Gullaby.

Roland's books went tumbling. So did the squire. Admittedly the squat man didn't have far to meet the floor, but he landed with a rather harsh thud.

"Now look what you've done!" Roland's tone accused more thoroughly than his words.

Onlookers, Miri included, sucked in a breath.

The squire's brows drew together, forming a bristly thunderbolt on his forehead. Roland was too busy to notice as he plucked his books from the floor, but Miri knew a storm would soon break.

When Roland reached to grab a book from the squire's lap, Gullaby beat his hand away—a loud, resounding slap. The kind that would leave red fingerprints across the back of her brother's hand for the next hour.

Roland recoiled, hugging the volumes he'd already collected. Miri stared, frozen in place at the pew box's door, unable to think of how to stop the horrid drama from escalating.

With a grunt, Mr. Gullaby planted himself upright, legs wide as if he'd not be toppled again by surprise. The glower he directed at Roland would have made a sane man think twice.

Roland merely sniffed. "You, sir, should watch where you're going. Now, give me back my book."

"You were the one who barreled into me!" The squire's nose, red during the best of times, deepened to the hue of a ripe tomato. "Book indeed. I ought to book you right in the head, that's what. Why … I ought to have you locked up, crazy fool."

"Need I remind everyone that we are in the house of God?" Bishop Fothergill closed in, and as he bent to retrieve the book in question, Miri's heart stopped.

She knew that leather cover.

As it flopped open to the first page, a wave of recognition rippled across Fothergill's face as well. "What the devil are you doing with Vicar Eldon's Bible?"

Roland squared his shoulders. "For want of a nail—"

"Please!" Miri stepped between the huddle of men. If Roland continued at this rate, he'd be rooming at Bethlem Hospital by teatime.

She forced a smile. "As you've said, Bishop, this is God's house. I am sure this is but a misunderstanding. Vicar Eldon left behind many things, and my brother has had the good will to safeguard each possession until his return. This is but one more to be stored safely away. If you don't mind?" She held out her hand.

Fothergill frowned but placed the Bible on her outstretched palm. She wrapped her fingers around it and turned to Roland. "Here. I am sure you will see to this book with care. And an apology would be in order as well, I think."

She waited, wide-eyed, every bit of her willing Roland to please, please, please beg the squire's forgiveness. Behind her, Gullaby cleared his throat. The bishop's surplice swished as he shifted his weight. Those parishioners yet watching held their breath.

Roland's jaw flexed once. Twice.

But he said nothing.

Without looking back, Miri was sure the squire's entire face was now red. Had she pushed everyone beyond the bursting point?

Roland's chest expanded, and after an enormous exhale, he said, "Pardon me, Mr. Gullaby."

Miri's heart didn't start, however, until her brother walked the length of the aisle and disappeared out the door. She turned to the men, who both wore scowls, one holy and one not, and discovered she'd been right. Mr. Gullaby's face would easily anger a bull.

"Do forgive my brother, gentlemen. He's not been well."

The squire exchanged a look with the bishop, then tugged down his waistcoat and straightened wrinkles from his breeches. At last he focused on her. "Your brother treads in dangerous waters, Miss Brayden. Dangerous and deep. See if you can talk some sense into the man."

Miri dipped a curtsey. She might more easily talk a chicken into giving milk.

❦

As Miri fled down the aisle, Ethan stepped from the harbor of an alcove. He suspected she'd not been in any real danger, not in the full sight of God and man. Nevertheless, he'd kept watch over the disturbing scene. Her brother really should have waited until after morning prayers to uncork his brandy—or whatever his choice of poison was. It didn't take a learned man to know drunken outbursts ought be saved for a different time and place.

A shaft of sunlight shone through the beams of an overhead window, casting the shadow of a cross at Ethan's feet. A wry smile twitched his lips. Listen to him—denigrating Roland for drinking on the Sabbath when he'd committed oh-so-much-worse sins no matter the day. He lifted his face to the bright rays. *Forgive me, Lord.*

Then, lengthening his stride, he caught up to Miri as she reached the door. "Allow me."

She passed through with a thank-you and a strained smile—one barely more than a slight upturn at the edges of her mouth.

"May I walk with you?" Before she could answer, he fell into step at her side.

She slanted him a glance. "It appears that you are, sir."

"Sir?" He lifted one brow and tilted his head, an expression he'd mastered as a young boy to garner sweets from the cook. "I thought we'd gotten beyond that by now."

Her gentle "humph" neither chastised nor encouraged—so he muddled on. "About what happened just now, in the sanctuary, I mean—do you wish to speak of it?"

A warm pink stole over her cheeks. "There is nothing to say."

"But Roland clearly was—"

"I can have no good word on the matter at the moment." She averted her face and spoke to the wind. "Let us change the subject."

"No."

Her step faltered, and she snapped her face back to his, the dimple in her chin deepened by her frown. "Let it go, please."

He'd recant if it would remove the hurt in her eyes, but not even he could erase that much pain. "I can't let it go. I see how your brother treats you, and yet your kindness toward him is nothing short of remarkable. Why do you protect him so? Is that not God's job?"

"Do not think to preach to me! You have no idea—"

"But I do. I know exactly the kind of man he is."

Her eyes widened, and he was hard pressed to know if the fire glinting in her gaze was from the sunlight or something deeper. "Don't fret, Miri. I told you your secrets are safe with me. Come, come, where is your faith and hope?"

"In whom do you wish it to be? God or you?"

He smirked. "I would not presume so much. And neither would you if you knew of my past, but we are not speaking of me. We were discussing faith and hope. Do you not think God capable of caring for Roland beyond that which you are able?"

"I don't argue that God *can* redeem Roland from his . . . situation." She stopped and turned to him so quickly, her skirt swirled with a swish. "The question is *will* He?"

She gazed at him as if his reply had the authority to raise the dead. The desperation in her voice, the strain of the muscles in her neck, why . . . he might almost believe she'd never voiced this question to anyone before—not even to God.

"Seems to me that if you knew the answer, if you could see and know the every movement of God, then I daresay you would have no need of faith. Perhaps the real question is …" He paused, knowing that what he was about to ask might very well broadside her with as much force as when Newton had asked him. "Do you trust Him? Do you trust in God alone?"

For a fair amount of time, she nibbled her lower lip, lost somewhere deep in thought. Either she bit too hard, or the action dislodged raw bits of undigested truth that didn't taste so good, for she winced.

Finally, she sighed. "To be honest, it's hard to trust in someone I can't see or touch, while a brother I love very much is coming undone before my eyes. Sometimes faith and hope are only words to me. Why cannot God simply come down here and be real? Something tangible. Flesh and blood and—"

"He did."

A simple rebuttal, really, but her lips parted at the revelation. And he knew exactly how she felt. How many times had Reverend Newton pulled the same one-two truth punch on him?

"I guess … I never … thought of it that way before."

"So the question remains. Do you trust Him?"

The fierce angle of her jaw softened. "I suspect that not only Roland's life depends upon my answer, but mine as well."

"And your answer is?"

She turned to resume their walk to the rectory.

His boots crunched on the gravel beside her patting slippers. Opposite sounds, but compatible in a soothing way, though he doubted she noticed. She was silent all the way to the front stoop of the rectory, where he could no longer follow. That he'd breached etiquette to travel this far to the main entrance could be construed as subordination to prying eyes. Hopefully there weren't any.

She gained the first step, so preoccupied that she probably would have been halfway to her chamber before noticing she'd left him behind.

"Miri?"

Her mouth pursed into a small *O* as she faced him. "My apologies. I fear I am not the best of company today. And … well, you've given me much to consider."

He grinned, happy to, for once, be on the thought-giving end instead of the receiving. "I don't claim to be a scholar, but this much is true. God loves your scoundrel of a brother infinitely more than you do. And you, Miri, are more precious to Him than life itself—"

Just as you are becoming to me. He swallowed back the words, but that did not stop the slow burn working its way up from his belly.

"Would that I had a faith like yours." She leaned toward him as if by nearness alone she could grasp belief from his pocket.

"Ask."

"But—"

He laid a finger on her lips. "Just ask. It's that simple—and that hard. Sometimes faith is a moment-by-moment thing."

The feel of her soft mouth beneath his fingertips scorched hot as a coal, and he jerked his hand away.

She frowned. "Is that a promise or a warning?"

"Yes." He turned and crunched down the walkway alone. Whether she knew it or not, she could lob her own powerful questions.

24

"Blast it!"

Nigel stubbed his toe for the third time on a jutting bit of moss-camouflaged limestone. His worn boot provided precious little protection where the sharp edge had hit painfully close to his ingrown toenail. One more run-in with a rock, and he'd rethink this stealthy approach into Deverell Downs.

Hopping on one foot, he lifted the other to examine the thin leather. His boot was scuffed and dirty, but the flash of his red sock didn't peek through any gashes.

He shook off the pain, then reoriented himself, aligning his route to keep the sun on his right shoulder—at least what could be seen of the sun through the forest canopy. He picked up his pace, taking care to also lift up his feet a little higher. The way the rocks increased and the woods thinned, he ought to make the village a hair past noontide. Smacking his lips, he could almost taste the slice of kidney pie that would soon be his. He might even indulge in a side of hasty pudding or some—

He sniffed. Strong cheese. A mature cheddar? No, more like Blue Stilton. With the wind out of the southwest, he lifted his nose that direction and snuffled like Duffy. Make that rotted Blue Stilton, quite sickening—and unfortunately familiar.

"Double blast." He worked up a mouthful of spit and nailed the ground, debating how much he really wanted to know. Not wanted, perhaps, but needed. Who knew when a corpse card could be played to his advantage?

Heading toward the stench, he scanned just above the forest floor, looking for a swarm of flies. Twenty paces off, he narrowed his eyes, then stopped and picked up a stick. It was surprising that some scavenger hadn't spied the free bit of firewood—

Or the body defiling a patch of spring growth.

Nigel squatted, an arm-and-stick's length away from a man's carcass. In a stage of putrefaction, not much of the fellow's waxy skin remained intact, and his human shape was deflated—almost like the poor soul was trying to sink into the ground for want of a decent burial.

Breathing through his mouth, Nigel poked about. Not many maggots remained, replaced by shiny-backed beetles. The blighter must have been here for a month, more or less. A large notch in the skull screamed either foul play or a topple from a horse.

After a few more prods, he uncovered a crucifix around the man's neck, and then he stood and cast the stick aside. "Holy or not, we all end up the same, eh mate?"

His stomach growled as he resumed his trek to Deverell Downs. He'd have plenty to chew over with the squire. Why, he might just ask the man to dine with him—pie and pudding, that is. He'd definitely skip the cheese.

⊷♾⊶

Passing by the kitchen door, Miri heard a sharp intake of breath, followed quickly by a low moan. She peeked in as a tray rattled against the counter. The cook hunched over it, kneading the small of her back with one hand. "Mrs. Makin?"

Caught in the act, the woman spun. Her face, usually flushed from range heat and manhandling dough, whitened with a wince.

Miri crossed to her side. "What is it?"

The cook straightened, or tried to, her trunk bent like a crooked branch. "All those hours at Ol' Joe's bedside, I'm afraid. Oh, not that I regret a minute of it, mind you. Happy I am that he's on the mend. A little liniment for me, and we'll all be right as rain. Well, exceptin' the bishop's horse, that is."

"Not any better?"

"No. It was a bad sprain, worse now that fever's set in. The way that man treats his animal …" A fierce frown creased her face. "Mr. Good's spent most o' the day out there. Not a bite to eat, either. I was just bringing him this—"

"Let me." Miri reached for the cloth-covered tray.

"'Tis not your place—"

"Truly, I don't mind. Now off with you. Go put your feet up and care for your back."

Mrs. Makin clucked her tongue. "You're a dear, that's what."

Miri smiled, masking her guilt. This noble gesture was more for herself than the cook. She'd wanted to speak to Ethan since their conversation on Sunday morning, but during the past few days there'd been no discreet moment to harvest.

Stepping out the back door, she paused and inhaled the sweet scent of blossoming daphnes. Their pale pink flowers stood out as stark little lights in the gathering dusk, cheery and hopeful. But as she walked farther down the path, nothing so merry showed on the rose bush. She sighed, yet pressed on.

Light spilled out the stable door, and she followed the glow inside. "Ethan?"

The smell of horseflesh, leather, and fresh straw greeted her, but nothing more.

"Hello?" she said, louder this time.

Ethan emerged from the shadowy end of the line of stalls. He stood, blinking, as one who couldn't quite fathom her figure in the meager light.

But oh, how aware she was of his form. Shirt loosened at the collar, his chest peeked out, solid and inviting. If he held her, her cheek could rest against him, right there, warm and sheltered and protected from—what was she thinking?

She jerked her gaze back to his face, angry at herself and even more at him. "Why do you not have a lantern at the other end of the stable?"

He lifted a finger to his lips.

Miri squinted into the dark behind him. "What's going on?"

Half a smile lifted his mouth, and he shook his head as he drew closer. "Nothing so clandestine as what might be running through your head at the moment. I have simply found that Champ rests easier in a dark and quiet stall."

"You're acting like a nursemaid, you know."

His smile deepened. "I've been called worse."

"Yes, I suppose you have."

"Did you come out here to ridicule me, Miss Brayden?" He folded his arms. With his sleeves rolled up past his elbows, the muscles of his forearms swelled, and she traced those lean lines with her eyes, over and over and—

"Are you all right?"

She swallowed and pulled her gaze back to his. "Of course. I ... uh ... I have brought you something to eat."

"Just like old times then, eh? Allow me." He stepped past her and shoved aside currycombs and hoof picks from the workbench.

She set the tray on the cleared bit of space, then hesitated. Palms moist and tingly, she ran her hands along her skirt. This was ridiculous. Why feel so jittery? All she wanted to do was talk to the man. Inhaling for courage, she turned.

But Ethan hadn't moved, and she practically bumped flat against him. She edged backward, until the workbench bit the small of her back.

"You are more skittish than Champ this evening." He raised one brow in his trademark fashion.

And breathing suddenly required a lot of effort. She looked past him, for if she focused on his inquisitive gaze, her words would lie in an unspoken heap. "I've ... uh ... well, I've been meaning to thank you. For our discussion, on Sunday morning, that is. I've been thinking, that is to say, I have thought, seriously, about all you said. You were right, you know. Very right. Almost too right, actually ..."

Gads! She sounded like an empty-headed ninny who couldn't put together two pence's worth of words if paid up front. She inched to the left. If she made a run for it now, she might be able to save face, or at least cool off her burning cheeks in the night air outside.

Ethan stepped sideways, blocking her escape. "Don't go yet. I should like to know what I was right about."

Not fair. The tilt of his head, the gleam in his eye, both rooted her to the stable floor. She could stand here forever and not tire of studying his expressions.

"Miri? Are you certain you're all right?"

"Right? Oh! Yes, of course. As I was saying, it was you who were right when you said it wouldn't be faith if I could see and know the every movement of God. I wrestled with that. I mean truly wrestled. It's a hard truth, leastwise for me. But I honestly believe that, yes, I can trust Him. Furthermore, I *will* trust Him."

He tilted his head the other way. "Even if things don't work out the way you hope?"

"Especially if things don't work out the way I hope, otherwise it wouldn't very well be trust, would it?"

He smiled. "Then I daresay your faith will be larger than mine."

"About that ..." She dared a step closer. "I am curious how you came to such a faith in the first place. You admit to being Will's friend, yet I know he did not lead the most ... pious lifestyle."

A shadow descended, dimming the gleam in his eyes. His throat bobbed as he swallowed, but he remained silent.

Miri sighed. She'd probed too deep, as usual. Roland might be crazy, but he'd always been right about her—ignorant and completely oblivious. She forced a light tone to her voice. "There's no need to answer."

"No ... no, I want to tell you. I've wanted to tell you for some time." Running a hand through his loose hair, he retreated a step. His eyes darted like a caged animal's.

"Then speak it. I am able to bear the truth now. Please, don't fear on my account."

He studied the low-beamed ceiling. Was he praying or stalling? His chest rose and fell several times before he finally fixed his gaze back on her. "It is not you that I fear for."

The slight pounding of a headache began in her temples. Men and their pride often gave her a pain. "I will not think ill of you,

Ethan. You have been nothing but kind to me, more of a gentleman than most. Whatever you might have been, you are not now."

A grunt escaped him.

She waited.

His jaw worked, though no words came out.

Whatever he had to say could not be good, not if it took this much effort to speak it. Her heart thumped faster, ramping up the pounding in her head. She ought to leave, but her feet would not move.

"When I first met Will ..."

He spoke so quietly, she had to step closer to catch what he said.

"... looking for a good time. Oh, I knew how to have a good time, all right. Three years his senior, I had the jump on knowing where to find women, drink, opium. My pockets had been well lined, but when that ran out, well ... we learned to steal, to cheat, and God knows we were already liars. Even so, debt mounted. Maybe because Will was younger, I don't know ... I guess I felt somewhat responsible for him, so I always took charge in any of our dealings."

"Dealings?"

He nodded. The ferocity of his stare sent a shiver through her.

"Let us keep it at that," he said.

Thousands of questions rose like dandelions on a field of green, but she bit her lower lip, and they withered.

"You cannot begin to understand the depths to which Will and I sank. Nor should you." Ethan shook his head, a faraway look in his eye. "I owed a fat sum of money to a crooked bailiff, and with no way to pay him off, I feared I'd rot in Newgate. Desperate, I roamed the streets to a better part of town and pinched the first purse I saw—or tried to. For the first time in my life, I felt remorse. No, not exactly ..."

A flash of a smile, the familiar Ethan, broke through as he rubbed his chin absently. "It was more like repentance, I suppose. I not only gave the woman back her purse but vowed I'd never pickpocket again. I didn't gain any money that day, but I became richer than I'd ever dreamed. How could I not share with Will the new hope God had given me? I ran back to Old Nichol, intent on changing my ways, but … funny how strong old habits can be."

Shame scoured the hope from his face, and he grimaced. "I thought, well, one last fling then, and Will and I would leave behind—"

His voice broke.

Tears welled in Miri's eyes, making her vision blurry. She should not have started this conversation.

"We never had the chance." The pain in his tone was raw. "Will never had the chance, and it's all my fault."

"Oh …" Her voice sounded thin, especially inside her head. Empathy choked her. She knew exactly how horrid he felt. How many times had she blamed herself for her father's death? She closed the short distance between them and laid a light touch on his forearm.

He shrugged her off. "Don't."

"Ethan, I am sure you are not to blame—"

"Do not deny me this guilt, Miri." His chest heaved, and the grief etched on his face stole her breath.

He spun and stomped toward the darkened part of the stable.

Miri stared at his retreating form, paralyzed by conflicting emotions. How exactly did one comfort a man who harbored such guilt—guilt that apparently had something to do with the death of her brother?

25

Ethan stalked into the shadows, willing the darkness to open its jaws and swallow him. He slammed his fist into the stall next to Champ's, again and again, eliciting a weak whinny from the horse. The impromptu boxing match against guilt, rage, and helplessness left him broken and spent. He staggered backward and leaned against the wall. Warm blood wetted his fingers. His split knuckles stung. A welcome pain. Too bad it didn't hurt worse.

Breathing hard, he closed his eyes. The stable disappeared, but not the ache inside.

Straw rustled, though not from within the stall. It grew louder, then stopped—next to him. The scent of violets floated above the baser smell of horseflesh.

His eyes flew open.

Miri stood two paces away. Even in the dark he could see the questions in her eyes—and worse, the fear.

Silently, she held out a rag. The way her fingers trembled made his every muscle scream to gather her in his arms.

Snatching the cloth, he wrapped his hand, then looked away. "You should leave now."

He should too. He never should have come to Deverell Downs.

"You encouraged me to trust in God, so allow me to return the favor. Will you trust Him? With your guilt, I mean." Her voice was small yet unwavering, her question holding all the power of a musket ball, piercing and possibly fatal.

His heartbeat pounded in his ears, but it didn't block out the words he knew the reverend would nail him with right now. Either he must believe his part in Will's death had been paid for on the cross, or his faith was a sham.

"God I trust," he said at last. "It's me I'm not so sure about."

Blowing out a long breath, he gazed back at her. She stood entirely too close, so beautiful it tore his heart and mended his gaping loneliness in one swift stroke. Desire spread through his veins—and sickened him. How could he long to hold her when she didn't even know the kind of monster he was? "Listen to me, Miri, I failed your brother. I failed him, do you hear? There is not one redeeming quality in me."

"Well, then, we are kindred spirits. I've been told the same of myself time and again." Pools glistened in her eyes a moment before spilling. "We all fail those we love."

He lifted his hand and wiped away her tears with the pad of his thumb. Her skin was soft, warm—and it took every scrap of self-control to withdraw rather than pull her closer. "Indeed. I have no doubt I would fail you."

She gasped, small but audible. "What are you saying?"

Crossroads were notoriously dangerous. Primal instinct urged him to run, leave as he'd warned her to, for if he spoke, there'd be no going back.

He searched her eyes, willing her to read the sincerity in his own. "I love you, Miri Brayden. I have since the day you slammed the kitchen door in my face."

There. He'd said it. And he felt nearly as exposed as the hour he'd first knelt before God. He raked back his hair and retreated deeper into the shadows. "Sorry. I don't suppose this conversation was what you had in mind—"

"Unexpected, yes." Squaring her shoulders, she advanced. "But not unwelcome."

He froze. Either she didn't have a clue as to what her words could mean, or this was a leftover hallucination. The nearer she drew, the harder his heart pumped, creating the same edgy feeling as before a brawl—but this was unlike any fight he'd ever been in. "I am nothing, Miri. You could have so much more. You should have so much—"

"I *want* nothing more."

The words, the whisper, the way her sweet breath landed on his face intoxicated as opium never had. His senses heightened, magnifying everything—her scent, her shape, the sound of his own blood rushing in his ears.

"I'll say it one last time." His husky voice grated on his ears. "Go."

"Where? To a brother who despises me? Who frightens me more than I can say?" She stepped forward, the fabric of her skirt brushing against his legs. "No. There is nowhere else I'd rather be than with you."

Time stopped as she stood there, so trusting and lovely that it hurt somewhere deep in his chest. He might never breathe again. Her gaze held his, steady, relentless, piercingly naked, until he almost cried out from the honest emotion shining there. Pulling her close, he hesitated, gauging her response. At the smallest hint of resistance, he'd open his arms and let her go.

She leaned into him, and all his willpower gave way. He groaned out the last of his restraint as her breath moved across his parted lips.

He lowered his mouth to hers. Heat shot through him, fierce as a summer sun, and roused the beast within. He cradled her head with both hands and deepened the kiss.

Miri's fingers ran the length of his back, upward. The trail burned into his skin through the fabric of his shirt. She shivered against him, small but urgent, fanning to life a fiery need low in his belly.

His lips strayed, running along her jaw, nuzzling her neck. She arched against him, each breath matching his, and he felt the exact moment their hearts beat as one. He could consume her here—now.

"Ethan …"

Little more than a murmur, his name on her lips slapped his conscience. He sucked in a breath and pulled back, releasing her as he might an armful of hot coals.

A deep flush spread over her cheeks, and her head dipped. "I am sorry. You must think me a harlot."

Crooking a finger, he lifted her chin, horrified to see a fat teardrop marring her cheek. "Please don't cry, Miri. I cannot bear it. You are nothing short of angelic. I am the one out of control."

She sniffed, several times, each one building on the last. "But … I should not have—"

"No." He cut her off. "I should not have. Not yet. We will do this the right way or not at all."

Her brow wrinkled. "I don't understand."

He leaned in until their lips were almost touching, then rested his forehead against hers. "I have nothing to offer you but this— every moment of every day, from now till forever. Will you … would you have me?"

Her sharp intake gave him so much pause, he almost didn't hear the breathless words that followed.

"Yes, oh ... yes!" She threw her arms around his waist, nestling her head against his chest. A complete fit. A perfect fit.

But as much as her response thrilled him to the core, all it showed was her regard for the Ethan Goodwin she thought him to be—not the opium-eating murderer that he really was.

If he didn't tell her now, he never would. He closed his eyes, summoning strength. *God, help me.* "Miri, there's something you should know—"

The sharp crack of a riding whip sliced through the air.

Miri twisted. Her cry pierced him deeper than a dagger.

Roland's black silhouette stood before them like a demon fresh from hell. "Whore!"

∾◦◦◦∾

Fire sliced across Miri's back, but that was nothing compared to the rage igniting in her soul. The taste of safety in Ethan's arms, the hope, the passion—all of it shattered into fragments. If Roland said another word, she'd never be able to gather the bits and patch them together. "How dare—"

Roland dug his fingers into her upper arm and dragged her down the stable's aisle, away from Ethan. Away from promise, from all that was good and right.

After two of her brother's long-legged strides, she stumbled sideways and crashed into the wall, dazed. A shadow whizzed past. Or were there more? She pressed both hands to the sides of her head and thanked God that He pumped air into her lungs, for surely she could not.

Angry growls, primal, savage, were punctuated by fists meeting flesh, crunching against bone and rending cartilage. She had heard that noise before, weeks and weeks ago, maybe months. Hard to tell, when all of time had been balled up and thrown away somewhere in the recesses of the dark stable.

A grunt so deep, the rushing of air from the bellows of a man's chest—and suddenly she knew exactly what had happened to Vicar Eldon.

"No!" She pushed off from the wood behind her and staggered into the lantern-lit work area.

Roland and Ethan faced off. Both crouched, bloodied and sweating—carnivores with a taste for fresh meat.

"Drunken son of a …" Ethan looked particularly wild-eyed as he circled her brother. "If you ever touch her again, I swear I'll—"

"Stop it!" Her voice sounded small, helpless against the murder that hung heavy on the air. She ran into the middle of them and flung out her arms.

"Step aside, Miri … this is not … your fight." Thick breaths broke Ethan's words. He wiped his brow but did not lose his warrior stance.

"You don't understand." And she didn't have the time to explain. She jerked her head to her brother. "Roland, please. Do not do this."

Roland observed her as one might gaze upon a face that is underwater, horrified as understanding slowly seeps in that this is no stranger that has drowned, but a loved one. Rising carefully, he reached out. "Come."

She stood firm.

"Come to me." Despair and gut-wrenching loss clouded Roland's eyes like a winter landscape. "Miri."

She took a step, pulled by the endearment yet repulsed by the years of his cruelty.

"Miri, don't," Ethan warned from behind.

Of course he was right. She shouldn't. So why did her feet move?

"No." Ethan darted between them, blocking her from reaching her brother.

Roland moaned, a wailing sound, like a great animal felled by a surprise blow.

She sidestepped Ethan, but he held out his arm. "I will see to him. You have my word—"

"But—"

"As long as I know you are safe, I will not harm him further."

Looking from Ethan, to Roland, then back again, she nodded, for truly what more could she do? "Be ... be gentle. He's all I have left."

"Not true, love. You have me now." Blood trickled from his nose, battered by Roland's fist, and he swiped it away. "But for your sake, I will take care."

She bit her lip. A single sob escaped Roland, and he dropped to his knees. After all the hurtful, hateful, beastly things he'd said to her throughout the years, why did her heart convulse? An urge to run back, gather him in her arms, sing his special lullaby, and rock him to sleep, gripped her so powerfully she hesitated.

"Do you trust me?" A pleading undercurrent flowed in Ethan's voice.

Her mouth twisted into a wry half smile, and she turned toward the door—just as Bishop Fothergill entered, flanked by a bevy of men.

The bishop planted his feet wide and placed his hands upon his hips. "What is this? A schoolyard brawl?"

"I can explain, sir," Ethan said.

The confidence in his voice astonished her. How in the world could he explain this mess?

Gullaby shoved past the bishop, followed by the magistrate, Mr. Buckle.

"Save it for the inquisition, Mr. Good ..." said the squire. "Or should I say Goodwin? You, sir, have some explaining to do."

Gullaby paused and pinned Roland with a look that sucked the marrow from Miri's bones.

"You too, Brayden. I can't wait to hear what you'll have to say." Gullaby lifted his hand and snapped his fingers, and four of the largest men came forward, as did the magistrate.

Mr. Buckle's voice boomed like cannon shot. "Arrest them."

26

Two men advanced on Ethan, one carrying a length of rope in a hand the size of a beef brisket. Ethan edged backward. Did they seriously think he'd let them truss him up like a Christmas goose with no explanation?

From the corner of his eye, he saw two others drawing near Roland. Shifting a glance the other way, he caught a glint off the bottle of liniment he'd been using on Champ. With a lunge, he grabbed the glass and cracked it against the stool's edge, then held it out as a jagged weapon. "What's this about?"

"Murder," said Mr. Buckle. "Now drop the bottle."

"No!" Miri cried.

The panic in her voice beaded a cold sweat on Ethan's brow. He should've told her long ago. Why had he been such a coward? What a laugh that he'd dared to think he could ever live as an honorable man. Regret closed in on him like the squire's henchmen, as shockingly real and inescapable as his past sins.

He splayed his fingers, allowing the bottle to fall, then nodded toward Roland. "Let him go. He's got nothing to do with this."

"To do with what? Ethan?" The question in Miri's voice drained all the fight out of him. She'd know now. Know and never trust him again.

He grunted as his arms were wrenched behind his back. Slivers of hemp bit into his wrists. Better to focus on that pain and study the scuffed toes of his boots than answer her. If he looked, the betrayal in her eyes would kill him.

"Bishop Fothergill, please do something!" Miri's tone was a nightmare he'd relive for weeks to come.

"There is naught to be done, Miss Brayden, other than a trial. I've had my suspicions all along, but today they have been borne out. The vicar's dead body has been found. Deeds done in the dark can never remain unexposed, and—"

"Here! Here!" Gullaby interrupted what would have turned into rhetoric of epic proportion. "Now move 'em out. Step aside, miss."

Ethan snuck a glance to where Miri stood, framed in the middle of the open doorway—a pixie of an avenging angel.

"There must be some mistake. Ethan"—her gaze met his and held—"tell them!"

"Saucy wench, that one, eh?" The man behind him lowered his voice to a lewd tone. "I wager she makes for a fine tussle in the hay, don't she?"

The slander burned like a wildfire through Ethan's veins. He jerked back his head and cracked his skull into the man's nose. The feeling of cartilage giving way satisfied in a twisted fashion.

The blow that came wasn't a surprise, but the kick that followed caught him off guard. Unable to catch himself, he crashed to his knees, then toppled onto the stable floor, face first. He gasped for breath, but his lungs forgot how to work. A boot ground into his back, compounding the pain.

Miri's cry hurt worse. "Let me go!"

"Release her at once." Roland's voice carried an eerie calm.

Ethan rolled, losing the foot on his back and winning a boot stab to his ribs. Too bad curling into a fetal position wasn't an option at the moment. He forced himself up to one knee and was as quickly knocked back down with a cuff to his head.

"Enough, Mr. Handy!"

The magistrate's command sounded a bit warbly, or maybe that was simply the ringing in Ethan's ears. He rose on shaky legs. His vision blurred, and it appeared he was surrounded by twice the amount of men—though once the stable stopped spinning, he saw only one of each person instead of two.

Miri stood near the door, wringing her hands, as if somehow she might wash the night clean of this chaos. The magistrate tipped his head toward Roland and his handlers. Roland stalked out unaided, pausing only long enough to say to his sister, "Carry on, Miriall, as you always do."

Before Ethan could make his thick tongue move, Mr. Handy and his equally helpful partner yanked him from the stable and halfway across the backyard. He'd had no time to say good-bye to Miri and likely never would. Remorse hammered as painfully as the pounding in his head.

"Up you go, maggot. I hope they tie the rope 'specially tight 'round your neck." Mr. Handy put some muscle into heaving him upward, above and beyond what was necessary.

Ethan plunged forward, smacking his chin on the wooden planks of the cart. Behind him, a door clanged shut, followed by a rough "Haw!"

The cart lurched, and Ethan used the momentum to swing into a sitting position. Either it was exceptionally dark in there, or he was about to pass out—possibly both, and either a good thing.

"Did you commit murder?"

The question shot out from nowhere and everywhere. Was God in the cart too?

"Well, Mr. Goodwin?"

Ethan lifted his head, then winced at the shooting pain in his jaw. Across from him, blacker than darkness, Roland hunched like a creature of the night.

The stunning realization hit him that Roland's words were not slurred, nor did the stench of spirits foul the close air. "You're not drunk."

Roland laughed, the rusty sound of a tool not often used. "Whatever gave you that idea?"

"Why else would you ..." Ethan's brain worked faster than his mouth, shuffling a deck full of Roland's freakish behaviors into some kind of hand to deal out. But a few cards were missing. "What have they got on you? There's no way they can link you to Thorne. Are you the reason the vicar is—"

"You are a strange mix of character, Mr. Goodwin. You smell of indulgence and privilege and the gutters. You're a gallant con, a gentleman clothed in degradation. Contradiction is in your blood."

Ethan's heart beat faster. The man had no idea how right he was. "And what are you?"

"Why ... a protector, of course. A protector of divine virtue and holy standard. I am a jealous lover of the church, sir."

"Jealous enough to kill?"

A snort traveled through the dark. Hard to tell if it came from Roland or one of the horses.

"That's the question I daresay everyone will be asking."

Ethan measured his words. Too many and the height might topple this entire conversation. "How will you answer?"

The groan of the wagon grinding over the uneven roadway was the only answer he received. Ethan leaned back, then thought the better of it when his skull bumped in time to the ruts. The wagon wheels mumbled a low-tone rant.

Ethan tilted his head—those weren't wheels.

"Threw it away, he threw it away. I warned him, yes, yes, I did. Lusting after a woman is one thing, but ... oh, the shame. The shame! Better to run away. Better to die. He knew my secrets. Shh. Shh! Yes, but how much worse are yours."

Roland's voice gained in intensity. "No! I will not speak it. No say. No say. I will not tell of your demons, and do not speak of mine. Leave, Eldon. I shall have to execute God's judgment. If your eye causes you to sin, pluck it out. Your hand, cut it off. Your manhood, sever it. Sever it, you hear? Or I will. Now ... leave!"

Acid burned a trail up Ethan's throat. Thank God Roland's hands were tied.

"Why are you still here?" Roland leaned forward. "You said. You said!"

Ethan swallowed the vinegar taste at the back of his mouth, then forced out calm words. "I am not Eldon."

"SHUT UP!"

Ethan closed his mouth. The cart swayed in silence once Roland's voice quit reverberating—

Until the night breathed a whisper. Many whispers. All of them one with Roland's breaths. "*Vos es fatum. Ego sum fatum. Fatum, fatum, fatum.*"

Reaching back to boyhood, just beyond his fingertips, Ethan strained to remember those dull Latin lessons. A dream? A dome? No.

As their bones rattled on the dark road to the inevitable, Roland chanted—doomed, doomed, doomed.

⁂

Miri clutched her shawl with one hand and a lantern in the other. Night air waged a brisk assault against her cheeks, and cold crawled up her stockings, fanned further by her swishing skirts. She hardly felt either. Feelings belonged to the living.

Pleading with the bishop had gotten her nothing more than a sore throat. She was done with him. Done with Mrs. Makin's clutterings and flutterings as well. Accompanied or not, she would find help from somewhere or perish in the trying. If she were gored while taking the bull by the horns, then so be it.

Off to the side of the road, a glowing pair of yellow eyes reflected her lantern light, then scurried back into the brush. An eerie appearance, but it failed to raise any gooseflesh along her arms. Her own safety mattered not a whit. Not anymore.

Deverell Downs was tucked in slumber as she crossed the stone bridge. Though she couldn't see the water in the dark, the shushing river below scorned her. Only highwaymen and women of ill repute went about at this owlish hour.

She quickened her steps. By the time she pounded on the apothecary's door, her breathing sounded as ragged as her knocking. "Mr. Knight!"

Pausing, she peeked into the window at the door's side. No light.

She set down her lantern and used both fists. "Open up! Do you hear me? Open this—"

The door yanked wide, and she stumbled forward.

Mr. Knight's arm righted her. "Good heavens. Is someone that ill?"

"No … I … my …" As much as she wanted to ask for his help, breathing took priority.

He retrieved her lantern and led her inside, then pulled his stool from behind the counter. "Sit."

The order might have been nothing more than a command to a dog, so empty did his voice sound. He folded his arms and leaned against the counter. His usual impeccable appearance was askew, with a woolen wrapper thrown hastily about his shoulders, covering an ankle-length nightshirt. His feet were bare. His hair loose.

"This is highly irregular, Miss Brayden."

She wondered if he had any potions or salve that might ease his frown.

"I have nowhere else to turn, sir. I thought that you might—"

"Why don't you turn to your hired man, miss? I am sure Mr. Good would be more than happy to help you." Mr. Knight's face—why had she ever thought it handsome?—tightened into a stern mask.

Miri massaged her temples. Jealousy wasn't something she had time to deal with right now. "He's been taken, along with my brother, and I don't know where. Please, Mr. Knight. Would you speak to the magistrate? A mistake has been made, but he will not listen to me. Neither will Mr. Buckle."

He cocked his head. "On what matter?"

Miri averted her eyes. "Murder."

If he sucked in a breath any harder, she'd be caught in a swirling vortex.

"Murder! Really, Miss Brayden." He stalked to the door and opened it. "I cannot help you with this matter. I am an apothecary, not a lawyer. I suggest you speak with the magistrate yourself. Now, good night."

Tears pressured her eyes to release them. Pride dammed them in. She stood so quickly, the stool tipped over and crashed to the wooden planks. By the time the noise stilled, she'd crossed the room and grabbed fistfuls of his nightshirt. "If there is any honor in you, Mr. Knight, you will help me see that justice is carried out."

"Contain yourself! Honestly, Miss Brayden, you are more than hysterical." He pried the fabric from her hands. "Again I say good night." With one hand, he shoved her backward, and the door shut in her face.

Out on the street, waiting for her with open arms, her old friend defeat embraced her, along with his companion—despair.

Miri's shoulders slumped. Now what?

27

Nigel slipped a finger between the cinch and the horse's belly. A little flappy, but tight enough. If the saddle slid and ol' Ethan boy knocked his noggin on the ground, oh well. The horse stamped in agreement, or maybe from his cold hands. Nigel rubbed his palms together, then blew into them. Blast this predawn chill.

Mounts readied, he led them from the stable. The moon had long since donned its nightcap, yet a cloudless sky with innumerable stars lit his path.

He tethered the horses near the door of the village lock-up—which was nothing more than a seldom-used storage shed abutting the back of the inn. Prisoners were simply not kept in Deverell Downs. They were either carted off or executed.

A chair sat empty next to the makeshift jail cell. Several bottles littered the dirt nearby. Apparently Mother Nature had called away the deputy on duty.

Nigel glanced at the locked door where Ethan lay on the other side. Was he sleeping? Pacing? Angry or bewildered? A slow smile lifted the corners of Nigel's mouth. One thing was sure—Ethan would be surprised to see a ghost.

He spun away and retrieved a sturdy club from the pack on the back of his horse. Running his fingers along the length, he admired the hard hickory. He smacked his palm a time or two, approving the way it slapped the dark around him.

"That you, guv'ner?" A lantern bobbed wildly around the corner of the inn, illuminating a whiskery man long in years and short on balance. He tripped and swung his arms wide, the light spilling one way, then another.

"Aye, it's me." Nigel kept his voice low and quiet. No sense tipping off Ethan and losing the element of surprise.

The keys at the deputy's side jangled louder the closer he came, and a waft of ale traveled with him. "Sure you won't be waitin' till sunup? Make for an easier time a-stayin' on the road."

The way the man bobbed and weaved, he could hardly stay on the path.

Nigel nodded toward the door. "I got men waitin' in London for this one."

Wiry eyebrows climbed up the man's forehead. "He that dangerous, guv'ner? Maybe you ought not go alone."

Spreading his feet wide, Nigel once again thwacked the club against his open palm. "I won't be taking any chances."

The old man swaggered over to the chair and set down his lantern. He retrieved a flintlock pistol from within the confines of his coat, then cocked it. "Me neither." Which might have been impressive had he not belched afterward.

Nigel scrubbed his face with one hand. "I'll handle this, mate. Just cover me."

"Righty."

He readied himself in a crouch while the deputy unfastened the lock. The hinges rasped as the door yawned open.

Only darkness tried to escape.

Nigel neared the opening, but his light didn't illuminate past the threshold.

"Grab the lamp," he whispered to the deputy and was tempted to add, "and put down that gun." The tipsy fellow could as soon shoot him in the back as Ethan.

Raising his club, Nigel waited until he could make out the shapes inside. His heart thumped against his ribs when he caught sight of a pair of unblinking eyeballs staring at him from a dark corner. He tightened his grip, prepared to beat back the man should he lunge.

The man didn't budge. The fixed gaze reminded Nigel of a stuffed lizard he'd once seen at a sideshow. His own eyes watered in response. Whoever lived in that body had already moved out, likely posing no threat.

Still, it paid to be careful. He took a tenuous step forward, as did the deputy with the lantern. Light stretched into the lower corners of the small shed, highlighting a familiar form. Legs sprawled, Ethan sat, leaning against the wall, head back and mouth open. Nigel squinted. Was that Ethan? The man's face was so swollen and bruised, it was hard to tell.

A smirk twisted Nigel's lips. That was him, all right. No doubt about it. Looked like ol' Ethan boy had been up to his usual shenanigans even in Deverell Downs. This was a member of the aristocracy?

"On your feet, Goodwin." He nudged Ethan with the tip of his boot.

Ethan's head bobbed, and he blinked. Several times. Surely it was hard to understand how the man you thought you'd sent to the grave suddenly took to walking the earth again.

"You!" The murder in Ethan's voice would have been enough to curdle Nigel's blood, but the primal rage that shone in his eyes frightened him more.

Nigel swung.

Ethan crumpled.

The man in the corner merely stared, and from behind, the deputy whistled. "Guess you don't take any chances, now do you, guv'ner? Did ye kill 'im?"

Nigel threw the club out the open door, narrowly missing the deputy, then grabbed Ethan's feet and pulled. Once outside, he dropped to his knees and bent over Ethan, listening.

What if he had killed him?

♠

Miri awoke with a start. The bed-curtain fabric she focused upon comforted after such a terrorizing nightmare. La, what an overactive imagination she harbored. Roland would no doubt accuse her of reading contraband novels if he knew the course her dreams had taken.

She turned her head on the pillow, relieved to escape the lump of her chignon—until she realized she never went to sleep without first taking down her hair.

Bolting up, she wobbled on her feet and reached to steady herself. Her arms tangled in the shawl she yet wore. The thick taste in her mouth, her rumpled skirts, and her dirt-encrusted slippers still on her feet all testified that she'd not experienced a nightmare. Roaming from Harper's to the magistrate's to the squire's, pacing outside the jail until threatened at gunpoint to leave the village, every shocking, torrid bit of last night had been real.

She stumbled to the door and leaned against it for support. Like the stabs of pain felt after the shock of an injury wears off, emotions jabbed her, increasing in intensity. Stunned disbelief. Betrayal. Fear. But what violated her heart most was the realization that moments after love had been offered to her, it had been snatched away.

Her stomach soured, and for a moment she feared the dry heaves that dogged her all the way home from the Downs last night would return. It wasn't fair. None of this was fair. How could everything she'd held onto slip through her fingers so quickly?

Closing her eyes, she whispered, "God, is this a cruel joke?"

Trust Me.

Her eyes flew open. Only her ragged breathing filled the room, nothing else. So why had she heard those two words so clearly?

And then, just as audibly, more came.

Sometimes faith is a moment-by-moment thing.

That was definitely a memory. She could still hear the warm inflection in Ethan's voice when he'd said it, the touch of his finger upon her lips.

Ahh, his touch.

She shoved down a sob as she remembered the sanctuary in his arms when he'd asked her to be his. If she dared relive that moment she'd never return, for she would dwell there, becoming as lost as her brother.

Roland! Dread shook her as she yanked open the door. She had to find him and Ethan before it was too late. Flying down the stairs, she grabbed the railing just in time to keep from smacking into Mrs. Makin.

The cook's hand fluttered to her chest. "Oh my! I wasn't expecting you to pop out like that."

"I beg your pardon, truly, but I am in a hurry." Sidestepping the woman, she descended the last two steps.

"You've gone and missed breakfast already. All this rushing about isn't good for the stomach. I fear for you, miss, all pale and drawn. Shall I make you some—"

"No." The thought of food gagged her. She glanced back on her way to the front door. "Do not wait dinner on me, either."

"But you should not—"

Whatever the cook had to say was shut out by the sealing of the front door. Miri's legs shook as she crossed the front drive. Maybe she should have grabbed at least an apple, but judging from the zenith of the sun, she was late enough already.

Hiking to the Downs took a lifetime, especially after a face-first tumble when she tripped over a rock. She lost a shoe but pressed on without bothering to reclaim it. Horrid imaginings drove her to move faster. What if Roland already wore a strait-waistcoat and was calling her name in some cold asylum chamber? Worse, what if he swung from a tree, feet dangling, noose about his neck? And Ethan—would he be hanging next to her brother? Why had he been charged with murder? He hadn't even been in the village when Mr. Eldon went missing. How could they possibly tie him in to the crime?

She pressed her hands to her head, only then realizing she'd forgotten a bonnet. A sudden longing for a reprimand from Roland gaped like a raw wound. If only things could go back to the way they were, she wouldn't mind his lectures so much.

The village was nearly as empty as it had been on her midnight trek. Most of the shops looked closed, and no wagons bumped along the main thoroughfare. Odd for a market day. Not so strange, though, considering that Roland and Ethan's inquisitions could yield enough gossip to feed Deverell Downs for years to come.

Outside the Cricket and Crown, a gaggle of women drew into a tight circle. And where vultures clustered, there would be found a body, or bodies, as the case may be—Ethan's and Roland's, no doubt. The public house's door was propped open, and a huddle of boys pressed their noses to the front window. Beside them, two men with pipes, smoke puffs collecting in a cloud above their heads, gestured toward the pub while they spoke.

As Miri approached this gauntlet, she faltered. Her appearance alone would give cause enough for shunning, but being blood-related to the indicted was worse. She stared at the patch of ground her steps ate, bite by bite, blinding herself to their raised brows and knowing gazes.

But it did not shut out their words.

"He's mad as a March hare, I tell ye. Likely runs in their family."

"It's all for show. He's a cold-blooded killer, I say."

"Moonstruck, that's what. The man is positively dotty, and I daresay so's she."

"Shhh! She might hear—"

As if she hadn't already. Miri frowned, escaping into the press of bodies filling the Cricket and Crown's main room. Most of the tables had been moved to the walls, providing plenty of space for the attraction. A murmur of hushed voices hung like a fog, punctuated by official monologues from ahead. The noise filled her ears, and in a layer below, heard more by her heart than her ears, Roland mumbled something in reply.

Fanning themselves toward the back of the crowd, Mrs. Tattler and Miss Prinn angled their heads together, whispering behind their raised fans. Miri gave them a wide berth as she wormed her way toward the front.

On tiptoe, she peeked over the shoulders of village men, hoping to catch a glimpse of Ethan or her brother. Mr. Knight stood in the front row, blocking her view from this angle, with Miss Candler at his side.

Miri darted sideways a few bodies and tried again. No good on tiptoe, but if she jumped just a bit, she saw fragments. Seated behind a table near the great hearth was Squire Gullaby, the magistrate Mr. Buckle, and Bishop Fothergill. There were also a few men she didn't know. Why could she not see Ethan or her brother?

The squire's voice carried loudest, managing to override the snippets of conversations going on about her. "The real question is gaol or the asylum. Though Mr. Thorne's testimony on the position of the body does not rule out foul play, it is certainly a moot point in light of the mental state of Master Brayden. I move to conclude this hearing by committing the man to the Sheltering Arms Asylum."

Miri's heart constricted. The truth she'd feared for so long had finally been shook out and hung on a line for the world to see.

"I concur, gentlemen," said Bishop Fothergill. "The sorry end of Mr. Eldon may never be known by man. But God knows, and His supreme justice will be carried out. Time will reveal Brayden's innocence or guilt, either in the complete restoration of his mind or a deeper plunge into the depths of insanity, according to God's judgment. Furthermore—"

"Seeing there are no objections"—Mr. Buckle broke into Fothergill's speech—"this case is closed. Mr. Knight, please step forward and sign the document committing Roland Brayden to the Sheltering Arms Asylum."

"No!" Miri shoved past the last wall of gawkers. The inertia tripped her up, and she flung her arms wide to keep from falling. "Please …"

Her entreaty stuck in her throat.

Time stopped.

So did her heart.

Roland was on his knees at the side of the table. He rocked forward and back, forward and back, a revolting reminder of his teetering mental balance. His hair hung in his eyes, and an angry purple bruise colored his jaw. Apparently it didn't hurt too much, for his lips moved, though no sound came out. His cravat was missing. His shirt was torn open. And a stain darkened the front of his breeches where he'd soiled himself.

Miri slapped her hand to her mouth, stifling a cry. As horrible as her brother had been to her, she'd never wish so much shame upon him. The magnificently terrible sight froze her in place. She wanted to look away, but her eyes would not turn aside. Was this how Roland felt, as unattached to his own body as she was to hers?

A sharp bang on the table was followed by Mr. Buckle's voice. "Take him away, Mr. Handy."

The same man who'd hauled Ethan off the night before grabbed the back of Roland's collar and jerked him up. Roland's eyes widened. His head swiveled side to side as if the sudden movement had loosened a fastening. Either he refused to cooperate or his feet mutinied, for despite the command of Mr. Handy, Roland did not budge.

Mr. Handy clouted him in the head. "I said come along."

"Don't!" Her heart broke afresh from the shocking transformation of her proud brother into a prodded beast. "Please treat him gently."

A sneer twisted Mr. Handy's face, and he shoved Roland forward.

Miri stepped up to the front table and planted her palms on the cool wood, hoping to mimic the intimidating stance Roland had used on her many a time. "Mr. Buckle, make him stop."

"The situation is beyond my concern now, miss. Yet there is another matter to be discussed, and by coming here willingly, you've saved me much trouble."

"I … I don't understand." Miri straightened slowly, conflicted between keeping an eye on Roland to make sure he was not further mistreated and paying attention to Buckle's words.

The magistrate shuffled through some papers. "Miriall Elizabeth Brayden, you are likewise summoned to an inquisition concerning the state of your mental capacities."

"What?" The room started to spin. "Me?"

"You are Miriall Brayden, are you not?"

"I … yes, of course." She patted down her hair, painfully aware that she probably presented no better an appearance than had Roland. Lifting her chin, she fought for composure. "Who brings these charges?"

"I do."

Miri turned toward the voice, though she needn't have.

The nasally tone said it all.

28

Horseflesh and leather. Hard to say which woke Ethan first—the smell or the feel. More likely it was the pain that cut through his stupor. Half his face ached as if every bone had been shattered. His hands were bound so tightly behind his back that, beyond the stretched sinew in his arms, he felt nothing from the waist down. With each plodding step of the horse that carried him, his belly rubbed raw against the saddle. For the life of him, he could not remember how he came to be hauled about like a gutted stag.

He arched his neck, hoping to gain some clues as to where he was and why. One eye refused to open. The other couldn't see much past the chestnut's shoulder.

"Hey!" His voice rang in his ears, making him dizzy. He laid his head back down, hoping the rising nausea would back down as well.

Another horse, farther on, blew out a snort.

"Whoa, now. Ease up." The command came from ahead and, while not particularly menacing, halted the mounts at once.

Ethan watched the patch of bracken beneath his horse slide to a standstill. Individual fronds came into view, followed by a pair of scuffed boots.

"Awake then, are ye?" The boots disappeared, stomping toward the back of his horse. "Off ye go."

Moments later, his world flipped, and he whumped to the ground. Pain spiked into body parts he didn't know could hurt, and he groaned.

"Gads, but ye're a soft-boiled dandyprat."

Ethan shook his head, trying to clear the fog that clouded his reasoning. Other sounds receded as the man's voice circled in his brain like a marble in a funnel. With each revolution, he came closer to identifying it. Round and round and—

He reeled to his feet. "Murderer!"

Nigel Thorne cocked a lopsided smile. "Killing a rat is hardly murder."

Ethan's gut churned. All the guilt he'd suffered over a crime he didn't commit twisted into a crazed desire to commit the crime. For one intense moment, war waged in his heart. The old Ethan would've thought nothing of lethal retaliation, but now ... could he really send a man into eternal damnation?

He bent and charged. Killing Thorne might be out of the question, but a little physical justice could not be denied him.

Thorne stepped aside, leaving one foot snaked out—which Ethan noticed too late. He landed face-first, stunned.

Thorne's laughter added more injury. "Seems I've got the upper hand once again, eh, Ethan boy?"

The fine thread between hatred and reason slowly unraveled. Ethan pushed to a sitting position, breathing hard. "Not for long, Thorne. I will see justice carried out for Will's murder. You'll be hanged. You hear me? Hanged!"

Thorne cast his head aside and spit a stream of tobacco juice, then ran the back of his hand across his mouth before facing him. "Who's to believe a known opium eater against the word of an upstanding lawkeeper such as me?"

"Upstanding? My sweet—"

"Tut, tut. Yer makin' yer shiner go even more purple."

Blackness edged in, darkening his slim hold on vision. He filled his lungs, time and again, until the light-headedness receded. "What's your game, Thorne?"

"No game at all, mate. More like a bargain, or a barter, so to speak. We'll agree that the murder of Will Brayden will go unsolved. I'll vouch for your innocence; you vouch for mine. In return for your silence and a stipend of … oh, let's say"—he glanced skyward, his lips moving as if numbers were painted in the clouds—"one hundred per annum. O' course I'll need an up-front payment of a hundred. That oughtta do 'er. In return, I won't pin the blame of ol' Will's murder on you."

Thorne's words made no sense. Mayhap he'd been hit in the skull one too many times. Ethan shook his head to clear it. "You're saying I should pay you to keep you from blaming me for something I didn't do?"

"It's like this," Thorne said methodically, as if speaking to a wee tot. "My face is known at court, yours in the gutters. A court of law won't waste a precious minute listening to your defense. It's that easy."

Thorne advanced and stood over him. "So what's it to be, mate? The gallows or a fat purse flung my way once a year?"

Blackmail? Ethan laughed, long and loud, then winced from the pain of it. The world started to spin again, and he let his mirth wind down like a spent top.

"You've wasted your time traveling here to drag me back. Even if I wanted to agree, which I don't, I haven't got a blessed halfpenny to pay you off." He frowned. Something still didn't make sense. "And you should have known that."

"You don't know the half of what I know." Thorne bent, his voice a raspy whisper in Ethan's ear. "But I wager my life you'll pay me good to keep quiet. Real good."

Turning his head, Ethan went nose to nose with the man. "Never."

"Ye'll change yer mind." Thorne's confidence was as strong as his breath.

Still, Ethan would not look away and appear the cowering dog. "What makes you so certain?"

"Newgate." Thorne stood. "A few nights in that hellhole and you'll change your mind, all right. You'll change it right fast."

Ethan locked his jaw, refusing to give Thorne the pleasure of seeing him grovel for mercy. Never! If Newgate would be the death of him, then so be it.

❧

An abnormal silence settled over the Cricket and Crown, magnifying the sound of Miri's heartbeat in her ears. As Witherskim stepped forward, rage shook through her. He glanced at her momentarily, as if she were of no more consequence than a dead fish at market. A slow burn worked its way up her neck until it engulfed her face. If she didn't speak now, she'd explode. "How dare you question my mental state?"

He raised his arm with a sweeping gesture, indicating her, but kept his attention solely on the panel of men before them. "The unkempt hair, the bedraggled garments, why look … this woman goes about wearing only one shoe. It is plain to see she cannot care for herself. Is not the flush of her skin, the wild cast of her eyes, even the way she clenches her hands into fists evidence enough that Miriall Brayden is not fit for society at large?"

Miri swallowed as she realized every person in the room fixed their sight on her. The gaze of the living God could not have been more terrible. At once, she loosened her fingers and smoothed the fabric of her skirt, forcing herself to remain calm. "I fail to understand how appearance is sufficient indication of one's suitability for society."

Licking a finger, Witherskim slicked back a hair that might have been out of place—if he'd not already greased it down with a tin of pomade. "It is enough that Miriall Brayden is a woman, and as such is prone to hysteria. An *unmarried* woman, I might add. And we all know"—he paused to meet the eye of each man on the panel in front—"that spinsterhood frequently upsets the natural fluids and functionings of a female's mind, leading to melancholia and derangement."

Miri's jaw dropped. "Is that what this is all about? Revenge? Just because I turned down your proposal, you have the gall to publicly accuse me of insanity? You're a bigger fool than I gave you credit for, sir."

He merely sniffed, completely ignoring her questions. "Additionally, several times she has cast her body against mine in an untoward manner. On one occasion, she even went so far as to bite my ear so that it bled. This woman is clearly as mad as her brother."

"Those are lies!" She whirled back to the table where Bishop Fothergill, Magistrate Buckle, and Squire Gullaby sat open-mouthed. "Surely you cannot indict me simply because of one man's accusations."

"Of course not, Miss Brayden," said Mr. Buckle.

Miri blew out a long breath. Thank God, reason and justice would prevail—

"There are two more men who would bear witness to your instability." Mr. Buckle rummaged through his stack of documents.

Miri staggered back a step. Two men? "Impossible!"

"Bishop Fothergill, if you would, please state aloud for this inquiry what you have seen," said Buckle.

The bishop stood, hooking his fingers onto the lapels of his waistcoat and puffing out his chest. "Since residing at the rectory, I have observed Miss Brayden in her natural state. At first, I detected no hint of abnormality, except perhaps for noticing she was a bit high-strung, especially around her brother. She was cordial to the point of perfection, yet her overall humor lacked. Noting such, this made it all the more peculiar when I caught her speaking to garden tools."

She stiffened as a shock ran through her. Fothergill wouldn't have to lie to make her appear a lunatic. He'd seen more than she'd ever wanted him to. "I can explain—"

"One day," he continued, "before God and man, I caught her in the act of spinning about the yard, arms wide, speaking gibberish."

"Listen to me—"

"And there have been many nights, allow me to restate—more than just once—I witnessed her roaming about the hallways like a spirit, an agitated spirit. Darting about at the most witching of hours and"—he paused, driving home his words with a terrible gaze— "most notably during the full moon."

Several gasps sounded behind her, each one adding an uncanny validation to the bishop's words. She slanted a glance toward the back door. If she ran full speed, could she make it?

"Are these things true, Miss Brayden?" Mr. Gullaby leaned forward, brows merging into a solid line on his forehead.

Miri bit her lip. Running away was clearly not an option, and neither was lying, though both were tempting.

Fothergill lifted a fat finger and aimed it at her. "This woman is cursed. Hers are not the acts of a sane and sanguine mind. The sins of the father have obviously been passed down upon both brother and sister. It is my opinion she be put away, that her influence will not taint this good community. Bad company corrupts good morals, as stated in—"

"Thank you, Bishop." Mr. Buckle cut him off.

"The book of Proverbs, chapter—"

"I said thank you, Bishop Fothergill." Buckle's voice cut through the monologue.

"And again in—"

"Enough, Mr. Fothergill!"

The bishop flipped out his coattails and sank to his seat, clearly rankled that his opportunity to speak had been cut short.

Witherskim's lies and Fothergill's truth settled on Miri like the beginning of a great sickness—heavy on her chest and foggy in her head. How could it possibly be fair that this panel of men should decide her fate? A disgusted sigh escaped her. Would she never be free of this lot in life?

She lifted her chin. "May I be allowed to speak?"

The magistrate eyed her an instant before turning toward the end of the table. "In due course. Mr. Knight, if you would."

She snapped her gaze to where the apothecary stood, still clutching the pen he'd used to seal Roland's future.

He did not meet her eyes. "As Mr. Witherskim has already pointed out, it has long been held that women are predisposed to hysteria, melancholia, and in the worst cases, derangement. Medically speaking, a woman's fluids are in a constant state of flux and can easily swell into the tide of mania. I witnessed Miss Brayden in such a state, just last night, when she accosted me quite forcefully."

Bowing her head, Miri studied the floor and shut out his words. With a whole profession to back him up, who would doubt his assessment? Who would believe in her?

Ethan.

The dull ache in her heart sharpened. So consumed with Roland, and now herself, she'd had no time to consider him. Where was he? Still locked up? Alone and cold or—

"Miss Brayden?"

She jerked up her head. The entire panel's eyes bore down on her, squashing the breath from her lungs.

"I said"—Mr. Buckle annunciated with large movements of his lips—"have you anything to say?"

Her mind went blank—no. More like numb. What could she say against lies and incriminating truth?

The only thing possible. She lifted her face and clipped her words so that the entire room might hear. "I. Am. Innocent."

"Very well," said Buckle. "If there is nothing more to add, Mr. Knight, would you please sign the committal document?"

"But—" Her tongue froze as she watched him dip the pen into a bottle of ink, allow a drip to land on a blotter, then set the nib to paper. Behind her, whispers flew around the room like swooping bats.

"No!" The panic in her voice struck a discordant gong in her head.

And stopped Mr. Knight's hand.

"I should like to call my own witness." She threw back her shoulders. "Mr. Ethan Goodwin will vouch for my character."

The room went silent again, except for a snort that came from Witherskim.

"Such a request provides witness enough." Magistrate Buckle stood, briefly nodding at Mr. Knight, then locked his eyes on her.

"Only a madwoman would ask for a murderer to speak on behalf of her character."

29

Ethan a murderer? Impossible. Miri wrapped her arms about herself, vainly trying to re-create the safety she'd felt in his arms. With each stroke of Mr. Knight's pen, she trembled more violently. Behind her, harsh comments and I-told-you-so's rushed from one end of the Cricket and Crown to the other.

"Mr. Handy, if you would." At Mr. Buckle's command, a man advanced toward her, the same man who'd clouted Ethan the night before. The one who'd dragged Roland away. She didn't stand a chance.

Miri spun and bolted into the press of bodies.

Fear choked her as physically as the yank on her collar. Stumbling backward, she darted her gaze from face to face, hoping—desperately—that someone would come to her aid. Pity glistened in a few eyes. Very few. Most squinted judgment.

"Help me!" Did that shrill voice really belong to her? "I am not mad!"

"Come along now, miss, peaceable like." A strong arm clamped around her torso, slamming her against Mr. Handy's body.

Her toes barely scraped the floor as he dragged her from the crowd. Nothing good ever came of being whisked away. Suddenly she was six years old again, as helpless to stop this from happening as the innumerable times her father had hauled her off for a beating.

"Noooo!" She wriggled, clawed, bit—anything to break loose.

Mr. Handy's grip tightened, squeezing the breath from her until shadows rimmed her vision. If only he'd squeeze tighter and end this nightmare.

Once outside, he hoisted her onto the back of a waiting cart. Roland huddled in one corner, hands manacled to an iron ring attached to the wagon's side—

Just like the one Mr. Handy clamped onto her wrists. She twisted. The metal bit sharp teeth into her flesh. Tears carved hot trails down her cheeks. "Please, don't do this. I swear I am not mad."

"Not for me to say, miss." Mr. Handy jumped down and walked the cart's length to the front, dismissing her as if she mattered less than yesterday's porridge.

Truth was, she did matter less. No one was left to care for her. That single, stunning thought made her cry all the harder as she welcomed the pain into her soul.

The driver yelled, "Hyah!" and the cart lurched forward.

Wiping her nose on her sleeve, she slumped onto the cart's wooden planks, the mirror image of her brother. He made no sound. No eye contact. Nothing. Did he know what was going on somewhere deep beneath the layer of madness? The vacant look on his face gave no hint.

Before the final dust of Deverell Downs rolled beneath the wagon wheels, Miri closed her eyes. Why watch the death of a dream? She'd never have a home of her own, nor any home, for that matter. Sniffling, she fought back another wave of tears.

The jarring motion of the cart, combined with exhaustion and despair, eventually lulled her to sleep. When she awoke, shadows stretched in the waning light. Roland was a dark ball, curled into the corner like a pill bug.

Pushing up, she peered over the cart's edge. The jostling ride was over. Mr. Handy and the wagon driver spoke in low tones with another man. Much gesturing ensued, and the conversation took on a more lively tone. None of them paid her any mind, so she studied what would be her new home.

A sprawling two-story brick building crouched uneasily on a crumbling foundation. Ivy strangled its walls. The roof slanted at precarious angles, as if the shingles wanted to jump off and run away. Windows, some barred, others boarded, dotted the facade like the grimace on a toothless hag. Above an iron gate that served as a front door, the words *Sheltering Arms Asylum* were engraved into a granite placard—only the *A* and *y* in the last word were covered over with creeping vines, making it the Sheltering Arms slum. How fitting.

The huddle of men broke. Mr. Handy and the driver swung up to unfasten her and Roland from the cart. In that one instant of freedom, she considered making a run for it. Roland wailed like a banshee. New cuffs were clamped onto their wrists, and the Sheltering Arms keeper led them along. Though her feet moved, she kept her eyes on the darkening sky all the way to the door. Who knew when she'd see it again?

Panic flashed through her, and she turned to Mr. Handy. "Don't do this. I am not mad, and you know it."

"What I know or don't know ain't the point. Orders is orders. Now move along." He urged her with a nod of his head.

Miri shut her mouth. Trying to reason with a big man housing a small mind wasn't worth the effort.

Once through the gate, they stopped and waited for the keeper's key to turn in the grate. Twenty paces more and they stopped again while he unbolted another iron gate, allowed them to pass, and relocked that one as well. This same routine played out yet one more time, until finally they entered a room. Roland needed to be persuaded with a shove.

The chamber was tired, with a worn rug at the center. More rag than rug, actually. In one corner near the ceiling, large curls of paint peeled off the wall. Dirty streaks ran the length of the single window, which mimicked the outside bars. The entire space was hardly large enough to contain the bench, bookshelf, and desk crammed inside.

A man entered from a side door. In two steps his legs covered the distance to the table, where he paused and folded his lengthy arms. Everything about the man was elongated, from the stretch of his nose to the stripe of his thin body. Stubbly black hair crowned his head and most of his face. He eyed the group, frowning. "Did you not tell them we are full up, Mr. Beeker?"

The fellow that had led them through the labyrinth shifted his weight from one foot to the other. "Naturally, Mr. Spyder. They would not be put off, though. And their paperwork is faultless." He stepped forward and slapped down several documents, emphasizing his point.

Looking from the documents to Beeker, Spyder pursed his lips. "You know Dr. Pembernip will be put out by this. He won't like it at all, I tell you. And Alf's gone home for the night. We can't properly receive inmates without Alf."

A small hope fluttered in Miri's stomach.

"Still …" Beeker shrugged. "They've got papers and all."

Spyder retrieved a ledger from the bookshelf and paged through it as he inched onto the chair behind the desk.

Miri took the opportunity to step forward. "Sir, there has been a terrible mistake. I do not belong here. Would it not serve us all well were I to leave?"

Mr. Spyder ran an ink-stained finger down the length of a page, nodding all the while, then rose. "Very well."

The tension in Miri's shoulders uncoiled. "Thank God. And thank you, sir. I am—"

"Very well, *Mr. Beeker.*" Spyder shot her a pointed look, then redirected his glance at the man. "If you could please summon Graves to my aid?"

"Yes, sir." Beeker disappeared out the same door Spyder had used.

Miri frowned. "But you just said you were full."

"None of your concern, miss," said Spyder.

"Surely you can see I am not mad, sir." She looked over at Roland, hoping Spyder would follow her gaze and make the contrasting observation.

Roland didn't disappoint. Spit bubbles gathered on his lips and dribbled down his chin.

Spyder shook his head and bent, his fingers scrambling across the parchments on his desk for a quill. "It is not for me to say."

"Make it yours to say. You obviously document the admitting. One less inmate to house would lighten your load, and I daresay your Dr. Pembernip would not be nearly as 'put out.'" She leaned forward, schooling her face into the most pleading of looks. "You would earn my eternal gratitude."

Spyder lifted his face, meeting her gaze, and scratched the black stubble on his chin. Slowly, he stepped away from the desk and crossed to Mr. Handy, stooping toward the man's ear. "Why did you bring this woman?" Though he kept his voice low, the small room projected it.

"Hysterics," answered Handy.

"Ahh," said Spyder, an all-encompassing "ahh" that clearly meant she'd committed a sin.

An unforgiveable sin.

"I am not hysterical!" She didn't shout, but it reverberated as if she had.

Roland snapped his head toward her and raised his manacled hands. Chained or not, he managed to point a finger at her. A stream of Latin flowed out of his mouth, competing with the bubbles. Loose hair covered one eye. The other glared at her. Passion possessed him, and he jumped atop the bench, swinging his arms like a scythe.

"Get down." Mr. Handy reached to pull Roland off. "You crazy nit."

Roland smacked him in the head.

Mr. Handy went for his throat.

"Don't!" Miri cried. She turned to Mr. Spyder. "Do something."

Barely flicking his eyes her way, he strolled back to the desk and sat.

Mr. Handy cut into Roland at the knees. Her brother fell forward, his face making a sickening crack against the floorboards.

"Please!" cried Miri.

Spyder lifted his hand, examined his fingernails, then nibbled on one as if there were no chaos erupting in front of him.

Roland wailed and flailed about. Blood snaked a trail down his chin from a cut lip. Handy kicked him.

"Mr. Spyder, do you intend to sit there and watch my brother take a beating?" Miri reeled back a step. "This is insane!"

"Exactly," he said.

At that moment, Mr. Beeker and an enormous fellow, presumably Mr. Graves, entered the room. Beeker handed Spyder a long stick with a loop of wire at one end, matching one that Graves held.

"Thank you," said Spyder.

He turned toward Miri, lifting the stick as one might a butterfly net. She threw her hands up—but too late. The loop cleared her head, settling on her neck. Wedging her thumbs between wire and flesh, she tugged.

Spyder yanked it tighter, as one might do to a naughty pug on the end of a leash, then looked past her. "Graves, the one on the floor is yours. Put him … somewhere. Good night, Mr. Handy. Mr. Beeker, see Mr. Handy out, would you?"

Then he pivoted and dragged her along.

The wire bit into the back of her neck. Either she followed willfully or got decapitated.

He tugged her through a door and down a dimly lit corridor. She choked on a scream. If rot began in one's bones, then the outside of Sheltering Arms had been an accurate indicator of the inside. Great patches of plaster from the walls lay in crumbles underfoot, leaving gaping holes that exposed the lath bones of the building. The floor rose and fell at whim, sometimes requiring a step up or down to resume walking. Soot darkened the upper halves of the walls and ceilings, adding a cavelike effect to the corridors.

Spyder paused, withdrew a key from his pocket, and opened a door. Monkey shrieks and howling gibberish shattered her ear bones as he pulled her through. The noise crawled through every part of her, invading the smallest spaces, then swelled until she might burst.

They entered a large area ringed with more doors. Each contained a slit at eye level, just enough to peek through. Nearing one, Spyder leaned forward for a look. The stick between them forced Miri to remain behind. A sharp thud jarred the door, and Spyder reared back, key in hand.

Gooseflesh rose on Miri's arms, and she was suddenly glad for the stick separating them. She had no desire to look through that peephole.

Another thud smacked the door. Louder. More violent.

Spyder set the key in the lock.

Was he seriously going to put her in there? Tears welled. Her throat clogged.

"Please …" That she managed to speak was a miracle. "Anywhere but in there."

He glanced over his shoulder at her. That he'd heard her choked voice was miracle number two.

The key slid out from the lock. Miracle three.

Miri exhaled a heartfelt sigh. "Thank you."

Spyder pivoted so fast, the wire cut into her neck. She ran to keep up with his long strides. They exited the big room with all its teeth-rattling noise and ascended a narrow stairwell. By the time they reached the top, she could hardly breathe. It opened onto a small landing with one door. A solid door with no peepholes, and no noise behind it except for—

Miri listened hard.

As Mr. Spyder inserted the key into the lock, a clicking sound came from the other side, like a crayfish scuttling backward over rocks. Many of them. An army with snipping and snapping pincers.

Fear stopped her heart as Spyder opened the door.

He yanked upward on the stick, freeing her neck, then reached to grab her forearm and threw her in.

Miri screamed.

The women looking back at her had no faces.

30

"Move it!" Nigel shouted, fed up with Ethan's belligerence. He gave him a hard shove to the shoulder blades and smiled when Ethan stumbled through the scarred door of Newgate prison. Once it clanked shut behind them, all his pent-up tension drained like waste down a sewer. Nigel circled his shoulders, stretching out the kinks, then tipped back his hat. Though he'd kept the brim low and his collar flipped up, he'd felt exposed trekking through London proper. Prodding an uncooperative prisoner attracted attention—a veritable calling card, letting Buck know he was back in town.

"This way." A guard motioned for them to follow down a sconce-lit corridor. The flickering light cast freakish shadows against the stone walls, and a dull haze filled the air. If ever there was a picture of hell on earth, this was it—especially with the added scrape from Ethan's chains against the floor. The moans muffled behind locked doors gave it a nice touch too.

Drawing alongside Ethan, Nigel nudged him. "We can still turn back. It's not too late. Just say the word ... er, sorry, mate. Forgot. Nod yer head."

Mouth gagged, Ethan fixed his stare on the guard in front of him.

"Pigheaded fool." Nigel flattened his lips into a sneer. "By this time tomorrow, you'll be beggin' me to get you out."

He cuffed Ethan in the head, delighted that it made the blighter stagger.

"In here." The guard directed them through yet another door, closer to the entrails of the jail. The deeper into the guts of Newgate, the more putrid the stench. Disease, waste, and death combined into a stink that violated the nostrils and ravaged the senses. Nigel flipped his collar back up and breathed through it.

They entered a large room with shelves upon shelves of leather-bound books. One lay open on a desk beside an ink bottle and several quills. Behind the desk sat a man, rather gawkish, with one eye that couldn't seem to decide which direction it should look. It roamed free, the iris romping about in its field of white, while the other eye hooked and reeled them in.

"Name?" he asked.

Nigel stepped forward. "Nigel Thorne."

It was a little disconcerting how one eye remained on Nigel while the other focused on the man's quill as he wrote in the book. The pen stopped scratching, and the man looked up. For the briefest moment, both pupils stared at Nigel. "Crime?"

Gads, was the man lazy of mind as well as of eye? "No, no. I'm not the bleedin' criminal. He is." He hitched a thumb over his shoulder.

The man's jaw jutted forward, baring a crooked rack of teeth, then he dipped his head and made an excessive show of crossing out his last entry.

"Name?" he repeated without looking up.

"Ethan Goodwin," Nigel answered.

"Crime?"

"Pending."

The pen froze in midair, and the man raised his head. "What's that supposed to mean?"

"Uh …" Who could think while watching an eyeball do loop-de-loops? "Probably murder."

Setting down the pen with one hand, the man corked the ink bottle with the other. "Who did you say you are?" he asked.

Behind him, Nigel heard the distinct scrape of chain against floor. Apparently he wasn't the only one Mr. Crazy-Eyed-Keeper-of-the-Books was annoying.

"I am Nigel Thorne, bailiff to the Crown, serving the parishes of Old Nichol, Ramsgate, and Walpole." He puffed out his chest and nodded toward Ethan. "And a bounty hunter, when needs be."

With raised brows, the man skewered both of them with a look—simultaneously. "Judging from the way you've got that fellow trussed up, I can see you're capable of fancy knotwork, but perhaps you're not familiar with the legal process. You can't go locking up a man based on probability."

Nigel's impatience swelled into anger. He widened his stance. No half-blind clerk would question his authority. "Of course I'm familiar with the legal process, and I said his charges are pending."

"What does that *mean*?"

"This!" Nigel rushed toward the table, intending to choke the blasted weasel until his eyes popped out. The guard's footsteps sounded from behind, forcing him to rethink his strategy. Instead, he thrust his hand into his pocket and pulled out a crumpled bill, holding it inches from the man's face. Neither eye would miss it at that distance.

The clerk pinched it with thumb and forefinger, then secreted it away like a squirrel with a nut. He uncorked the ink, picked up the quill, and mumbled as he wrote, "P-e-n-d-i-n-g."

"Duration?"

Nigel glanced back at Ethan. Cold steel glimmered in his gaze. Good thing he couldn't voice that rage. Persuading such a mule could take longer than he thought. He turned back to the desk. "Indeterminate."

Crazy eye slapped down the pen. "Believe it or not, Mr. Thorne, Newgate has certain standards, one of which being accurate records. I must know the expected length of sentence, or how will we know when to release—"

Nigel held out another bill.

The man plucked it away as fast as the first. "Indeterminate," he said under his breath as he wrote.

Chains rattled again. Nigel ignored them. "Now about this man's stay, I'd like it to be ... memorable."

"Hmm ..." Tapping the quill against his chin, the man let both eyes wander. "Memorable as in holiday to the countryside, or as in suffering through a severe case of the pox? Either way, it will cost you."

Nigel's anger flared as out of control as the man's ridiculous eyeball. He emptied his pocket and slammed the contents down on the table. "A pox on you and on Ethan Goodwin!"

He spun and stalked out the door, not giving the record clerk or Ethan a second glance. He had half a mind to leave him in there to rot. No one would know or care. He didn't slow his long strides until the grey fortress spit him out onto the street.

"See? That man can't get outta there fast enough ... hey—hey, Thorne!"

"Hey, Duff," Nigel answered before he turned around, so familiar was the snuffling voice.

Duffy's long snout twitched, usually a sign he was thinking hard. Either that or Nigel smelled funny, which could be the case after the last few days of hard travel. Duffy held the collar of a ragtag boy in one of his hands and scratched behind his ear with the other. Yep, definitely thinking hard.

"But I thought you were gone. What you doin' in Newgate of all places?" Duffy's arm stretched as the boy made a run for it, yanking him back without a pause. "Did you find that fella you were lookin' for finally?"

"O' course. I always find my man. Ol' Ethan Goodwin is locked up at last."

The boy snaked up his head and stared at Nigel. Raw contempt sizzled like burning coals in the lad's gaze.

An eerie chill shivered up Nigel's spine. "Quite the l'il criminal you got there, Duff."

"What … this?" Duffy's big teeth shone, and he leaned forward, lowering his voice. "I'm not really going to jail him, just put the fear o' God in the boy for fighting in a street brawl in Old Nichol. Some kind of scuffle over sweeping rights and—ow!"

Duffy jerked up his hand. Nigel reached to grab the little hooligan, but the thin material of the boy's shirt ripped off. Knees pumping, the lad zigzagged down the street.

"Ow, ow, ow!" Duffy pressed one hand against the back of the other. Blood rained down each of his fingers. "The blighter bit me good."

Nigel whistled low. "You better get that looked at. Human bites is worse than a dog's. I learned that one the hard way."

He rubbed his forearm over the ridge of a poorly healed scar. "You ought to know better than to drag around a street waif, especially one from Old Nichol. Since when does anyone care about street fights in that slum?"

"A reverend started some kind of holy reform down there. Trying to save souls, I guess. Cockamamie idea, if you ask me. Some souls ain't worth the savin'. Anyway, it's riling up some of the residents. They're starting to care 'bout things like brawls and brothels and such. Ain't wantin' 'em, that's what." Duffy paused and lifted his top hand to peek at his wound. Blood oozed afresh. He blanched and pressed it tight again. "I got to go."

Nigel watched the hedgehog toddle off. Even in a hurry, the man waddled.

He turned and headed the opposite direction, down Canal Street to his own flat, all the while thinking on Duffy's bit of news. If Old Nichol was getting cleaned up from the inside, then the brothel madams, the gin guzzlers, or the gamblers couldn't be happy about it. Preachers were bad for business. He scrubbed at the itchy days' growth on his chin. A little holy water would flush out the vermin, all right, forcing them elsewhere … which could be to his advantage. Maybe Buck was gone already. If not, it wouldn't be long.

He practically skipped home, his burden so lightened. A shave, some sleep, and a meal, yessir … he grinned, returning Lady Luck's smile.

The stink of cabbage past its prime and one too many onions greeted him as he entered the flat. He tiptoed past Mrs. Spankum's door. The old girl's cooking rivaled the stench of Newgate's. He climbed the first set of stairs, cresting the top of the landing, then paused, listening intently. Though everything was as it should be, a peculiar scent mixed with Spankum's dinner—danger.

He spun. The stairwell was empty.

"Pish." He grumbled, ashamed at acting more doltish than Duffy. After the second set of stairs, a distinct floorboard creaked behind him. He wheeled about. "Look, if it's about the rent ..."

The stairwell remained empty.

He stomped up to the third floor, slamming down his boot on each step to prove that fear was a bug to be squashed, not run from.

"Lady Luck, that's what. She's smilin' on me now, she is. I'll spring Ethan tomorrow, collect his money the day followin'. Lady Luck's my little gal, she is," he mumbled to his door, the pep talk lifting his spirits once again. "A shave, some sleep, a meal, ahhh."

Entering his room, he gasped.

His bed, his table, even his lucky elephant—gone. All that was left were some brown water stains on the plaster beneath the windowsill and coal dust in the hearth—just dust, no coals.

"What in the—"

"Down payment."

He whipped around into a crouch.

Buck filled the doorframe. "I come for the rest."

A lump lodged in Nigel's throat. He swallowed. It stayed. "Two days. Two more days is all I need and—"

"Yer time's up, Thorne." Buck pulled out a knife with a very long blade.

The flay-your-flesh-from-your-bones kind of blade.

Nigel ran a shaky hand across his brow. It came away wet with perspiration. "See here, mate—"

Huge veins popped on each side of Buck's neck. "I told you once before, I'm not your *mate.*"

Buck charged.

Nigel turned tail and ran. Shards of glass ripped his skin as he dove through the window. He rolled onto the roof, stopping just before the edge. A shudder ran through him at the thought of what might've been. Apparently Lady Luck was still with him after all.

Buck blasted out after him.

Now what? Peering over the roof's edge, he almost vomited. A straight drop to the cobblestone three stories below would break his neck.

Behind him, Buck growled.

Staying put would mean a slit neck. He scampered sideways, then darted up to the peak of the roof.

A sneer grew on Buck's face, increasing with each of his deliberate steps. "I got you now, Thorne."

"Think again, *mate!*"

Buck bolted toward him.

Nigel sucked in a breath, then ran full speed downward. Just before the edge, he sprang. If Lady Luck truly was his woman, he'd sail across the gap and land on the neighboring roof. Buck would never be able to do that, the big lummox.

Stretching straight out, Nigel reached for the opposite roof, fingers ready to grasp and hold on for the inevitable collision.

He reached.

And clutched nothing but air.

The world shot upward. His stomach, his kidneys, his heart and liver, all his insides ran up to his mouth, as if each organ might independently climb to safety. He flailed, wondering if rolling on impact would help.

A sharp crack sounded somewhere at the base of his neck. Everything went black.

Rolling would never again be an option.

❧

"In you go, maggot."

The guard jabbed Ethan forward, the momentum too much for his shackled feet. He thrust out his hands and landed on all fours. Fiery pain shot along each lash mark on his back, and he sucked in air to keep from passing out.

Behind him the iron door slammed shut, the screech of its hinges raking his eardrums. A lock slid into place, and then the walls closed in. Darkness smothered him. All the wretched reality of Newgate sank to the pit of his soul. His worst nightmare come true—and for a crime he didn't commit.

Anger trumped panic.

He bolted up and swung around, chains clanking. Throwing his weight against the door, he hammered his fists. Hard. Bruising knuckles. Splitting skin.

"Let me out! I am innocent. Innocent! Thorne's the guilty one, not me. Let … me … OUT!"

Pummeling the cold metal, he suddenly understood why a trapped fox would gnaw off its leg to get free. If it would do any good, he'd beat this door until all he had left were bloody stumps for fingers.

"God, this isn't fair." Though he couldn't see it, he shouted at the sky. "You hear me? It's not fair!"

"God don't live here, boy."

Ethan whipped around, startled by a voice as agreeable as rocks in a tin can. The only light in the cell came from an air vent high up on the wall, and that from a mere hand's breadth of space. He thought he could distinguish dark forms around him. Then again, maybe not. But now that he'd stopped making noise, he could hear the blackness breathing.

A touch swept along his right arm. He jerked left.

"Skittish one, this," the darkness snorted.

A waft of air fanned his face as if something flew by. Close.

He swatted at it. "What do you want from me?"

Fingers reached out from the abyss and brushed the length of his left leg. He jerked right.

Dry laughter wheezed in and out from mouths he couldn't see.

"Make this easy, boy, and it won't hurt so much."

The flesh at the nape of his neck rose. He crouched, waiting. Whispers circled, coming from everywhere at once.

Then stopped. Silence filled the black space. No whispers, no talking, no breathing, as if all life had been driven from the room.

The cell was a crypt.

Ethan's heart pounded in his chest, his throat, his ears, unbearably loud and out of control.

"Where are you?" His question hung like a noose—

And squeezed the air from his lungs. He crashed to the floor beneath the weight of countless men atop him.

This time when darkness came, he didn't mind.

31

Miri sat on one of the benches lining three of the walls in her cell and closed her eyes. *Are You there, God? Do You know where I am? Do You even care?* She scrunched her eyes tighter, pretending to be any place but here in Sheltering Arms.

Huh. What a name. Sheltering Arms, the great sanctuary and haven for those suffering brain illness, was nothing more than a jail. No ... worse. It was a warehouse, storing the unwanted or those too embarrassing for polite society. A great pantry, with jars of forgotten humanity, left to dwindle and rot.

In the four days since she'd arrived, she'd had no contact with the outside world or the staff of the asylum—except for the crony that brought gruel and emptied the waste bucket once a day. Though Miri pleaded for news of Roland's welfare, the woman ignored her. She began to despair of ever knowing, and desperation was a crueler companion than the inmates around her. When Ethan told her that sometimes faith was a moment-by-moment thing, she hadn't really understood.

Until now. With every breath, she fought to trust anew that somehow, good would come of this plight.

Resting her head against the wall, she opened her eyes and sighed. Careful not to focus on any of their faces, she watched the women around her. Shapeless blanket gowns hung loose on their thin bodies. None had hair. Her initial fear and revulsion had given way to curiosity, leastwise toward one in particular.

A sprite of a girl named Lil sat on a bench across from her. Miri smiled. The girl waved in return, then resumed conversing with another. Eight or maybe nine years old, she displayed the mildest form of the affliction marring the faces of the group. Only one gap split open from her upper lip to her nostril, making her nose slightly tipped and flat. She could speak somewhat in a nasal monotone, though with much effort and concentration, and it was hard to understand.

Instead of such verbal gymnastics, Lil and the other women snapped their fingers and intermittently clapped, a primitive yet unique language structure. As near as Miri could tell, not one of them showed any outward signs of madness. None acted as erratically as Roland. To the contrary, they'd treated her with kindness. Yet she understood why they were locked away. The smallest glimpse at their abhorrent faces would bring a grown man to his knees.

One woman's mouth extended into both nostrils, with no upper lip and no way to ever close the gaping hole. Pink skin with reddish veins, moist and plump, was visible to deep recesses that ought not be seen.

Next to her, another woman's jaw jutted the opposite direction of her mouth, a slanted affair, with misshapen lips that in one corner appeared to be attached to her ear. A few wore perpetual smiles, curved splits in the flesh with tongues that lapped out like a dog's. Except for Lil's, everyone's teeth were helter-skelter, some missing altogether, others with extra, all malformed into spiky pillars or flattened nubs.

Here in this patch of poorly carved jack-o'-lanterns, Miri felt pretty for the first time in her life—and the feeling shamed her. She was no better than Roland, superior only because of noting the impediments of those around her.

The grate of a key in the lock pulled her from her thoughts and pushed the women toward the back corner in a huddle. Their fingers snapped up a frenzy, clicking and snipping some kind of warning. Would it be safer to join them or remain where she was?

She rose. Too late.

The door opened, and every hand dropped.

Mr. Graves stood on the threshold, gripping the hated stick and wire device. No one moved.

He lifted it and faced Miri.

Her throat closed at the thought of the wire biting into her skin. Tender flesh still smarted on the back of her neck from when Spyder had dragged her here.

"There is no need to yank me about. You have my word I will follow you," she said.

He did not lower the stick. Neither did he advance.

"Look"—she lifted her wrists, iron cuffs still attached—"do you really think I'll be any trouble?"

The stick hesitated in midair, then lowered.

Graves stepped aside, nodding for her to exit. He relocked the door and, without a word, grunted for her to follow. As they descended the stairwell, Miri braced herself for the clamor of the big room.

But even prepared, she winced when they entered.

Occasional howls pierced the air, awful in pitch, though that didn't curdle the blood nearly as much as the undercurrent. A continuous drone babbled, passionate and charged with energy. The many voices blended into one foreign monologue of cries for help.

"*Oh, the worms! The bloody worms again. They're crawling. Crawling! Somebody get 'em off!*"

"*Mum? Mum? Whyn't you come for me, Mum? I done like you tol' me. Be quiet! Don't tell me. Make her stop. Make her stop!*"

"*Me stockings are too tight. They choke me, they do. I can't breathe. I can't breathe!*"

Miri sped ahead, drawing a small measure of security from Mr. Graves's broad back. The depth of insanity hidden behind those doors disturbed her like nothing else. What a blessing she was not locked in with—

Sudden understanding stole her breath, and she gasped. In the midst of the most hellish place on earth, she'd been granted peace and safety in the company of women neither mad nor violent. Her cellmates were dreadfully disfigured, nothing more.

One stunning thought shone brighter than the rest: God knew exactly where she was and had provided accordingly. Though the standards differed from what she expected, it did not negate the provision. The very name of the asylum took on a whole new meaning. No matter where on earth she or Roland or Ethan may be, they were not out of God's reach. Her trust level swelled, and she mouthed a silent "thank You" to the One watching over her.

The frenzied noises faded as they wound through the maze of corridors and locked gates, but her heart didn't pound as hard as the first time she'd passed this way. Peace held her as securely as the irons on her wrists.

At last they entered a room smelling of camphor and something that left an immediate brassy taste in her mouth. Mercury, perhaps? Many jars and instruments lined a rack of shelves, most unidentifiable—except for the one clutched by a singular-looking man in a long, white jacket.

Miri retreated a step.

"No, no, come on in. There's nothing to fear in here," he said.

Liar.

The man who spoke held a silver pair of shears, shinier than those she used in the garden, though every bit as large.

And sharp.

⟶⟝⟞⟵

Sandwiched between two guards, Ethan stumbled up the last two steps on a twisting staircase. He flung out a hand, catching himself before falling.

"Move on!" the guard behind him snapped.

"If speed's what you want, then take off the chains."

A whip cracked an instant before a searing stripe opened across his shoulders.

"You say something, bait?"

Ethan arched his back but kept his mouth shut. Better to save his venom for Thorne. No doubt that's who had summoned him—finally—from below. How long he'd been in here was hard to say. Days and nights didn't exist in Newgate. Only pain. Time was measured in beatings and blood.

He squinted as they crossed the corridor. A torch burned in a sconce near the door. After the blackness of his cell, the light hurt.

One guard led him into a chamber while the other remained on watch outside. A table with two chairs totaled the sum of furniture in the small room, but a booming voice filled it completely.

"Ethan, lad!"

Caught up in a bear hug, Ethan winced until the man let him go. "Reverend, you are a sight for sore eyes—and I do mean sore."

Newton laughed. "At least they've not beat the humor from you. Sit." He nodded at one chair while he sank onto the other. "I didn't think it possible, but you look worse than last time we met, boy."

Ethan smirked, the side of his face stinging from the sudden movement. He could only imagine how he must look, let alone smell. "What are you doing here?"

"Saint Matthew writes that our blessed Lord said, *I was naked, and ye clothed Me; I was sick, and ye visited Me; I was in prison, and ye came unto Me.'* You just provided an opportunity to carry out the work of our Lord."

"Glad I could help out." Ethan shifted in the chair, and his shoulder burned a retort.

"Hah!" Newton slapped the table. "Salty as ever, eh, boy?"

The reverend's voice thundered like a squall at sea, but to Ethan it sounded as comforting as a mother's coo. He hadn't realized how much he'd missed this man. "How did you know I was here?"

Newton rubbed a hand over his bald pate and sat back. He appeared as relaxed in the depths of Newgate as in the pulpit at St. Mary's. "There's nothing God can't reveal."

Ethan's brows rose. "God *spoke* to you?"

"Speaks to me all the time, boy. Through His Word."

"Right. So you read in one of your gospels that Ethan Goodwin's in Newgate. Go visit him." Some of the venom he'd stored for Thorne spilled out. Instant remorse hit him hard, and he looked away. "Sorry. I didn't mean to say—"

"No offense taken. Prison has a way of sharpening a cynical edge, even in the mildest of men. And you were never mild to begin with. I heard about you on the streets, lad. Talk spreads faster than the pox in Old Nichol."

He jerked his face back to Newton's. "What were you doing in that hellhole?"

"Jesus came to storm the gates of hell, boy. What better place to stir up a tempest of a revival? Why … I owe it to you for bringing Old Nichol to my attention."

Ethan snorted. Not many would be so thankful for an introduction to that place. "You're incorrigible. You know that, don't you?"

A grin dawned on the old man's face, deep crevices appearing at the sides of his mouth. "That's not the first time I've been called such, and I daresay not the last."

"So tell me then"—Ethan leaned forward, trying hard to ignore the hot sting of the lash marks on his back—"what is the talk?"

Newton cast a glance at the guard by the door, then nudged his chair closer. "Word is you killed a man. Your friend Will Brayden."

Slamming both fists on the table, Ethan shot up. "I did not!"

"Watch it, bait," the guard warned.

Ethan blew out a long breath and slowly sank, welcoming the accompanying pain. But inside, he yet raged. "I swear to God, I didn't do it."

"Swearing to God holds eternal consequences, son."

"I know."

"Do you?"

The reverend's eyes bore into his, as if Ethan stood before the living God in flesh.

"I did not murder Will Brayden. Nor anyone else, for that matter. Not yet, anyway." Without willing it, his hands curled into fists. "But if I ever get my hands on Thorne—"

"On whom?" asked Newton.

"Nigel Thorne." He spit out the name like a bad piece of meat.

Newton cocked his head. "Why would you say such a thing?"

"He's the one who killed Will."

"Hmm …" Newton studied the ceiling and went back to rubbing his head. "That does present a problem."

"Why?"

"Thorne's dead himself."

Ethan flinched, the news a direct hit. The trouble that man had caused him in life would be manifold with his death.

He thought it, but Newton spoke it. "So you're charged with a murder you say Thorne committed. It'll be your word against a man who can't defend himself, and a lawman at that. I have a feeling the judge will see it as a desperate attempt on your part. Were there no witnesses?"

Despair grabbed him by the throat and squeezed. "None," he whispered, sinking back.

Neither of them spoke. What else was there to say? It was hopeless. And what of Miri? She'd never know what happened to him. He hadn't even gotten to say good-bye.

A rap on the door broke the silence.

"Time's up," said the guard.

"Don't fret, lad. If anything, you're in the best position of all." Newton rose and rested his big hand on Ethan's head. "When we're at our weakest, God's at His strongest. We serve a powerful God, boy, and last time I checked, He was still on the throne. Do you believe that?"

Did he?

Ethan closed his eyes. He had to.

God was his only hope.

32

Miri's eyes locked onto the scissors gripped in the man's hand. Her newly formed peace played tug-of-war with fear, and she retreated another step.

"Oh, do these make you nervous?" The man laid the shears on a table behind him. "There. Now come. Let's chat."

Her gaze traveled from the man's hands to his face. His skin, the color and texture of porridge, suggested he'd suffered a particularly vile case of the pox in the past. A distinct bone structure stood out in contrast to dark eyes that sank in. It appeared his skeleton thought it should make an appearance before being closeted away in some casket.

"Don't be timid." He smiled, his flesh stretching tighter over his jawline.

A skeleton that talked. Miri shuddered.

"You see, my dear, I like to get to know my patients first."

"Before what?" She didn't want to know, really, but the words tumbled out nonetheless.

"Before treating them, of course." He nodded at Graves. "Remove her shackles, and then you are dismissed."

Graves produced a small key, and she held out her hands. Her arms floated upward when the heavy cuffs came off.

The man in the white jacket pointed to a chair with wide arm-rests. "Have a seat. We shall get to know one another, shall we not?"

Other than his ghoulish appearance, he appeared to be a gentle-man. Rubbing her wrists, she crossed the room and sat.

"You are Dr. Pembernip?" she asked.

"One and the same," he answered.

"I am—"

"Yes, I know. Miss Miriall Brayden." He lifted a brow. "I wonder if you are as interesting as your brother."

She leaned forward. "Please … how is he?"

"Delightful!"

Miri blinked. Roland and delightful mixed together like lemon juice and milk.

With his chuckle, Pembernip's jaw moved as if it had become unhinged. "Your brother put Alf out of commission in record time. Record time! Which reminds me, I must apologize for your lack of proper admittance. Alf usually handles such matters. I am here only once a week."

He angled his head toward her hands. "May I?"

Her wrists did look bad—skin rubbed raw, swollen and red. And the man did have *doctor* attached to his name. She bobbed her head. "Very well," she said.

He examined one wrist, then the next, his touch probing yet light. "Those irons should have been taken off days ago."

"I should never have been admitted in the first place, Doctor. My commitment is based on lies against my character, my behaviors, even my virtue."

He reached for a jar of ointment on the table beside him. "One man's lie is another man's truth, my dear."

"You don't understand. The men who put me here did so out of spite and ignorance. I am not mad."

Dabbing a bit of the gel on one of her wrists, he did not look up when he answered. "It's always our adversaries who are the mad ones, is it not? Other hand, please."

Her skin felt soothed even if her emotions did not. If nothing else, at least the doctor knew what treatment to offer.

"Clearly you can see that my sanity is intact," she said.

"I would suggest that sanity is an illusion, albeit a very persistent one." He paused, looking up, his dark eyes wells of mystery. "We are all mad in some respect, especially when the cause is perceived as sufficient."

Miri sighed. She was getting nowhere.

Pembernip released her hands and screwed the lid back onto the jar. The scent of lanolin lingered long after it was sealed.

"Now then, for your own safety and comfort, you'll find a gown on the other side of that screen." He pointed toward a woven bit of wicker framed in a corner. "Though you are housed with a gentle lot, which I must say was a rare act of nobility on behalf of Mr. Spyder, the rest of the inmates would as soon skin you alive to get their hands on such a fine dress."

Miri glanced at her plain jaconet skirt. This was fine?

"If you don't mind," he said.

Of course she minded. The man was as crack-brained as those he attended. Still ... with no immediate possibility of escape, the wisdom of blending in might be the better part of valor. She rose, taking her time to cross the room as she studied its one window. The bars were too narrow to crawl through, too strong for her to bend, unless she might find a metal rod somewhere for leverage.

"Sorry to rush you, Miss Brayden, but you are not my only patient today. Move along, if you please."

"Of course." She stepped behind the screen, hidden from view but not from hearing. "About my cellmates—"

"Tut, tut, they're family now, not cellmates. You may call them sisters."

She cringed as she undid the buttons on her bodice. Sisters? "Right ... well ... they are obviously not the most beautiful of women, yet I find no fault in their mental capacities."

"Bravo, Miss Brayden. An astute observation and very, very correct."

"Correct?" She forced the coarse gown over her head and, fingers shaking, fumbled with the drawstring at the neck. "You admit to it, then?"

"I detect an element of surprise in your voice, if not disdain."

"Should I not scorn the fact that you have locked up perfectly normal women—aside from their looks, that is?" The fabric chafed against her skin as she emerged from behind the screen. Rage threaded along each finger, pulling her hands into fists. "That's insanity! Why would you—why would anyone—commit such a heinous act?"

"Now, now, don't fret so. It's not good for your constitution." He approached her, cautious in step and touch, and gently laid a hand on her arm. "Please, sit back down. I shall explain, I promise."

She gnawed the inside of her cheek, casting a last glance at the window. What other choice did she have?

"Much better." He lowered to a chair adjacent hers and smiled. "You see, there is a fine line between normalcy and lunacy. It is not up to you or me to define where that line is drawn. It is simply my duty to treat those who find themselves on the wrong side of it, and your duty to oblige."

"Who decides—" She lowered her voice, for her shrill tone screamed hysteria even to her own ears. "Who decides, Doctor, where that line is drawn?"

"Why … whoever holds the biggest stick at the time, my dear." His smile widened, sharp and toothy. The kind she'd seen in nightmares. "It's always about power, you see. Who has it, who does not. Surely you know that, especially being a woman."

"But that's not right!" The anger his sentiments stirred would not be tamped, and heat rushed to her face. "We all enter the world in the same way, and leave it likewise too. That some live in freedom while others are locked away, through no fault of their own, is injustice at its worst."

"There, there, this discussion is agitating you." He clasped her hands in his own, rubbing little circles on the tops with his thumbs.

She yanked them away. "How can you sit idle in the midst of such wrongdoing?"

He reached for her hands again but this time did not try to hold them. He set them on the chair's wide arms. "Take some deep breaths. In and out. That's the ticket. In. Out."

Against her will, her lungs rebelled, taking on the rhythm he set.

"That's it. Very good, Miss Brayden. I have complete confidence that once you settle in, you'll find Sheltering Arms to be quite the haven. The insane are not without their charms, you know."

She clenched the armrests to keep herself from punching him in the nose. "I do not plan on settling in. I don't belong here any more than you do. In your honest medical opinion, can you find one reason to say that I am mad?"

"Not a bit of it. I find you refreshingly clear-headed and intelligent. There is nothing feeble minded about you, Miss Brayden."

Her knuckles regained color as she relaxed her grip. Finally. Someone other than Ethan on her side.

"Furthermore," he continued, "I look forward to many more conversations with you."

He flipped her arms over and snapped on two clamps, locking her wrists to the chair. From a shelf behind him, he pulled out a box of sharp instruments.

Miri's heart seized. Though the gown she wore hung loose, her chest constricted. "What are you doing?"

"First, I'm going to bleed you," he said.

The room started spinning.

"First?" she asked.

He ran a steel blade across her flesh, near the crook of her elbow. Her skin gaped, and she saw the different layers inside her arm before blood poured out.

Dr. Pembernip held a porcelain bowl beneath the flow. "Then there's the purging, of course."

Miri detached from her body, floating to the corner of the room, somewhere near the ceiling.

"Pur … purging?" She didn't feel her lips move, though the shaky voice she heard could be none other than her own.

Pembernip's skeletal grin exposed every tooth in his mouth—on both jaws. "Yes, yes. All body cavities must be expunged. Clearing the body helps clear the mind. Miss Bray—"

Miri soared through the ceiling, up to a black, black sky.

◈◈◈

Prodded along a brick-walled passage, Ethan shuffled forward with twenty to thirty other prisoners. Now and then a guard whacked a club against some straggler. A grunt and a curse followed. Ethan kept up but couldn't blame those who didn't. Newgate would sap the strength of a stallion, a fact testified by the gaunt faces and withered muscles on the men around him.

But Newgate was behind him now. Herded into a semicircular area—much too small for the pack of them—here he would wait for the call to trial. The Old Bailey butted up against the jail, turning the gears of justice in a swift if not grinding fashion. There appeared to be thirty, maybe forty men awaiting judgment, but the Lord Mayor would be through with them all in plenty of time to have tea with his mistress. Ethan had heard that the average trial lasted at most seven or eight minutes, and at the rate they called out men's names, he didn't doubt it. Today he'd be set free—or hung from the gallows.

And there wasn't one thing he could do about it.

"When we're at our weakest, God's at His strongest."

Ethan snapped his gaze around the pathetic group. Who'd said that? The man nearest him scowled so darkly, bootblack couldn't have painted his face any fiercer. No one else paid him any mind. Either they were too caught up in their private miseries or too busy mustering bravado to notice him.

He shoved his way to the outer edge of the stinking cluster of bodies. Leaning against the masonry, he mulled over the words he'd sworn he'd heard. Then remembered Newton had told him that. Newton, the man of God. The man of eternal optimism.

That was Newton, but who was Ethan Goodwin?

A wretch, that's who. A shackled, dirty, wasted excuse of a man.

He closed his eyes, shutting out the hopelessness around him. Too bad it did nothing to remove the hopelessness within. "I am nothing, God. Weaker than weak. Please show Yourself strong, just as the reverend said."

"Goodwin!"

His eyes flew open.

"Ethan Goodwin, over here!"

The men parted more easily this time, probably glad it was his name that'd been called instead of theirs. In a way, he was glad too. Better to end the not knowing.

A squabby-looking court clerk stood at the door opposite the one Ethan had entered. "You Ethan Goodwin?"

"I am."

"This way."

Flanked by a guard, he trailed the short official down a shorter corridor and entered a large courtroom teeming with people.

Coming in from the side, he caught only the profiles of the twelve men seated on the jury. Below them in a gallery and above them in balconies, spectators leaned forward, gawking. The farther into the room he went, the harder it was to see. Four brass chandeliers burned bright, assaulting his eyes. He squinted at the judge on the raised platform ahead of him, trying to determine what manner of character held his fate. Hard to tell, especially when the clerk halted him midaisle and positioned him in a dock front and center. A large glass mirror, attached and angled from the ceiling, caught the sunlight and focused it onto his face. Highlighted by the reflected light, everyone clearly saw his own character. And after so many days locked in a cell, what a sight that must be.

"The honorable Lord Mayor Kenyon presiding for the City of London in the case of Ethan Goodwin," the clerk called out.

Courtroom chatter lowered to a dull drone. "Ethan Goodwin, you are indicted for the willful murder of one William Brayden on March the fifth. How plead you?"

"Not guilty!"

"Mind your tone in court, sir. Who brings these charges?"

"I do."

Ethan turned his head. To his left, an enormous hedgehog stood on its hind legs. He rubbed his eyes, chains clanking. Sweet heavens, he was losing it.

"Name?" asked the clerk.

"Duffy. Harry Duffy, constable, east end."

"State your case."

The clerk sat while Ethan tried to remember who in the world Duffy was. Surely out of his many run-ins with the law, he'd recall such a peculiar fellow.

"I bring this case, Lord Mayor," Duffy said, "on behalf o' me partner and friend, Bailiff Nigel Thorne, now deceased."

"You have firsthand knowledge of the crime?"

The judge's question wafted a fresh breeze of hope toward Ethan. Only Thorne and Will had been in the alley that night.

"I was not present on the night of the act, but Thorne was," said Duffy. "He contacted me shortly thereafter. He'd been stabbed in the side by Mr. Goodwin."

"Proceed," said the judge.

"Right." Duffy rolled back on his heels and lifted his chin, a stance he'd surely practiced to look important. It didn't work. "As told to me by Nigel Thorne, bailiff and partner—"

"You've already established that, Mr. Duffy."

"Right. On the night of March the fifth—"

"The date has been duly noted. Proceed with what we don't know, Mr. Duffy."

"Right." He paused to scratch behind his ear.

Ethan relaxed for the first time in … how long had it been? No matter. The longer Duffy talked, the better his chances of freedom.

"So as I heard it," Duffy finally said, "Goodwin owed Thorne a fair amount o' money. Thorne went to collect. Goodwin's friend, Brayden, apparently owed Goodwin some money as well. Goodwin wanted to get his money from Brayden to pay off Thorne, see? When Brayden refused, Goodwin got angry. He pulled a knife on 'im, that's what. Thorne saw it all. Goodwin stabbed him so as not to have any witnesses. He run off then, he did, run all the way to Bedfordshire. I was the one who ferreted out that little nugget."

"That's a lie!" Ethan shouted.

The judge's gavel cracked. "Silence, Mr. Goodwin."

Ethan scowled at Duffy. The man didn't even notice. He was too busy smiling at the judge, his yellowed teeth peeking through his dark beard.

"Allow me to restate, Mr. Duffy," said the judge.

Ethan turned his attention back to the man who held his life. Powder from the judge's shoulder-length wig speckled his black robe. Pale blue eyes surrounded by even paler skin suggested that the man considered sunshine a novelty to be avoided. His ferocious tone left no doubt that he took his position seriously.

"As I understand it, Mr. Goodwin owed Mr. Thorne money. Mr. Brayden owed Mr. Goodwin money. When Mr. Brayden refused payment, Mr. Goodwin murdered him in front of Mr. Thorne. Mr. Goodwin then thought to kill Mr. Thorne and leave the area. Is this correct?" asked the judge.

Duffy clapped his hands. "Oh, yes! Oh, that's very good, Lord Mayor. That's exactly what I—"

"Enough, Mr. Duffy."

Duffy deflated into his seat.

"A few more questions, if you don't mind, Mr. Duffy."

He shot up as if he'd sat on a beehive. Buzzing comments flew from the spectators and jurors while Duffy straightened his surcoat.

The judge banged his gavel again. "I should like to know the content of the character of Nigel Thorne."

"A fine law man, my lord. Dedicated, he was. And none finer when it came to thief catchers. He could sniff 'em out quicker than a beagle—"

"We get the point, Mr. Duffy. And the defendant, Ethan Goodwin. What do you know of him?"

Ethan held his breath. This could make or break him.

"Why …" Duffy scratched again. "He's gutter trash, sir. A known opium user, gambler, and thief." Duffy leaned forward, waggling his eyebrows. "Lived in Old Nichol, if you know what I mean."

"Thank you, Mr. Duffy. You may be seated."

The judge aimed his gaze at Ethan. He'd been wrong. The color of the man's eyes wasn't pale blue. It was ice.

"You've already stated your position on the murder of William Brayden. What of stabbing Mr. Thorne?"

"Yes, but—"

"Gambling?"

"I, uh—"

"Opium use?"

Each accusation cannonballed into him, tearing down the weak wall of hope he'd constructed.

"Thievery?"

He hung his head. Hair fell forward, hiding him in darkness. He'd done them all.

God, forgive me.

"Did you have a hand in Mr. Thorne's recent demise?"

He might have, if given the chance. He opened his mouth, but the clerk spoke. "Records show, my lord, that Ethan Goodwin was imprisoned at the time."

"Very well. Jurors, do your duty."

The world stopped, leaving a gaping, jagged hole where Ethan's life hung, suspended somewhere high above the consulting jury. Air was thin. Belief, thinner. And what of the trust he'd prattled about to Miri?

A vapor.

This would be a good time to pray, but what to say? *Lord, I'm scared to hang? God, I don't want to die? Give me a second chance?*

His shoulders sagged, drawing him closer to the pit. He'd made a mess of his life, and now it was too late. He blew out a long breath, exhaling the last of himself, every wicked bit.

"Your will be done, Lord," he whispered.

From the jurors' gallery, a single, deep voice called out. "We have reached a decision, Lord Mayor."

33

Ethan stood alone. Exposed. Naked in a way that the rags he wore would not cover. Is this what it would feel like on judgment day?

"Guilty as charged, your honor."

The foreman's words sank deep, settling low in his belly. He'd hang for this—for a crime he did not commit. The injustice of it ignited a holy anger, and he started to shake, loosing his lips. "I did not kill Will Brayden!"

"He's right," a booming voice called from behind.

Pandemonium erupted. Spectators stood, leaning over each other to catch a glimpse of the new arrival. Duffy and the clerk argued something about witnesses. Even the jurors broke rank, craning their necks like worms popping from the ground.

Though Ethan thought he recognized the voice, he turned to look. The guard beside him cuffed him on the head before he could make sense of it.

"Face the judge, or I'll whop you again."

His ears rang from the blow. The judge's pounding gavel didn't help.

"Order! I will have order in this courtroom!"

Like petulant children, the spectators continued to thrum, albeit at a more respectable level.

But apparently not quiet enough. The judge's eyes went from ice to glaciers. "What is this about? And mark my words, sir, this had better be of import."

"I have a witness concerning the case of Ethan Goodwin." Newton's volume, no doubt about it.

"Witness!" Duffy cried. "That boy's a—"

"Enough." The judge banged his gavel again. If he ever lost his job, he'd make a fine carpenter.

Ethan shook his head, clearing out the random thought. Why could he not focus on the pertinent?

"This is highly irregular." The judge's brow furrowed, and he crooked a finger toward the rear of the room. "Nonetheless, step forward, boy."

If he slanted his eyes, Ethan could see just far enough without turning his head to notice a ragamuffin walking a death march.

Giving an exasperated sigh that ruffled the curls on his wig, the judge leaned over the bench. "Come, come! We've not got all day. What have you to say, boy?"

"Awuzairsuh."

"Louder, lad."

"I was there, sir."

Ethan cocked his head, careful to keep the movement a notch below smack worthy. Recognition, though slow in coming, was a surprising guest. What could Jack the crossing sweep possibly have to say?

"I see'd it happen, I did."

Rummaging through a stack of disordered memories, Ethan tried to reconstruct that horrid eve. Sick. Opium. Money. Fight. Death. Jack hadn't played into it at all. Why would the boy lie on his behalf?

"Tell us what happened," said the judge.

"Hethenanwil thaycumin—"

"Speak up, boy!"

Jack took a big breath, but he did not look up. "Ethan an' Will, they come in late. To the alley, I mean. Tha's where we stay. It were drizzly an' cold. I'd curled up a'ready. Ethan, he were sick, hacking up a fit, and tripped o'er me."

It all came back. Stunning. Clear. Every last detail. Ethan's mouth opened, more from a need for air than to speak.

"Then that bast—"

"Watch it, boy. You're in court," warned the judge.

Jack pushed his toe around in little circles. Ethan felt as chagrined as he. If Jack couldn't use his street language, how would he speak?

"The ba ... uh ... bad man, Thorne, he crawled out o' the shadows, grousing about some coin. Ethan tol' him he din't have it. He tol' him plain as I'm a-tellin' you. Din't stop Thorne from pullin' a knife, though. Ethan din't see that. Will did. He took it, took what were meant for Ethan."

The boy's toe stopped.

So did his words.

When had the courtroom become so quiet?

The judge tapped his chin with his index finger, obviously in thought. But what exactly was he thinking? How much value would he place on a street sweeper's word? Finally, he folded one hand over the other, fixing his terrible gaze on the lad. "Then what?"

"Ethan, why he were awful mad, he was. His friend a-bleedin' in the alley and all. He hauled off and stabbed Thorne a good one, but it weren't no killin' blow. Ethan ranned off. Scairt, I guess. Don't blame him. I would be too. And Thorne, why he stumbled away late in the wee hours. The watch don't call out in Old Nichol, but I knowed the night were terrible spent by then. Tha's all what I got to say."

The judge looked from the boy to Ethan. Jurors, at each other. The spectators blinked.

A fierce glower tugged down the corners of the judge's mouth. "If this were true, boy, then why did you not report it to the authorities sooner? Why this sudden and last-minute testimony?"

Jack shriveled, shoulders hunched, chin tucked. "Eyewer skairtoe—"

"You will lift your face and speak clearly to this court, or I will swap you for Goodwin here and now."

Jack's head jerked up like a marionette's. Beneath a layer of grime, his skin blanched. "I … were … scairt … o' Thorne!"

The judge frowned. "Those above the law have nothing to fear, boy."

Jack's lower lip jutted out. "Thorne weren't above no law. He'd as soon slit my throat as he did ol' Will's."

"Do you publicly malign the character of a law man?"

Jack's toe circled furiously. He looked over at Ethan, then the judge. "Yes, sir. I do."

A wave of whispers and mumbles rolled from one end of the courtroom to the other. The gavel cracked.

"Very well. Far too much time has been spent on this case as is. Boy, report to my clerk immediately. I have need of a staff member brave enough to speak truth under pressure. As for you …" The judge focused on Ethan.

Those weren't glaciers for eyes. They were pools.

"I find Ethan Goodwin not guilty of the crime in the murder of Will Brayden. You are acquitted, sir. Next?"

The guard unlocked his fetters.

The clerk told him to move.

Newton clapped him on the back and urged him away, for a new prisoner was already vying for his spot.

His body went through all the motions of freedom, but his mind would not—could not—pull it off the table and hold it. Just like that, the nightmare was over? He felt shaky and clammy and—

"... hear me?" Newton shoved his face into Ethan's. "Lad?"

"I'm ... I'm free?" The words tasted sweeter than a raisin cake.

The reverend's laugh boomed, earning a serious round of gavel banging from the judge.

"Come on." Newton angled his head. "Let's take this outside."

Life and light and hope, too long held at bay, surged through him. He breathed a prayer, thanking God that His will hadn't included death this time, then smiled. "Yes, my friend, I should love to take this outside."

He fell in beside Newton. They strode to the Old Bailey's front door, each step bringing him closer to fresh air and daylight. He'd never take such blessings for granted again.

"Not so fast, Mr. Goodwin." A man rose from a nearby bench. Narrow shouldered but tailored to perfection, he held a hat in one hand and an ivory-headed walking stick in the other. "A few words with you, if you please."

Of course. He should've known. Trepidation sank to the bottom of his gut. This had been far too easy of an escape. "The judge said I am free to go."

"And freedom implies choice. Will you choose to humor me, sir? I have a carriage waiting outside."

Ethan shot a glance at his companion. Newton raised his brows but said nothing.

The choice was his alone.

∽⚬⚬⚬∾

Miri slapped her shoulder, then scratched, hard enough that the coarse fabric bunched beneath her fingernails. Ahh. Relief for one blessed moment. For the past week, ever since she'd put on this natty gown, her skin crawled. Literally. Head lice she could deal with, but fleas? She shuddered for the hundredth time. And for as many times, wished down the wrath of God on Witherskim, Knight, and Fothergill for putting her here.

Her movement caused Lil to stir. The girl shifted, keeping her head on Miri's lap. She seemed so tired lately. Withdrawn. Not snapping away like her usual self with the other ladies. Perhaps she'd given up.

Not that Miri blamed her. What was there to look forward to other than bleedings, purgings, and just for fun, the occasional blistering?

The door opened, but Miri didn't bother to look. Too much effort. Come to think of it, fatigue was beginning to weigh on her as well.

In came the crony, gruel bucket in hand. The shuffle of her feet didn't sound quite right. Too forceful, too deliberate.

Miri glanced over, then did a double take. The woman dragged the gruel pot with both hands as if it weighed eighty stone. Her collar draped open, and her sleeves were pushed up, exposing wiry arms with a pink rash flushing her skin. Her mobcap wilted, and beneath it, her hair lay plastered in streaks against a glistening forehead.

Miri nudged Lil. The girl sat up, rubbing her eyes. "Look," whispered Miri.

Lil stretched, all the while following the crony with her eyes.

The woman stopped midroom, releasing the bucket. Grey paste slopped over the rim. She straightened and revolved in a slow circle, both hands to her head. Was she trying to keep her brains in or the snapping of the women out?

Miri stood. "Are you well?"

The woman turned toward her voice. Her mouth opened, and her throat convulsed. Either she was going to speak for the first time ever, or she might throw up.

Neither. She crumpled.

All the women rose at once, gathering around her—but not too close. She smelled bad. Sick bad.

Fever bad.

"We've got to get some help." Miri looked to Lil. "You know the corridors better than I. Will you come?"

Lil shrank.

As did Miri at the thought of trying to weave her way alone amongst the maze of hallways. She held out her hand to the girl. "It's all right, Lil. We'll stay together the whole time. I promise."

The girl hesitated, glanced at the crony, then slipped her fingers through Miri's. Trust added an intensity to her brown eyes—hopefully it was trust and not the beginning of a fever.

Miri led her down the stairs, along the corridor, then stopped where two other hallways converged. "Okay, Lil. You guide us from here."

"Where?" Lil's nasal tone sounded like a goose honk.

Good question. Where should they go? Though he was a doctor, Miri had seen more than she ever wanted to of Pembernip. Probably Mr. Spyder would do. Too bad they couldn't both just run off. Escape. But that would leave Roland—

She grasped Lil's arm. "Do you know where the men's quarters are?"

Lil scrunched her face, then finally nodded.

"There first. Then Mr. Spyder's office. Lead on, Lil."

The girl tugged her to the right instead of the usual left, then down a stairwell. The temperature cooled as they tromped down another set of stairs. The air took on a damp, earthy quality, like a root cellar, only … Miri sniffed. Rotted. Sickly sweet and acridly so.

The staircase opened onto a small area, no bigger than the rectory's pantry. The floor was dirt. A torch sputtered in an iron holder attached to the wall. Miri's stomach knotted. She'd never seen a dungeon before, but she could imagine none worse. This was where they kept her brother? Wasn't this supposed to be an institution of rehabilitation?

Miri lunged for the door and yanked the knob. Of course it didn't open. That she expected it should made her realize she'd resided at Sheltering Arms one day too many.

"Roland!" she yelled, then pressed her ear against the wood. No answer. No cry. "ROLAND!"

Nothing.

Miri turned, hope dashed to small bits.

Lil stared, wide-eyed.

"You think I'm mad, don't you?" Half a smile lifted her mouth. "Mayhap I am, Lil. Come on. Let's go."

Retracing their steps, they wound back up to the main floor and entered more familiar territory. Miri braced herself, as always, for crossing the big room. So far, no matter how much she expected it, the noise shocked her afresh each time.

Lil darted forward.

Miri stopped.

Gooseflesh rose along her arms. Her neck. Her legs.

Silence filled the great room, like the sudden absence of crickets chirruping just before a tempest hit. Stillness so complete, it lived.

What would she see if she dared look into one of those doors' peepholes? Wild eyes staring back, empty and unblinking? Madwomen cowering in a corner from only God-knew-what? Piles of corpses?

Without a step, her eyes traveled from door to door, coming to rest on the largest. The portal to freedom.

And it gaped open.

Lil plowed into her, wrapping her arms tight around her middle.

Miri ran a hand over her shorn head. "Don't fret, Lil," she whispered. To speak aloud would corrupt the balance of the universe.

They scooted across the room, out the door, and sped down the corridor.

Then froze.

At their feet lay a shirt, heaped as if thrown in a hurry. Stripped off and cast aside on the run. Like the wearer couldn't wait to get the thing off.

Lil trembled against her.

Farther ahead lay a bare-chested man. A big man. Mr. Graves.

Miri tiptoed closer with awkward steps. Lil was a growth against her.

"Mr. Graves?"

He turned his head, but not to her voice. Sweat ran in rivulets down his temple. A rash, darker and angrier than the crony's, covered his chest and arms—nowhere else, though. Definitely not the pox.

Miri tightened her arms around Lil. Either this was a simple case of the measles or ...

Typhus.

34

Ethan glanced out the carriage window, ending the conversation between him and Mr. Spindle. What was the point? Though Ethan lobbed question after question, the man returned no answers of substance. The fellow belonged in parliament.

His shoulder bumped against the paneled wall of the coach as they rattled along. Tasseled curtains slapped his cheek when they rounded a corner. Finer houses lined this street, and if they held their westward course, they'd become grander still. But where they'd end up, and why, rankled him as much as the clattering wheels.

Perhaps he'd made a mistake in coming. The longer he tarried in London, the longer it would be until he saw Miri again. With Roland taken away, how was she faring? A wry smile twitched his lips. No doubt much better than he had.

At last the coach stopped swaying. The door opened from the outside, and Ethan waited for Spindle to exit.

Spindle angled his head. "After you, sir."

Sir? Surely this was a joke. He studied the man's pinched face for a trace of humor. Not a muscle twitched.

Fine. Ethan stepped from stair to gravel. The drive led to an enormous brick Tudor. Sun glinted off so many panes, he blinked. Whoever owned this mansion didn't care a fig about window taxes.

Marble lions flanked the main door. Spindle grabbled hold of the knocker and rapped it against a brass plate with a fancy, engraved *W*.

The door opened immediately. Apparently the footman had nothing better to do than sit on a cushion behind it and wait for a rap—and by the looks of his plush livery, that's exactly what he did. From the tips of his gilt-cord shoulder knots down to his white silk hose edged in lace, the man was nothing more than a bauble.

"Mr. Spindle and Mr. Goodwin to see Barrister Wolmington." Spindle handed the footman a card.

So they were seeing a barrister. Which law had he broken to earn a visit to the man's house?

The footman glanced at Ethan, hesitating longer than protocol allowed. Not that Ethan blamed him. Fresh from Newgate, he didn't quite fit the décor of the place.

Spindle cleared his throat.

"This way," said the footman, shaken from his musing. He executed a perfect military pivot, then led them through a foyer big enough to hold a state dinner. All the while, he rested his gloved fingertips upon his nose. Ethan lifted his arm and sniffed. Did he really smell that bad?

The footman parked them in a sitting room off to one side. As soon as he left, Ethan turned to Spindle. "I'm not sure what your game is, but we both know I don't belong here. There's no need for charades on my account. If I'm in some kind of trouble, just tell me now and get it over with."

Spindle flipped up his coattails and took his time settling on a chair. At last he looked up. "You are very direct, sir."

"And you are not."

A thin smile drew up the corners of Spindle's mouth. "I daresay you are an astute judge of character, sir."

Ethan swept a hand from head to toe. "Do I look like I deserve the 'sir'?"

Spindle choked, coughing so hard he pounded his chest. Ethan fully expected him to dislodge a fur ball.

The footman returned, giving Ethan the evil eye as if he were to blame for the red-faced Spindle. "The barrister will see you now."

Spindle stood, yet again deferring to Ethan to precede him.

Ethan fell in step behind the footman, and when he did, the man lifted his glove to his nose once more.

"Don't worry," Ethan said. "You're not downwind of me."

The man's shoulders stiffened.

Ethan smirked.

They entered a room done in burled maple paneling and port-colored carpeting, much smaller than the sitting room and foyer combined. Pipe tobacco scented the air. Tooled leather wingbacks occupied the space in front of a large desk. Next to it sat a man, his foot propped on a padded stool. He was shriveled, like an empty walnut shell that'd been tossed aside.

"Banes." His voice suggested much more strength than Ethan would credit him. "You are dismissed for now, but do not go far. And for heaven's sake, stop covering your nose."

The barrister frowned, then turned to them. "Cheeky fellow. Rather a good looker, though. You'll not find one taller or with better turned out legs." He nodded at his own foot. "Forgive me, gentlemen, if I don't rise. Flare-up of the gout, I'm afraid. I see you've found your man, Mr. Spindle."

"Indeed, sir," answered Spindle.

"Good. Good. Your documents are all in order there." He pointed to a stack of papers on the far side of the desk, then gazed at Ethan. "Do sit, Mr. Goodwin. This shan't take long, but you'll be much more comfortable seated."

Ethan lifted a brow as he sank onto a chair. Why would a barrister be concerned about his comfort? He ran his fingers absently over the fine upholstery and leaned forward. "Can you tell me what this is about?"

"You look rather amused, Mr. Goodwin. Is this really such a novelty for you?"

"Your pardon?" Ethan asked.

"Wealth," the barrister answered.

Ethan snorted. "I wasn't aware that gout affected one's eyesight. Surely you can see—at least your footman did—that I am not a wealthy man."

The man waved his hand as if he flicked a fly, then glanced at Spindle. "Are you prepared, sir?"

Spindle gave a curt nod. "Quite."

"Then proceed," said Wolmington.

Ethan sat back and folded his arms. "By all means."

"As I have noted, you are very direct." Spindle positioned himself in front of Ethan and leaned back against the desk, looking down his nose at him. "Not unlike your father."

Ethan rolled his eyes and stood. "If that's what this concerns, count me out." He turned to leave.

"Please, sir, if you would but listen."

Spindle could have no idea what he'd just said. Ethan wheeled about and jammed a finger against the man's chest. "Listen? You mean like how my father listened to me? The family butler paid me more attention than that man! Why should I listen—"

"Your father is dead, sir."

Ethan's hand dropped. Dead? The word bounced like a rubber ball. The more he tried to grasp it, to feel it, the more it ricocheted about. He should be sad. He should be overcome, or undone, or ... something. Though he tried, searching every nook inside him, he felt nothing. The part of his heart that should be welling with grief was bone dry. Parched white bones, long dead.

He relaxed his jaw, unaware until it loosened that he'd been clenching his teeth. "You've wasted your time dragging me from the streets. My brother, Richard, will see to everything. He always does."

"Your brother is deceased as well."

The ball bounced back, springing and jouncing so that his breathing turned irregular. Weak in the knees, he sat. "What happened?"

"Highwaymen," answered Spindle. "Your father liked to travel rather ... ostentatiously, making for a tempting target."

Ethan rubbed his eyes, pushing back the headache screaming for release. "That's putting it mildly. My father was a pompous, prideful—"

"Sometimes sorrow is best expressed in silence, Mr. Goodwin," interrupted the barrister.

The reprimand, though disguised, slapped his anger down to size, and he nodded. "Point taken. Go on, Mr. Spindle."

"As I was saying, Lord Trenton and your brother, Richard, were to attend a state affair. It ran late. They should have taken lodging, but there was a hunt early the following morn, one your father was loathe to miss."

Of course. His father always made time for entertainment, just not for his second son. Ethan stood and paced the small room, hoping to walk away from the bitterness nipping at his heels.

"They were on a stretch of road in Sherbourne. Apparently Lord Trenton refused the highwaymen—"

"Refused?" Ethan stopped in his tracks. What a fool.

"I cannot say it was the most prudent of decisions—"

"Let's call it what it was, man. Pig-headed. Greedy. Asinine!" He glared at Spindle as his words echoed off the walls.

Spindle tugged at his collar.

"You are upset, Mr. Goodwin. Might I suggest you resume your seat?" asked the barrister.

Ethan ran a hand through his hair. He didn't want to sit. He wanted to run and run and never—

"This belongs to you, now." Spindle cut through his thoughts and stepped toward him. "Hold out your hand, sir."

Spindle shook open a small velvet bag and dropped a heavy golden ring onto Ethan's palm.

And that's when it hit.

He staggered back to the chair, the ring breathing life into memories he'd long ago thought dead. The few tender moments. Some laughter, sparse but real. Sanguine days from early childhood. Things he didn't want to remember, because to do so would remind him just how big his loss really was.

Just like that, no more family. How many times had he wished for this? Now that the moment had arrived, the relief he expected to feel was overshadowed by a remorse so strong, it bound his heart. He hung his head. A fine sweat dampened the hair on his brow. This signet belonged to his father, to Richard. It always had and always would.

He held out the ring to Spindle. "Take it. I was never trained for this. I was the black sheep put out to pasture. I can't—"

"You are."

Looking up, he locked eyes with Spindle. "You don't understand—"

"You are Lord Trenton now, Ethan Goodwin. That's all there is to it."

Though it'd been the smallest of possibilities all along, he never dreamed the title would fall to him.

And likely neither had his father or Richard.

Ethan burst out laughing, hard enough that tears wetted the creases at his eyes. If God could make a carpenter into a Savior, a slave trader into a reverend, why not an opium addict into an earl?

"Are you all right, sir?" Spindle leaned forward, concern accentuating his pinched features.

"Probably not," Ethan managed between laughs.

"There are a few documents to sign. When you're ready, that is."

"I'll never be ready. Oh, don't frown so, Mr. Spindle." With one hand, he scrubbed his face, wiping away the last of his mirth. "I did not say I wouldn't sign."

He'd be a fool to turn down an opportunity such as this. Pushing out of the chair, he took up a quill from the desk, then scratched his signature where the man indicated.

"You know, Spindle." Ethan set down the pen when finished and eyed the man. "I meant it when I said I don't have a clue as to how to run an estate."

Spindle cocked his head. "Are you asking for my assistance, sir?"

"Begging is more apt."

"Direct and humble." A smile softened the tight lines of Spindle's face. "I think we shall get on famously, my lord. I accept."

"Good." He stepped over to the barrister. "I'm … uh … not familiar with operating on the acceptable side of the law, sir, but from now on, I intend to."

Hearing his own words struck a chord deep within. Here was his chance—the one he'd mused about in a church sanctuary a lifetime ago—to lead a respectable, God-fearing life. Closing his eyes, he silently prayed. *Amazing, God. Simply amazing. You have done above and beyond anything I could have planned. Thank You.*

"Are you all right, Mr. Goodwin?"

He blinked. The barrister's brow furrowed at him. Half a grin lifted Ethan's mouth. "Yes, sir. I believe that I am, or will be with your help."

The barrister's eyes sparkled. "You've got style, my lord, and a bit of cheek. I like that in a man. I should be happy to assist you any time." Without rising, he reached to a side curio and rang a bell for the footman, Banes.

Ethan took the hint and crossed to the door. "Thank you both, gentlemen. It's been a rather eventful day."

"I daresay," said Spindle. "I shall file the appropriate documents, then contact you, my lord."

Banes entered. Before following him out, Ethan turned to Spindle. "So … what exactly do I do now?"

And behind him, in just above a whisper, the footman said, "Might I suggest a bath, sir?"

⁀⊙⊙⁀

"Come on, Lil. Please? For me?" Miri propped the girl up and held a spoon to her mouth. Most of the thin broth dribbled down Lil's chin, but some slipped past her deformed lips. Miri couldn't blame the girl for not wanting to drink the foul stuff, especially if it tasted half as bad as it smelled. It made Miri's own eyes water just to serve it.

Lil's chest fluttered. Miri set down the spoon and eased the girl's head to the pallet. Lil blinked up at her, then slowly closed her eyes.

Miri closed hers as well. *Please, God, don't let her die, nor my brother. And wherever he may be, please watch over Ethan.*

How long she sat there, she couldn't say, but long enough that her head bobbed, jerking her awake. She rose, careful not to jar Lil, then stretched and arched her back. Though fatigue numbed her mind, the muscles along her hips and spine had plenty of feeling— sharp and relentless. She pressed her hand to them and kneaded. Bending over pallet after pallet was getting to her.

Surveying the big room, she tried to think of whom she might have missed. Most of the women were here now, laid out like bits of cloth on a drying field. A few remained in their rooms, babbling as usual, but the overarching sound in the great room had changed to lungs gasping for breath and pain-filled moans.

A fickle lover, Sheltering Arms had exchanged its embrace of madness for death.

"Miss Brayden." Dr. Pembernip summoned her from the doorway with a crook of his finger.

She wound her way through the maze of pallets, her feet unaccountably slow. Looking down, she fully expected to see someone holding onto her ankles. Funny how far away the floor looked.

"I've mixed up a new batch of powders." He held out an envelope. "Stir this in with the broth, and we'll see if it doesn't put everyone to rights."

The pungent scent of garlic wafted up, tickling her nose as she grasped the envelope. A sneeze shook her whole body.

The doctor cocked his head. "How are you faring, Miss Brayden?"

She threw back her shoulders, refusing to wince at how it jolted her back. "Let's see … I'm locked in an asylum against my will, forced to care for women who are dying right and left. I am bone-tired and could use a long soak in a tub of rose water. Other than that—"

"Delightful!" A smile covered half his face. "So happy to hear it."

Nettlesome man! She frowned.

"Oh, don't fret, my dear. I have not forgotten our bargain. Soon this will all be but a memory for you."

She swept a hand across her brow. Her fingers came away damp. "See that you don't, for I shall hold you accountable, sir."

"No doubt. Very well, now have at it. Try out those powders on the women, and I'll tend to the men."

Miri touched his sleeve before he could turn. "My brother?"

Pembernip patted her hand. She should probably feel patronized but couldn't work up the effort.

"Intriguing as ever," he said, "and wholly, completely healthy. Thus far, at any rate."

He turned away, and Miri watched him go, relief rendering her motionless until the groans of the women behind her broke her stupor. Fortified with a deep breath, she spun and retrieved the cup she'd left by Lil, then zigzagged to the other side of the room where a large pot sat. Dumping in the contents of the envelope, she stirred, pausing to sneeze yet again. She stirred some more, trying to remember what to do next, but who could think when it was so stifling in here? Oh, for a cool breeze.

Setting down the spoon, she fanned herself. The action made her sleeve snuggle down to her elbow.

Her hand faltered to a stop.

She lifted her forearm inches from her eyes, mouth dropping. So did her stomach. She stared, mesmerized in a freakish way.

Thousands of tiny red pinpricks dotted her skin.

35

Ethan climbed the steps of St. Mary Woolnoth's, the summer sun warm on his shoulders. He paused at the spot where he'd collapsed on his last visit and lifted his face to the sky. Heat warmed his cheeks, gratitude his soul.

So much has changed, God. Thank You.

He pressed on and pushed open the scarred oak door. Some churches kept strict hours, but not this one. Newton would have it no other way.

Charlie, the warden's boy, was busy scraping wax from a candle stand in an alcove off the foyer. When he saw Ethan, he stopped so suddenly that the wrought-iron stand wobbled. "G'day, sir. Show you to the sanctuary?"

"I came to see Reverend Newton, lad. Can you tell me where he is?"

"I can do better than that. I'll lead you." The boy wiped his hands on his shirt and scooted past Ethan, eager as a puppy after a bone.

Ethan grabbed Charlie's collar and gently tugged him back. "I wouldn't want to take you from your work. You can simply tell me. No doubt I'll find my way."

The boy darted a look around, then cupped a hand to his mouth, whispering for only Ethan to hear, "I don't mind a bit, sir. Scrapin' wax is my least fav'rite duty."

"I see." He knew that look of desperation on Charlie's face, a reminder of hated tasks in bygone days. He relented with a nod. "All right, then. Lead on."

They skirted the sanctuary and entered a side door, then descended a stairwell. Foggy memories of the last time he'd been here, sick and on the run, left an unpleasant taste in his mouth.

Charlie stopped and knocked on a door, opening it after hearing a hearty, "Enter."

A booming voice met Ethan's ears before he could cross the threshold.

"Well, well." Newton rose from a chair, twirling one finger in the air. "Let's have a good look."

Ethan held out his arms and turned. His cutaway jacket, fashionable yet not gaudy, fit him well. Brass buttons were enough glitz for him. He'd chosen quality fabrics, refusing all ruffles, laces, and frills. Just because he was an earl didn't mean he had to look it. He lifted one brow. "Satisfied?"

"Only God satisfies, boy." The grin Newton flashed bordered on wicked. Was that allowable for a reverend? "Or should I say *my lord*?"

"You may say what you please." Ethan strode to the man and clapped him on the back. "But I won't answer to it, not from you."

Newton laughed, the bellow filling the room like a tidal wave.

"At least you smell better." The reverend pushed an empty chair toward him and took the other. "I suspect you came to talk of things besides your appearance though, eh?"

Ethan sat, smoothing his palms along his thighs. Suddenly this courtesy call didn't seem nearly as trivial. He'd known the man for what, five, maybe six months?—and in that time his respect and affection for the reverend had grown deep roots. Pulling away might leave a bigger hole than he imagined.

He swallowed back a swell of sudden emotion. "I came to say good-bye."

His sober proclamation robbed the smile from Newton's face. "I thought as much."

"Did you?" He locked eyes with Newton, wondering how this one man could know him through and through, more intimately than his father ever had.

"Aye, lad. Besides the fact that you're a high and mighty land-owner now, I suspect there's a certain young lady ye'll be wantin' to claim. Am I right?"

The thought of claiming Miri, of making her his own, burned a fire through his veins. He pulled at his neckerchief for air. "Aye. That you are. And none too soon for my liking."

"I should like to meet her someday." Newton's eyes twinkled. "She must be a fair treasure."

Ethan took a deep breath. The man couldn't have spoken a truer word. Everything about Miri was fair, from the way the sun glinted copper strands in her curls, to the curve of her cheeks and softness of her lips. But she possessed far more than beauty. Nursing him back to health, caring for him at the risk of her own censure … how many other women would take in a vagabond, especially one bearing tidings of her brother's death?

He nodded. "She is a treasure, indeed."

Impatience urged him to his feet, and he offered his hand to Newton. "For that and other reasons, I must make haste. But I could not leave without a good-bye, my friend. Your words of faith have been a lifeline. Without you, I …"

His throat clogged, and he had to work to clear it. "I'd still be on my way to hell, were it not for you."

"Don't thank me, lad, thank—"

"I know. And I do." Ethan glanced at the ceiling. "Thank You, God."

Newton clasped his forearm. "Keep that up, no matter the circumstance."

"I shall."

"You promise?" The man's grip tightened on his arm. His tone took on an unmistakable urgency.

Ethan cocked his head, studying the reverend's sea-grey eyes. A storm brewed there, one his answer would either quell or unleash. How curious and ... unnerving.

"I promise," he said.

Newton's head bobbed. "I hope so, lad. I hope so."

Ethan frowned. What was that supposed to mean?

❧

The pain in Miri's head competed with the ache in her muscles as she pushed up from the stool. A wince twitched her cheek. Even her bones hurt, down to the marrow. How much longer could she keep this up? She steeled herself against giving in to a coughing fit and willed her feet to move. She'd keep this up until each of these women was well, that's what. Then Pembernip would have to honor his word to set her free.

Focus on that, girl. Focus. Better to set her mind on that than on the chills shaking through her limbs.

She wound her way to Lil's pallet, an easier route now that so many bodies didn't block the path. Thank God Lil wasn't one of those resting six feet under behind the asylum. Kneeling by the girl's side, Miri set a cool cloth on her forehead. Lil's eyes opened, bright and clear.

Miri smiled. "You're better!"

Half the girl's face lifted, the biggest grin she could likely manage.

"Oh, Lil." Miri's words traveled on a sigh. "I've been so afraid."

The girl reached out and patted her hand. Her fingers felt like ice, causing a sudden shiver.

Lil's eyes widened. "You're sick?" she honked.

Panic increased the pounding in Miri's head. No! She wasn't sick. She'd probably heard the girl wrong.

"What's that you say?" Dr. Pembernip's voice asked from behind them.

How had she missed his footsteps? Miri stood on legs that wobbled like a foal's.

Pembernip grasped her arm. "Are you well?"

How did he do that? He stood inches from her, but his voice was in the other room.

"I'm fine." She jerked her head aside. Her voice was out there too.

He crooked a finger under her chin and turned her face to his. "Perhaps I should be the judge of that."

To give in to the horrid sensations attacking her senses would break their bargain, and she'd never get out of here. Summoning all her strength, she pulled away. "I said I am fine, Doctor."

He nodded, but a shrewd gleam lit his eyes. "As you say, my dear." He glanced down at Lil. "I see your patient is recovering nicely."

Relief should have eased the tension clawing into her shoulders. It didn't. "Yes. I think Lil is ..." She scrunched her brow, trying hard to remember. "Lil is ..."

"You were about to say?" asked Pembernip.

Exactly. What was she talking about? She pressed her hand to her forehead, willing her thoughts to gel.

"Miss Brayden?"

She startled. *Pull yourself together, girl.* "Yes, I meant to tell you, we need more ..."

Licking her lips—oh, how dry she was—she tried to think beyond the hammering in her skull. They were out of something. Something important. She was supposed to ask him for ... Think. *Think.*

" ... not good. Not good at all." Pembernip's voice ran off to the other room again, though his eyes burned into hers.

No, that wasn't right. The only thing burning was her.

At least the floor felt cool as she folded onto it.

36

Ethan pulled hard on the reins, halting his horse in front of the rectory. Glancing up at a window, he pictured Miri, nose pressed against the glass, waiting for him. She'd run out the door any minute now, arms open wide, and nestle against his chest. Never to part again. He smirked at the irrational expectation, then slung his leg over the saddle before his mount completely stopped. He'd have a fair amount of explaining to do before he could expect such a reaction as that. The horse blew out a snort. Apparently the fast clip he'd ridden from London wasn't appreciated.

He took the steps three at a time, reaching the door in five long strides. His heart pounded as loud as his fist on the oak frame. Oh, how good she would feel in his arms. How sweet she would smell.

No one answered.

"Hello?" He banged harder with the heel of his hand. It smarted, but no matter—Miri waited on the other side.

"Miri!" He'd hammer loud enough to be heard in the garden if he had to—

That's it. Mayhap she tended her garden out back on such a fine, late summer morn. He dashed down the steps and sprinted around the corner.

Gradually, his feet slowed. Across the field, some pony carts, a wagon or two, and several tethered horses congregated close to the sanctuary. A chorus swelled out the open door. Idiot. He'd given no thought to the day of the week.

He straightened his riding jacket and smoothed his breeches, brushing off the dust from the road, then crossed to the church. Slipping in the door, he remained at the back, straining for a glimpse of Miri. With everyone standing, he could not see past the heads of taller men in the last rows.

But he got a grand view of the vicar up in the pulpit. He was a bald, sweaty sort, red in the face and gullet, with a long neck, like a turkey in a holy smock. How odd. Where was Fothergill?

The hymn ended, and the man lifted his hand in blessing. After a passionless benediction, pew doors opened and feet shuffled into the aisles. That must've been some sermon. Ethan leaned to the right, desperate to catch a glimpse of Miri.

A voice came from the left. "Good day, sir. I don't believe we've met. I am—"

"Magistrate Buckle." Ethan recognized the voice and turned.

The man's face screwed up as he tapped a finger to his chin. "You are … no. Don't tell me. I feel I know you."

Squire Gullaby joined his side, wide-eyed. "Mr. Goodwin?"

Their shock, while amusing, hindered his search for Miri. He gave them a curt nod. "Gentlemen, please excuse—"

"How you have changed!" Gullaby's eyes traveled the length of him, landing on his signet ring. "And for the better, I might add."

"Yes," said Ethan. "Now, if you'll ex—"

"But how did you"—the squire stepped up to him, his head

barely cresting the top of Ethan's shoulders. He aimed a fat finger at him—"meet with such fortune?"

Ethan knew that look well. Even more, the tone. Generally, though, he'd been guilty of the theft the question implied. Not this time, nor ever again. He lifted his chin, making the squire appear all the shorter. "My father, Lord Trenton, has recently passed. His estate is now mine."

"*Lord* Trenton? But that would make you …" Understanding registered on the squire's red face, and he retreated.

"Exactly." With a look he'd seen his father use a thousand times, Ethan dismissed him and peered over the man's head for Miri. By now several others had gathered around as well, making it impossible to see as far as her pew. "As I've said, gentlemen, excuse me."

The smell of horehound and onions broke through the crowd, preceding a stick figure dressed in a velveteen jacket and striped socks. "What's going on here?"

Ethan rolled his eyes. Just what he needed. Witherskim. "Nothing of your concern."

Recognition twisted Witherskim's face, bringing his nose to an even finer point. The man ought to dip it in ink and make a fine living as a scribe. "You!"

Ethan frowned. He didn't have time for this. "I'll say this one last time. Slowly, so that you might understand." He nodded at the fellow. "Please excuse me. I should like to speak with Miri Brayden."

"Hah!" Witherskim's egg breakfast traveled on his breath. "She no longer lives here, Mr. Good. Oh, that's right. It was Goodwin, wasn't it?"

"Stand down, man." Gullaby disguised his warning in a cough.

A failed attempt, for Witherskim shot forward a step. "I remember now. Goodwin, the murderer."

Gullaby sing-songed without moving his lips. "Be careful."

Witherskim merely snorted. He either didn't listen or didn't care. Probably both.

Neither did Ethan. Leastwise not the words about himself. "What was that you said about Miri? She no longer lives here?"

"That strumpet—"

"Mind your tongue, Witherskim." Gullaby did nothing to conceal his warning this time.

And Witherskim was too stupid to shut up. "That trollop—"

Ethan advanced, fists clenched at his sides. Though he'd like nothing better than to give the man a fat lip, he restrained the urge. Not in a church. "I believe I made you apologize to the lady once before."

Witherskim rolled back his shoulders and tipped his chin. "Not this time."

Ethan grabbed him by the lapels, lifting him off his feet. "*Every* time."

The crowd stepped back.

Witherskim blanched. "Put me down."

"Apologize!"

"She's not even here, man!"

Ethan twisted the fabric in his hands. Where could she be? And why? Questions buzzed like pesky flies. He leaned into Witherskim's flushed face. "Where is she?"

"Put me down and I'll tell you, you big ape!"

Ethan splayed his fingers and let the man fall.

Immediately, Witherskim set about tugging down his waistcoat and straightening the crumpled fabric, pausing only to direct the evil eye at both Ethan and Gullaby.

"Where is Miri Brayden?" Ethan looked from man to man.

A fine sheen of perspiration glistened on the magistrate's brow. Gullaby's neck and face deepened in color. Both pressed tight their lips.

Only Witherskim answered, still fussing with his rumpled collar. "She's in the Sheltering Arms Asylum, caged up with that half-wit brother of hers."

Ethan's blood ran cold. An asylum for her brother made perfect sense, but ... "Why on earth would she be there?"

Witherskim stretched to his full height.

"Don't do it, man," Gullaby cautioned from behind, loud enough for all to hear.

A haughty smirk pulled up the right side of Witherskim's mouth. "Because a strumpet deserves to be locked away. I simply made sure she got what she merited."

The ice in Ethan's veins turned to fire. He flung out his arm, collecting Witherskim in a headlock, and dragged him out the door.

They weren't in church anymore.

Ethan shoved him, and the man stumbled forward, flailing like the village idiot along the walkway. A collective gasp sounded behind them.

Witherskim caught his balance and turned, fists raised. When he advanced, Ethan swung low. A solid blow to the man's abdomen doubled him over. One last kidney shot would end all of Witherskim's slurs against Miri forever. Just one, quick jab.

He clenched his fists tighter. Giving in to the rage shaking through him would make him no different than Thorne—no different from the man he used to be.

God help me.

Drawing in a shaky breath, Ethan spun and tromped across the grounds. Emotions roiled through him too fast to name as he rubbed his bruised knuckles. His sweet, sweet Miri in an asylum? The thought punched him harder than the blow he'd dealt Witherskim.

Dear God, please—he stopped midprayer and dropped to his knees.

There, on the side of the path, lay the rosebush Miri had babied. It was dead.

❧

"Papa?"

Miri bolted up. Impossible. His bones had long ago turned to dust. Yet he seemed so real. So near. A dark figure, just around the corner, his coattails fluttering on the breath of wind created by his passing.

"Papa, is that you?"

She reached out her hand. Slow. Tentative. Like wanting to touch a loved one's corpse, desiring yet abhorring the idea.

There. Cold fingers wrapped around hers.

And pulled.

"Papa, I don't want to go."

The chill crawled past her wrist and spread up her arm. She shivered. She'd been cold before, but not like this. Never like this. The grip on her hand tightened.

"No, Papa."

Why would he take her where she did not want to go? Papas should be trustworthy. Good. Defenders of their little lambs.

But her papa had been different.

Fear slid across her shoulders like the wintery breath of death. With her free hand, she touched her face, horrified that it might be gone already. Her fingertips came away wet. Would she weep forever? His gentle tug turned into a yank. She jerked sideways, closer to the darkness. The cold. She was losing ground, and she knew it. The frigid embrace sank deeper. Squeezing. Seeping into her lungs and stealing her breath.

"Papa, I love you," she whispered, "but let me go."

A December wind gusted, freezing the hairs on her arm, beading up ice drops on her eyelashes, and settling into her heart.

Too tired to struggle, Miri lay back and, in giving up, rested in her Father's arms.

37

"Hyah!" Ethan leaned close to his mount's neck, urging the animal forward with each dig of his heels. Its mane whipped back and stung him in the eye. The left side of the world turned watery. He blinked away the moisture but continued at a reckless pace. Slowing down was not an option. Not now. Yesterday's mishap had already eaten a glutton's portion of time. Replacing a lame horse on a Sunday had proven as big a challenge as scaring up an honest man at a cockfight.

He flicked the reins, and the horse shot ahead, leaving behind a trail of dirt clods. Sweat trickled down his face, tasting salty and gritty. By the time he reached Miri, he'd look no better than the first time he'd knocked at her door.

"Watch it, ye scurvy prigger!"

Curses pelted him like arrows as he swerved to avoid crashing headlong into a wagon. The side of the cart grazed his calf as he tore past, yet he daren't try to stop now. Howls and strange titterings followed him, sounding like a cage full of monkeys. He glanced over his shoulder while his horse pressed on. It was a cage of monkeys. Man-sized. What in the world?

No time to wonder now, not with only half a league remaining to reach the asylum. *Soon, Miri, soon.*

The lane narrowed, but he pressed on. What had she felt on this same road—fear? Anger? If only he'd been there for her. A frown soured his mouth. He'd built his life on if-onlys, and a poor foundation that had turned out to be.

No more, God willing.

At last the road spilled onto a wide gravel drive in front of a ramshackle building. Chaos filled the yard. Wagons and carts. Drivers and guards. Shorn-headed sacks of bones with big eyes. Some laughed hysterically. Others stared, dazed and vacant. Most made noise. So this is where the cartful of monkeys had originated. Was this an outdoor asylum?

His horse shied sideways, and he pulled the reins taut. Not that he could blame the animal. The anthill of activity spooked him, too.

With a poke to the horse's ribs, he forced his mount over to the driver of the first wagon. "What goes on here?"

A stream of tobacco juice shot out of the man's mouth and nailed the ground. He swiped the back of his hand across his face, leaving behind a brown smear at the side of his lips. "Closin' 'er down. Movin' 'em out."

"Where? Why?"

"Not my job to know, jes' to do."

Frustrated, Ethan rode on to the next cart in line, eyeing the load of wild-eyed scarecrows in the back. All men. No Miri. Thank God.

"Can you tell me what's happening?"

The driver shrugged. At least he didn't spit. "Can't say as I can."

Ethan grit his teeth and moved on. Women sat in the back of this wagon. He slowed, searching face after face, dread and hope roiling in his gut. Eyes, most vacant, some wild, burned in their sallow faces. None the amber of Miri's.

He repeated the process three more times, each driver as clueless as the one before. After searching the last wagon, with no sign of Miri and none the wiser about the commotion, he wanted to hit something.

He threw back his head and shouted, not caring that he blended in with the rest of the lunatics. "Doesn't anyone know what's going on?"

"Of course, sir. I do."

Ethan yanked a hard right, wheeling his horse about. On the front stoop of the asylum stood a little man with a big nose. Ethan immediately dismounted and closed the distance between them.

"Well?" Ethan asked.

The man blinked at him. "Well what, sir?"

Ethan folded his arms to keep from punching the man in his protruding bull's-eye. "Why the carts? Where are they taking these people?"

The short fellow had to look up when speaking or be forced to address Ethan's chest. "Sheltering Arms is closing. All inmates well enough to travel are being transferred to Bethlem Hospital."

"Well enough?" Fear edged out anger, creeping into places in his heart he didn't know existed. *Dear Lord, not Bethlem.* "Tell me, what of Miri Brayden? Is she—"

"Can't tell you that, sir."

"Please." His voice cracked. He'd drop to his knees and beg if he had to. "I must know."

"Oh, it's not that I won't tell, sir, it's that I can't. Mr. Spyder keeps account of the inmates, not me. Though I daresay his records are a bit haphazard at the moment."

Ethan grabbed the man by the shoulders. "Take me to him."

The man's face paled. "Oh, no. Oh, never, sir. Why ... haven't you heard? There's typhus afoot. Wouldn't do to expose—"

"*Take me!*"

The man jerked back his head as if he'd been popped a good one. "Well, can't say as I didn't warn you properly."

They wound through several locked gates and corridors. With each step, Ethan's concern grew. As did the stench. Death crouched in these corners. He could smell it. It hung from the ceiling, clung to the walls, reached out unseen fingers and brushed against anyone passing by. This was where Miri lived?

He swallowed a lump of terror.

Please God, don't let her die.

The man led him into a worn cracker box of a room. Peeling paint. Toothpick furnishings. A window so grimy it lit the area in perpetual twilight. Ethan scowled. He'd slept in better rat holes.

"Mr. Beeker! What is the meaning of this?" An abnormally long-limbed man rose behind a plain oak desk, pointing a finger at Ethan. So this was Spyder. Apt name. He was a daddy longlegs in human form.

Ethan spoke before the shorter fellow could answer. "Do not blame your man here." He nodded toward Beeker. "I insisted."

Spyder opened his mouth. "But—"

Ethan advanced and lowered his tone. "With much force, which I hope I will not have to employ with you."

Spyder eyed him from head to toe, obviously measuring the threat, then looked past him to Beeker. "You may go. I'll handle this." His suspicious gaze darted back to Ethan. "I must say I do not appreciate such incivility, Mr. ... what did you say your name was?"

Annoyed at wasting so much time, Ethan brandished his biggest weapon—his title. "Ethan Goodwin, Earl of Trenton." Though it rolled off his tongue easily enough, hearing it was still hard to swallow.

Spyder stiffened, then mumbled to himself. He lifted a finger and pointed to a bench. "Have a seat. My apologies for the general disarray. I'm afraid you've caught us at a bad time."

Ethan huffed. Who did the man think he was fooling? "From the looks of this place, it's been bad for quite a while."

"Yes, well—"

Ethan held up a hand. "Don't bother. I don't care. I came for Miri Brayden, nothing else. Is she here?" Steeling himself for the answer, he sucked in a big breath.

Spyder's thin shoulders lifted. "I don't know."

"What?" Ethan's voice filled the room. He shifted his weight, rattling the inkwell on the desk. "I thought you were in charge."

"Mostly."

"Mostly? What is that supposed to mean?" This was turning into an ugly dance, swapping one ignorant partner for another. Ethan ran a hand through his hair, tempted to pull it all out. "I was told you would know."

"As I said, mostly." Spyder lowered to his seat and shuffled through some papers. "I have lists of the departing, the dying, and the dead, not the full listing but—"

"But you have some?" Ethan stepped up to the desk.

Spyder looked at him with the same expression he likely gave every lunatic that entered this room. A frown pulled at his mouth. Not angry, rather ... disgusted. Like the discovery of manure on the bottom of his shoe. "Lord Trenton, I may be a bit short-staffed in the midst of this crisis, but I am not incompetent. Naturally I have some of the lists. I am trying to tell you that they are not complete."

Impatience spread along every nerve, a consuming cancer that made him jittery. "See if her name is there."

"You really ought to come back later, my lord. These documents are not—"

"Do it!" Ethan planted his hands on the desk, jarring the inkwell cover from the bottle. It rolled off the table and crashed to the floor.

Spyder pursed his lips, twitching them one way, then another. With precise movement, he reached over to a drawer and slowly pulled. He removed a pair of spectacles and a bit of cloth, then rubbed one lens to a fine sheen before moving on to the next.

Something snapped inside Ethan. Loud, almost crackling, like a shoulder joint ripped from a socket. His voice, however, remained deadly calm. "Mr. Spyder, if you do not hurry along, I will lunge over this table and personally add your name to the dead list. Do you understand?"

Spyder paused his polishing and narrowed his eyes. "Hostility is a sign of madness, you know."

"Fine. Then lock me up and I'll reach Miri all the sooner. But when I do"—his hands curled into fists—"you'd better pray I find her whole and hale."

Setting his spectacles on his face, Spyder rifled through a stack of papers. "Name?"

Ethan growled. "Brayden!"

"Ahh," Spyder murmured while running a fingertip the length of a document. Toward the end, his hand stopped. "Hmm."

Ethan held his breath.

Spyder's lower lip jutted out. Then his finger was on the move again, finishing out that listing and skipping over to the next.

The rustling paper slapped Ethan's senses. Everything prickled. Spyder's breathing grated shreds of flesh off him. Nothing should take this long.

"Huh," Spyder grunted. "Looks like …"

Ethan willed the man's words to continue, hoping, dreading, dying a thousand deaths.

"Brayden. Brayden. Yes, here it is." The man looked from the document in his hand to Ethan.

He really ought to be able to figure out what that look meant, what those eyes were saying from behind the glass walls. But he couldn't. He wouldn't.

Yet he had to know. "What …" Thick emotion, hot and dusty, strangled him. "… what list is the name on?"

Spyder removed his glasses, setting them and the document on the desk. The fine lines at the corners of his eyes turned down. "Perhaps you ought to sit, my lord."

Ethan froze. Rigid. Numb. He felt small and useless. A discarded heap of impotent bones.

"Just tell me." An old man's voice. His.

Spyder pushed back his chair and stood, meeting Ethan on a field for a game he did not want to play. The man's lips moved. Eight words came out. Arrows, swift and sharp, keenly aimed to stop his beating heart.

"The name Brayden is on the dead list."

38

Dead list. The *dead* list? How could he understand that? The phrase echoed over and over. The dead list. The dead list. Each time it circled, he tried to grasp it for meaning—and came up empty handed.

"My lord, are you all right?"

His heart still beat but only from habit—a custom his body didn't know it should stop. Everything faded until all that was left was a pinpoint of light—and that not very bright. He tensed, muscles taut as bowstrings, then waited. Hold. Hold. Like a frontline infantryman anticipating the charge.

Snap.

Loss opened a mouthful of razor-sharp teeth and bit, swallowing him whole.

He staggered backward until his body hit a wall. Snippets of things Miri had said floated in the air around him. He reached, pulling memories to his breast, trying to keep them all from flying away. He'd lose them in this space. *God, don't let me lose them.*

"Sometimes I get scared, but not with you. Never with you."

"Were you scared, Miri?" he whispered. "I wasn't there, my love. I wasn't there for you."

"We all fail those we love."

"I failed you most of all, my sweet, my love. I failed you!"

"There is nowhere else I'd rather be than with you."

"Then don't go, Miri. Please—" His voice broke. "Don't leave me."

If he tried hard enough, strained and pleaded and pretended, mayhap he'd sense the feel of her in his arms, her touch caressing the length of his face as she had that fateful eve in the barn. *Please, God. Please.* A ghostly tingle ran along his jaw, his neck, spanned his shoulders, and settled deep into his heart.

Then it vanished.

Completely.

"Miri, come back! Come back to me. I never said good-bye." He jerked his face heavenward. "God, I never said good-bye."

His legs gave way, and he sank. Gravity was a monster, pushing him down. Flattening him. Good. He'd sink and sink. Burrow under the earth. Find his beloved and lay with her. Forever.

A sob rose like vomit, ripping out his throat, severing soul from body. "Nooo!"

"Are you all right, my lord?"

He felt his hand lift. Someone patted it. Maybe.

"What's going on here?"

The words meant nothing to him. Words would never mean anything again. Nothing would.

"He came asking about an inmate. He's not taking it well at all, I'm afraid."

What kind of gibberish was that?

"Move aside, Mr. Spyder. This is my line of work, after all."

Something nudged him.

"Sir?"

A stinging slap jerked his head. But it didn't matter. Not anymore.

Fingers pried open his eyelids. Hot breath fanned his face.

"Hmm … appears normal. What did you say happened, Mr. Spyder?"

"He came in here asking about a Miri Brayden. Insisted I look up her name, though our documents are far from complete, as you well know. I did find it, however. On the dead list."

Dead list. Dead list. There it was again. Circling. A vulture looking for a carcass to pick clean, gnaw on the bones, suck out the marrow—from Miri.

Ethan started rocking. What else could he do? The sorrow welling inside would not sit still. It raged and ranted, prodding him to movement.

A strong arm restrained him.

"But that's impossible, Mr. Spyder."

"Why's that?"

"I just came from the woman's bedside. She's well on her way to making that list of yours, but she's not there yet."

Slowly things came into focus, emerging as one swimming up from a great depth. Murky at first, then taking on form. Ethan sucked in a huge breath.

"Well, well, an amazing recovery." A skeleton with skin crouched next to him.

"What did you say?" Ethan's voice was rusty.

The skeleton peered at him, assessing him from one end to the other. "Mr. Spyder tells me you are searching for a Miriall Brayden, yes?"

She was here? Alive? His heart swung on a pendulum, the extremes making him queasy. He shoved the man away and bolted up. The room spun. He flung out a hand and balanced against the wall. "Where is she? Take me!"

"Calm down, sir. I assure you she's receiving the best care I can administer. There's nothing you can do. Taking you to her would only endanger your health."

Grabbing handfuls of the man's shirt, Ethan shoved him backward. "I don't give a flying fat rat about my health. Bring me to her!"

The skeleton's thin eyelids stretched over bulging eyes as he blinked.

"Now!" Ethan's voice rumbled, the harbinger of a black storm about to unleash.

"As you wish," said the skeleton.

"Dr. Pembernip, I am not at all certain that's wise."

Ethan let go of the man and growled at Spyder, stomping toward him.

Spyder held up both hands, retreating.

"Wise or not"—the doctor straightened his shirt—"there's no reasoning with a man in a state such as this. Believe me, I've seen it many times. Were we not closing down this asylum, you can be sure I'd admit him for observation. As it is ..." He glanced at Ethan, then turned. "Come along."

Ethan followed close behind. He'd run ahead if he knew the way. The place bore an eerie resemblance to Newgate. Dark. Dank. Foul smelling. No wonder disease roamed these halls.

A million things ran through his mind as they went. How near death she might be. How much she'd suffered already. How he'd ever be able to forgive Witherskim for putting her through all this.

Led into a large room with pallets on the floor, he recoiled from the stench.

The doctor glanced over his shoulder at him. "She's right over ... You look a bit green, my lord. Are you sure you want to—"

"Lead on." It was hard to let words flow out past the vomit welling at the back of his mouth.

"Over here." The doctor lifted an arm, allowing Ethan to pass.

His gait hitched, much the same as when he'd visited his mother's deathbed as a small boy. No! He threw back his shoulders. This was *not* the same. It couldn't be.

In front of him sat a girl. Her waxen face looked as if it had been placed too near a candle flame and melted. Part of it, anyway. Disfigurement and beauty mixed in such a grotesque combination, it pulled at him. He stared, mesmerized, wanting to look away but unable to.

The girl turned from his open stare.

What kind of horrid joke was this? Ethan shot a glance at Pembernip. "That is not my Miri."

"Of course not." The doctor looked past him. "Lil, run along now. This gentleman is here to see Miriall."

The girl rose, leaving a clear view of the entire pallet. No wonder he'd missed her. A mud-colored blanket clung to the shape of a cadaver curled into the fetal position.

This was Miri?

He peered closer. No beautiful curls adorned that shaved head. Amber eyes did not shine out of those shrunken sockets. The Brayden high cheekbones looked as if they'd climbed higher to escape the hollowed cheeks beneath.

Miri. *Dear God.*

Ethan dropped to her side and gathered her in his arms. A bundle of kindling could not have been lighter. Holding her close, he gasped. Urine and sweat violated her trademark violet scent. Oh, what she must have suffered.

He stood, clutching her to his chest, and faced Pembernip. "Lead me out."

The doctor rested his hands on his hips. "You can't be serious. Moving her now is much too risky. She's close to delirium, and once that sets in—"

"Lead me." Ethan measured his words, each one a threat ready to strike. "Or I assure you, you'll wish you had."

Pembernip lowered his hands and lifted his palms in a shrug. "I see. There … is a certain procedure, sir, that—"

"Hang your procedures! And hang you as well." He stomped toward the door they'd come through earlier. He'd find his own way out or be damned in the trying.

Miri moaned. Her perspiration soaked into his shirt. If he didn't get her some real help soon, the grief pooling just under his skin would flood over him again. He'd lived through that once.

Never again.

39

Ethan cradled Miri as the coach's wheels jolted out of a huge rut. Several inches cleared between his bottom and the seat, and he smacked his skull on the roof before landing. Silently, he cursed the beastly roads and worse carriage. A rubber ball caught between two paddles would be less bruised.

Pushing against him, Miri rose. Her face twisted as she darted a glassy gaze from one wall to the other.

Ethan shot his head out the window and yelled, "Faster!"

A low-hanging tree limb rushed toward him, and he jerked back his head just as the branch raked the coach's side.

"Roland?" Miri's voice was a thin piece of glass rattled by the wind, on the sharp edge of breaking.

The first time she'd done this, hope made him giddy, thinking her fever had subsided. But then Pembernip's warning of delirium barreled back, grinding that hope to a fine dust. Now he merely allowed her to look one way and another before drawing her against him.

"Shh, love. Soon. We'll be there soon." He doubted his words meant anything to her. Neither did his presence. And that cut deep.

"Rest now." He caressed her hair as the coach jostled along. Stubbly patches scraped against his fingertips, and he grieved afresh that her curls adorned a rubbish pile somewhere.

She sank to his lap, poured out like water from an urn. Since leaving the asylum, the day and a half of travel had taken more than she had to give. How much she had left, only God knew.

Please, God. That prayer, his breath.

With Miri quieted, he gazed out the window. Afternoon sun dappled through a thick hedgerow. Each shrub stood at attention, shoulder to shoulder. A living fence, marking one field from another. Darby's wheat. Jonesey's rye. Trenton farmers. Trenton lands ... home.

A home he'd not seen nigh on fifteen years.

He sat back, leaving the curtain swinging, and aimlessly ran a finger along Miri's arm. So many threads of emotion twisted inside, the sorting might unravel him. Sorrow over his father's and brother's deaths tangled with regret that he'd never reconciled with them. Years of anger and hurt. All this balled together in the pit of his stomach whenever he thought of his new position as lord of an estate. Many would depend upon him. How would he manage without fouling things up?

Please, God. That prayer, his breath.

At last the coach lurched to a stop. The door opened, but he sat as still as Miri. Once he set foot on Westford Manor's drive, a bridge would span from past to present. Could he cross it without falling off?

"My lord?" The driver poked his head through the door, nodding toward Miri. "If ye'll hand me yer lady, I'll hold her right proper till yer out on yer feet."

Ethan lifted Miri into the man's arms, then sucked in a breath as he peered outside. Westford Manor, brick-faced, lace-curtained, overhung with scrolled soffits and slate tiles, looked exactly as he remembered. The ivy thicker, the yews taller, but the house ... the same. Many a woman would pay a king's ransom to age half as well as this. He jumped down, both feet tamping onto Trenton soil and the demons of his past.

Retrieving Miri from the driver's arms, he rested his cheek against the top of her head. "We're home, love," he whispered.

Gravel crunched beneath his boots, memories swelling with each step. Above, third window to the right, was the escape he'd used on many a night to sneak out from his chamber. Off to the left, a hedgerow where he'd stashed cheroots stolen from his father's study. And if he bypassed the main entryway and followed the drive behind to the carriage house … no. Better to not even think of the wicked acts he'd committed in those shadows.

Shoving down each memory, he climbed the stairs and paused in front of the door. Should he ring the bell, knock, or just walk in? With Miri in his arms, knocking and ringing were out of the question, and he couldn't very well open a locked door.

So he kicked against the paneled mahogany. Unconventional but effective.

A ruddy-faced servant, cheeks splotched as if recently slapped, opened the door. Before Ethan could introduce himself and explain the situation, the man spoke. "The charity hospital is two towns over. In Middleton. Good day."

The door swung shut. Just like that. Without so much as a "who are you?" or "how are you?" Ethan scowled. He'd like to slap those cheeks himself.

This time, he kicked harder.

When the servant appeared again, his neck matched his face. "This is a private home. Go away—"

"This is *my* home, if you please."

Miri stiffened in his arms, and he lowered his voice. "I am—"

"You are lost. I know the members of this household, and you are not one of them. And especially not her." The servant curled his upper lip as he glanced at Miri. "Now go away."

The door slammed. The knocker rattled—and Ethan's boot thrusts kept it rattling. "Open up!"

Miri moaned. He recanted of his volume, but not his intent.

A great sucking noise filled the air as the door flew open. Red-eyed, the servant yelled, "Do not force me to—"

"I am Ethan Goodwin, you—" Ethan bit back a few coarse names. "I am the Earl of Trenton, lord of this manor."

"And I am the queen mother. Good day."

Bracing for the pain, Ethan shot out his foot and wedged his boot between door and jamb. When it hit, he bit down. White hot hurt cut into his ankle and spread up his leg, and he gasped.

The servant flung open the door. Were it not attached to the hinges, it would've been a deadly projectile. "Are you mad?"

"Just about." He ground out the words between the throbs in his foot. "Think, man. The earl had an heir, one that Mr. Spindle sought. He found me in London, and now I am here. Do you really want to chance angering me if I am who I say I am?"

The man narrowed his eyes. At least he didn't slam the door.

"If you let me in, I vow I'll go no farther than the sitting room. You can call on Dobbins to confirm my identity."

The man's brow furrowed. "What would you know of Dobbins?"

"Listen, you baldy-cocked—" He forced out a breath, along with a few other choice names. This fellow ought to be protecting the crown jewels in the Tower—or better yet, residing as one of its prisoners. "Dobbins is the butler, Mrs. Pandy, the housekeeper. Should you like me to continue?"

The man merely sniffed. "Anyone could know that."

If his hands weren't full of Miri, he'd throttle the oaf. "Yes, but anyone could not tell you to look three floorboards over from where you're standing, to the left. There's a gap between slat and baseboard. Wiggle it and lift. You'll find a child's handful of shiny pebbles. It's where I kept them as a boy."

Though the man's mouth dropped, he didn't budge.

But Miri wriggled against him.

"Do it!" Ethan ordered.

The fellow sprang into action, darting sideways and bending low.

Miri burrowed her face into his shirt. This delay could not be comfortable for her.

"Sorry, love," he whispered.

When the servant finally straightened to full height in the doorway, his cheeks were purple stains on a white canvas. Not simply a sheepish look, but an entire flock of contriteness settled over his face. "My apologies, my lord. I am so very sorry to have doubted—"

Ethan shook his head. "Just let me in."

"Of course," the man mumbled as he stepped aside. If he had a tail, it would be tucked tight between his legs.

Favoring his tender foot, Ethan brushed past him, calling as he went. "Send for Dobbins."

"Anything you say, my lord. Anything at all, sir." Other hangdog comments followed him toward the sitting room. Ethan cringed, unsure which annoyed him more—pompous disdain or this new bootlicking tactic.

Miri struggled against him, and he increased his pace. The scent of lemon oil greeted him as he crossed the threshold. Memories haunted this room. Too many heated words echoed in his heart. He'd have to face these ghosts, but not now. Not with Miri limp in his arms.

He settled her onto the chaise lounge, a ragdoll in need of care. Pressing his lips against her forehead, he soothed. "Back soon, my sweet. Rest easy."

He strode from the room, ignoring the leftover pain in his foot. "Dobbins!"

A man rounded the corner farther down the hallway. Dobbins's height, Dobbins's size, but oh … was it really Dobbins hiding behind that faded skin, wrinkled tight in some spots and hanging in others? His chest tightened as it suddenly hit him just how much he'd missed this man.

"Master Ethan, good to see you, sir!" Dobbins dipped his head in respect.

Ethan smiled. "And you." The truth of those words dredged up pleasant recollections tied to the butler, countering the bitter. Good ol' Dobbins. He patted the man on the shoulder. "There is much to say, but for now, I would have you send for a doctor."

The old butler assessed him, a practiced flick of the eyes that might catch a scraped knee or flush of sickness. "I hope all is well, sir. I have an urgent matter I wish to discuss."

"Your urgent matter will have to wait." He stepped aside, sweeping his arm toward the sitting room. "I am fine, but the new mistress of Westford Manor is not."

Dobbins looked past him, then craned his neck farther. "Sir?"

Ethan followed the butler's line of sight with his own eyes, and his heart stopped. With long-legged steps, he strode to the center of the sitting room. The bolster from the chaise lounge lay on the floor, the chair completely empty. He spun. No Miri.

Alarm spread a fire in his veins.

Please, God. That prayer, his breath.

⤲⤳

"Roland?"

Hugging herself, Miri padded along, feet sinking into plush carpeting. Someone must've paid a small fortune for that. Funny how she could feel her feet but not her head. It was probably somewhere nearby, floating about like a giant soap bubble. If it popped, would she disappear?

That's right … Roland had disappeared. He floated somewhere too. She had to find him, tether him to her wrist on a very long string, and then all would be right with the world. Or … maybe not. He might yank her around. Take that great string and spin, orbiting her in an endless circle. Round and round and—

Her stomach seized, and she doubled over, moaning.

Then she floated again. Her whole body, not only her head. She landed somewhere warm, and strength embraced her.

"Dobbins, go now!"

The words rumbled beneath her ear, an earthquake of sorts. Too loud for worms. Too deep for crickets. It didn't smell like dirt, more like … sandalwood. She pressed her face against this soft ground and felt … nothing. Her soap bubble had caught on a gust of wind, taking her on a wild ride. She held on tight—

But bubbles were notoriously slippery. It would be easier to just let go.

Should she?

40

A scritching noise, like metal drapery rings forced along a rod, jarred into the abyss where Miri huddled in a ball. She startled, tightening further, then slowly uncurled, loosening one joint at a time. After being cold and cramped for so long, stretching felt wonderful.

"Awake then, are ye?"

Miri's eyes popped open. Bright sunshine assaulted her, and she squinted.

The silhouette of a woman grew in size, taking on features as she bent over the bed. Judging from the crinkles at her eyes and pucker marks near her lips, she had many years tucked beneath her mobcap. Hair the color of a bleached mainsail framed her pinked cheeks, and her mouth pulled into an agreeable line. All in all, a safe-to-share-your-secrets-with kind of face—but one completely unfamiliar.

"Quite the scare you've given me, dear."

Did she know this woman well enough for such an endearment? The woman's voice, while sweet, did not ring any former-acquaintance bells. Miri searched her memory. Did she know the woman at all?

"And you fairly frightened the life out of m'lord."

Miri nibbled her lower lip. Who was "m'lord," and why would a chit of a woman like herself frighten him? The woman must be mad. That's it. Just one more lunatic in the asylum.

"Now then, shall I plump you up and get you some broth?"

Plumping brought to mind a fattened goose before the slaughter, or beating the lumps out of a cushion. But the mention of broth rippled a hunger pang through her tummy. "Yes ..." Her voice came out like water through a seldom-used pipe. "Yes, please."

The woman's smile widened. "That's the spirit!"

She thrust a strong arm beneath Miri's shoulders and lifted. With her other hand, she scooched up the pillows and settled Miri against them. If that was plumping, Miri rather liked it. She sank against the soft backdrop.

"There. Comfortable?"

"Yes, but ..." Miri's brow tightened. The woman's question confused on more levels than one. Why she'd care about her comfort was anyone's guess. Bare necessity topped the list at Sheltering Arms—not comfort.

Unless she wasn't at the asylum anymore.

Shifting, she gazed past the woman's concerned face. Sunlight bounced off a crystal chandelier, polka-dotting the walls with bits of rainbows. Miri blinked. Hopefully that explained it and she wasn't in for a doozy of a headache.

Two overstuffed chairs and an upholstered settee lounged in front of a bay window. Against one wall stood an enormous wardrobe, and near it, a full-length looking glass on a frame. Gracing the other wall were a glossy writing desk and a washstand. In stolen moments, she'd read of such fine places in novels. Was this some kind of fantasy, then? A snippet of something she'd gotten lodged in her mind? Then again, mayhap she'd died and gone to heaven. Or—

Perhaps she'd gone as skippity-nippy loony as Roland. She stiffened. "Where am I?"

"There, now. Don't fret." The woman smoothed her fingertips along Miri's brow. "You're safe at Westford Manor."

"Westford Manor." Repeating the name didn't help. It sounded pleasant enough but was completely foreign on her tongue. How had she gotten here? And why? Miri drew up the blankets to her chin. "Whose house is this?"

"M'lord Trenton's, of course." The woman's eyes narrowed with concern. "You're looking a bit pale, dear. Perhaps you ought to lay back down."

"No." Miri drew a big breath, suddenly light-headed. Heaven, madness, or fantasy, she wanted to remain bolstered up in this fine, faery-tale room.

The woman angled her head. "You are certain?"

"Yes …" Her strength drained, swirling down into the mattress, the pull of it irresistible. "I'll just … rest …"

"I thought as much." The woman's voice faded.

As did the room.

When it came back into view, blue-grey light filtered through the windows. Shadows stretched into odd shapes, none resembling a mobcapped woman—at least not on the wardrobe side of the room. Fighting with a tangled sheet, Miri kicked it back and rolled over.

Then gasped.

In a chair at her bedside sat a man, head tipped back, eyes closed. Stubble darkened his jaw, the skin beneath pallid, as if he'd wallowed in an ashbin. Color deepened in half circles beneath his closed lashes. Either the dusky light granted him no favors, or he'd not slept in a very long time. His white shirt was unfastened at the collar, his loose hair brushing its edge. Dark hair, rumpled from an endless amount of being raked back, over and over, just like Ethan used to—

Her breath caught, trapped in a net of recognition and longing. Impossible. Sudden empathy for Roland welled, for she could not deny the madness that must be skewing her perception. What a bittersweet way to lose the last of her sanity. She sighed, giving in to the horridly wonderful vision.

The man's head snapped forward, then turned. When their gazes met, something quivered in a deep part of her—a place she'd been saving all her life.

"Miri?" His voice had aged a thousand years since she'd last heard it. "Are you …"—his throat bobbed—"well?"

She reached, desiring to wipe away the lines that troubled his brow. That, and to see if she dreamed. "Are you real?"

He captured her hand in both of his and squeezed. "Very real, my love."

A warm smile spread across his face, and he eased from chair to bed. He sat so close, she rolled nearer to him from the sag in the mattress. Her fever must be back. She was burning up.

His hand trembled as he brought her fingers to his lips. As he kissed the top of each one, a hot trail burned along her arm, running straight to her heart. This was real. And if not, she'd choose to live here anyway.

Closing his eyes, he whispered against her fingertips. "Thank You, God."

Miri swallowed, shaken by the depth of emotion radiating out from him. "Indeed."

He lowered her hand and pressed her palm flat against his chest, right over his heart. A steady beat pumped hard beneath his shirt.

The connection brought tears to her eyes, and she soaked in his strength, his presence. She could bathe in this moment. Dive into that brown-eyed gaze and never surface again.

But too many questions held her back. "How did you know where to find me?"

His jaw tensed. A corded muscle stood out on his neck. She'd seen that look on Roland too many times not to read it as anger. Even though this was Ethan, her dearest beloved, she shrank into the pillows.

"Witherskim informed me," he ground out.

Witherskim? Would she never be finished with the man? She frowned, searching her memory for missing pieces. How could Witherskim have told him anything when Ethan hadn't been there during the inquiry? "How did you ... they took you away. They called you a murderer."

He smirked. "They called you mad."

"They lied!" She shifted, trying to rise. That accusation had violated her one too many times. "You've got to believe me. I—"

"Shhh." He crooked a finger and ran his knuckle along her cheek. His touch soothed in ways she couldn't begin to understand. "Of course you are not mad. Neither am I a murderer, love." He trailed his finger down to her chin, then over her lips.

She shivered.

"And we shall never listen to them again, shall we?" he asked.

"Yes ... I mean, no." Who could think with the gentle stroke he ran all around her face?

"All is well, then." He leaned closer.

She breathed in his scent—sandalwood, earthy, masculine—the smell of warmth and safety. Inches from her, he paused, gazing at her with a yearning that both frightened and thrilled.

"Miri." Her name, his soul, entwined in that one husky word.

His mouth touched her brow, light yet entirely intimate. A meeting of more than flesh and blood. Her heart beat erratically, and she felt a tremor shake through him. If his lips moved lower, what kind of passion would be unleashed?

Which is exactly what he must've realized, for he shot to his feet, chest heaving. "I should let you rest."

He strode to the door and disappeared before she could answer. Prudent reaction. A sensible, chivalrous, wise bit of behavior.

But one she would mourn for the rest of the night.

⌬

Air. Cold or frigid, ideally. Ethan rubbed a knot at the back of his neck as he descended the stairs and headed toward the front entrance. Here he was, running away again. Apparently some things would never change. A smile twitched his lips. But this time, oh how different the cause. Yes, a long walk in the cool of evening ought to calm the parts of him Miri had stirred.

"Excuse me, m'lord." Off to the side, Dobbins stood near the sitting room door, light shining merrily behind him. "This cannot be put off any longer."

Ethan frowned. "Are we expecting guests?"

"No, sir." The butler folded his hands together, then as suddenly unclasped them. A small thing, really, but completely out of character. Something was wrong.

A crazy, horrible thought niggled at the back of Ethan's mind. In bringing Miri here, had he brought typhus along as well? "Are you well, Dobbins?"

"Quite, m'lord." His hands disappeared behind his back, and he shifted his weight.

Old liar. He'd never seen the fellow so unsettled. "Very well." Ethan swept past him into the sitting room. "What is it?"

Ethan stationed himself at the mantle, eye-level with a carved wooden box. His desire for opium was pretty much nonexistent, thank God, but the urge to light up one of the cheroots in that box made him rethink where he stood.

"I've been trying to have an audience with you ever since you arrived. Rather unsuccessfully, I might add." Dobbins lifted a decanter, lamplight turning the liquid into a burnt honey glow. "Brandy, sir?"

Would this entire night be one snare after another? He licked his lips, swallowing this new temptation as well. "No, thank you."

"You might need it." The butler lifted the stopper and poured.

Two glasses.

Alarm shot through him. "What on God's green earth is this all about, man?"

Dobbins delivered his drink. When he handed it off, the glass shook. He said nothing of it as he looked up into Ethan's face. "You've been so preoccupied with your lady, sir, that I've taken the liberty to deflect most household matters. You are required to journey to Bainbridge tomorrow, however. That's one bit of business I cannot attend to. And what I have to tell you cannot keep until your return."

The butler doubled back and collected the other glass. Then lifted it to his lips.

The breach of protocol was stunning—and grounds for dismissal. Ethan slugged back one swallow, let the drink burn down his throat, then set the glass on the mantle. He crossed to a chair, sat with elbows on knees, and leaned forward. "This is more than Bainbridge. Have at it."

A hint of a smile lit the butler's face. "You are not at all like your father, sir."

"Thank you."

The butler smiled in full, then drained his glass and returned it to the tray. Straightening his jacket, he neared the settee but did not sit.

"You might as well take a seat, Dobbins." Ethan smirked. "As long as you're collecting them, what's one more liberty?"

Dobbins gave a somber shake of the head. "Thank you, but no. I shall not indulge beyond your limits. I fear what I have to say might very well see me packing this night."

Ethan's brow shot up. His thoughts flitted about, a swarm of mayflies that would not land. "Your gravity is unprecedented, Dobbins."

The man sighed, looking years beyond his age. "The topic I wish to discuss will not be welcome."

"Which is?"

"About your father, sir."

Any leftover amorous feelings stirred by Miri fled—the mention of his father accomplishing much more than a walk in the evening air ever could. "Go on."

"I think I may say, sir, it is no secret that bad blood ran between you and my former master." Dobbins drew in a large breath. "And I know why."

Ethan scrubbed his face. He wasn't even sure he knew the reason why. "What are you talking about?"

"Your father, God rest his soul, did not … could not … dote upon you—"

"Dote!" Ethan leaned back, folding his arms. "The man could hardly stand to look upon me."

"Yes, well, that was because ..." The butler wiped a gloved hand across his forehead. "You were a constant reminder of his infidelity. A regret he took with him to his grave."

Ethan's jaw dropped. A million questions shattered his existence. Just like that. Poof. No more Ethan Goodwin.

"Oh, don't get me wrong, sir. He loved m'lady Trenton, loved her like a saint, for so she was. It was simply one terrible indiscretion, fueled by too much excess, as you know he was wont to do."

"An indiscretion that resulted in ... me?" Voiced aloud, it sounded even more absurd. He shook his head to clear it.

"Yes."

That one word landed like a cannonball, sending out a ripple that touched every memory he owned. How could he begin to view the past through these spectacles? Who was he? He lifted his head and peered at Dobbins. "Why?"

Dobbins's brow wrinkled. "Not quite the question I was expecting from you. Why what, sir?"

"Why did he keep me, raising me along with Richard? Why even admit to my birth? Why not simply dispose of the woman who bore me? Send her away? Pay her off?" He cringed at the suggestion, a cruel blow to any woman. Despicable conduct, to be sure, but more common than a halfpenny.

"Because of m'lady Trenton."

"My—" The name *mother* died on his lips. She wasn't. She never had been. The woman he'd assumed as his own flesh no longer belonged to him. Just one more grievance pitched on top of a lifelong pile of injustices. He raked a hand through his hair.

"Then who was my mother? What happened to her? Where is she now?"

"Your real mother"—was that a quiver in Dobbins's voice?—"died in childbirth. It was m'lady Trenton who insisted you remain here, sired as her and your father's own."

Ethan searched the old butler's face. Was he making this up? Was this all some kind of trickery? For what means?

Dobbins did not so much as flinch beneath his gaze, and gaze at him he did, for a very long time, scouring every line for movement, for truth. "Why was I not told this before?"

The butler's mouth pressed tight, his lips disappearing for an instant. "Your father made me and m'lady swear to secrecy. It was his one condition for keeping you on. He would not have m'lady's name besmirched by flaunting his tryst in public. Now that he's gone, now that they're both gone, I felt it your right to know, sir. And rest assured, the secret dies with me."

The information pummeled him, beating him into a shape he could not recognize. He rose on shaky legs. One more question, and he'd burst out of here. Walk and walk. Lose himself in the night air—whoever he was. "How do you know all this? Why would my father reveal such personal information to you?"

Dobbins's jaw worked for some time, and Ethan stared at it in dreaded anticipation.

"The woman, your mother, was a scullery maid in this household." Dobbins's voice softened. "My sister."

41

Miri pressed her forehead against the bedchamber's windowpane. Yesterday had been the first she'd truly felt her old self, and now that she regained strength, boredom reduced her to watching raindrops squiggle down the glass. Fat, steady droplets wept from a grey afternoon sky. If she listened really hard, she could hear Roland's stern voice in the roll of thunder.

"Idle hands are the Devil's workshop, woman!"

Her sigh fogged the glass. Would she ever hear his voice again?

Did she really want to?

Conflicted, she turned away, pressing her fingers to the cool spot on her brow—the same spot Ethan's lips had warmed well over a week ago, now. Where was he? Why had he not been to see her? She walked a fine line between hurt and anger. Next time she saw him, she'd either slap him in the face or run into his arms.

She paced the length of the rug, as useless a pursuit as when she'd questioned the young maid about Ethan. The girl, Anna, didn't know him. Nor much of anything else, for that matter. She was newly hired and, while she liked to talk, was not well versed in the ways of Westford Manor.

A light knock rapped on the door an instant before the girl appeared. How come when she thought of Ethan, he didn't pop in as magically?

"Oh, miss!" Anna rushed in, hands wringing. Her apron strings flew behind her like streamers as she dashed across the room. "There you are."

Miri furrowed her brow. "Where did you think I'd be?"

"There's no time. Come." She pulled out a cushioned stool next to the vanity, almost tipping it over. "Let me see what I can do about your hair."

"Don't bother." Miri ran a hand over her shorn head. "I hardly have any. Besides, why would you want to? What's going on?"

"M'lord has returned, miss. And straight off, he's asked after you!" Her freckles fairly danced across the bridge of her nose. "He should like to see you in the sitting room directly."

Palms suddenly moist, Miri wiped them on the borrowed day-dress she wore. Of course she'd known the time would come when she'd face the lord of the manor, and that the opportunity would answer many of her questions. But apprehension of the unknown rankled her all the same.

"And I don't mind telling you, miss, he's quite the gent. Spoke right to me, he did. To me! Imagine. I never heard of such a thing." A deep blush chased away Anna's dancing freckles.

Miri pursed her lips. What manner of man was this fellow? Rescuing half-dead nobodies from insane asylums and dialoguing with servant girls was rather unconventional—and downright scandalous.

Anna stepped closer, reaching to straighten Miri's collar and puff up her sleeves. "He's a real looker, too. Tall and dark-haired. He's got the kindest eyes I've ever seen."

"You"—Miri smiled at the girl—"are entirely smitten with the man."

One hand of Anna's hands flew to her chest, the other to her mouth. She retreated a few steps, eyes wide.

Miri laughed. "I promise I won't tell a soul, don't worry."

Anna lowered her hands to her stomach. "Thank you, miss. If Mrs. Pandy knew, she'd let me go, she would."

"If the master of this house is half as wonderful as you claim, I daresay he'd not allow her to dismiss you for mere admiration."

As the logic of Miri's words sank in, a grin grew on the girl's face. "That's right!" She skipped to the door and held it open. "Come along, then, miss. I fancy you'll take to him just as I have."

"Very well." She spoke more for Anna's sake than from belief. Crossing the chamber, she paused in front of the looking glass. A goose-necked waif stared back at her. The pale blue daydress added pallor to her skin and hung on her frame as if it had been clothespegged to her shoulders. Her hair, too curly to lay flat and too short to spiral downward, frizzed out like an ill-trimmed boxwood. She frowned, the expression even less attractive. Typhus had robbed her of the small cask of beauty she owned.

"Come, miss," Anna called from the threshold. "You don't want to keep m'lord waiting, do you?"

"Yes, actually." She would not mind at all if he waited until her hair grew out and she put on some weight. But Anna's gasp ended that thought. She stepped from the glass. "I'm only jesting. Lead on."

Rich paneling and crystal wall sconces adorned the corridor they traveled. The stairway sported a curved balustrade that felt like glass to the touch, and her slippers sank into thick carpeting on each step. The lord of Westford Manor apparently appreciated exquisite décor. What could he possibly want with her?

On ground level, Anna turned right. Miri slowed, memorizing every detail. When she did leave here, as surely she must, she wanted to remember everything, revisit the place in her mind as one might an old friend.

Passing by a closed set of mahogany doors, she heard a voice boom from behind. Not angry or reprimanding, more like a rattle-your-chest kind of loud. Even so, she cringed, a leftover habit from dealing with Roland. Would the master of this home speak to her in such a fashion?

She scooted ahead and trailed Anna into a large room. Framed art dotted the walls, elegant sceneries of rolling hills and vast valleys. An enormous Persian rug anchored a plump sofa, matching chaise lounges, and two chairs in front of a hearth. This was no sitting room. The sheer size and opulence of the place could house the queen and her ladies-in-waiting for an afternoon tea.

"You're to wait here, miss." Anna dipped a small bow and disappeared out the door.

Miri opened her mouth to call her back, then slowly closed her lips. She couldn't very well hide behind the apron of a servant, and a young one at that. Blowing out a long breath, she ran a finger aimlessly along the back of the settee. No doubt once this Lord Trenton saw her, he'd realize the mistake he'd made. He'd send her away, and she'd go … where?

Despite herself, she smiled. From rectory, to asylum, to manor house, would she never escape the same old problem of finding a home?

Footsteps sounded behind her. She forced herself to turn around when what she really wanted to do was run away. As her eyes landed on the man who entered, her breath caught in her throat.

The room shrank as Ethan's presence filled it.

⁓⦿�⦿⁓

Three paces beyond the threshold, Ethan paused, drinking in the sight of Miri. Her eyes, overlarge in a gaunt face, gave the appearance of a lost little girl, but her skin tone was decidedly rosier than last he'd seen her. She was a living, breathing miracle, thank God. The longer he stared, the more gratitude both filled and crushed his heart.

Her lips parted, but she remained silent. Did she sense the tension that stretched his every muscle? No. Of course not. How could she possibly know that this would be the day she'd either walk out of his life or become a permanent part of it?

Releasing his clenched jaw, he forced a smile. "It is good to see you're up and about."

He closed the distance between them and took both her hands in his. Soft. Frail. Vulnerable. Desire hammered as strong as his pulse. Good thing he hadn't pulled her into his arms. "How do you feel?"

She matched his grin. "Much better, thank you."

"I am happy to hear it." His voice came out huskier than intended. He released her fingers immediately and retreated a step. He'd never get the truth out standing so near her.

"Shall we sit?" He angled his head.

She looked past him to the door. "Do you think we should?"

"Why not?"

"Well ... I ..." She returned her gaze to his. Was that fear or longing that glistened in the depths of her eyes?

"I suppose," she said, then crossed to the front of the settee and sat.

He joined her, near enough to read her face, but not too close. Temptation deviled him enough just being alone with her. "There is much to say."

"I agree."

The trust in her tone sliced through him, for she would likely recant of it soon enough.

Folding her hands in her lap, she leaned toward him, as she might a confidant. "I've been wondering where you've been, why you'd gone. Or for that matter, how you came to be here in the first place. I asked about you, but Anna, the new maid, she did not …" She paused and cocked her head. "Why are you looking at me like that?"

"Like what?"

"Like … I don't know. Like I might suddenly disappear or something. It's a little disconcerting." She glanced over her shoulder.

Was she dismissing him already? Taking a deep breath, he steeled his resolve. "Miri, there is much I must tell you. Will you listen? To all of it, I mean?"

She snapped her face back to his. "That sounds a bit ominous."

"It is."

Biting her lip, she studied him. "Very well."

She lifted her chin, an action she'd often employed when he'd seen her face Roland—and he hated that she looked upon him so.

He stood and paced the length of the settee. "I pray you'll pardon my abruptness, for there's no easy way to say this. You know my past is jaded, for I've hinted at such before—"

"There is no need to speak of it."

"I must. I owe it to you. To us … if there is to be an us." He stopped and turned toward her, drawn by her sudden silence.

She sat motionless, the picture of innocence and purity. Her hair, short and curly, crowned her head like a halo. "I don't understand."

"I know." He dropped to his knees. She deserved the truth eye to eye. Where he'd draw the courage to speak it, he had no idea.

Please, God, help.

"I was ..." He blew out a disgusted sigh as memories assailed him. All the wicked things he'd done paraded across his mind in a macabre kind of dance. How he hated to defile her like this. "I was the vilest sort of man, Miri. A user. An abuser. Women, drink, opium—"

"Ethan, no—"

"Yes!"

She gasped, wincing as if he'd slapped her.

His gut twisted, knowing he was the source. "I'm sorry, love." He lifted his hand toward her cheek, stopping a breath away from contact. Should a canvas so pure become tarnished by his touch? He dropped his hand to his side.

Half a smile curved her lips. "There is much in my past I'm not proud of. But if God has forgiven you, who am I to do any less?"

Her willingness to absolve him so forthrightly stole his breath. Remarkable. No saint could be purer. Still, his shoulders sagged. How could he be fully forgiven for speaking only half the truth?

"You look as if the weight of the world is your mantle." Her smile faded. "Ethan, did you not hear me say I forgive—"

He held up his palm, halting her. "There is more."

Rising, he resumed his back-and-forth path in front of her. He should have told her this long ago, before he cared. Before he loved.

She stood and blocked his path. "What's done is done. I don't need to know—"

"It's about Will."

She cringed, looking at him as if he might strike her at any moment.

And what a blow his words would be. Would she strike him back? Faint? Run? Gripping her upper arms, he held her in place. "I owed money. Lots of it. Money I'd gambled away. When the man came to collect, I didn't have it. Your brother, my dearest friend—" His voice broke, and he sucked in a breath. "Will died taking a knife blade meant for me, Miri. It's my fault he's dead."

She shrank beneath his touch. Horror rippled across her face, followed by grief and hurt. Pain he'd caused. He'd do anything, say anything, to remove it.

But all he could do was stand before her, powerless. Weak. Impotent. Abhorring the hurt he'd caused.

He released his grasp and wheeled about. "Now you know. I won't blame you if you walk away."

But if she did, his heart and his future would leave along with her.

42

The truth of Will's death, of Ethan's part in it, opened a fresh wound in Miri's heart. That her younger brother had died through no fault of his own brought tears to her eyes—tears that spilled over as she watched Ethan retreat to the hearth.

He stood, back toward her, one hand gripping the marble mantle as if he laid hold of Calvary's cross. She reached for him, then slowly let her arm fall. Whatever kind of black guilt weighted those broad shoulders could not be soothed by a mere touch. Not from her.

Please, God, give me the right words.

Setting aside her own sorrow, she took a deep breath. "Whatever you once were, Ethan, you are not now."

The muscles beneath his surcoat flexed, yet he did not turn.

Emboldened, she stepped forward. "I meant it when I said if God has forgiven you, I can do no less."

He spun, chest heaving. Hope and terror flickered in his eyes. "This is your chance, Miri. Now that you know what I am, what I've done, you're free to go. But if you stay …" He closed his eyes, his voice barely audible. "God, if only she could stay …"

Unbridled emotion moved across his face, so pure it shivered through her. "Oh, Ethan … I could never leave you willingly. Part of me would die. Do you not know you own my heart?"

His eyes shot open, red-rimmed and intense.

"Besides ..." She swallowed, worrying the fabric of her sleeves with restless fingers. "Where would I go? I'm not even sure where I am, exactly."

A slow grin spread across his face. In three great strides, he pulled her close. "You are home, love. Home."

All the warmth and safety she'd ever longed for wrapped around her with that one word. She leaned against him, letting his warmth and strength soak into every frightened, lonely fracture in her soul. A tingle ran the length of her back—right along the scar from the whip Roland had wielded the last time Ethan held her. What would happen if Lord Trenton discovered them so entwined?

She pushed away.

Ethan's grin faded. "Second thoughts already?"

"Not at all, it's just that ..." She glanced over her shoulder. No imposing earl filled the doorway—yet. "What if the master of Westford walks in?"

"The ... who?" He cocked his head and studied her, much the way she'd eyed Roland many a time.

"Pray do not look at me so. I speak of Lord Trenton, of course. And you, sir, have yet to tell me how you came to be—"

His laughter cut her short and likely could be heard clear into the corridor.

"Shh!" She folded her arms, all business. "He might hear. I fail to see what is so humorous."

"Miri"—he smiled— "I *am* Lord Trenton."

She frowned, irritated that he'd pick such a time for shenanigans. He should know as well as she, if not better, that a capricious noble could ascribe any manner of punishment for those below his station. "Don't be ridiculous. You are Ethan Goodwin."

"Exactly." Reaching for her, he rested his hands lightly on her shoulders. A rogue twinkle lit his eyes—one that increased her pulse.

"My father, Robert Goodwin, was the Earl of Trenton. He has recently passed on, leaving me sole heir. I offer you not only my heart, Miri, but all I now own as well." He nodded at the grand room about them.

"Your ... father?" Ethan's face faded, or maybe the room was fading. Even her voice sounded far away. "I had no idea ... but ..."

She spun, needing air, or a seat, or something to hold onto. Catching sight of her reflection in a windowpane, she shuddered at the ugly scarecrow. How unfair. How unjust.

"This changes nothing between us, Miri."

He couldn't be serious. She whirled to face him. "It changes everything!"

He flinched as if her words slapped him. "Why?"

"Look at this." She flung out her arms. "Look at me. I don't belong here. I am a ruin. You can't possibly want me—"

"I can." He stepped toward her. "And I do."

Her eyes welled, and the closer he drew, the blurrier he looked.

"Remember the day we met?" His voice was low, caressing. He stood so near now that when he breathed, the edges of his shirt brushed against her bodice. "You looked beyond the grime, the stench, the ruin that was me, and saw the man inside. What you are on the inside, Miri Brayden, is more beautiful than a simple man such as I can ever express. Believe me when I tell you ..."

He cupped her face, forcing her gaze to meld with his. "I want nothing more than you."

His eyes burned into hers, and she bit her lip, the pain a testament to reality. Did he really mean it? Dare she believe him?

One of his brows rose, the handsome, endearing gesture she'd come to love more than anything. "Do not question my sincerity, for I mean every word."

Despite herself, she smiled. "How well you read me."

"Like none other."

His tone raced a thrill up her spine. The words were entirely too intimate.

Loosening his hold on her face, he ran a knuckle along the length of her jawline and back again, never varying his gaze from hers. "So will you have me, even if I am not the penniless jack-of-all-trades you thought me to be?"

Who could think beneath such a touch, let alone speak?

"Yes," she whispered.

He bent, the warmth of his mouth heating her forehead. "You are altogether too tempting."

His lips moved against her brow as he spoke, and she lifted her face.

A groan sounded from deep in his chest, and he stepped back. "No more ..." He drew in a shaky breath and squared his shoulders. "No more kisses until we can finish what we start, love, for I would have all of you."

The respect she held for his integrity and honor dimmed only slightly with a shadow of disappointment. "And when might that be?"

He grinned, the light of which warmed her through. "Now."

Her brow crinkled. "What?"

"Come along." He grabbed her hand and pulled her into the corridor.

She held on tight. His long strides tugged her forward at a fast pace. She'd tumble face-first if she let go.

"I believe you asked me where I've been. While you were on the mend, I was off to London." He slanted a glance at her but did not slow. "And I brought back a friend."

At last he stopped in front of the closed door she'd passed earlier, then winked at her. "Someone I'd like you to meet."

He pushed open the door and swept his arm. "After you."

Winded and confused, she took a few tentative steps, then paused. The paneled room smelled of tobacco and leather. Books lined two of the walls with a hearth on the third. Floor-to-ceiling windows adorned the fourth, silhouetting a stout old man dressed in a black cassock who turned at her entrance.

"Well, well ... you must be Miri," his voice boomed.

The same voice she'd mistaken as Lord Trenton's. So ... who was this fellow, and how did he know her? "Forgive me, but—"

Ethan's arms wrapped around her from behind, a possessive embrace—and entirely welcome. "Miri, meet the man who's helped save many a soul, mine included: the Reverend John Newton."

"Reverend?"

"Aye, that I am, lass." The fellow shrugged, his grizzled eyebrows raising. "Among other things."

Miri turned in Ethan's arms, and the fire in his stare settled low in her stomach. For the first time, she felt just one of her brows lift in perfect imitation of his.

Ethan pulled her against him, resting his chin atop her head. "I wasn't jesting when I said I would have you now."

Her cheeks heated at the implication.

Behind her, the reverend cleared his throat. "You always were in a hurry, Ethan lad, always in a hurry. But in this case, I understand why. Shall we be about it, then?"

Loosening his hold, Ethan pulled from her, though his gaze never left. Hope. Joy. Love. All these and more shone in the light of his smile. "What say you?"

"I say"—her own smile deepened—"yes."

43

5 months later - London

Miri stepped from the coach, relying on Ethan's grip to steady her wobbly legs. A tingle ran up her arm, familiar yet surprising. After five months as Ethan's wife, his touch still elicited a schoolgirl response from her.

His gaze sought and held her own. "You are certain of this?"

She lifted her chin. "Yes."

"Very well." He looked past her to the driver. "Wait here."

"Aye, m'lord."

Placing her hand on Ethan's offered arm, she drew strength from the muscle beneath his tailored sleeve.

While they waited for the porter to open the outer gate, she glanced up at the soot-blackened walls of Bethlem Royal Hospital— Bedlam, to those in the know. From one window, way up high, a blanket-gown flapped in the wind between the bars, looking for all the world as if it dared an escape. In front of her, crowning the gate-posts, two statues writhed—Raving Madness and Melancholy—the extreme expressions of insanity. Mouths abnormally twisted, eyes unblinking ... which expression would she find on Roland's face when she saw him?

"Miri?"

Ethan's voice pulled her from her trance. "Hmm?"

"After you, love." He nodded toward the porter, who stood tapping a foot on the other side of the gateway.

When they'd both passed through the narrow opening, the man swung shut the gate and locked it. "This way." He loped across the frost-packed dirt, keys jingling.

Miri lifted her skirts, not only to keep her hem clean, but simply to keep from tripping in her haste to keep up.

Ethan glanced at her as they walked. "If this is too much for you, just say the word."

She smiled. Such love and concern shone from the depths of his brown eyes, that her breathing hitched. "You fret like an old lady."

He huffed but thankfully did not slow his steps. Persuading him to bring her here had proved as big a challenge as a wrangle with Roland himself. Truth be told, now that the dismal structure loomed in front of her, second thoughts made her queasy. She pressed one hand to her stomach, grateful Ethan didn't seem to notice, for he'd call off their appointment in a heartbeat.

They entered an arched cove with niches cut into each side. Life-size wooden figures of young beggars stared at her, holding out large jars. The inscription above them read,

Pray remember the poor lunatics
and put your charity into the box with your own hand.

Miri placed a light touch on Ethan's arm.

He snapped his gaze to her, alarm widening his eyes. "Are you—"

"I am fine, but may we ..." She angled her head toward the donation pots.

Ethan lifted his hand and ran his fingertips the length of her face, leaving her weak-kneed.

"Of course, love." From a pocket inside his greatcoat, he retrieved some coins and tossed them in.

The porter scowled and tugged at a mouse-colored neckerchief. "Not that it'll do any o' them half wits a thimble's worth o' good. You ask me, all these crackpots"—he hitched a thumb over his shoulder—"ought to be put down like a lame horse."

The cold-hearted sentiment sent a shiver through Miri—one that Ethan apparently noticed.

Ethan stepped toward the man, a full head taller than the fellow. "I don't remember asking for your commentary. Lead on."

A poorly disguised sneer twisted the man's face as he turned. Miri eyed her husband, unsure if he'd pursue any recourse for such insubordination. He met her eye—

And winked.

She returned his smile before passing in front of him. Porter ahead, Ethan behind, Miri passed through a skinny door into an even narrower corridor. The closeness of the walls squeezed her chest and must surely have been squeezing her husband's broad shoulders. Was this some kind of precaution to prevent a wild stampede of escaping lunatics?

After climbing a few stone stairs, they entered a large hall ringed with doors. Placards embellished with bare-bottomed cherubs lined the walls, listing benefactors who'd done more than throw in a coin or two. Too bad the funds had not been spent on upkeep. The carpet runner was threadbare, the plaster so dirtied, it looked like snuff, and the sour stink gagged her.

Miri sucked in a breath and held it. Brilliant. That would last for only so long. Bypassing her nose, she inhaled and exhaled through her mouth.

But when they passed by an enormous iron-grated door, she stopped breathing altogether.

"Miriall!"

She jerked her face toward the bars, expecting to see Roland's face pressed against them. No human form stood there, but a very real entity reached out—the ear-shattering clamor from second-floor.

While she'd expected the noise of the mad might trigger some recollection of Sheltering Arms, she was totally unprepared for the terror that crawled along her skin then burrowed in. Shrieks, moans, groans—all wormed into her ears, unearthing awful memories. A tremor ran through her. Then another. And—

"Miri!" Strong arms wrapped around her from behind, turning her to face a furrow-browed Ethan. "I feared this would be too much for you. We're leaving. Now."

"No, please." Resting in his embrace, hearing his steady low voice, she allowed the tension in her shoulders to loosen.

Ethan frowned. "Why is this so important to you? Mr. Spindle is more than capable of—"

"I have to do this myself, Ethan. I *need* to do this myself." She paused, biting her lip. How to explain something so crazy? Not a week passed when she didn't wake up in a cold sweat, having dreamt of Roland. And it always ended the same. He'd curl into a ball and roll away, stealing her along with him. Her fear was that if she didn't find out for herself what had happened to him, the nightmares would stalk her the rest of her life. Irrational, really. Too irrational to speak aloud in the middle of a hospital for the certifiably insane.

So she blinked with what she hoped were guileless eyes. "Please, Ethan?"

He blew out a long sigh. "If I see you falter one more time, I swear I will not be swayed. Understood?"

"Yes." She smiled. "I love you."

He smirked. "Your charm will not change my mind, either."

"You, sir, are a——"

"Mr. Barker will see you now." The porter's voice cut through their conversation. Ethan released her, and she turned to cross the corridor.

Upping the tempo of his tapping foot, the porter stood with one hand propping open an oak-paneled door.

Miri and Ethan swept past him through a small anteroom and into a larger office. Behind a paper-strewn desk, a man in rolled-up shirtsleeves rose.

At their backs, the porter announced, "My Lord and Lady Trenton, meet Mr. Barker. Mr. Barker, my Lord and Lady Trenton." The sparse introduction ended with the bang of the door as the porter left.

Stepping aside from the desk, the man bowed to Ethan. "My apologies for Hawkins's manners. After managing lunatics all day, well ... you can imagine. Happy to make your acquaintance, my lord." He turned and bowed his head to Miri. "And yours, my lady."

Miri fought the urge to look over her shoulder when hearing the title.

"Please, be seated." Mr. Barker resumed his chair behind the desk while they sank onto leather-covered seats, sturdy yet worn in spots. "How may I help you?"

"After much investigation," Ethan began, "it is my understanding that the former patients of Sheltering Arms Asylum were brought here. My wife and I seek one inmate in particular. Roland Brayden."

"Yes, yes. That is true." Mr. Barker batted aside one pile of papers and reached for another. As he fanned through them, Miri's hope grew. If she could just see her brother, know he was all right, she would rest so much easier at night.

"Hmm." Barker set down the stack of documents. "He is not listed, which means he was not admitted."

"But we were told …" Miri frowned and leaned forward. "If he wasn't admitted here …" A thousand questions raced through her mind—only one made it past her lips. "Then where is he?"

The grooved lines on each side of Mr. Barker's mouth softened. "We accepted all the survivors, my lady."

"Survivors? Then he … Roland is—"

"I am sorry, m'lady." The pity on Barker's face stunned her into silence. Her hand flew to her mouth, stifling a cry. Roland dead? Grief shook her, the force of it breathtaking. As often as she'd wished to be rid of him, now that her brother was gone, she recanted.

Tears burned her eyes, a few overflowing. Warm fingers gripped her shoulders, urging her up and into Ethan's ready arms. Wrapped in his embrace, she laid her head against his shirt.

"I am so sorry, love." His voice rumbled in his chest.

After a polite intermission, Mr. Barker cleared his throat. "My condolences m'lord, m'lady."

Drawing in a shaky breath, Miri at last felt ready to step from Ethan's side. "Thank you, Mr. Barker. At least now I know, and for that I am grateful."

He nodded. "Is there any more I can do for you?"

"You've done all you could." Gathering an arm around her waist, Ethan pulled her close, "My wife and I thank you for your time."

Ethan led her through the door and into the anteroom. Barker's horrid words replayed over and over. Would she be stuck with that now instead of the dreams?

We accepted all the survivors, all the survivors ...

What an awful death Roland must have suffered. It'd been bad enough watching typhus ravage Lil—

We accepted all the survivors.

Miri gasped, wrenching from Ethan's hold. She sped back to Barker's office and planted her hands upon his desk. "There was a girl. I know she survived. I nursed her myself. She was young, maybe eight or so. Lil ... I don't know her surname. Is she here? She looks like this." Miri jammed her finger into her upper lip and pushed up so high, her eyes watered.

Mr. Barker recoiled, mouth agape.

Ethan's hands rested on her shoulders and squeezed gently but firmly. "You've had enough for one day." He spoke into her ear, then aloud to Mr. Barker. "My apologies, sir. My wife is—"

"No need to apologize. I think"—Barker's eyes widened—"I do believe I know ..." He shuffled one paper to another pile, then two, and finally lifted a third, scanning it with his index finger. "A young girl, you say, rather keen, quite intelligent, really, but slow in speech ... yes. Lillian Ashenhurst was a Sheltering Arms inmate. She currently resides here."

Miri spun and wrapped her arms around Ethan, tipping her face to plead with her eyes. "We can't leave her in this place. You rescued me. I know you could—"

"You're insufferable." His soft tone belied his words. Looking past her, he spoke to Barker. "What procedure must we follow to see to the release of this girl?"

"The discharge of any patient must be sanctioned by the governor's subcommittee."

"And they meet when?"

"Just missed it, I'm afraid. They won't meet for another month, m'lord, though the entire process can take upward of a year."

"A year!" Miri's arms sank along with her spirits. Poor Lil. Trapped through no fault of her own.

Ethan glanced at her, then angled his head toward Barker. "Is there no other way around it?"

Barker's brow furrowed. "Well … I suppose if you got a barrister to sign a Writ of Liberation."

"A barrister, you say?" An odd gleam lit Ethan's eyes.

The man nodded. "Yes, I've seen it done a time or two."

A slow grin spread across Ethan's face. "Thank you again, Mr. Barker."

"Can't say as I've done much for you, m'lord. Nevertheless, you are quite welcome."

A little annoyed at the smug set of Ethan's jaw, Miri hesitated before giving in to his offered arm. Upon reaching the main hall, her frustration crescendoed along with the din of the lunatics upstairs. She stopped and turned to Ethan. "If we could just—"

"Shh, love." He set a finger on her lips. "I know it seems hopeless, but I have a plan. Or rather, I suspect, God has. While we're in town, I was hoping to introduce you to a recent friend of mine. Barrister Wolmington."

Miri's brow crumpled beneath the weight of confusion. "A barrister? Your friend? But you can't possibly know—"

"Do you trust me?" He lifted one brow.

Any shred of reserve vanished. She leaned toward him. "Completely."

"Excellent." He drew her close with one hand while the other slid down to rest low on her belly. "Now, Mrs. Goodwin, I am taking my family home. Any objections?"

At his touch, something deep inside fluttered, and not just a thrill. Wonder pulled her lips into a smile, and she clasped her hand over his. "The babe might think otherwise, but yes, husband, I am ready to go home."

CPSIA information can be obtained at www.ICGtesting.com
Printed in the USA
BVOW06s1503051013

332778BV00001B/7/P